COMBUSTION

Visit us at www.boldstrokesbooks.com

COMBUSTION

by

Daniel W. Kelly

2012

This Trade Paperback Original Is Published By
Bold Strokes Books, Inc.
P.O. Box 249
Valley Falls, NY 12185

First Edition: November 2012

CREDITS
EDITOR: CINDY CRESAP
PRODUCTION DESIGN: SUSAN RAMUNDO
COVER DESIGN BY SHERI (GRAPHICARTIST2020@HOTMAIL.COM)

Prologue

Jeeves always felt invigorated after a night of servicing Masters Lamond and DuPont: so alive, the blood coursing through his veins, igniting fire in every extremity. The next morning, he was incredibly aware of how pumped his muscles were, even before he tackled his workout duties for the day.

His maintenance exercise routine was quite specific and always took top priority to mansionhold chores. Above all, Masters Lamond and DuPont expected every inch of him to be defined and hairless, shaved and waxed by in-mansion groomer Samson, except for a perfectly trimmed patch of pubes above Jeeves's seven-inches of uncut cock. So each morning, his first order of business included yoga with Phillip, the in-mansion yoga master and colonic therapist (to limber up), then a grueling training session in the state-of-the-art gym with Don, the in-mansion chef and personal trainer (to bulk up). After that, it was on to cardiovascular work in the enormous pool (to tighten up). Only then would he begin the menial mansionkeeping duties (cleaning up).

Jeeves, in his usual servant's attire—a jockstrap—entered the Masters' suite, laundry basket tucked under one arm. He could still smell the bitter taint of the previous night clinging to the ice-cold air molecules in the darkness. Masters Lamond and DuPont preferred their room extra chilly, to keep them cool during the sweat-inducing sexcapades and to give them a reason to cuddle under their thick comforters come time for sleep—when Jeeves would be dismissed to his servant quarters down a narrow hall nearby.

Jeeves had slept wonderfully last night, that evening's session having lulled him into pleasant dreams of comfort, security, protection, and trust—the psychological stimuli that had accompanied his physical interactions with his Masters. It had been an extra treat for him, for his Masters had invited Phillip the yoga instructor and Garth Healy the "foot master" to participate, beginning with the tongue bath.

Jeeves had been instructed to lie on his back on his Masters' king-sized bed, completely naked in the chilly room, the dark patch above his cock and the thick, dark streaks of brows over his eyes not enough to provide any natural body warmth. Master Lamond and Master DuPont had begun by each taking one of his fingers between their lips and covering it with a slick film of warm saliva. This would quickly begin to cool and dry as they moved on to the next finger, slowly working their way up the muscles of Jeeves's arms with the thick flats of their tongues, nuzzling into the sensitive shaved area of his armpits. At the same time, Garth, who was responsible for the smooth-soled perfection that was Jeeves's feet, had taken each and every toe into his mouth, licking between them, sucking on the heels, over the raised hardness of the ankle, and then working his way from toe to "head." And finally, Phillip started at Jeeves's center, first sending a burst of tension through Jeeves's taut stomach muscles by circling just the tip of his tongue around the knotted nub protruding from Jeeves's navel before slathering every crevasse and cranny of Jeeves's torso and nipping at his nipples.

Jeeves had absorbed the attention with his epidermis, the wetness of tongues and mouths evaporating into it in segments. The tongues had lapped at his face, over his lips, nose, eyes, cheeks, across the smooth surface of his shaved head, poking and prodding at his ear canal. Finally, when it was time to flip him, the process had begun all over on his rear side: up the backs of his legs into the sensitive crook behind his knees, painting the hairless nerves at the nape of his neck, filling the valley that was his spine, tenderly gnawing at the meaty flesh of his firm butt, and at last, finding the treasure that was the possession of his Masters—his asshole. It had been taunted and teased, tongues dancing around it as hands held him open, trickles of saliva drooling into it.

And then the feast: an entire euphoric experience of erotic cannibalism. He'd been a slab of meat being devoured and marinated all at once, his flesh tight with drying saliva and tender from masterful nibbles.

After the men had had their fill of him, it had been his turn to have his fill of the men. Master DuPont had scooted to the edge of the mattress, used his fingers to hold his thick erection straight up, and instructed Jeeves to lower onto it. Jeeves had done as told, feeling every dense inch puncture and stretch him as he breathed deeply to make the full insertion as swift as possible, not wanting to make his Masters wait to be inside him completely. He never complained of pain or begged for careful or slow penetration to accommodate his own comfort level.

When his rim was finally against the thick bush of golden brown hair covering Master DuPont's balls, he'd been instructed to open up that tightness and ride. Master DuPont's meaty hands had clenched Jeeves's cheeks and pulled them apart to open the ass cleavage, the big arms wrapped around him motivating Jeeves to lean down for a stubbly, scratchy lip lock with his Master. It was just as Master DuPont had drained saliva from Jeeves's glands that the second cock forced its way into his already aching asshole. He'd groaned loudly into Master DuPont's mouth as Master Lamond mounted him, making room between Master DuPont's thick cock and Jeeves's upper ass cleft for a thin but quite long cock that swiftly pushed its way further into Jeeves's bowels than Master DuPont's head could ever reach. As Jeeves had experienced the sore yanking apart of his sphincter muscles and the abrasive rubbing that preceded, Phillip and Garth had climbed up onto the bed as instructed, Master DuPont chucking Jeeves's chin as a signal for Jeeves to drop his jaw. Both of the other men slipped into his mouth at the same time, yanking his facial cheeks in both directions as the two cocks poked for pleasure within his oral orifice.

The love had been all around him, all up in him. He had been the focal point of all these older men, all of them burly and coated in masculine layers of hair that he was denied the right to grow. And it had been magnificent. Although there was very little the muscles in his mouth or rectum could have done to drain the orgasm from any of these men, it hadn't been necessary. His caverns had brought pleasure rushing to the piss slits of all four men, not exactly simultaneously, but close enough to leave him dripping from both ends within no time.

And now, he was here to clean up any mess left from the previous night's emissions. His anus was still blazing with soreness as he went around the gigantic suite picking up any stray garments that had been removed the night before. He knew exactly which ones belonged to which men. He filled his laundry basket, also grabbing the used designer cum rags that had been left in a corner to dry into starchy roughness. As he rose back up, in the shadowy darkness he could make out Master DuPont alone in the bed: his stony facial features as he lay with his eyes closed, his well-developed physique sprawled across the center of the bed on top of the thick comforter, the frigid air having drawn his nipples to plump dollops. Jeeves's cock jumped in his jockstrap as he took in the vision, wishing he could wake his Master with a suckling, but a voluntary pleasuring would be partially to satiate his own desires, and he only wanted to serve.

Jeeves could see the broad, tall frame of his other Master showering in the luxury bath, the bright interior lights within bouncing off the creamy brown and gold tones that adorned the space, contrasting with the lush tropical plants that trimmed the entire room.

The water stopped. Jeeves's cock jumped again. Master Lamond would be entering the room naked any second, expecting Jeeves to have pulled the drapes across to reveal the gorgeous view of the trees and shore of Kremfort Cove, a vision that made it impossible to believe what lay in the urban jungle beyond the gates of the estate. Hopefully, his Masters would allow him to straddle each of them in turn like a breakfast tray and arch his back to reveal his bruised and battered asshole so they could apply their natural oral salves as they all enjoyed the view that faced them at the foot of the bed. The routine was one they called "break-assed in bed," and variations on the position were loaded with ridiculous double entendres like "over easy," "sunny side up," "side of sausage," and "sticky buns"—the kind of silly-speak at which only the intimately involved could laugh. And provided his Masters were satisfied with his performance the evening before, they might even let him at last release the swelling swirls of white that were straining inside his scrotum. If not, he would have to work harder to earn a release by pleasing them with whatever they had planned for him this evening.

Jeeves quickly moved to the thick blue drapes with gold trim, which looked more like the curtain on a grand opera stage. Hearing Master Lamond's bare feet plucking along the heated bathroom floor, he grabbed the thick pull cords at the end of the drapes.

As he drew them across the rod in one quick yank, the glorious morning sunlight streamed over the ocean beyond and into the room, catching Master Lamond's long, lean, and muscular physique as he stepped into the room naked, toweling his head of thick white hair.

And on the bed, Master DuPont did not stir as his entire bulky physique burst spontaneously into flame.

CHAPTER ONE

Long, late September shadows of dawn were just creeping through cascading weeping willows that signified to Deck Waxer that he was most definitely at Weeping Manor. He kept his car a reasonable distance behind the modest handful of emergency vehicles that drove in a procession up the road, which was covered in willow dust from the trees that stretched lazily across it from either side. This was not the welcome wagon he had anticipated when he arrived at the mansion of television and film power couple Hayes Lamond and Ben DuPont, with whom he'd become fast friends during a summer vacation.

Deck drove his car around the side of the house to a carport as Lamond had instructed during their phone conversation soon after the horrific and mysterious demise of his partner. As Lamond had planned, Deck was met by a man: a man with a horse's mane of hair nearly down to his ass and a body like something off the cover of a romance novel.

"Hi, Deck Waxer," the pretty man said as Deck opened his car door. "I'm Samson. I'm the personal groomer of Weeping Manor. Mr. Lamond asked me to take you right upstairs. We'll go through the rear entrance and take a back set of stairs so we won't be stopped by the police."

"Okay," Deck said, reaching to open the back door of his car.

"We'll get your bags later," Samson said. "Mr. Lamond could really use you right away."

Deck followed the muscular bubble ass that bounced just beneath the long locks of Samson's hair. He was led inside through winding halls and up a spiraling staircase. Finally, he was greeted by the familiar sounds of a crime scene.

"It's right in there," Samson said, pointing to a doorway through which numerous criminal investigators were passing. "I…don't want to go in there."

"I get it," Deck said. "Thanks, Samson."

After Samson disappeared down a hall, Deck waited for just the right moment when no men were entering or exiting the room, then slipped in. Despite the chaos in the elaborate bedroom, his eyes were immediately drawn to an African-American woman who looked like she should be portraying Mama in the musical *Chicago*. A form-fitting black dress suit with a blazing red shirt underneath couldn't contain the buxom, bodacious figure. Tight curls formed a layer of stylish black moss over her head. Her round cheeks were glowing with golden maple highlights. She definitely looked like she could belt out a magnificent jazz number if the spirit moved her.

Deck wasn't quite ready to deal with her because he wasn't sure how she was going to react to seeing him. He hadn't expected they'd come face-to-face this quickly. He had hoped she'd first hear rumors of his arrival in Kremfort Cove so it would soften the blow. Or better yet, that she might actually be happy to have him in town.

She still hadn't noticed him. She stood at the beginning of a small corridor that branched away from the bedroom, her arms crossed. As she stepped back, Deck braced himself for her to spot him, but he quickly realized her attention was focused on two men coming from that narrow hall. He immediately recognized the white hair of Hayes Lamond. Lamond was holding the hand of his young, twenty-two-year-old servant, Jeeves. Jeeves looked unusual in a white T-shirt and jeans, at least to Deck, who had only seen him wearing a jockstrap for the entire time he had spent with Lamond and DuPont during their summer vacation.

Lamond released Jeeves's hand as they stepped into the brightly lit bedroom, both of them blinking in response to camera flashes as photos were taken of the crime scene. The bursts of light didn't stop them from noticing a thin man with large rimmed glasses using some sort of forceps to place a lone foot into a clear bag.

"I can't look at this!" Jeeves exclaimed.

Lamond pulled Jeeves into his chest and peered over his shoulder at the African-American woman.

"Do we *really* need to be in here, Commissioner Anderson?" Lamond asked.

"Hey!" Commissioner Anderson barked at him, making crime investigators around her look up from their duties. "You tell us your partner just burst into flames before your eyes and the two of you happened to witness it, I need both of you to point out to me exactly how this all went down. So now, I want to hear *his* side of the story." She gestured to Jeeves. "How exactly are you two connected here?"

"He's part of the live-in staff," Lamond replied coldly.

"Do you hold hands with all the help?" Anderson raised an eyebrow quizzically.

"He's like one of the family," Lamond shot back.

"Is he in the will?" Anderson didn't let up.

"What are you implying?" Lamond asked, and even Jeeves pulled his face out from his chest to look at her with disbelief.

"I'm just trying to get the facts here." Anderson raised her thick arms defensively.

"The fact is, my partner of twenty-three years has turned into ashes in a room that has been completely untouched by fire," Lamond growled.

"Hayes?" Deck finally spoke up, putting power behind his voice to enhance its deep tone. He knew damn well there was no other way to go into a conversation with his old (or former?) friend Yvette Anderson.

Lamond, Jeeves, and Anderson all turned to look at him.

"Oh, for Buddha's sake!" Anderson rolled her eyes. "What the hell are you doing here?"

"Want me to remove him?" a towering black cop with a full mustache asked her from his post at the door, looking Deck up and down.

Anderson sighed and rolled her eyes a second time. "No. He's okay. For now. Waxer, could I ask what in the world you happen to be doing at the scene of this crime in my city? The last I heard, you were gonna move to Canada and open an agency."

"Nice to see you too, Yvette." Deck tugged the front of the T-shirt that hugged his belly and swayed over to her.

"That's Commissioner Anderson," she corrected him.

Deck ignored her and hugged Lamond tightly.

"You know each other." It was a statement from Anderson rather than a question, as if she wasn't surprised.

"Yes, we know each other," Deck responded flatly, not going into detail about how they had met in Provincetown a few months ago. "Jeeves, I'm sorry."

"Thank you, Sir Waxer," Jeeves replied as he wrapped his arms around him.

"Uh, Waxer. This is police business. Would you mind making yourself scarce for a while?" Anderson interrupted the consoling.

"I'd like him to be here for this," Lamond said, holding on to Deck's hand. "He's a detective and may be of help in this case."

This time, Anderson muttered her standard "oh, for Buddha's sake" under her breath, squeezing her crimson-painted lips together with frustration. "Fine. But after we're done talking to your butler friend, what is it—"

"Jeeves," Jeeves answered.

"Are you *kidding* me?" Anderson asked.

"Ironic yes, but that's really his last name," Lamond said.

"Well, after we're done taking Jeeves's statement, I want to talk to *you* alone." Anderson pointed an already blood red fingernail in a hooked claw position at Deck, and now it was he who was rolling his eyes.

Lamond kept his long arm draped over Jeeves's slumped shoulders as Anderson made him recount everything that had happened, from the moment Lamond "allowed" him to leave his room until he walked back into the large bedroom only moments before DuPont burst into flames—flames that did not spread to the sheets, mattress, furniture. Nothing. Anderson asked if any of them smoked in bed—cigarettes or stronger. The answer was a firm no. She asked if DuPont had felt ill at all the night before, if his behavior had been erratic or unusual lately, if he had been involved in outside activities lately—from social to sexual. Every question was answered negatively by both Jeeves and Lamond, neither ever even looking at each other as if to non-verbally corroborate their stories and responses.

"Boss, it's all the same as before." The foot-retrieving man with the large-rimmed glasses pushed them up on his curved nose in an unassumingly cute Clark Kent way as he called over to Anderson.

"Thanks, Zimmerman," Anderson said, nodding.

Zimmerman, her forensics expert, packed up his tools, gestured to his assistants to clean up, and headed out the door.

Deck tried to slowly back away from the circle he was in with Anderson and the two men she was interrogating. He felt sharp jabs in his shoulder as Anderson grabbed hold of his T-shirt, halting him in his tracks.

"Aah-hah-hah!" Deck stuttered, cringing. "You got a load of shoulder hair in there!"

"Where do you think you're going?" Anderson glared at him.

"Bathroom?" Deck offered as an answer, knowing full well she knew he was planning to do some interrogating himself—of the forensics expert.

"You leave Zimmerman alone. He's got a serious case to deal with here, and only a bunch of interns for help," Anderson said. "In fact, Lamond and Jeeves, I thank you for your time. Some of my officers will need to ask you a few more things. Is there any place I can talk privately with your friend Mr. Waxer for a moment?"

"Yes. Fifth door down the hall on the left. It's the study. Incredibly peaceful and quiet, like it's in its own pocket of existence in this giant home," Lamond said.

Anderson dragged Deck to the described location, past an elaborate collage of Michelangelo art on the walls of the hall. As soon as she had slammed the French doors closed behind them and turned to him in the tranquility of the large study, which was more like a giant library, they destroyed the tranquility with a simultaneous barking outburst.

"How is it that you always seem to find trouble—"

"It's my business when a friend is in trouble—"

Standing practically nose-to-nose between two elegant colonial easy chairs, they began to laugh after the unison "trouble."

"You look good, Yvette," Deck said, long dormant affection for a friend of the past creeping to the surface as his lips twitched into a smile.

"You're getting gray. And red," Yvette noted, brushing a finger across his beard. "And a little belly too!"

"It's hard as rock!" Deck said defensively, blushing. He pounded the swelling area pushing against the torso of his T-shirt. "Feel it! It's all muscle."

Yvette gave him a "whatever" eyebrow with which he was all too familiar. "So. You're still single?"

"Now and forever," Deck said, proud of his bachelor status. "And you?"

Yvette looked uncomfortable for a split second and then shrugged. "From the minute I saw those hazel eyes and that thick brown hair in our freshman year criminal law class, I was ruined for other men."

"Hey!" Deck said, flashing the exact charm that had drawn Yvette to him in the first place in college. "I *never* led you on. I told you from the start I was gay."

"And I lied and told you I just wanted to be your hag," Yvette said. "So that I could follow you all over campus and go to the clubs with you and watch you dance shirtless."

"Wow," Deck said. "I guess I did ruin you for other men."

"Well, you didn't ruin *you* for other men. You could still make some lucky man happy now and forever," Yvette said, almost sadly. "When you're not driving him up a wall. Which is what I can see you're going to be doing to me. Why exactly are you here?"

"I was hoping you could give me a job on the force," Deck said. The incredibly dirty look Yvette gave him made it clear that he was dancing around sensitive territory with that joke and that she was probably hoping he'd come to give her a great big apology. But he'd only get to that when he was sure she might accept it. So he leveled with her. "Okay. I do freelance investigative work."

"No, no, no. Don't do this to me, Deck," Yvette said, putting a hand on the tight curls at her temple.

"They *need* it, Yvette," Deck argued. "Lamond is trying to help clean this place up and feels it could benefit from my—"

"That's what the Kremfort Cove Police Force is for," Yvette cut him off. "We can take care of our own business."

"This is a gay district of the city, and yet the violence against gays is off the charts, and none of the perpetrators are being apprehended."

"We have open cases. I've got my best men working on it," Yvette said, the defensive one now.

"*I* was your best man in Chicago, Yvette," Deck insisted.

"Until you went all Kolchak on me!" Yvette exclaimed, clearly irritated. "Remember the unsolved murder case? Your werewolf theory that got you kicked off the force and made me a laughing stock because I brought you in? I was pretty much pushed out of the assistant commissioner position. Which is why I ended up in this hellhole."

"That case never was solved," Deck said bitterly.

"That doesn't mean it was a werewolf," Yvette said. "You harassed that poor man who lost his partner. But he went on with his life, got over his partner's death, met a great man. They moved up into the woods together to get away from the urban monsters and back to nature. Sometimes, you just gotta let things go, Deck."

"And at other times, you gotta take care of business, especially when no one else seems to care."

"Look, I'm telling you. Don't get involved in this case. You're out of your jurisdiction, publicly and privately. I don't want to see you poking around these crime scenes." Yvette scrunched her face together, realizing she'd said too much.

"It's not the first time!" Deck said. "You don't think Hayes Lamond is a suspect in this case. How many have there been?"

"He already told you all about the deaths, didn't he?" Yvette asked. "Just because he may have called you here to help doesn't mean that he or his boy toy or any of the staff in this entire mansion is off my suspect list for this particular case. In the months since these Hollywood types have moved here, things have been weird in Kremfort Cove. All the gays down there are drawn to this damn place and its promise of beautification for the entire district."

"So you admit things have been weird, huh?" Deck asked. "So the other burn cases, have you considered pyrokinesis?"

"Don't *even* go into that Stephen King territory with me, Waxer."

"Come on, Yvette. This is obviously pretty confounding to the police. It's not every day the commissioner of the force makes a personal appearance at a crime scene. So the other victims who went up in flames, is there *any* evidence they've been up here to enjoy some of the luxuries?"

"Oh. We both know it's more than the gym, pool, and outdoor bar that's luring men to this place," Yvette said.

"Come on, Yvette! You know I can help you in a way that no one else can, and you know I've gotta do this as a favor to a friend who just lost his partner," Deck pushed.

Yvette stared at Deck skeptically. "You really want to investigate magic and voodoo after everything that happened in the past?"

"What kind of freelance investigating do you think I was talking about?" Deck asked. "I was never going to get back into law enforcement after that. So I'm making paranormal investigation my career."

Yvette's jaw nearly dropped to her big boobs. "I think you're really crazy. But hey. You do whatever you need to do, as long as it doesn't interfere with police business. But you're not getting *anything* out of me. And damn you, Deck Waxer, don't be poking around any of my men, verbally *or* physically, to get any information from them. And if you *do* stumble upon any actual real clues that exist on this plane of existence, you get on the phone to me immediately. And don't touch evidence!"

She whipped out a cell phone and held it up, waiting for him to do the old zapperoo to exchange numbers. He dug his own phone from the pockets of his baggy shorts and gave her a little Bluetooth action, then she pulled the French doors apart.

Numerous officials were littering the hallway. Deck noticed the big, black, mustached cop standing in a corner with a shorter but equally bulky white cop with a head of thick mahogany curls and matching goatee.

"Boss, we're pretty much done in here. They're going to set up sleeping arrangements in another room for a while," the black cop informed Anderson. He introduced himself to Deck with a gleam in his eye. "I'm Officer Soloman. This is my partner, Officer Bembury."

Deck shook the strong hands offered and made intense eye contact with both men. But all visual and hand contact was severed by Yvette, who pushed between them. "Let's go, Deck."

She pulled him away, again by the shoulder of his T-shirt, leaving Soloman and Bembury staring.

❖

"You've got a large screen TV, Blu-ray, and your own surround system, all remote controlled. You have your own private Jacuzzi bath as well," Jeeves said. With all the law enforcement gone from the mansion, he was in his jockstrap, the way Deck best remembered him and much preferred him. He carried Deck's bags into one of dozens of lavish guest suites and placed them at the foot of the bed. "Every room has its own…"

Jeeves pointed to a modest hearth set into a wall on the other side of the room and fronted by two easy chairs. "Even though nights are getting colder, Master Lamond asked that we remove the wood supplies from all the rooms for now."

"I understand. Thanks, Jeeves," Deck said gently as he dropped his share of the bags beside the others.

"Big king-sized bed." Jeeves patted the hard, firm mattress and smoothed the surface of the lush comforter. "And there are gorgeous weeping willows right outside the window."

Jeeves moved to draw the drapes as if it were a routine he'd acted out for guests numerous times. But as he grabbed the decorative rope to pull them apart, he jumped back as if burned and swung the rope away from him. The knot at the frilly end thudded against the wall. Jeeves turned sheepishly to Deck.

"Sorry, Sir Waxer," Jeeves said.

"You don't have to apologize. I totally understand," Deck said.

At that moment, Lamond entered the room. "Everything okay?"

"I'm sorry Master Lamond. I had a moment…" Jeeves explained.

"I think you need to release," Lamond said.

"No. Not today. It's not right, after what—"

Lamond silenced him with the wave of a hand. "It will relax you and help you expel some of the negative energy. It will be your way of welcoming our guest too."

"Okay. Thank you, Master Lamond." Jeeves nodded.

"Enjoy, men," Lamond said then disappeared, leaving the door wide open behind him.

"What is he—" Deck asked as he turned back to where Jeeves had been. "Whoa! What are you up to?"

Jeeves had climbed onto the bed on all fours, and now his tightly muscled butt, evenly tanned due to his constant nudity, was swelling and parted, his bright pink perianal area raised to the forefront of the space between his cheeks.

"Master Lamond needs me to release and insists that I allow you to enjoy the rewards."

"Let me just get the door," Deck said, never one to hesitate with this type of invitation.

"Master Lamond prefers that there be no sexual modesty or private passion in his home," Jeeves explained, anxiously swinging his hips with impatience to be relieved. "As long as that's okay with you."

"I'm gonna like it here," Deck said, moving toward the booty on the bed.

He grabbed the collar of his T-shirt and began to slide it up over his chin. His belly button was just sticking out from the bottom of the shirt when he heard, "Please don't."

He dropped the collar of the shirt, slipping him right back into his T-shirt. Jeeves was looking over his shoulders and ass pleadingly at Deck. Deck self-consciously stuck a finger under the shirt and into his bellybutton to see if there was unappealing lint trapped in the hair, but finding it empty, for the second time in two hours he proved he wasn't fat by pounding on his belly. "It's hard as rock!"

"What I mean is, it makes me hotter when I'm the only one naked."

"Oh. Okay," Deck said, embarrassed at having acted insecure about his tummy, even though it *was* rock hard.

Moving to the gaping ass crack, Deck kissed one of the creamy caramel cheeks, feeling the solid muscle underneath.

"Uumm," Jeeves sighed. "Please, sir, may I have three fingers?"

"You don't need any warm up?" Deck asked the back of the beautiful young bald head that was facedown on the bed.

"Just some moisture if you'd like," Jeeves said. "I prefer the immediate intensity."

Looking at the dilated asshole, which had created a flat pink surface with a dark dip directly in the center, Deck used a talent he had for flattening his fat tongue out into a wide spit sponge, then ran it wetly over the smooth surface.

"Thank you, sir," Jeeves groaned. "Please, sir, fill me."

Deck locked together the three center fingers on one hand and placed the conjoined tips on the hole. Without hesitation, he pushed right in, feeling slight resistance from the first sphincter.

"OH! Sir! Thank you, sir! I'm so SORE!" Jeeves cried out, which told Deck everything he needed to know. Jeeves had been fucked but good the night before, and his asshole was protesting against any further abuse.

"Let me in there," Deck said, forcefully twisting and turning his fingers within the warmth.

"Sir! It won't take long! I want so badly to release for you!" Jeeves cried.

Deck didn't want to miss out on this. The muscles inside Jeeves's rectum were crushing his fingers. Unable to remove them, he managed to twist his body into a position as if he were going to drop under a limbo stick and brought his back somewhat clumsily onto the edge of the mattress between Jeeves's dangling feet. Using his legs to hold himself in the position, Deck slid up on the mattress to get his head into the space between Jeeves's thighs. Jeeves's shaved, tensed balls and erect cock brushed across Deck's face, scalding hot, and dripping with precum. Deck wiggled his way in and finally used his free hand to guide the erection into his mouth. He then wrapped his arm around Jeeves's thigh so he could push the three fingers of his other hand into the hole, using Jeeves's prostate as a lever to bring Jeeves's pelvis down onto his face.

"*Sir Waxer!*" was all Jeeves could manage, as if trying to warn Deck of the coming flood.

Jeeves's hips convulsed spastically. Deck felt the rigid cock in his mouth swell and then tangy wetness was filling his mouth, but mostly slipping smoothly down his throat.

Finally, every ounce was consumed. Jeeves dismounted and circled the bed to stand in front of Deck, who was still in limbo over the edge of the mattress, his arms now stretched out on either side of him to hold him in place.

"Sir Waxer, would you like me to—" Jeeves began. Then he took note of the large wet spot at the stretched and taut center of Deck's shorts, where his crotch was widely parted so his legs could carry the weight with even distribution. "Wow. Did that happen by itself?"

Deck blushed. "Swallowing is my thing. Kind of like you wanting me to stay dressed."

"You'll need to clean up now. I can bathe you," Jeeves said.

"Okay, but first, could you help me up?" Deck asked, and Jeeves politely offered a hand for him to grab. Using every swelling muscle in his legs and deltoids, Deck righted himself (with audible pops in his knees), feeling the blood draining from his face.

"Come," was all Jeeves said, taking Deck's large, hairy-knuckled hand in his and pulling him into the bathroom.

Part of Deck felt guilty soaking in a relaxing hot Jacuzzi tub while having his body washed by a young man who had just lost one of the most important men in his life. When Deck had first met Lamond and DuPont, they had told him Jeeves's story. He had been kicked out on the streets of rural Arkansas by his parents because of the humiliation *they* felt after he'd been beaten into unconsciousness by members of the high school baseball team because he got an erection in the locker room. Jeeves had hustled at roadside truck stops to get money for a ticket to the supposedly glamorous gay urban jungle. Two months later, Masters Lamond and DuPont had taken him away from a man who was trying to pimp him out—and beating him right on the streets of Kremfort Cove. They'd given him a home, a job, and a sexual role that seemed to make him feel a sense of worth, perhaps even of love and acceptance.

From the tub behind him, slick, soapy fingers tightly kneaded Deck's nipples, which protruded half an inch from his areolas as a result of years of yanking.

"That's wonderful," he sighed, closing his eyes and dropping his head back.

A warm, wet mouth snuggled between his beard and mustache to latch on to his lips. A tense tongue played with his own, so he sucked on it lightly and steadily. Jets shot pressured streams of water against his naked muscles, and Jeeves scooped puddles up onto his chest to rinse off the suds while holding the lip lock. Deck needed to get himself one of these servants. Only problem being, there was clearly an emotional bond between Lamond and his "boy." *Not* what Deck wanted out of any relationship.

Suddenly, Deck felt cool air nipping at his flesh, crawling swiftly down the length of his torso then slipping down off his bent knees and spreading evenly over his thighs and calves as the water began to drain from the tub.

"Done already?" he asked, opening his eyes as Jeeves moved away to grab something from a nearby shelf of creams and lotions.

"No. Have to wash your cock still," Jeeves said matter-of-factly, holding what looked like a cake decorating tube in his hand. "Would you mind doing the honors and just squirting some of this in me?"

Without waiting for a reply, Jeeves climbed into the tub, feet on either side of Deck, and bent over, once again revealing that delicious fuckhole. Deck placed the smooth, rounded tip of the tube against it and pushed inward, meeting no resistance, then squeezed the tube. Jeeves, in the meantime, flicked a switch on the side of the tub that corked up the drain again, leaving the water at a level just below Deck's big hairy balls, the pubic strands swishing with the waves of the water. Deck decided on his own that he'd filled up the young man enough and removed the tube, dropping it onto the lip of the tub.

"You're definitely ready again," Jeeves said, taking in the hard cock that lay across Deck's swelling lower abs. He turned around and faced Deck, water splashing around in the tub as he repositioned himself. With his sculpted hairless legs on either side of Deck's bigger bearish legs, he began to squat, reaching one hand back to raise Deck's cock to a vertical position. "Don't worry. It's all natural herbal liquid soap, so it won't sting your pisshole."

Deck wheezed in surprise as the creamy liquid inside Jeeves allowed for a smooth, snug place to park his cock as Jeeves sat right down on it.

"DAMN! Didn't see that coming." Deck smiled at Jeeves, whose face was only inches from his now.

With his hands on Deck's fuzzy shoulders, Jeeves began to ride up and down, using his soap-filled crevasse to clean Deck's cock.

Deck reached his bushy arms around the lean musculature of the beauty bouncing up and down on him and grabbed chunks of the firmly tensed cheeks that were parted by his hardness. He found the soapy tender flesh sponge that glided over his shaft and sunk his fingers into it. "Damn, you're good at this. Does Lamond make you do this for every guy who walks in the front door?"

Looking over his shoulder, Jeeves had placed his two strong hands on each of Deck's calves so he could lean back, using them as leverage, his erection and bald balls bouncing between his straining thighs. He turned back to Deck and looked him squarely in the eyes and said, "Master Lamond does not make me do things with anyone he knows I wouldn't want to. He knows you're just the kind of poppa bear I like."

Deck blanched at the comment, only partly flattered. "Wouldn't you say I'm more like an older brother bear?"

"Nasty. That would be incestuous!" Jeeves laughed, missing the point. "You want that kind of action, you need to visit the Glouster twins. And have cash on hand."

"Sounds interesting," Deck wheezed as the friction was beginning to build on his cock. "Aaaahhhh, that's niiiiiiice. So where can a guy get a drink—and some information around these parts?"

Jeeves was no longer doing a jackhammer riding, but was instead slipping up and down with slow, controlled sphincter squeezes. "Dirty Harry's."

"Wanna take me there tonight?"

"I'd love to, but I want to be home with Master Lamond tonight. Believe me, any other night, I'd be honored to be at your side. If I was free, I'd be all yours. But some other lucky guy is going to get you."

Jeeves had shifted forward again, and now had his arms wrapped around Deck's neck. Their faces were intensely close.

"I don't do that sort of thing," Deck countered.

"You just haven't met the right man yet." Jeeves looked directly into Deck's eyes, and his words were filled with assurance.

"You...got...the wrong....GUUUUY!" Deck grunted as Jeeves's rectum sucked a load of juice out of him. He heaved, his nipples darting around like torpedoes with each gasp.

Jeeves clamped his mouth once again over Deck's and they kissed, Jeeves stroking his own cock blindly, finally catching his entire second load in his other palm. Without hesitation, he brought the contained expulsion up and cupped his hand over Deck's mouth. Deck sucked and lapped hungrily at the familiar flavor.

When Jeeves was confident that his hand was clean, he slipped it to Deck's chin and stroked his thick beard. "I envy the man you fall in love with."

Deck abruptly broke the intimacy of their proximity, lifting Jeeves off him and scrambling out of the tub in nearly one movement. He grabbed a towel and began drying off as he exited the room. "I told you, it's never gonna happen."

❖

"You don't know what this means to me," Lamond said as he sipped tea around a gorgeous marble table in a Victorian parlor, "but I told you, I could hire someone to take care of all this."

Deck had just hung up the phone, finishing the last of the arrangements for the wake, which would be taking place *in* Weeping Manor, which was just plain strange to Deck. But the couple had been non-denominational, not to mention that, according to Samson the personal groomer, there weren't exactly any funeral homes yet in Kremfort Cove, and only one church that was still getting established and not ready to open its doors yet.

Deck sat back down with a checklist in hand, quickly swiping off his reading glasses and hanging them from the collar of his T-shirt. "It's pretty much all done already. I also had Commissioner Anderson's people do some PR, releasing the news to the media with detailed information about the wake being held at the home you haven't sold yet on the West Coast. There isn't much in the way of public knowledge that you have relocated here permanently, so the decoy story will have the media poking around there while we keep things quiet on this coast so your celebrity friends can attend. The only other thing I need is a list of loved ones to call—"

"They all know," Lamond said flatly. "My boys all know. We are a very tight-knit community here. When something happens to one of us, word spreads fast. It's what Ben and I were trying to do. Turn this place around and create a safe haven for all the young men who came here to get away from the evils back home. When we got here, it was a gay ghetto, still at the mercy of the predatory souls of straight people. The police force hasn't been much help in getting things on track. It's an evolution. It's going to take time. I've got a new division of an established gay advocacy organization moving into the city in a month to help with this. And I'm working on finding wealthy men to buy up all these abandoned manors on the coast, to bring hope—and money—to Kremfort Cove. Right next door"— Lamond gestured to the west wall of the room—"Pale Shelter Estates. It is being renovated by a fantastic man named Proc. He's gorgeous too. We met in England. He was looking to come back to the States. His partner just isn't the worldly type and wanted to be back home in a more urban setting. I told him of all these incredible mansions along the coast, he tripped here to stay with us in the spring, and he was sold. My Ben was ecstatic. He felt the dream was moving forward. We were going to single-handedly be responsible for cleaning up an entire city and making it into a gay Mecca. It was truly going to be a home for lost souls. And now, I lost my soul…"

Lamond put a hand over his perfectly tweezed, silver eyebrows to pull himself together. Deck shifted uncomfortably in his plush chair and tugged unconsciously at the belly of his T-shirt. Conveniently, a large presence entered the room to break the silence.

"You need anything, boss?" asked a deep-throated, towering Latin man.

"Deck," Lamond said. "This is Don, our chef."

Deck immediately recognized the sexy man, who was a former football player. He was in tight silky black eighties shorts, black flip-flops, and a dark gray Everlast shirt that looked like something from the *Flashdance* era. The torn off sleeves dangled over Don's swollen bi- and triceps. The collar was a jagged outline that draped loosely over what looked like a thick black wool sweater. But on closer inspection, Deck realized it wasn't. The man's shoulders and chest were absolutely covered in thick black hair, well up to his Adam's apple. At that point, it broke off into scruffy five o'clock shadow that was about four hours early, generously circling Don's luscious lips and shadowing the area under a wide, prominent, arrow-shaped nose that allowed room for two extremely long nostrils. His deep-set black eyes were shadowed by a long unibrow (apparently, he hadn't gotten the plucking treatment from Samson), and the thick hair on his head was smoothed back with a glistening gel. Below the shorts, a forest of hair crawled all the way up the tree-like thighs, almost as if his pube bush was spilling out of his shorts. Even his big feet, visible through the mesh of sandals, was not immune to the hair, with tufts coating each and every toe.

"Please just make sure you get a list of Mr. Waxer's dietary needs," Lamond said as he placed his empty teacup on a platinum tray so Don could cart it off to the kitchen.

Don looked over to Deck, who had been mesmerized by the flopping bulge banging against the silky material of the shorts, extremely close to the bottom lining. Clearly, Don didn't believe in underwear.

The silence alerted Deck to the attention being on him, and as he looked up to see slight smirks on the faces of Lamond and Don (who both obviously knew what the distraction was) he tried rewinding the little tape machine in his ear canal. Something about dietary needs. That was it.

"Uhm…I have some food allergies," he responded, looking Don in the eyes while patting his belly.

"I feel ya. It comes with age," Don said.

"I'm only thirty-nine…" Deck began, but Don clearly didn't really hear.

"When you get a chance, just drop me a list. I'm pretty much in the kitchen for the rest of the day."

"Okay," was all Deck could think to say. "Hey, Don?"

Deck had stood as Don turned to leave. "What up, cabrón?"

Deck was bewildered by the foreign word.

"It's Peruvian for big faggot or big cocksucker or something." Lamond waved it off. "Trust me. He uses it endearingly."

"Okay." Deck shrugged, feeling a little thrill in his own shorts at the big man calling him a big faggot. "Don, any chance you could show me where a place is called Dirty Harry's tonight?"

"Hell, yeah. It's a date." Don grinned.

"Well, I didn't mean it was a—"

"Say ten o'clock. I'll meet you in the front hall," Don said. Without another word, he left the room.

Deck turned back to Lamond quickly.

Lamond couldn't help but muster a laugh. "Believe me. He doesn't think you were asking him out on a date. He's just a huge flirt."

"Oh. Okay." Deck practically went limp with relief.

"So I take it you're starting your investigation at Dirty Harry's," Lamond said, standing. "That's a good place to start."

"Yeah? Why's that?" Deck asked, taking in a wall covered in ornately framed photos.

"Because Dirty Harry's is the first place people look when they want to investigate bad things happening in Kremfort Cove. Which is why Harry and his partner Jimmy are both on my side in this war over the future of this city. Harry's been trying to run a clean establishment for years, and it's really turning around, expanding, becoming more classy, but he still gets the riffraff in there—including 'straight' men from the suburbs looking to solicit the same young men they pushed to the fringes of society for being open about who they really are."

It was surprising to Deck to hear an aggressively political stance being taken by a man who had been so free, fun loving, and sexually charged when they'd first met while vacationing. Perhaps it was just a side of the man he hadn't gotten to know in the few short days they'd been partying and via cyber chats ever since. Or maybe Lamond's hurt about the loss of his partner needed an outlet for venting.

"Gorgeous, aren't they all?" Lamond spoke passionately as he moved next to Deck and put an arm around his shoulder to enjoy the framed photos with him. "These are our boys. All the beauties who make Kremfort Cove something special." He tugged Deck to one picture in particular for a closer look. "Look at these two. Isaac and Will."

"They're stunning," Deck said, gazing into the frozen faces of the youths who had their heads pressed together as they smiled for the camera as if they hadn't a care in the world.

"Seventeen and nineteen. So young, innocent, and filled with life. Met them during a business trip to New England. Bizarre story. Isaac lost both parents and Will became his legal guardian. They have a fortune together and a gorgeous home. I urged them to consider moving to a plot here on the coast, but they are so very happy being alone together, not interested in outside influence. Which is why we couldn't get them to have any fun with us. Monogamy hasn't taken its toll on them yet."

"I feel ya, cabrón," Deck said the word before he could stop himself, then looked at Lamond. "I can't pull that off, can I?"

"Not at all," Lamond said. "Although, your humility is adorable."

And, as was the case with many men Deck encountered, Lamond couldn't resist the urge to tug on the whiskers on his chin.

Here it was, not even the end of September and big, bearish Deck was feeling a chill in the air. Jeeves had shown him that he could control the air temperature in his own room using a thermostat in his walk-in closet, so he made sure to set it at a comfortable seventy-two before leaving for a night on the town.

Pulling on a thermal long-sleeved shirt after a quick shower, Deck stood in front of a large mirror in his room, legs squatted slightly to hold his jeans up at the knees while he smoothed the shirt over his pelvic area. He tugged the jeans up and over the shirt to tuck it in. This was one of his favorite cuts of jeans. It felt somewhat elastic around the waist, yet right below that it hugged his groin and buttocks. The cute young man who had helped him at Old Navy had claimed it was because Deck was thinner around the waist than around the butt area because of his muscles. He'd been flattered to hear the word thin being spoken about himself by a twenty-year-old, which had given him all the more reason to treat the young man to a swallow session in the fitting room.

As usual, Deck's mind was on sex. The swell pushed against his jeans. He had a feeling that would be a pretty standard condition while he was here in Lamond's sex-charged environment. He may be pushing forty, but Viagra was not in his foreseeable future.

His thoughts were broken by a barely noticeable noise. He looked around the quiet room and tried to follow the sound. He put his ear to the closet. Nothing. He stepped into his bathroom, but the sound seemed even farther away. Finally, he moved to where Jeeves had slid the drapes aside earlier. They were now drawn. Deck drew them aside to reveal the glass doors and the blackness beyond the panes. As soon as interior light struck the glass, the sound stopped.

"Hm." Deck hummed, sliding one glass door open and stepping out onto the balcony. Just as he noticed a small table and two chairs off to the side, he was surprised by the sound of fluttering in a nearby weeping willow tree. He felt foolish as his heart recuperated and the swaying branches slowed to the speed of the slight breeze. "Frickin' birds."

Deck's nipples shrank beneath his thermal shirt. It really was chilly at night. He could hear the strong currents of the ocean breaking against the cliffs in back of the mansion. Along the pitch-black horizon, a hint of a yellow glow from the moon reflecting off the water brightened things up. The moon must be somewhere on the other side of Weeping Manor, because all he could see was darkness above. Looking over the solid cement pillar railing of his balcony, he couldn't make out the forest from the trees that he knew were there. But he could make out a tiny burst of light a couple of acres away, right over the tree line.

"At least this farsightedness is good for something," Deck muttered as he easily took in the little spotlight of activity through the trees.

A porch light had been turned on at the mansion on the next tremendous plot of land. Within the reach of its glow was the tail end of a large truck. Deck could make out two figures, one large and dark, the other lean and ghostly pale, pulling out a ramp at the back of the truck. Then both climbed the ramp into the truck and within moments reappeared, carrying a tremendously large piece of furniture, perhaps a china closet or hutch.

The movers disappeared from view momentarily. Deck breathed in the salty smell of ocean carrying on the wind and hugged himself. The figures reappeared within the light, empty-handed. The bigger figure climbed the ramp again as the other waited alongside it. Deck was amazed at his eye for detail; it was like he had 20/20 vision from this distance. He was sure he could make out chiseled features on the snowy white complexion of the one watching the bigger dark figure work. When the hulking figure emerged carrying what looked like a monstrous chair, the smaller figure waited until the man and chair had disappeared into the house before mounting the ramp.

The pale white figure suddenly stopped at the center of the ramp and turned to look right at Deck.

Deck had made himself comfortable, leaning on the cold stone slab of the railing, but now he stood upright, chills tugging at his spine, and stepped back.

That's when he felt his waist being grabbed by heavy hands. He let out a terrified "What the—" More chills attacked in response to the fingernails-on-a-blackboard sound his heels made on the cement below them as he spun around.

Something large eclipsed his view of the inside of his room.

"Geez, cabrón!"

"Don! What the fuck! You scared the shit out of me!" Deck hissed as he swallowed hard, grabbing the huge muscular forearms clinging to his waist and noting the fingers that had swiftly found their way into his belt loops. Of course, that also helped steady him and prevent him from flipping backward over the railing and into the waiting branches of weeping willows below.

"Sorry." He smiled sort of dumbly. "Didn't mean to. It's five after ten. I wanted to make sure you were okay. Thought maybe I had slipped up with your list of food allergens at dinner."

"No. My stomach is fine. Really," Deck said, ironically noticing it was still doing turns from his recent scare. "Dinner was phenomenal."

"I take this healthy eating stuff seriously," Don said. "Let me cook for you for a few days; you'll forget you ever had food allergies." Don changed gears. "Oh. Proc and Wilky are moving some more stuff in."

Don moved around Deck and pointed to the light in the darkness. "Surprised they didn't ask for some help again. I guess they figured I wouldn't be up to it considering what happened with boss DuPont."

"Those are the new owners?" Deck asked, moving up beside Don. "Moving stuff in at night?"

"Yeah. They got the stuff coming over on boats from England. Time differences and all, by the time the boat docks here as compared to when it leaves there, it's always at night."

"I don't know how they can see anything in all that darkness," Deck noted.

"The place was built in the center of a big pine forest. That's why it's called Pale Shelter Estates. The mansion itself gets barely any sun. They're gonna have to cut some of that stuff back with winter approaching. Being at this elevation and on the water with no sun exposure, that place will cost a fortune to heat," Don said. "Hell, they cut down enough trees; they can have all twelve fireplaces in there blazing all winter. It would give a great smell to the place, cut down on some of the stale air that's been trapped in there all the years it's been abandoned. Can't wait to see what he does with it. It's going to look beautiful. If I had to be with one man for the rest of my life, that's the way I'd want us to live."

"You ready to go?" Deck interrupted Don's musings.

"Yeah. Let's blow this joint." Don mischievously grabbed at the crotch of his too tight camouflage pants.

As Deck moved to follow the incredible Latin hulk back inside, he turned once more to the spotlight in the darkness. If his eyes weren't deceiving him, he could swear the man who had remained frozen on the ramp was now raising a hand in a wave.

"Wait for me." Deck tried to sound casual as he hurried behind Don and grabbed the shoulder strap of his black wifebeater. Or so he thought until they entered the light and he realized he had missed the strap by about an inch. In his hand was a thick bush of body hair. Don didn't even seem to mind the tug.

CHAPTER TWO

"Geez. Couldn't Hayes have put in some streetlights around here?" Deck huffed from the passenger seat of Don's Ranger—a vehicle as big as the man driving it.

"He's thought about it. But there's something majestic about driving up this dark dirt road toward a giant beacon of light at the top of the hill." Don gestured with his chin toward the reflection of Weeping Manor in his rearview mirror as they pulled out of the side parking area of the mansion and onto the road.

"It sure is majestic," Deck said. "It's like a mountain resort."

"That's what he and Ben were going for. Each wing has dozens of rooms, so they could house a maximum number of people. They wanted to save the western gay world, take in all the strays, clean them up, nurture them, give each one a job and a home all in one—"

"And have more playthings to fill their sexual needs," Deck interrupted.

"Wait until you see The Caves!" Don said excitedly in response to the topic, not catching Deck's attempt at irony—and investigation. "It's like paradise down there. Before he started producing films, Hayes was one of the best set designers in the film industry, so he created imaginary fantasy worlds, from your typical dungeon to kings' courts. I've done some role-playing like you can't imagine."

"I can imagine. I'm looking forward to getting down there myself." Deck rubbed his beard thoughtfully.

"It's the best. Of course not at the moment because of Ben's death, but usually, The Caves are open to the public weekend nights after dark. Guys from all over the city come to party. I'm telling ya. Living at Weeping Manor is the life." As if to punctuate his statement, Don punched a remote button connected to his visor, which opened large metal gates they'd just approached at the front border of the Weeping Manor property. Not actually an opening to any kind of fencing, these gates were essentially just for aesthetics—attached to large stone pillars.

"How did you end up working for Hayes and Ben?" Deck asked as the Ranger pulled through the now open gates and onto the road that would lead to the thriving part of town: a community expanding with plenty of storefronts and apartment rentals that were quickly driving up real estate costs.

"I assume you know about me being outed and how it ruined my football career and all?" Don referred to a hugely publicized scandal from two years ago, and Deck bobbed his head in response. "That's when I was getting all that extra attention with my healthy cookbooks, which were selling like crazy. Right before the shit hit the fan, PontMond Enterprises had contacted me about doing a cooking show. That's when I became friends with Ben and Hayes. We're still working on putting the show together, and plan to market it to one of the gay cable networks. Probably gonna film it right in the kitchen at Weeping Manor. I'm telling you. These guys saved my life. Here I was, just hitting forty, and then I saw my life and fortune crumbling down around me."

Deck quickly did the math. Forty when the shit hit the fan two years ago. Don was older than him! But even in the faint glow of dashboard lights, Deck could make out Don's muscles, which looked flexed even when they weren't. He unconsciously wrapped his thick arms around his upper body to get a sense of his own barrel chest and substantial arms underneath the soft layer of "safety padding," as he called it.

"Check it out. This is when we get to the happening side of town. There are great antique and art stores coming in here, some great restaurants, a couple of clubs, a movie theater. You'll see. A couple of years, and this place is going to be huge. A total destination spot like Chelsea or the Castro."

"The hotties are out tonight," Deck noted as they drove past a brightly lit coffee shop. Men of all ages and lifestyles, from club kid to leather daddy, were spilling out into the street, chatting, sipping from cardboard cups, smoking, and cruising.

"Wave," Don said as he beeped his horn and rolled down both windows, letting in cool night air.

Deck could hear and see the reaction of all those conglomerating on the sidewalk. There were smiles, returned waves, hoots and hollers, and campy comments like, "I got a tight end for you right here, Donny!" But the biggest surprise was when a coiffed looking blond walking a poodle called, "Donny! Got yourself a daddy?"

Don giggled, beeping like he was acknowledging the truth of the statement as they turned a corner. Deck slipped into something of a pout. He was more than two years younger than Don!

"Whoa. What's happening?" Deck perked up as a cloud seemed to descend on the street. The streetlights even appeared to dim to a dull glow and litter began to blow across the asphalt, which was showing signs of potholes and cracks. Most of the storefronts and warehouse doors on either side of the street looked derelict, and shadowy figures hung out in doorframes, slipping back into the darkness as the headlights picked up their silhouettes.

"That's what happens when you turn the wrong corner. You end up in the broke breeder zone. The city is not quite where they want it to be yet," Don explained, and Deck assumed by "they," he meant Lamond and DuPont, who seemed to be the unofficial mayors of the town.

"Ben was going to run for office." Don read Deck's thoughts. "They need more cooperation within the legal and government branches. Even some of the businesses are being difficult with them, because they actually thrive on the sleaze factor. But not Dirty Harry. He's all for it."

Deck could see why. After only two shady blocks, they were met with more life—good fun *nightlife*. A lone strip mall's parking lot was filled to capacity, and everyone seemed to be heading for the sparkling glass doors under a bright fluorescent red sign with the words Dirty Harry's emblazoned on it. It was basically swallowing the 7-Eleven sign next to it whole.

"Harry and Jimmy bought out a bunch of vacant stores on the strip and expanded this tiny bar into *that*. And this parking lot used to be a junkyard," Don said as he pulled into a gorgeously paved stretch across the street from the club.

Don had to drive fairly deep into the lot before finding empty spots. Groups of men cruised the Ranger as it drove past.

"Things are hopping," Deck noted.

"Wait until you get inside," Don said, steering into an empty spot.

❖

"It's wall-to-wall!" Don shouted to Deck as lights and music assaulted eyes and ears.

"Is it always like this?" Deck shouted back. He noticed as they plowed through the crowd that men of all ages were giving Don nods, pats on the shoulder, and strokes on the arm. Clearly, they had all heard about Ben Dupont's death and were silently sending their condolences. *Or are they just copping feels and not even noticing me?*

"There are a lot of regulars from The Caves here," Don explained as they moved to a quieter corner by a bar. "It's like Weeping Manor is the center of the universe to these guys. It's where they go to get away from it all. It's home."

"Hey, Donny," a delicious black bartender dressed only in tight white jeans said as he placed napkins down on the bar in front of Don and Deck. "Didn't expect to see you out here tonight. How you holding up?"

"Hey, Lox. Let's just say I can definitely use the usual," Don replied. "What you drinking, Decky?"

"Uhm, I'm fine. Doctor says I should stay away from that stuff. It's poison to my GI tract." Deck waved it off.

"Eh, forget that tonight. Tomorrow morning, we'll visit Phillip, the colonic therapist, and he'll suck that poison right out of us. How about a simple lite beer?"

"Yeah. Okay," Deck said, wondering why the chef/personal trainer automatically suggested a *lite* beer.

"You like to experiment?" Lox asked Deck, his dark eyes gleaming as he stroked his thin, perfectly sculpted goatee, which beautifully framed his swollen lips.

Deck detected dancing in his jeans. "You know it."

"I got a great new import beer. You're gonna love it." Lox flashed his pearly whites and Deck nearly melted.

"Sounds good." He raised one lip flirtatiously.

"Damn, Decky! The boys are checking you out big time!" Don nudged Deck, who was rolling up the sleeves of his thermal shirt to show off his powerful, hairy forearms.

"Really?" Deck grinned broadly.

"Hell, yeah. You're fresh meat. Heck, even Old-Timer is snaking you, and he probably hasn't gotten it up in like thirty years." Don gestured to a *real* old-timer slumped lazily at the end of the bar, big purple bags under his wrinkled eyes making him look like a sad puppy dog.

"Gee. I'm flattered," Deck muttered.

"I don't think he ever moves from that spot. In fact, I think when Harry remodeled this place, he had to just build everything around the old geezer," Don joked.

Lox handed them their beers, throwing Deck a wink.

As Deck sucked on the bottle, his thought was, *my stomach is going to be on fire tomorrow.* His thoughts were interrupted when he sighted two stocky, domineering men standing off in a corner. Deck recognized them: Soloman, the top-heavy, mustached black cop who had been guarding Lamond's bedroom door that morning, along with Bembury, his shorter pale-skinned buddy with the mahogany curls and goatee. They were both eyeing him, heads close together as they spoke conspiratorially, either sizing him up or feeling somehow threatened by him…perhaps even suspicious.

"You don't want to run into those two in front of the Seven-Eleven next door," Don said as he caught the looks being tossed across the sea of men. Then he finished with a mysterious, "Or maybe you do," before putting down his beer and grabbing Deck's hand. "Let's dance off some of these calories."

Trying to figure out why two cops grabbing coffee at a 7-Eleven could be ominous (other than the fact that it wasn't a doughnut shop), Deck watched the thudding legs of his ex-football player escort pounding the floor as men parted to let him through. There was the slightest jiggle within the tightness of the camouflage pants that gripped Don's bubbly butt. The black wifebeater was glued to his physique, sucked in at his indented lower back and stretching across his huge delts, the material blending with the hairy shag of his exposed shoulder skin. Don had no insecurities about it, and no one seemed to be disgusted by it, even the young, hairless fellows they cut through as they entered the swirls of bright colors and immersed themselves in the pulsing, heart-pounding beats.

How the hell is this big lug going to dance? Deck wondered, waiting to see if Don would break into some sort of bad 1980s Guido dance. Instead, he was shocked as the stony hard body turned elastic, Don melting into the gyrating bodies all around him as if dancing was his natural form of release.

A former club junkie himself, Deck should have felt at home on the dance floor, but he sort of needed to step on the welcome mat first and wipe the soles of his shoes to warm them up, especially considering it had been so long since he'd been a resident in this environment.

Don's soul was wiping up the dance floor and whipping the heads of all the men in the vicinity in his direction. His lithe moves were mesmerizing, luscious. Deck focused on feeling the music like he used to, letting its invisible strings seep inside to move him like a marionette. He went for the old standby, sticking his thumbs in his front belt loops so his arms could hang lazily as he swiveled his hips back and forth to the rhythm. He could feel the jeans clinging to each ass cheek as he jutted them left and right in time, and the heated, soft abrasion of the inside material as it rubbed gently at his genitals, stimulating them into a welcome half-hardness that displayed itself nicely.

Don looked deeply into Deck's eyes and winked playfully as he attached himself to Deck's rhythm. He reached out and stroked Deck's fuzzy jaw then leaned in and whispered, "You're so damn cute and sexy."

His lips nipped at Deck's, which only further crowded the crotch of Deck's jeans. When Don pulled away, Deck glanced around to see if any of the observers noticed the head-turning hunk making the moves on him.

Instead, most heads had turned away from them. Four very different hotties, in nothing but white towels, climbed up on the monstrous speakers in each corner of the dance floor, bumming out the numerous flamboyant club kids who had been on the platforms trying to hog the strobing spotlights. The DJ kicked into an anthem that was clearly a crowd favorite, for everyone let out a cheer and arms flew into the air with just the first few synth stabs and booming beats.

Deck's eyes were drawn to a body that glowed like porcelain on the speaker nearest to where he and Don were dancing.

"Come to Papa!" he exclaimed, then got flustered as Don grinned at him. "Did I just say that?"

Don threw a hairy arm around his shoulders. "Don't sweat it, cabrón. Welcome to the mindset of the over-forty crowd."

"Ugh!" Deck huffed.

"You wear it fantastic." Don ruffled his hair. "All this decade does is separate the men from the boys. Consider yourself a man."

"Three more months!" Deck corrected him.

"My mistake…kid," Don teased him as they got back on the beat, grabbing each other's waists.

Deck couldn't take his eyes off the lean meat gyrating above him a few feet away. There was absolutely no body fat, so what little effort seemed to be put in at the gym easily revealed every smooth muscle. An almost hairless, eight-pack stomach was split down the center by a sculpted black line of hair that ran from bellybutton down to a hidden area beneath the towel. Sharp, square shoulders topped off the long torso nicely. And the face was that of an Asian beauty with a touch of some other ethnicity mixed in that somewhat diluted his heritage while paradoxically enhancing its finest qualities. The young man's pearly white skin was accented by tight eyelids and lashes, thin black lines for eyebrows, and a shaggy, spiked head of dark hair. Deck latched on to every detail of that face, from the gaunt cheeks and protruding cheekbones to the small yet puffy lips that curled into a closemouthed smile.

The black eyes, so concealed yet so wide open, so soft yet so forceful, seemed to be staring right at Deck, busting him non-verbally for gawking. Deck looked away quickly, not wanting to seem like one of those dirty older men who has nasty thoughts of domination in his mind. Or one of those older white guys who preys on young Asian men as if he thinks he has some power over them simply because of the social stereotypes. *I'm no potato queen.*

Deck focused on the gorilla of a man with boyish charm right in front of his face: so different, yet so equally delicious. Don locked eyes with him and they glided together in time. Just as the warmth was coursing through him, a determined, aggressive, cherubic young man in only a tight pair of brown corduroys slipped between them to be the meat in their sandwich.

Deck's erect cock head was burned by every ridge of the corduroys through the material of his own tight jeans as the kid's tight ass sawed away at him. On the other side of the slice of spicy salami, Don was getting completely mauled. The kid was attached to Don's face, his hands yanking feverishly at Don's perfectly sculpted, cheesy eighties Guido coif. Suddenly, Deck was feeling quite deflated. How the hell had he become the third wheel—or more like the flat spare tire in the trunk? As far as this kid was concerned, he and Don could have been a couple—a monogamous couple. The sparks had been flying intensely between them a split second before the kid had decided to join them. It was apparent the kid's goal had been more to jump Don and get Deck out of the picture. What happened to Deck being the fresh meat? The object of all the regulars' desire?

Don seemed really into the attention, the action, or both. His hands slipped off Deck's hips and landed on the kid's corduroy waistband. Deck peered down as Don's hands weighed on the material, and the kid's smooth, pert, tight tan ass cheeks began to pop out the top. This was his cue to leave them alone. He released his hold on Don and silently danced away from them, not looking over the kid's shoulder at Don, not looking around to see if nearby dancers had witnessed the scandal. As a result, his eyes immediately crept upward, and to another scandal taking place, involving the Asian go-go boy on the speaker.

A total burnout type with scraggly hair and beard, a gaunt physique draped in a heavy metal band T-shirt and acid washed jeans, was reaching up to the towel that hugged the Asian dancer, who currently had his back to the crowd to show off his cute little wiggling behind.

There was an urgent nag in the pit of Deck's stomach as he sensed a bad situation about to occur between the clearly intoxicated burnout (probably something worse than an alcoholic intoxication) and the Asian dancer. He tried to push through the crowd, but he didn't get far before the burnout's arm was up the back of the dancer's towel.

It was obvious that a humiliatingly invasive action had been taken against the dancer's derriere. There was a sudden blur of movement, men could be heard shouting out, some were pointing as they stopped dancing, and several large bouncers seemed to burst out of nowhere to grab the burnout. But these bouncers weren't fast enough to save the burnout's face as the Asian dancer instinctively reacted to an unwanted anal probe. He had swung his body around swiftly while jumping away from the assault, one of his lean, muscular legs automatically lashing out. His shoed foot made contact with the side of the burnout's head, sending the scrawny man into the crowd.

Before the burnout could pick himself off the floor, the ferocious bouncers had done the job for him. He probably would have been better off staying down there, curled in a ball. He was savagely ripped away from the crowd and out of sight as a sleek and beautiful young blond man in a tight T-shirt and black slacks pointed and yelled angrily, his face red with fury. He then turned to the Asian dancer on the speaker, reached a hand up, and helped him climb off the box. They spoke for a moment, then the blond placed a hand gently on the dancer's bare shoulder and escorted him out of the high traffic area.

As they disappeared from sight, Deck caught a glimpse of Don, who seemed to have lost his score in the crowd during the drama, and was now peering over heads as if searching for Deck. Deck wasn't in the mood to deal with it right now. His real urge was to find out how the dancer was doing. He slipped off the dance floor quickly.

A wall of blackness suddenly obscured Deck's lock on the Asian dancer and the blond stunner escorting him away from the crowd. A line of huge black men, each in a black suit and dark sunglasses, walked menacingly through the crowd, and Deck found himself essentially rolling off their log-sized arms. None of them paid any mind to the annoying white bear skimming over their bodies.

Deck finally found his balance and stepped back, bumping into other clubgoers who had parted as if by telekinetic command to let the black men through. Deck glanced around. The entire tone in this area of the club had changed. He could almost see all the patrons stiffening—and not in the good way. It wasn't like there was racist air in this club, which was a melting pot of all urban jungle tribes, yet it appeared that every man in the vicinity made sure to keep one eye on the clan of black bodybuilders with *The Sopranos* attitude.

"Who are they?" Deck asked the closest person, a young guy with a fruity umbrella drink in hand.

"Black Mafia," the fruity umbrella drinker whispered with a combination of nervousness and delight at the scandal of it all. "They're so hot...."

They were indeed scalding. And also quite threatening as they gathered in an imposing circle in a corner by the bar, making Old-Timer look even meeker in his hunched position on his bar stool, although Old-Timer didn't seem all that terrified by them. He was the only one—other than Deck, who'd dealt with these types of posers enough in his years in law enforcement to see right through their disguise to their dependence on mob mentality for strength and confidence.

Deck moved to where the Black Mafia was gathered near Lox's bar station. Deck would be damned if he was going to let a block of solid dark chocolate keep him from getting another drink (and some answers) from his drop of sweet milk chocolate, Lox. Although, even at six foot, Deck was dwarfed by their presence. He smoothly slipped between the massive group, giving them one of his best charming grins. "'Scuse me, guys. Just wanna get a drink."

Next thing Deck knew, his knees were crashing onto the floor, absorbing the brunt of his weight. But the pain was nothing compared to the tweezer-like grip on his nipples. From his kneeling, submissive position, he looked up, and naturally, the biggest, blackest of the bunch was the one milking him. He had to bite down to fight from crying out.

"You must be new in town." The monster leaned down to nearly touch noses with Deck. A thick black beard practically meshed with

Deck's, and the spice of an Altoid poured from between those puffy purple lips.

"That feels great," Deck said through gritted teeth. "Wanna get a room?"

The burn shot through his pecs as the squeeze got tighter than he could imagine. He fell forward, but was stopped when his cheek hit a hefty piece of meat inside the crotch of the man's tailored black pants. The flesh seemed to grow hard against his cheek. The man was getting off on this.

Finally, Deck's battered nipples were released, and he was pushed away. His head landed in the hands of the men behind him. He bravely looked directly into the sunglasses of the leader of the pack, but his peripheral vision made him well aware of all the patrons trying not to look at the scene, for fear of finding themselves in the same position.

"You know who we are?" the monster asked from his towering upright position.

"Black Mafia?" Deck went for an ignorant joking tone from his kneeling position.

His jaws were pried apart by large black hands tearing at his whiskers. A thick glob of spit saturated the inside of his fear-dried mouth. Then his jaw was forcefully clamped shut by the many hands gripping his face.

"That's right, faggot. You like to swallow?" the monster asked in a deep, calm, almost seductive tone.

Deck just bobbed his head in response, not losing eye-sunglass contact.

"You may want to get yourself a police escort out of here tonight."

Deck was tossed aside by his head. He grabbed the side of the bar so as to avoid landing flat on the floor. He looked over to see the mob disappearing nonchalantly through the intimidated crowd.

Suddenly, a black hand dropped down from above. Deck flinched until Lox's gorgeous face followed. Lox was hanging over the bar, offering him assistance. He took it and was swiftly brought to an upright position. He winced as his thermal shirt rubbed against his bruised nipples.

"You okay?" Lox asked, hurriedly handing Deck another beer. "It's on me. To numb the pain."

"Thanks," Deck wheezed as he gulped down the offered cold bottle.

"Well, I was thinking you could put it on your nipples, but that will do too. I'd suggest you stay away from the BeNelly brothers," Lox said as he wiped down the bar.

"They're brothers?" Deck asked of the mob of about eight men. Lox grinned. "Broth-as."

"Oh," Deck said in understanding. "So is that a sample of the straighties terrorizing the town?"

"Uh…sure…straight…" Lox murmured before quickly changing the subject, as if uncomfortable talking about the BeNelly brothers. "What happened to Don Wand?"

Deck's other eyebrow raised. What an intriguing nickname for him. "Uhm, I guess he got lucky. So that dancer, the Asian guy."

"Adorable, right?" Lox smiled. "Name's Maru. Jimmy took him back to his dressing room. Apparently, someone went overboard on the dance floor."

"Maru," Deck repeated the name quietly. "Yeah. I saw what happened."

"Here's Jimmy now." Lox pointed. "Hey, Jimmy! Want you to meet Deck. He's a guest of Lamond's. Deck, this is Jimmy. He's Dirty Harry's partner."

"Nice to meet you," Jimmy said, extending a well-built but not over-pumped arm. "Sorry about the drama. It happens. Closet cases still crawling in from the fringes. But things are starting to clean up around here."

"How's the kid? I mean, the young man. The dancer." Deck tried to sound nonchalant.

"He's getting used to that shit. I just try to keep an eye out for him. He's been through some hard times, and I want to save him from going down the path I went down," Jimmy said. "He needs to find someone to take care of him like Harry took care of me."

"Can I meet him?" Deck asked, a little too anxiously, possibly sounding like *he* wanted to be the one to "take care of" Maru. "I'm a detective."

Why the fuck did I use that as an excuse? Deck kicked himself inside.

"Oh. Right. The Ghostbuster guy. Ben DuPont was telling us at dinner last week that you were coming to stay with them." Jimmy paused. "Damn. I can't believe he's gone. Well, I guess you know then that Maru lost his partner the same way."

Deck was used to having such shocking information revealed to him unexpectedly, so played it cool. "Yeah. I mean, I don't have to speak to him now, but maybe you could give him my card?"

As Deck was digging into his pocket for his wallet, Jimmy waved it off. "No. It's cool. Believe me, he's so ripped apart about this thing, he'd be more than willing to talk to someone who's going to seriously look into it and not accuse him of murder like our wonderful police force did."

Now I'm getting somewhere, Deck realized as Jimmy led him away.

❖

"Nice place," Deck said, keeping his eyes focused on the tight derriere of Jimmy as he lead the way down a glamorous hallway.

"Wasn't like this when I first met Harry," Jimmy explained. "He's dedicated his life to making this his dream club. Here's Maru's room."

As Jimmy knocked on a gold painted door, Deck enjoyed the view as various sizes and shapes of go-go boys passed in and out of doors in their thongs or towels, smiling and winking at him.

"Not in there?" Deck asked at last as Jimmy pressed an ear to the door, calling Maru's name.

"I hear his Christina Aguilera CD playing. He's obsessed with her and keeps the discs locked up in his trunk when he's not in there, so he's gotta be in there," Jimmy said. "Hey, Maru! It's me, Jimmy! You okay in there?"

"He's in there, probably blasting his *Burlesque* soundtrack and dancing around," a Latin stud said as he strolled by, and although his body was mostly hairless, he reminded Deck that Don "Wand" had no idea where he was right now.

"Thanks, Chale." Jimmy pulled a ring of keys from his pocket. "Okay, Maru! Naked or not, we're coming in!"

Indeed, Maru was naked. But modesty was the least of his problems right now.

"What the fuck?" Deck bounded past Jimmy at the sight of the lanky body swaying from a wood beam, the towel that had recently been around Maru's waist acting as a noose.

Deck righted a toppled chair that Maru had obviously jumped off and climbed it, ignoring the throbs in his knees from his recent run-in with the BeNelly brothers. "Grab him!"

But he needn't have barked the order. Jimmy was already wrapping his toned arms around the legs and lifting to relieve the tension in the towel as Deck began to rapidly untie it.

Questioning, curious, and shocked voices filled the doorway as Deck and Jimmy worked quickly, until finally Maru was flat out on a plush purple throw rug. Employees of the club who had been in the vicinity were piling into the room.

"Guys! Get back!" Jimmy demanded, rounding them up within his arm span. One dancer broke past him and ran to a small window to open it.

Deck pinched Maru's petite nose, slipped an arm under his back, and arched it, then pressed his lips firmly against still warm and moist lips.

Onlookers watched as Deck gave Maru intense, focused mouth-to-mouth.

"Come on! Breathe for me!"

And Maru did. There was some coughing and sputtering, and his compact skull began to roll slightly back and forth, the slit eyes opening slowly, dazed but quickly refocusing.

The irony was not lost on Deck when Cher's voice burst into a chorus of "You Haven't Seen the Last of Me" on a nearby boom box. Deck, one arm still under Maru's bare back, wrapped his other around Maru's head and stroked his frazzled dark hair. "You're okay. I've got you."

Breathing heavily, Maru looked almost dreamily into Deck's eyes and then weakly said, "If you'd gotten me a little sooner, I wouldn't have done that."

Deck was almost sure he caught a hint of flirtation twitch at Maru's lips even though he had basically just had a near-death experience. Confident Maru would be okay, he hurriedly turned to the concerned group that had gathered. "He's gonna be okay. No need to call the—"

He watched as Jimmy ended a cell phone call.

❖

"Oh, for Buddha's sake! Waxer, how is it you managed to be at the scene of two crimes in one day?" Anderson grumbled as she entered Maru's room just as all the other players in the emergency call were exiting, including a broad-shouldered, bearded EMT who had examined Maru. Also in attendance was the off-duty black-and-white cop team that had been in the club earlier and had been sought out by a concerned go-go dancer who knew they were still in the vicinity.

"Hell-O. *Saved* the kid's life, didn't kill him. This wasn't a crime." Deck looked at her pointedly. "It was an accident."

"A suicide attempt isn't an accident," Anderson corrected him.

"Where are you taking him?" Deck asked. Maru had been escorted out by some of Anderson's cronies.

"Down to the station for questioning, and probably psychological counseling."

"Questioning for what?" Deck wondered if he was being oversensitive because he was feeding off the energy of those in the area who felt the cops in Kremfort Cove were anti-gay. "He hasn't done anything to anyone."

"You don't know anything about this guy—"

"His partner burst into a puff of smoke just like Ben DuPont," Deck cut her off. "And apparently, it has torn him up to the point where he needs a little compassion and understanding."

"Don't get cute with me, Waxer." The fiery hot fierce club diva of twenty years ago surfaced unintentionally.

"Come on, Commissioner Anderson." Deck tried to tap into their old chemistry. "Isn't this a bit cliché? The big black brute of a police commissioner bullying the crafty, reckless detective incessantly even though it's obvious he's going to be the one to solve the case in the end?"

"Deck, I have business to take care of," was all she said as she walked out.

"Wait! Can I come? As Maru's guardian?" Deck suggested.

"Someone's got a Daddy complex." Anderson turned back to him with a wicked eyebrow raised. "It works for you. But the answer's no. You can come pick him up in about two hours. I'll tell him to expect you."

"Uh…no! That's okay. I want to surprise him!" Deck called after her as she disappeared.

The large black trunk in Maru's room had gold edges and ancient Oriental symbols painted in vibrant colors. Deck kneeled on the floor and unlocked it using a convenient tool on his key chain that had been an essential friend since his days on the police force.

The inside smelled surprisingly clean and fresh. It was neatly organized, with several smaller boxes nestled on the right and various books, a photo album, and an array of Christina Aguilera CDs (including the slightly out of season Christmas disc) filed neatly on the left. Deck took out one of the small wooden boxes and lifted the lid.

Inside, there was a strip of condoms, packets of sample lubricants you could grab from a fish bowl at any porn shop (and probably out of a bowl on the restroom counter right here in Dirty Harry's), and several neatly folded G-strings. Deck unthinkingly slipped a finger around the string section of a leather one and lifted it out of the box. For an instant, he imagined the thin material nestled between the crack of Maru's ass. He quickly pushed the thought out of his head and moved the box from his lap and onto the floor, carelessly tossing the G-string at it before closing the lid blindly. He refocused on the large trunk.

He found a photo album snuggled between two books. Short and sweet, it seemed to begin with Maru's childhood. Many photos featured a young Asian boy with a short, thin, and very beautiful Asian woman. She could have been a model, but it appeared she opted to be a loving mother. Chronological pictures showed the young

Maru growing, learning to ride a bicycle, appearing in school plays, graduating high school. The last few pages looked post-college, Maru glowing with happiness, often in the arms of a very cute man who looked to be of German descent if Deck's guess were correct. They were a gorgeous couple, eye and hair colors contrasting perfectly, the age difference just a small enough gap to keep the man from looking like a sugar daddy.

Deck tucked the photo album back between the two books that had held it in place. Then he noticed the binding of the books. One was *On Death and Dying*, a classic about grief. The other was entitled *Touched by a Guardian Angel*. Deck wasn't familiar with it, so he examined it closer. He noticed some dog-eared pages and flipped to the first. It was a chapter on learning how to communicate with your own guardian angel. The next chapter focused on visualizing your guardian angel. And the third, a chapter very close to the back of the book, was entitled "Becoming a Guardian Angel." The pages in this chapter were the most worn, as if the chapter had been referenced frequently.

Deck shuddered at the thought. It pained him to have to put the book back in with the other items that all clearly gave dimension and identity to Maru. Items that made him seem so alive.

As he was slipping the first small box he'd removed back in place, ready to remove a second box, Deck heard the door opening. He dropped the box inside and swung the trunk lid closed, but he knew he was never going to be able to get the lock on in time to appear innocent.

He spotted the leather G-string beside his knee. He had missed the box when he'd thrown it back. He hurriedly squished the minimal garment between the tight slit of his jeans pocket and put on his poker face.

"Deck, you're still here—" Jimmy began as he walked in, and then saw Deck slipping the lock into the loop on the trunk.

"Oh. Hey, Jimmy," Deck said, rising but not clicking the lock closed. "I'm trying to find some sort of clothing to bring Maru. I'm sure he doesn't want to leave the precinct in those medical scrubs they let him borrow."

"That trunk was unlocked?" Jimmy asked suspiciously. "He always keeps it locked up."

Deck shrugged. "Maybe he was doing something in there right before he...well, you know. There were some CDs. He was probably in there for those."

"Yeah. I guess so." Jimmy moved into the room. He knelt in front of the trunk and clicked the lock in place. "He's really private about his personal belongings. He keeps all his clothes in this closet back here."

Jimmy circled around a privacy screen that separated a corner of the room from the main area. Deck waited as Jimmy picked out jeans, a shirt, underwear, socks, and a jacket and slipped them into an empty knapsack that hung from a hook in back of the closet.

"You know, I can take this stuff down to him. I planned to go pick him up myself," Jimmy said as he handed Deck the knapsack.

"No problem. I feel kind of responsible for the kid after what happened. Wanna follow up with him, and be there in case the cops give him any trouble. I was a cop before I went private."

Jimmy held tightly to the bag for an instant as Deck tried to take it from him. "You're not looking to just interrogate Maru more about this, are you?"

"No. I'm not," Deck said honestly and something must have softened in his face.

"You like him, don't you?" Jimmy asked, letting go of the knapsack.

"I...don't know him," Deck's voice faltered. "I'm concerned. About everyone around here. It breaks my heart to see so many of us struggling like this just to survive."

Jimmy smiled. "Now I see why Lamond and DuPont spoke so highly of you. You're a man after their own hearts. Let's exchange numbers. I'd appreciate it if you two would call me when he's released and you're on your way back."

"Back here?" Deck asked as they both pulled out their cell phones to enter each other's info. "Won't you be closed by then?"

"Harry and I have a penthouse suite upstairs. And Maru has been sleeping here." Jimmy pointed to a nearby couch. "It's a pullout. Maru was a full-time student, and his partner was the breadwinner.

So when he passed, Maru needed a job and a home. I offered our guest bedroom, but Maru said he just really needed space by himself and didn't want to get in our way. After tonight though, I don't think I want him alone down here, so I'm going to insist he come sleep upstairs in the guest bedroom."

"I think that would be best," Deck responded before reciting his cell number for Jimmy's waiting fingers to enter.

Chapter Three

D amn Don for just leaving me."
Deck walked through a dark, grungy, industrial area of town. He was partially kicking himself. He had spitefully told Lox earlier that if Don should come to the bar, Lox was to give him a message that Deck had gotten lucky and would find his own way home. When Deck had eventually checked in with Lox to find out where the police precinct was, Lox had informed him that Don had indeed come by to determine Deck's whereabouts because it simply was not Don's style to ditch a friend at a club for a trick, especially when he was playing chauffeur to a guest of Lamond.

Deck felt so vulnerable as he passed large lots filled with Mack trucks, alleys filled with garbage bins, and chain link fences behind which sat monstrous canisters of unspecified substances, although some of them had the cliché skull and crossbones on them. *This whole friggin' part of the city needs to have one of those at every stoplight.*

Deck nearly pissed himself as ten-foot-high gates rattled furiously, accompanied by a vicious growl. The chain and padlock on the gate stretched to maximum width as a large, wet, steaming black nose was forced through the gap.

Deck had already leapt into the street at the threat of an attack.

It was a dog: a big, mean guard dog. Not surprisingly, only two dog breeds came to mind that it could possibly be, and both were black with rust markings. In this case, it was a Doberman, not a Rottweiler. A long snout breathed through the gate posts, and Deck could make out the angry glistening eyes on the other side of the fence as he slowly circled out into the street.

"Run home to Master Damien like a good devil dog," Deck suggested politely, and got a vicious bark in response. But he noticed that the dog wasn't even looking at him. Those angry eyes seemed to be focused off to his right.

Deck turned quickly to see yet another generic dark alley across the street. He glanced back at the dog. Those angry eyes seemed to morph into orbs of fright. The dog whimpered and ran off.

"That *can't* be a good sign," Deck huffed as he picked up his pace, getting as far away from that alley as fast as he could.

A little farther down the street, along the relative safety of a graffiti-covered brick wall, the spray-painted words "All fags burn in hell with AIDS" was not a very inviting sight in this dark side of Kremfort Cove. Deck recalled Don's description of the "broke breeder zone" earlier, and he sensed he was moving into the heart of it. Tall tenement buildings seemed to rise into the dark sky above as they paradoxically showed signs of crumbling to the ground as a result of neglect. The projects were such a scary place to *walk* through. He couldn't imagine what it was like for the low-income people who actually *lived* there.

As Deck passed under a streetlamp glowing a sickly pale pink/yellow, he saw fluttering shadows on the cracked pavement. His head shot upward. Around the blinding center of the streetlamp bulb, he could make out some sort of creatures doing flying somersaults. Hella big bugs? Or birds? A Doberman behind a gate might be unnerving, but unidentified flying creatures that were free to dive-bomb you at any moment were somewhat more disturbing.

These blocks were so creepy that even the freaks didn't come out to play. It was absolutely, bone-chillingly desolate and quiet. Deck could hear his own footsteps rebounding off the wall beside him. As he reached a corner, he crossed his fingers that the street name would be one that had been in the directions Lox had given him. He uncrossed them to give the sign the middle finger.

"Fuck!" Deck said. "I'm so fucking lost."

He turned the corner and continued on past more brick and mortar. And then he heard a high-pitched squeal that rebounded through the localized area of this concrete jungle.

Ahead was an alley: a very well lit alley. There was no mistaking the dancing colors on the wall leading into the alcove. It was a fire. Without a thought for his own safety, Deck sprinted the twenty feet or so to the alley, bracing himself for the sights of a human being burning to death as he rounded the corner. He tripped over numerous piles of trash littering the narrow alley, targeting large flames that were dancing up ahead. Just as he was reaching his destination, he came to a screeching halt. Actually, it was more of a screeching tumble, as a result of none other than the most cliché of situations. Deck slipped on a banana peel and came crashing down on a lumpy and less than cushiony pile of trash bags.

Deck hurriedly tried to get up for the mere purpose of returning to completing his original objective, not because he was embarrassed to have been seen taking a fall by two pairs of eyes. It took him a second to realize the high-pitched human sounds had stopped.

"Fuck off, pervert!" a gruff and hoarse voice croaked. "Unless you're gonna pay to watch. Hundred bucks."

Deck looked toward the fire. The fire wasn't incinerating a person. It was burning a pile of trash inside a big metal trash bin. Next to the big fire, on a bed of more trash was...

"Oh! So sorry. Sorry. Really. I...I thought you needed help..." Deck started as he tried to comprehend the sight before him. It was clearly an old black man, naked except for a lot of white hair and alley filth coating his skin, on all fours and making good use of the pale and equally grime-coated ass of a much younger white guy.

"You wanna help, that'll cost two hundred." The white kid looked over his shoulder with a smile, orange firelight bouncing off his already yellow teeth.

"Nah, I'm good." Deck put his hands up as a barrier to shield himself from the mere thought of it. "You two have a good time."

Is it wrong that I'm comforted to be back in the gay area of town?

Deck pretty much sprinted out of the alley faster than he had gone into it, making sure to leap over any stray banana peels. Finally, he was back on the desolate street and headed the way he had originally been going. *That's more doggies and doggy style than I needed to come across in one night.*

The air was split by two ear-piercing screeches from back in the alley. Under any other circumstances, Deck would have run to check on the homeless men, because it sure sounded like they were screaming bloody murder, but their sexual act had sounded similar before he'd even interrupted them. All he could assume was that they were having quite the simultaneous experience.

Farther ahead, Deck spotted lights: glowing signs, like maybe some businesses, perhaps only a cheap motel or something. But any life was better than none.

Scratch that. Deck saw a most unwelcome sign of life. From alleys between buildings on each side of this street, large black figures emerged, standing still once they locked on to him.

A couple of BeNelly brothers.

Deck turned abruptly as if he actually meant to cross the street at the intersection rather than to turn the corner.

Halfway across the road, he caught a glimpse of moving figures in his peripheral vision. There were two more BeNelly brothers coming from the other direction, fast, trying to steer him toward the two that already waited. He broke into a run, straight ahead as soon as he hit the other sidewalk, cutting down a street with only one functioning streetlight.

It was like he'd stepped into the twilight zone. Apparitions slipped from shadowy alleys and doorways. It was an almost storybook scenario. Four figures in flowing sheets appeared. But instead of your typical white-cloaked ghosts, these were covered in black sheets. Deck's heart nearly stopped. The flowing sheets seemed to float down the street toward him.

Feet were pounding the pavement behind him. He didn't look back. He saw an opening between buildings and plunged into a route that held no guarantees of escape.

He dodged a couple of garbage cans. He felt blind. He couldn't believe darkness could be this...dark. He grabbed along the wall to his right, trying to keep up his speed while hesitantly using his feet as feelers.

He needed to break this straightforward path. The BeNelly brothers knew this city. They would know where this alley let out. But what about those other things? With the sheets on? What the fuck were they? Could they walk through walls? Would one suddenly pop out of one of the brick structures he was running between? His skin crawled at the memory of the frightful vision. His heart pounded overtime. He strained his eyes, looking up for any sign of a fire escape.

Finally, his fingers, raw from scraping along a brick wall, dipped into a window frame. A slice to Deck's hand signified that the window had been shattered. Panting, he slipped his arms out of the knapsack on his back and used it to target the fragments of glass he could see in the limited moonlight. Once they were cleared, he hoisted himself up and in. He really should have put the knapsack back on instead of trying to climb in with it in hand. It slipped from his grasp and dropped to the ground outside the window. He couldn't even see it now. And he sure as hell didn't have time to go back out and get it. Especially after he heard a bloodcurdling scream echo down the alley. He banged his head on the window frame in his hurry to get all the way in and hopefully out of sight of the numerous enemies—living or dead—that were following him. If he was lucky, maybe one of the BeNelly brothers had fallen victim to one of those sheeted things.

Inside, there were squeaks and scurrying. God only knew what rat party he had just interrupted. Dust mites munched at his nostrils. This was insane. He could not see a thing. There was the mere suggestion that windows lined the far side of this derelict building, so he headed in that direction.

Please let there be no huge hole in the floor, he thought as he used his feet as feelers once again. "Things" were kicked aside. Animate or inanimate, he had no idea, but some objects were definitely heftier than others.

Stale air burned his eyes, which were wide open in the darkness. A glow of yellow light beckoned him. His hands groped at emptiness. The yellow took shape. A window. He was almost there.

A hand grabbed his leg. He cried out, looking down, kicking out. Yellow glinted off irises.

"Suck ya' dick. Hundred bucks," a voice slurred from the darkness.

It's the same guy from the alley, Deck thought, recognizing that voice. But that was impossible.

"Two hundred, we let ya help," another voice came from the dark, sounding more enthused and energetic. Fingers clawed at Deck's other leg.

"No! Sorry," Deck hissed as he yanked away from the grasping hands.

It can't be them. That was a few blocks away. And they'd need night vision to see me in here. Deck's mind was throbbing with fear and confusion at the same tempo as his pulse and heartbeat as he finally reached the window on the other side of the building. He looked out and saw a sign of humanity—a bodega across the street, some sort of clothing outlet, and farther along, an auto repair shop. He glanced carefully out the shattered window, as far as the eye could see in either direction. No sign of any big BeNellys. Or any ghostly demons.

Deck glanced quickly back into the black interior of the building. *Are those two homeless fuck buddies following me? How fast can they move?*

He managed to get the window up without having to shatter the remaining jagged edges of glass, which would be a sure way to announce himself. He climbed onto the rotten, skeletal windowsill. Somehow, the ground level had dropped on this side. It was a nice twelve feet below. He hoisted himself onto the sill and leapt. And felt something yanking him back.

"Aaagh!" he cried, sure the teleporting homeless fuck buddies had gotten hold of him. But then there was give as his weight flew forward. It was like he was being whipped with a cat-o'-nine-tails. His thermal shirt had gotten caught on some sort of sharp protrusion on the window frame, but the threads weren't strong enough to hold his weight and tore violently as he plunged forward, his intended graceful leap getting slightly twisted.

"Awwwgh!" Deck groaned when his feet caught the rest of his body. That stung like a mother. He managed not to crash on his palms and knees like a little kid though, which was a positive.

He righted himself and looked at the tattered remains of his shirt, which was more like a sash barely covering his torso as it draped over his shoulder. He glanced back from where he'd come. Up above, snagged on a splinter of wood, was most of his shirt. He dared not look long enough to see if those two horny homeless men would suddenly pop their heads through the window and offer to give him the whole shebang for three hundred bucks.

Feeling the sweat cool on his bare upper body as he yanked the tattered scraps of material off and tossed them with the other piles of filth in the gutter, he glanced around hurriedly, saw no ominous pursuers, and bustled across the street to the bodega. Interior night lighting was on, but the place was empty, with heavy-duty metal bars blocking the windows. Such a tease. Inside, rows of cookies, chips, condiments. It all looked so civilized, yet so out of reach.

The clothing outlet was hardcore, with solid metal gates allowing no opportunity for window-shopping.

Next, there was a large yellow sign blazing the words: Otto's Auto. *Evil Otto,* Deck thought of the dangerous bouncing head from *Berserk,* one of his all-time favorite video games when he was young. The damn sinister video smiley face had cost him mounds of paperboy quarters back in the day in its relentless pursuit.

And speaking of…across the sidewalk, a long shadow suddenly stretched past Deck, as if not only catching up to him, but passing him to prevent him from reaching refuge. He sprinted for the auto shop, praying that someone was there.

As Deck approached the gas pumps, he couldn't believe what he was seeing through the glass of the main office of Otto's Auto. Not only were the lights on, but there was a man inside—who was clearly deep into something.

A thick, ruddy-complexioned man with a gleaming bald head, bushy, sharply edged sideburns that sprouted from just beside his ears, and a severely shaped goatee barely separated from those sideburns, was standing behind a low counter, the front zipper of his mechanic overalls open to below the belt line. He seemed to be glancing down at his own round, hairy pecs as he yanked on his nipples. But just above the height of the counter, Deck could make out a thick head of hair moving toward and away from the bald man's crotch.

The bald man's facial muscles scrunched together, his lips pursed in an incredibly masculine way. His hands dropped from his nipples and clutched the back of the head facing his crotch as he thrust savagely at it.

Just as the bald man seemed to be gasping out the last of his lust, Deck's foot accidentally landed on tubing running along the pavement near the pumps, tolling a chime that usually signaled the arrival of someone needing a fill-up. Right now, the only person getting filled up was whoever was on his knees behind that counter.

Deck froze with the tubing still pressed under his sole. He didn't know what was more dangerous—the possibility of being worked over by the BeNelly brothers, dragged to the depths of hell by the mysterious sheeted figures right out of *Ghost*, or caught spying by the mean looking mechanic in the office. The choice of who nabbed him first was taken from his hands.

There were echoing clanks in the silence of the night as the bald man, steam nearly pouring from the ear holes right beside his hyper-sideburns, undeadened the deadbolts on his glass door, eyes glaring at Deck.

"You like watching, you fucking perv?" The burly man stepped outside and pounded toward Deck, his overalls still completely unzipped, revealing body fuzz matted with sweat.

"No…" Deck stammered, stepping back, arms raised defensively as he glanced over his shoulder at the same time. "I'm being followed! Can you let me in? Please?"

"You're serious," the bald man said, his arm already gripping the back of Deck's neck as if to rough him up.

"Yeah," Deck said, finally noticing how out of breath he was as he puffed heat directly onto the bald man's face, feeling it bounce back at him.

"Come on. Get inside." The bald man dragged Deck by the scruff of his neck while looking suspiciously up and down the street. Once inside, he locked the glass doors behind them.

"What's going on?" a burly bearded man asked from behind the counter.

"You're—" Deck began, recognizing the man who was still in his EMT uniform.

"Oh yeah! You're the guy who saved Maru's life," the man said, moving toward a closet in a corner of the room. "What happened to your shirt? Partied it up after being a hero?"

"It's a long story. But I got these big groups of mean looking black guys chasing me—"

"BeNelly brothers," the bald man cut in.

"Yeah," Deck said, not wanting to come across as crazy with any ghost talk.

"Luckily, all they got was your shirt. You don't want to get on their wrong side," the EMT said, emerging from the closet with a large Otto's Auto T-shirt, which he handed over to Deck.

"Thanks," Deck said, slipping his head into the well-worn material, very conscious of the two men staring at his naked torso as he did.

"Looks like they almost got away with your nipples too," the bald man noted as the shirt was just wrapping around Deck's neck.

Deck followed his eyes while grappling to get his arms into the short sleeves. "Damn! They sure did. Guess I'm already on their bad side."

Deck had two nasty purple nurples. He became very aware of how bruised they were as the material of the T-shirt was pulled over them. He winced.

"Nice tight fit. I'm Otto, by the way, and this is my partner, Teddy," the bald man said.

They moved into a smaller circle and shook hands.

"Deck," Deck said as he glanced closely at the two visions of brawn. His eyes eventually landed and locked on a sparkling liquid pearl at the bearded corner of Teddy's mouth. He turned red-faced. "I apologize for…interrupting you guys."

"Too bad we didn't spot you a few minutes earlier." Teddy smiled, and Deck watched the pearl stretch slightly.

"You're new in town," Otto said. "The guys must have been all over your ass-liciousness at Dirty Harry's."

Now Deck was sort of wishing he *had* arrived a few minutes earlier. He couldn't take his eyes off that gleaming beacon of white on Teddy's lip. He ran his tongue around his own lips to moisten them.

Otto followed Deck's gaze until he spotted the object of the fixation. He reached to Teddy's mouth and plucked the glob of goo off Teddy's beard with one index finger. "You got a little something there, Teddy Bear," he said before continuing, "Something I think the Big Deck wants."

Before Deck could react, the gritty finger covered in cum swooped toward his mouth and slipped between his lips. He instinctively sucked on it, tasting just a hint of the bitter blandness that was being overpowered by the grime of auto fluids that had worked their way between the miniscule grooves of Otto's fingerprint.

Deck sprung to life below. He could so use this right now. But he really needed to get to the police precinct. He grabbed Otto's thick arm and held it still, knowing he should pull it away, but savoring the contact.

Otto's finger slipped teasingly out from the saliva pocket that had formed right behind Deck's lower lip. "Wanna come home with us tonight?"

"Guys, I would so love to, more than you can imagine, but I gotta get to the police precinct to pick up the kid—Maru." Deck looked to Teddy for willpower.

"Yeah. You're right." Teddy showed strength. "We'll take a rain check though."

"You got it." Deck smiled. "Right now, I'm totally lost. Am I anywhere near the precinct? I can't be wandering this area all night. I got the BeNelly brothers on my ass."

They jumped at the tolling of the gas pump bell.

A bright white pimped out Hummer with tinted windows had just pulled into the front of Otto's shop.

"Oh shit," Deck muttered as an intensely black man, who was even bigger than the biggest of the BeNelly brothers, stepped out of the driver's seat of the Hummer, which sprang up about a foot with the loss of all the muscle mass. The guy could be a professional wrestler.

"That's no BeNelly brother I ever saw," Teddy said as he stepped behind the counter and placed one hand on a nearby phone.

"Stay cool, guys. I'll handle this," Otto said.

Deck looked over to Otto, who *still* hadn't zipped up his overalls. At the crotch of the seam, a thick mangled bush of pubes sprouted right at his lower belly. A lug wrench must have been conveniently lying around. Perhaps Otto had been interrupted by the arrival of Teddy and just tossed the tool aside in his excitement to get some head. He was now wielding the wrench as he approached the door.

"It's cool, man." The big black guy stepped away from the glass door, hands up in the air to show he had no weapon. "I'm here for Deck Waxer."

"No shit!" Otto called through the glass, lug wrench still held high as he looked into the stony strong features of the man with the giant neck and tremendous Neanderthal body. "You're gonna have to get through me first!"

"I'm his neighbor!" the man yelled. "Hayes Lamond's new neighbor."

Otto turned back to Deck, who had stood his ground in front of, but up against, the counter. Behind it, Teddy had the phone receiver held to his ear, finger already prepared to dial for help.

"Oh. Wait. Yeah. I think he's one of the guys I saw moving furniture earlier," Deck said quietly.

"Well, could you be a little more certain before I let the guy in? He's fuckin' BIG," Otto pointed out.

"Ask him his—" Deck began, then realized he was acting like a chicken shit. He stepped up beside Otto and asked himself. "What's your name?"

"I'm Wilky. My man is Proc."

"Wilky and Proc. Yeah. He got the names right." Deck shrugged, recognizing the odd names of the couple Don had mentioned earlier on the balcony. "Let him in."

The huge hunk of man had to bend to get in the doorway.

"Damn, you're a nice big one." Otto seemed to objectify any man in his presence. "You doing anything tonight?"

"Taking Deck back if he needs a lift," Wilky said. "How come I ain't seen you guys at The Caves?"

"We haven't really gotten around to getting up there for those parties," Teddy now joined the conversation. "We like things a bit more intimate."

"And damn!" Otto exclaimed. "We wouldn't want to have to share you with anyone else. Except Deck here. Imagine the four of us—"

"I really gotta get to the police precinct." Deck stopped the fantasy from forming. "Wilky, why are *you* out here looking for me?"

"Hayes called us. Said you was sorta missing in action," Wilky explained. "So I offered to come looking for you. Don's out also. I just tracked you down first."

"Yum. Don Wand," Teddy said. "I cough up a hairball just thinking of him."

"Guys! Please," Deck truly begged. "Can we just keep it in the pants for tonight? And can *someone* drive me down to the precinct?"

"I gotcha." Wilky's huge hand landed on Deck's shoulder.

Deck felt like a dwarf next to the near seven-foot Wilky. "I don't want to impose. It's really late."

"No prob." Wilky waved it off. "I'm a night person."

Deck quickly exchanged phone numbers with Otto and Teddy, thanked them for saving his ass, and then stepped through the black night and into Wilky's white Hummer.

❖

"And there goes the block where I think I made the wrong turn," Deck said as he looked down an ominous street the Hummer was passing.

"Don't wanna be going down there in the *daytime*!" Wilky laughed.

"Especially not with the Black Mafia chasing after you," Deck said, then blushed at the race specification.

"BeNellys after ya?" Wilky scoffed. "You send 'em my way. I suck their asses so good they be my bitches for life."

"I'll keep that in mind," Deck said. "For more reasons than one."

"Funny man." Wilky grinned, and Deck was amazed at the sort of adolescent charisma beneath the hard exterior. He also couldn't help but notice how Wilky's dialect seemed to be comprised of contemporary Ebonics with "proper" English sprinkled throughout. It added to his magnetism.

Light began to fill the streets as they continued driving, and finally, they passed the anxious energy of a medical building. Right past it there was more anxious energy to be had.

"Here we are." Wilky gestured with his head to a well-lit parking lot filled with police cars.

"I couldn't have been any closer," Deck practically muttered to himself.

"I'll wait out here," Wilky said after pulling into a spot.

"Thanks. I owe you." Deck threw the passenger door open.

"We'll dine together," Wilky responded, and Deck looked over to see his brilliantly dark eyes blazing with hunger.

"All you can eat." Deck smirked, then closed the door, glowing with pride at all the promises of action he had racked up in the past half hour. *I still got it.*

"What are you doing here?" Maru sounded incredibly confused when Deck entered the quiet office in which he had been sitting alone. Deck had expected some sort of broken English, but instead he heard plain old everyday generic English.

"I brought you your clothes," an empty-handed Deck said.

Although looking weary and tired, Maru raised a thick, perfectly plucked eyebrow at Deck.

"But I lost them," Deck confessed. "It's a long story. Let's just get out of here. I'll take you home."

"What? You think just because you theoretically saved my life I'm going to be your slave boy?" Maru shot back. His expression and tone were hard to read. The question came out as exhausted, bored, unsurprised, insulted, and maybe a little flirtatious.

"I just—I meant—I came to bring you back to Dirty Harry's," Deck stammered.

"Don't do me any other favors," Maru muttered, uncurling from his slumped position on the wooden chair in front of a detective's desk. He was still in the clothing he'd been covered in by EMT Teddy at the club—oversized scrubs that hid his thin, tight physique. "I sure hope you didn't lose my favorite pair of jeans."

"Yeesh! I'm sorry for being concerned!" Deck huffed as they exited the office and headed down a long hall toward the front of the precinct. "I had to pull a lot of damn strings to get you out of here. They were going to send you away to a loony bin."

"You're a cop?"

"I was. So I know people."

"I bet you're a spy because they think I'm in on this suicide club thing." Maru rolled his eyes.

"Suicide club? There's a suicide club?" Deck became all business.

"I'm not talking to you about this. I have the right to remain silent."

"I'm not trying to spy on you. So I'm not gonna ask any questions. But the bottom line is, we have to get you some professional help. Because they're going to be following up with you. *And* me."

"*We* don't need to do anything," Maru said as they stepped into the main lobby of the precinct, where cops, hustlers, drunks, druggies, and general thugs were all involved in their nightly routines. "You got a cell phone? I want to call Jimmy and Harry to tell them we're on our way."

Deck dug into his pocket, where he had stuffed his phone after exchanging numbers with Jimmy. As he yanked it out, something black went flying across the room, then skidded to a stop between two four-inch platform heels.

Deck's mouth went dry. It was Maru's leather thong. It had gotten caught on his phone.

"HUNN-Y BEEAARR!" a drunk drag queen attached to the platforms cooed as she tried to bend down to grab the thong, nearly dropping the little lap dog cradled in one arm. "I'd love to see your big hairy man ass squeezed inside those!"

Maru hurried over to the thong and snatched it up before the drag queen could gain enough equilibrium to pinpoint it.

"Bitch, this was a gift from me to my papa, and I'm the only one who's going to be seeing every gray hair on his fat hairy man ass in it!" Maru growled.

"Sooor-ry!' the drag queen swayed in both stance and voice as she turned away with her chin in the air.

Maru held the leather thong between two fingers, putting on a show for all the cops and criminals who were now gawking. "Now let's get home, Daddy, so you can slip this baby right between your cheeks—"

Deck snatched the thong and shoved it back in his pocket, as there was a combination of snickers (from straight cops) and catcalls (from gay hustlers) in the station. He grabbed Maru by the arm and began to drag him to the exit. He only half noticed a pretty boy in handcuffs being led by a cop past the drag queen, whose dog began to yap anxiously.

"Shut the rat up!" an officer behind the front desk was barking back at the dog and drag queen just as the precinct door closed behind Deck and Maru.

Once the cool late night air hit them, Deck growled, "I can't believe you just did that to me!"

"That's what you get, you perv," Maru responded. "But if it's any consolation, I'm sure your fat, gray-haired ass would look damn good in my thong."

Deck smacked away Maru's hand as it grabbed the back of his Otto's Auto T-shirt and lifted it up so Maru could get a look at the goods.

"It's not funny, Maru! I have to work with those people in there and be taken seriously if I want to figure out what the hell is going on in this city." Deck was fuming.

"I'm fucking sorry!" Maru exclaimed as they neared the white Hummer and Deck opened the back door for him. "Well, while you're busy investigating me and this town, *Detective,* could you possibly find out who killed my boyfriend?"

❖

That was about the most Deck was going to get out of Maru that night. After Maru and Wilky said hello, Wilky suggested that Deck join Maru in the back of the Hummer for the return trip to Dirty Harry's. Deck tried to apologize to Maru, but he waved it off and suggested they just ride in silence because he was really tired.

After calling Harry and Jimmy to tell them he was on his way, Maru stared out the window for a moment, but before long, he drifted off to sleep. In the flashes from streetlights, Deck took in the flawless, angular features of Maru's face, and the red bruising around his neck where the towel had done its damage. He sighed with sadness.

The sound seemed to send a nocturnal message to Maru, who rolled away from the window as if he were in a bed. His forehead came to a rest right against Deck's bicep, his two gentle hands caressing Deck's forearm.

Deck tried not to look down at Maru's soft breathing as he felt the hairs tingle on his arm.

I knew I shouldn't have had those drinks, he thought to himself, mentally blaming the internal warmth he was feeling as a very different painful heat that often burned inside his digestive tract after too much gluttony.

Maru stirred awake and slowly rose off Deck. "Wilks, can you drive around back? There's a private entrance for employees."

"Got it. I called Harry a moment ago, and he told me he'd meet us back there since you got no keys," Wilky spoke into the rearview mirror.

They came to a door that quickly swung open. Harry and Jimmy were waiting, both in comfy nightwear. Maru climbed out of the Hummer and Deck followed.

"I can manage from here," Maru said, stopping Deck in his tracks. "Well, I guess I should thank you for saving my life, but look at the life you brought me back to."

With that, Maru walked off, into the waiting arms of Jimmy and Harry, who offered quick nods of thanks to Deck over his shoulder.

Deck circled the Hummer and climbed into the passenger's seat. He'd had to fight the urge to call out to Maru, to offer to take him away from this life, to invite him to stay at Lamond's place.

❖

Since Deck didn't have a remote control for the front gates of Weeping Manor, Wilky actually drove into Pale Shelter Estates and took an inconspicuous path that branched off of his home's driveway and eventually led right through the pine forest to Weeping Manor.

"I can't thank you enough, Wilky," Deck said as he stepped out of the Hummer in the ornately landscaped carport of the Lamond mansion and leaned back into the vehicle.

"It's the neighborly thing to do," Wilky said. "After things have settled down following the funeral, Proc and I would like to have you and Hayes over for a visit, although, we still got so much work yet to do at Pale Shelter."

"Well, if you need any help moving furniture, painting, or anything, let me know," Deck said. "Have a good night."

Waking to the door, Deck realized Wilky was going to wait to make sure he got inside safely. He mounted the steps between gorgeous gold lanterns and quickly punched in the code Hayes had given him to disarm the digital alarm and lock system hidden behind a doorframe panel. He gave one last wave of his hand before closing the door. He climbed up the steps, heading for his room—noting the actual burning that was indeed a result of the limited amount of alcohol he'd consumed hours before. *Damn sensitive stomach.*

CHAPTER FOUR

When Deck opened his eyes the next morning, the enveloping sheets, comforter, and fluffy pillows begged him to just bask in their warmth longer. But he was pressured by the awareness of being in a new place—someone else's place—and not knowing what the daily protocol was in this environment. He wasn't sure if he was expected downstairs for breakfast or if people just kind of came and went as they pleased.

Deck got out of bed, immediately longing for the luxurious sheets touching his naked skin, and padded his way to the bathroom to begin his morning routine. Before long, he was under a cascading rainforest showerhead. It was quite invigorating, and there was something so freeing about standing in a Jacuzzi tub in the middle of a giant room instead of being squished in some dark shower stall.

He lathered himself with one of the botanical body washes in a caddy by the tub, enjoying the almost slippery lotion as it glided over his hairy muscles. He paused at his paunch, poked it with an index finger, and got a little frustrated at the slight sinking feeling before he hit hardness. Seemed no matter how little he ate or how much he exercised, that thin layer of padding didn't want to go away.

Deck quickly moved on. His hands found a much more appropriate place for a little extra padding: his buttocks. He rubbed them with his slippery palms then slapped the large surface area of each cheek, laughing as he imagined Don the chef doing the slapping.

"Someone's in a feisty mood today!" a cheerful but calm voice said from behind Deck.

Deck spun in shock to find Phillip, the compact and lean yoga instructor/colonic therapist, standing there dressed in a pink preppy shirt and pleated gray pants, both of which showed off his incredibly thin and lean body.

"Uhm…" Deck stammered, his modest cock poking its way out from his bush of pubes.

"If you can't turn yourself on, who can you turn on?" Phillip said politely, grabbing a blanket-sized towel from a warmer rack on the wall nearby. "Come, rinse off and I'll take you for your first internal rinse."

It was so odd how people just nonchalantly invaded your privacy in this place like it was no big deal.

A few moments later, Phillip was leading Deck, now in a cozy robe Phillip had handed to him after watching him rinse and dry off, through a maze of hallways, taking them farther and farther away from the heart of the mansion.

"Where are we going? I don't know if I could find my way back. These halls are all starting to look alike," Deck admitted. He had to take back his words when they turned a corner into a hall lined with inset fish tanks and terrariums. A soothing tropical soundtrack seeped down from above.

"Welcome to the Zen den." Phillip's voice was so lulling he could probably put you at ease even if the mansion was on fire. "It's purposely isolated from the other areas of the mansion to keep you focused on your inner spirit."

Past the path of natural habitats was a plain room with soft gold walls and no decorations. Lined up from left to right were four odd contraptions. They looked sort of like examination tables you'd see in a doctor's office, but it was as if all the meat of the tables had been left out. There were two padded posts on what would be the far corners of a table, then a gap that would have been the surface of the table, and finally, a long padded podium creating the width of the table's closer corners. Deck also noticed flat stainless steel basins sitting on the floor between the various components of these examination tables. Along the wall behind each of the four tables was what looked like slot machines with various large knobs on them.

"What's all this?" Deck asked.

"The detox tables," Phillip said, as if it were obvious. "I just need you to come around here, disrobe, and place your knees right in these little valleys."

Now Deck saw what this was all about. It was basically reversed stirrups. Once his knees were firmly in place in the valleys of the back posts, he would lean over them and his upper body would land on the podium-like contraption, which was actually not as high as the posts. He was about to be on all fours, elevated off the ground with his ass in the air.

Oddly, getting into such a vulnerable position was no problem in front of Phillip because the man seemed so sterile and doctorly. Smiling warmly and continuing to show little reaction to Deck's nakedness (it was almost insulting!), Phillip took the robe from him and hung it on a nearby hook, then placed one hand on Deck's elbow, the other on his back, and steered him onto the two posts.

"You're getting the picture," he said as Deck reached his hands across and placed them on the cool leather of the podium. Phillip was still holding on to him to make sure he retained his balance. "Now, notice the crevasses in this part of the table. Your chest should fit snuggly in here, and your arms will drape naturally into these two grooves."

Deck followed the clear instructions. It was so freeing. He felt his ass cheeks split apart behind him and his jewels dangling wildly between his anchored thighs, hovering about four feet above the stainless steel precipice below.

"That's it. Notice these lower ledges"—Phillip steered Deck's arms—"are for you to comfortably relax your arms so you feel well-balanced. And now, you can just place your forehead in this comfy headrest."

Phillip adjusted the doughnut-shaped headrest on its axis where it connected to the chest rest, until Deck's body felt perfectly contoured. Phillip crouched below headrest level to look at Deck's face. "How's that?"

"It's great," Deck replied, breathing in what must be the natural herbal scents Phillip probably used to shower and shampoo. "What's with the bedpan down there?"

Phillip giggled. "That's not a bedpan. This is an absolutely mess-free process. That is for men who have particularly sensitive prostates, or those who wish for a happy ending. Don finishes off his detox that way. He should be here momentarily, but I'll prep you in the meantime, so I can get him ready as soon as he arrives."

Happy ending. I'd like to have me one of those too after those missed opportunities last night.

"Have you ever had a colonic before?" Phillip asked from somewhere behind Deck, who could hear him keeping busy, opening doors of a cabinet back there and tearing something open.

"No, but I thought these things were done while you're on your back," Deck replied from his place on the headrest.

"Traditionally, in public service practices, it is for modesty purposes," Phillip explained. "But in actuality, lying on your back is just not a very natural way to move your digestive muscles. This is a much more appropriate way to get things flowing, which I determine is an issue with you from looking at the food restriction chart you gave Don."

"You're good," Deck said, truly impressed.

"Okay, now, it's almost time for the insertion. I use only sealed, sterile tubing equipment for each colonic, and I actually use a larger nozzle than the ones used in public practices. It's five inches long, but is much thicker and shaped just like a diamond butt plug. This way, it locks in once it passes your sphincter so you don't need to worry about it slipping out during emptying. Plus, it widens the rectum to allow for fuller flow."

Deck just didn't know how to respond to that, so he said nothing.

"Okay, I'm going to clear a path for better visibility," Phillip was saying.

There was a puff of air power that parted Deck's crack hair like a leaf blower flattening a fresh lawn. *The guy just blew on my asshole!*

"Good, good. Muscles are all contracting naturally back here, and now the target's in sight."

"Could you do me a favor and pluck any grays you see back there?" Deck only half joked, but it got a conservative chuckle out of Phillip.

"Now. This is going to be a little cold. I'm going to apply some lubricant," Phillip spoke in time with a squishy squirt, and then his finger was painting Deck's perianal area with the chilly goop. "Great looking anus for a man your age. Fresh, pink, healthy, tight. And you're dancing for me again. This should be a fairly easy insertion."

There was a second squishy squirt, and this time Deck lifted his head out of its resting place to look back. Over the fuzzy mounds of his ass (he had to admit, it was a nice big round sight to behold from this perspective) he could see Phillip, wearing white rubber gloves that caressed a large diamond butt plug as described. It was attached to a long plastic hose that extended to the slot machine on the wall.

It looked like Phillip was masturbating the plug between thumb and index finger, but he was actually coating it with lubricant. Holding it up for Deck to see, he asked, "Not that big, right? I'm sure you'll handle it like a pro."

"Only one way to find out," Deck said, turning back to his headrest. "Just be gentle."

He felt the invasive first poke of the butt plug, and slightly tensed up.

"Now, I'll need you to breathe into your butt," Phillip explained, placing his free hand around the side of Deck's waist, as a man might do when he's grabbing you to slip his dick inside you.

Deck focused until he was able to feel his rectal muscles contracting in time with his breaths.

"Excellent. Now make them slow and deep, relax your whole body, and things should begin slipping right in," Phillip spoke softly, and Deck felt the light pressure being put on the object as it began to move smoothly inside him.

And then it began to widen.

"Whoa," Deck huffed, feeling himself being spread apart, his anal walls trying to resist the assault.

"You're doing great. We're almost there. Just keep breathing."

Deck took a deep, lung-expanding breath, conscious of the weight on his gut as it expanded toward the floor from its midair suspension. There was a loud pop, and his entire body jumped forward at the sudden thump against his insides.

"Uuuh!" he gasped, his eyes widening in surprise, which gave him a better view of a huge stream of precum that shot from his now erect cock. He was convinced he heard it drip against the shiny steel basin as it reached bottom.

"Very *good*!" Phillip sounded so pleased.

"I—I have a sensitive prostate," Deck murmured, humbled by the experience of having this oh-so-clean-smelling, polished professional take him into the realm of excitement unintentionally. *Does he get off on this at all?*

"I *see* that!" Phillip said with a restrained impressed tone.

He wants me, Deck told himself.

"Mind If I join you?" a deep voice came out of nowhere.

Deck's head popped up from the headrest. Before him at the doorway, in a similar towel, was the bulky body of Don, smiling, his teeth sparkling within the confines of his unshaven morning face.

"That answers the question about your top/bottom status," Don said, pointing to the string of pre-excitement as he sauntered over to the table next to Deck.

"I have a sensitive prostate!" Deck argued. The quiet, sterile, isolated atmosphere Phillip had created was shattered now, and he felt so vulnerable. Part of him wanted to spring up, yank the big fat plug out of his ass, and jump back into his bathrobe. But he was afraid any hasty move in this bizarre contraption could cause some serious damage on dismount.

"Mm. Looking good," Don said, standing behind Deck and examining the tubing jutting from between his ass cheeks. "Fits perfectly."

"Get outta there!" Deck growled over his shoulder. "Phillip, can you get him out of there?"

"Don! Really! You're spoiling the calm!" Phillip scolded him as he ripped open a second package of tubing and began to attach it to the machine that coincided with Don's table. "Now please just get in position for me."

Deck watched as Don stripped down, going from plush white to plush black. Don was essentially an animal head to toe, front to back. Deck was amazed at the amount of prowess with which he carried himself, not a hint of shame at his ape-like appearance. The black, perfectly patterned coat looked darker in the crevasses of rippling muscle, which helped to show off the definition that could easily have been obliterated by all the hair.

And Deck could now witness the reason for the nickname Don Wand. Thick, long, and covered in a long cape of foreskin, Don's cock was already rock solid erect, weighed down by the density. Deck gazed at it longingly as Don mounted a table contraption swiftly and easily. Two giant fur balls of butt burst out the rear as Don's center was pulled down toward his own steel basin, which caused his back to arch wonderfully.

"You can stop drooling now," Don said, turning in his headrest to look at Deck.

Deck quickly ran his tongue around his lips to be certain before responding. "I'm not drooling."

"I didn't mean from your mouth," Don scoffed, mischievously directing his attention to Deck's cock. "Cute cock."

Cute?

"It gets the job done." Deck feigned confidence in his mere five inches.

"I don't doubt it does," Don replied. "I love them short and plump."

Is he throwing me backhanded compliments or is he serious?

"Okay. Enough chatter." Phillip hushed them. "Don, spread so I can see what I'm doing."

Now Deck nearly did drool from his mouth. Big, macho, Latin Don followed the orders of thin, gray-haired, bespectacled Phillip with the pleasant scent and passive voice.

Keeping his coconut pecs in place on the chest rest, Don brought his swelling arms back and grabbed his bulbous cheeks to pull them apart. Deck watched Phillip's thin lips purse quaintly as he blew into Don's crack—three times being necessary to clear a path this time. Don sighed with pleasure.

As Phillip lubed up Don and the butt plug, Deck looked at the bear-like man next to him and thought that if he had to have a hairy back, why couldn't it be one even coat like Don's instead of the ridiculous patches he had: on his shoulders, below his laterals, and down the center of his spine.

Don kept his cheeks apart for the insertion. His chest heaved, lifting him further from the precipice below as he swallowed everything Phillip had to feed him. He let out a long, sighing moan as the butt plug disappeared inside him.

"Niiiiice," Don said at last when the butt plug locked into place.

With the long tube flowing out of Don's ass, Deck couldn't help but think that it now looked like the big hairy beast had a tail.

"Okay. Deck, since you are new, I'm going to explain," Phillip said. "I will be flowing comfortably warm water into your system at a very slow and steady pace. At any time in the process, you may feel the need to evacuate, so you just need to say 'now' and I will reverse the flow and you can drain. Then when you are done, we will begin the flow again. During your first time, it is not uncommon for you to have short fills. Okay?"

"Yes." Deck nodded in his headrest, bracing himself for the flow to start.

"Fill up, Phillip!" Don exclaimed.

There was a wet gush as the two machine nozzles were spun. Deck did indeed begin to feel the warm water coursing into his gut, making him feel incredibly full incredibly fast.

"I gotta go!" he gasped after less than a minute.

Don snickered beside him. "Amateur."

"Very good. But you just need to say 'now,'" Phillip said after reversing the flow. "Don. Stop provoking him. We want him to release all the tension."

Deck sure felt it releasing, as something inside him spasmed uncontrollably, relieving him of the bloated feeling. It was magnificent. He accidentally wheezed with the sensation of letting go of all that made him uptight.

"He's feeling it," Don said.

"Definitely. That's wonderful. Shall we fill again?" Phillip checked.

"Yes," was all Deck could manage, already feeling like the wind had been knocked out of him—or more appropriately, *sucked* out of him.

The warm water flowed back in, smoother this time, like there was space inside to accommodate it. When Deck signaled with a "now" a few minutes later, his gut muscles retracted more gently after the reversal. Phillip gave him another "Good."

Don was still in the midst of his *first* fill. Only after Deck was ready to release for his third time did Don give the okay for himself.

"Damn! That was only like ten minutes!" Don grunted as he was flushed.

"Don is one of our record holders," Phillip explained as he turned the water back on for them both. "He has gone as long as thirty-five minutes. Quite the strong colon."

One more fill for Don was the equivalent of two more for Deck.

"Deck, you're doing amazing," Phillip said as they both released at the same time.

"I challenge you to a fill," Don said, looking over at Deck, the two of them in midair with their asses up and long tubes hanging out of them as they glanced into each other's eyes.

"You're on," Deck said. "Phillip, fill up."

"Don," Phillip chided him. "This is not a competition. Deck, do what feels natural. When you're ready to release, you release."

"Okay," Deck said, but made no promises to his digestive tract.

"Both of you just close your eyes, breathe slowly and steadily, and feel everything expanding inside," Phillip said quietly, turning the dimmer down in the already softly lit room. It was as if he wanted this challenge to happen despite what he said.

Gallons of water flooded their systems. Their bellies swelled (Deck peeked at one point and saw that even Don's incredibly tight abs had expanded into a big undefined dome over his steel basin).

"Feeling...full?" Don huffed.

"Fuck..." Deck paused to tense his gut muscles against the cramping pressure, "...you."

"OOoooohhhh!" Don suddenly moaned as a wave hit him.

"Fuuuckkk!" Deck cried, his beard soaked in sweat.

"Relax, men. Breathe in," Phillip said, and then all fell completely silent again.

"Damn!" Deck groaned as he was clutched with cramps. "DAMN!"

"You need to release?" Phillip asked.

"NO!"

"Give it to us, Phillip! Give it to us good!" Don begged, surrendering completely to him.

"Deck, I'm serious. You should probably let go," Phillip said after only about twenty seconds more.

"UUUUUHHHHH!" Deck growled. "Nooooo!"

Now his voice had become high-pitched.

"What's the time?" Don huffed.

"Thirty-one minutes," Phillip said, hands on both nozzles.

"I'm letting him off the hook," Don wheezed. "Make it a happy one!"

Phillip expected as much, and already had an open jar of Elbow Grease on the cabinet between both colonic machines. In one swift motion, he reached out, turned both nozzles, dipped his gloved hands in the grease, stepped between them, reached under them, and began to jerk.

It was like the sound of the ocean waves as sphincters burst open on either side of Phillip. He was masturbating both their cocks, and they howled gutturally as their insides clenched violently. The force against their prostates as they flushed was so powerful it curled them into fetal positions that were prevented from a complete closing by the nooks of the tables that held them in place.

It was now a competition of moans and groans as Phillip's slippery, expertly rhythmic stroking took only seconds to bring the cum gushing forth for them both. Thick gobs of white cream splattered noisily into the steel basins, shaking the very core of their chakras. Their muscles strained as they hugged their tables in ecstasy. Their heads turned to each other and they watched the gut contractions squeeze their facial expressions together, their locked eyes bulging with abandon—drool even slipping from between Don's lips.

Face heated and flushed, Deck gritted his teeth. A shot of his ejaculate went kamikaze on Phillip's shoe beneath him. He could see the muscles in his own stomach clenching and tightening back up as he emptied out.

Phillip made sure both cocks were fully spent, squeezing them right down to the head to get out every last drop, particularly from the folds of Don's foreskin. They both went lax on their tables, gasping for oxygen. They stared at each other almost lovingly, as if they had shared an intimate intercourse *together.*

Without warning, Phillip, who had returned to his station behind them, wrapped his hands around both nozzles, and pulled them swiftly and steadily from their asses with wet pops. Deck's aching sphincter protested before sealing up lazily.

"Bastard!" Don growled. "Gets me every time!"

"Good work, men," Phillip said calmly, and actually patted them both gently on their asses. "Feel free to shower up in back."

He walked between their tables again, and without looking back at them, removed the rubber gloves and threw them in a trashcan near the door before exiting.

❖

The shower room was beyond a barely noticeable alcove in the corner of the colonic room. Unlike a typical gym locker room shower setting, this place took you away like the old Calgon commercials. Overhead showerheads and warm light drenched Deck's body as he glanced around the edges of the room, which were vibrant with live potted tropical plants. It was like showering in the great outdoors. The entire back wall of the room was a glass window looking out on the cliff and ocean behind the mansion.

Deck moved to a round ceramic birdbath in the center of the room to grab one of the all-natural body lotions, but Don's hairy knuckles beat him to it.

"Let me do that," Don said, not flirtatiously, not mischievously. It simply sounded like he wanted to do a friend a favor.

As Don's thick hands massaged lotion onto Deck's back, penetrating muscles that had gotten a bit sore from his acrobatics the night before when being chased by the BeNelly brothers, Deck could feel Don's eyes on his ass.

"Amazing. I feel ten pounds lighter after that colonic." Deck made small talk.

"You look it."

"What the fuck is that supposed to mean?" Deck scowled, turning around to look at Don.

Don's face registered surprise. "Sorry. It was supposed to be a compliment. You look fantastic."

"But normally, I'm a little chunky around the middle or something?"

"No. You're meaty and delicious." Don reached out and brushed fingertips lightly over Deck's knobby-sore nipples then pulled him in closer.

Deck nearly melted against Don's rock hard torso, his head crashing lazily against one pec. His beard tangled with the swirls of hair on Don's pec as his mouth latched on to a nipple with infantile security.

Deck's wet suckling caused Don to moan lightly and pushed him into action. He began covering Deck's back in suds, slowly working his way down toward Deck's ass, his palms finally slipping over Deck's cheeks and clenching the dense wet flesh, His head slipped down into the crook of Deck's neck. They panted in the hot drizzle of water as they savagely sucked the moisture out of the stubble under each other's chins.

"I want you so bad, cabrón," Don whispered in Deck's ear. "So fuckin' hot."

"As hot as the guy you hooked up with last night?" Deck couldn't filter out his thoughts.

Don broke away from him. "Hey. I'm not the one who left you at the club because I hooked up with someone else. I was out half the night looking for you to make sure you got home safe. The streets sure as hell aren't cleaned up enough for someone unfamiliar with the lay of the land to be wandering around at night by himself."

They were both rock hard, but Deck could see Don quickly going flaccid within the confines of his foreskin. And he wanted so badly to get into it with Don, to at least have his chance to return the lathering up, to feel those giant muscles. "Hey. I know. I'm sorry. I had a bad night. Look, I didn't hook up with another guy and leave. I just told Lox to tell you that."

"I know. He told me," Don said, reaching for the body lotion again. He began lathering up his own body and Deck realized he had blown his chance. "You did an amazing thing last night. It's a testament to your character."

"Thanks." Deck was truly flattered to have someone who seemed cocky and confident throwing him a compliment. It seemed to break the tension between them, even if it didn't reset the mood.

"So I know you got in late last night, but if you can get up early enough tomorrow, you can join me and Jeeves in the gym for our early morning workouts before the regular crowd gets in at nine."

"Regular crowd?" Deck asked as they both scrubbed bubbles of shampoo into their hair.

"Yeah. Hayes opens the gym to the public. No fees. But it is an exclusive membership that he and Ben offer to only select men— you know, all the ones you'd want to sleep with. Which hasn't made the Glouster twins happy. They got a whole petition going and everything."

"Who are these mysterious Glouster twins?" Deck asked as they dried off with hot towels in an alcove off the shower room.

"Gorgeous European muscle boys who own the only gym downtown. Identical in every way. And they have quite a business going, because they also put on shows if you get the premium membership. Thing is, Ben and Hayes have lured all the prettiest men up here, and now the only ones coming to see the show are all the slobs and messes who aren't paying to use the gym equipment, just to see the Glouster twins' double-headed dildo show."

"I'm gonna have to check into that," Deck said mostly to himself as he wrapped himself in the giant towel.

"Yeah. I've seen it. It's hot," Don said, misunderstanding Deck's intentions. Don didn't bother to throw a towel around his waist as they left the showers and re-entered the colonic therapy room.

Looking much like a perfectly fit, neatly groomed show dog, Lamond was now on one of the colonic tables being filled by Phillip. He glanced up at the sounds of them entering and the corners of his lips raised with genuine happiness. "What a great sight for morning eyes. You boys all purged?"

"Yes, sir," Don said.

"I was in desperate need. Good for the soul. Helps with the letting go process," Lamond said before uttering a "now" to Phillip. His finely toned body convulsed smoothly as he flushed and continued, "Either of you need a fluff while I fill?"

"Anything to make you happy, boss," Don said, moving forward and waving his now erect, uncircumcised cock toward Lamond's head.

"I'm okay for now. Got some stuff I wanna get done before the wake this afternoon." Deck wasted his breath, for Lamond had already placed his head back into the headrest and was getting his mouth fucked by Don.

Deck just nodded politely to Phillip, who stood in the back watching the action nonchalantly from the stool on which he was perched by the colonic machine, his hand waiting patiently on the fill/flush knob.

Weeping Manor is just otherworldly, Deck thought as he exited.

❖

Definitely took a wrong turn. Deck passed large potted bonsai trees covered in white Christmas lights, on either side of a narrowing doorway.

He came to a screeching halt on the black-and-white tile floor on the other side of the threshold, and he almost lost the towel wrapped around his waist.

Samson, the Fabio-like beefcake groomer, was just finishing with a client it seemed, and getting a pretty good tip in the end. The giant steroid-head of a man was on all fours in the middle of the floor of a large hair salon, surrounded by clumps of freshly cut dark hair. He was naked, revealing that the only hair on his body was the huge mane cascading from his skull. And that mane was currently tied in a thick French braid and being tugged on by a lean and buff kid with a buzzed head who was clearly riding Samson's big muscle ass.

"You like when I yank that beautiful hair?" the militant kid asked as he leapfrogged the beast beneath him, using the French braid for balance and leverage.

"OH! YEEEEEESSSS!" Samson cried. "Open that hole so my tail will fit in there!"

With that image firmly burned into his imagination, Deck tried to quietly back out of the room before they detected his presence, but he crashed right into a large rack of hair care products that went rolling across the floor.

"Deck Waxer!" Samson cried as if it were Deck fucking him up the ass. "Come let me shave that gorgeous head of hair and beard! The more clippings the better!"

Samson clawed at the floor to grab some of the clippings already there and tossed them in the air like confetti with a big smile on his face.

"No, thanks!" Deck responded as he turned around to run out. "I want to put off baldness for as long as I can!"

The last thing Deck heard as he scurried down the hall in his towel was Samson crying, "It's so dry! Please squirt more conditioner on it!" And Deck was pretty sure Samson wasn't talking about on his hair.

❖

Deck stepped back into his room—now sunny, which meant Jeeves had been in to pull the drapes aside—whipped off his towel, and tossed it onto a nearby chair just as he heard the grinding buzz of his cell phone in vibration mode. It was on the wooden bureau doing doughnuts like a motorcycle spinning out in the dirt.

He snatched it up. The ID window above an unfamiliar phone number displayed the name Kim, M.

"No idea who that is," Deck muttered to himself as he punched into the call with his thumb.

"Hello?"

"Deck Waxer?"

"Yeah. Who's this?"

"It's Maru."

"Oh! Hi!"

"Are you making fun of the way my people speak?"

"What? I…no, I wasn't. I was—"

"I'm just messing with you." There was an adorable short giggle on the other end.

Deck found himself scrounging through his bureau for at least some underwear, as if it were inappropriate to be speaking to Maru in the nude. He tripped into them and nearly bashed his head into the edge of the bureau. The phone almost slipped from his hand, but he clutched it desperately.

"You still there?"

"Yeah. Sorry. I almost dropped the phone," Deck said, his face burning with embarrassment. He pulled the dryer-shrunk tighty-whities up until they squeezed snuggly around his big ass.

"Hey. I just wanted to call and apologize to you about my attitude last night. It's not your fault you prevented me from a fate better than life. You didn't know."

"I want to see you," Deck blurted out, his mouth immediately going dry. *Dammit, I have to change that filter in my brain. It's totally clogged.*

"You really are a dirty old man."

"Nah. I'm not old," Deck quipped dryly, hoping to break his own tension while hinting at flirtation.

"I like my men dirty."

"Um, so do you think we could meet tonight and talk? I'll take you out for coffee," Deck said because dinner would have sounded like a date. "I just want to help."

"That's so kind of you. But if you do it for me, it'll be murder."

"I take suicide very seriously," Deck said harshly.

"I feel the same way about murder."

Deck was completely speechless. He felt part sadness, part anger, part disgust at Maru's attitude. He didn't know what to say. Maru seemed to sense the effect it had on him and cut into his thoughts.

"There's an amazing Asian teashop downtown. We can go there after the wake tonight."

"You're coming to the wake?" Deck was surprised.

"It's the least I can do to thank Lamond for all the invitations to come live there. I'll just thank DuPont when I see him in hell."

"So I'll see you tonight." Deck chose to ignore the suicide insinuation about seeing Ben DuPont in the afterlife.

"I'll be looking for you."

Deck said his good-byes and hung up. He was shocked to realize his heart was fluttering. And he was rock hard erect.

CHAPTER FIVE

Way back at the rear of Weeping Manor's first floor was a ballroom. The staff had converted it into a temporary funeral home environment with lovely white wooden chairs set up like theater seating across the polished hardwood floors. Extravagant floral arrangements lined three walls, with the fourth wall covered in a collage of photos showing the wonderful life and times of the gorgeous Benjamin DuPont. A rich maroon runner carpet branched off to this wall of life from a main strip that ran directly to a pedestal in the front of the room. A golden chalice sitting on the pedestal was filled with the ash remains of Ben, which Lamond planned to sprinkle out over the cliff at the edge of his property.

Deck was in a suit and tie lent to him by Don. He was self-conscious because it felt loose in all the wrong places (shoulders, chest) and tight in all the wrong places (waist, ass—although Don had been overjoyed that the suit pants clung to Deck's buttocks).

The large, windowless room had its elegant wall sconces and lavish chandelier dimmed to a morbid glow, with many candles scattered about. Right now, those candles far outnumbered the attendees at the wake. Deck was able to count seventeen heads, not including himself and Don, who were manning the entrance greeting people. All those in attendance were either strolling about the room, looking at the collage wall, signing a guest list on a small stand in a corner, or in intimate groups chatting and sipping wine that was being poured by waiters. All those in attendance were also men, mostly very handsome men ranging from their early twenties to their fifties.

"I expected so many more people," Deck whispered to Don, afraid that his voice would echo in the room.

Don was busy adjusting his tie around his ridiculously thick neck. "Ben and Hayes tend to hang out with a night crowd. The evening service will be packed."

Deck sure hoped so, considering the couple was so prominent in the entertainment world and this community, which they were doing their damnedest to make beautiful.

Much to his surprise, the next person who entered, outlined by blinding daylight shining in from a crystal clear hallway picture window that looked out on the grassy gardens of Weeping Manor, was Commissioner Yvette Anderson. She was accompanied by several cops, including the black and white cops Soloman and Bembury, both of them looking mighty sexy in their cop uniforms. With Anderson's black pantsuit still showing plenty of buxom cleavage and a hot cop on each arm, Deck couldn't help but think of her in their former life together, twirling on the dance floor for hours without taking a break. She'd been quite the club diva, and that persona was still hiding beneath the gruff exterior. With her uniformed entourage, he could picture her busting out a chorus of "It's Raining Men."

"What're you laughing at?" She looked at him with annoyance as she walked by. "This is a funeral."

"Humor is good for the grieving soul," Deck commented, stifling his hint of a chuckle.

"Don, so sorry for your loss," Anderson said, ignoring Deck and firmly shaking Don's hand.

"Not much sun in here today," Deck said to the hot interracial cops, pointing at glasses so dark they blocked any sign of emotion.

"Cute," Bembury muttered, brushing past Deck with a heavy shoulder.

"Jeez. What's their problem?" Deck asked Don after Anderson and her men took to the maroon carpet.

"It's all part of their personas," Don said. "They live in a fantasy world."

Before Deck could ask what that fantasy world was (or how he could enter it), Jeeves (formally clothed once again) entered with Philip, and they parted to let Hayes Lamond pass between them.

His suited form surrounded by a white halo from the picture window behind him, Hayes Lamond looked absolutely majestic and strong in his grief with not the slightest hint of a crack in his armor.

But then that halo of white turned a deadly shade of burning orange. Hayes Lamond was surrounded by flames.

❖

Men inside the ballroom-turned-funeral-parlor began screaming and pointing. Lamond looked confused, until Officers Soloman and Bembury bolted back up the runway and pushed past him.

"I'll call the fire department!" Bembury shouted, grabbing his cell phone as fiery colors began to ignite on his face.

"Come ON!" Soloman roared at the handful of other cops, who were in no rush to respond to the emergency situation. His deep black skin appeared to darken in fury as he shot Commissioner Soloman a glare of frustration.

Everyone in the vicinity had rushed to the giant window in the hall and stared through it as a giant rainbow flag that was suspended between two weeping willows outside burned intensely, swiftly consuming a message that had been sprayed in bold black letters over the vibrant prism.

BURN IN HELL FAGGOT ASSED CRACKERS!

"My willows!" Lamond cried as the flames began to work their way up to the droopy floral branches.

"We'll get it!" Don assured him, running off with Officers Soloman and Bembury. Outside, it seemed Lamond's gardeners were already on it, running at top speed across the lawn with hoses.

"Look! There!" Jeeves shouted, pointing out the window to thick vegetation beyond the fire as sprinklers ignited across the grounds, dousing both the flames and the many men on the lawn fighting the fire with hoses.

Deck, who had been ready to follow Don's small but heroic group, stopped and looked to where Jeeves gestured.

Black-cloaked figures burst from the bushes and began running down the hill beyond the trees.

"Oh shit!" Deck gasped, recognizing the ghostly figures immediately in the daylight.

Anderson was standing right beside him, and she glanced up at him with curiosity.

"They look like the KKK," someone stuttered from the line of onlookers as, outside, Don, Soloman, and Bembury joined the gardeners in fighting the fire.

"The black KKK," a studious-looking African-American man said nervously.

Deck glanced at Anderson. She did not look happy. But Deck wasn't sure if that was because of the criminal act taking place on her watch or because of the young black man suggesting that other black men were responsible.

"Hayes, it's absolutely crazy of you not to have this place fully fenced with a high-level security system," Anderson argued as she, Deck, and Lamond sat in the parlor, Lamond once again sipping tea that Don had brought him.

"Commissioner, I have security on the house itself. If I cordon off my property, I'm sending too many negative messages to the men of Kremfort Cove. I'm telling them that I don't trust them. I'm telling them I need to be segregated from them. It implies that I'm better than them. I'm not. I'm one of them."

"But you're also a high profile businessman in the entertainment industry. You've got celebrity friends visiting you all the time. That makes you a prime target for everything from the paparazzi and crazed fans to struggling men downtown who feel a need to make you suffer because you're more of a success than they are. Remember what happened to Versace?"

"You're getting off point here, Anderson," Deck cut in. "He wasn't targeted by gay men. This was clearly a hate crime."

"Deck, you know as well as I do that the people in this community are quite aware of the tensions that have arisen between them and my force. Some activist group could be doing this intentionally to stir up panic about bias crimes and make my police force look bad."

"Maybe. But if you assume that's the answer, you're just feeding into it," Deck shot back.

"Stay outta this, Deck," Anderson said, standing. "You got gay men mysteriously catching on fire all over town, and now some disguised, chicken shit group with some sort of message delivered with flames showing up on the property of a man who is creating a lot of change, very fast, and it's not sitting well with *all* of your people—"

"They used to be yours too," Deck said softly.

"I'm just trying to help," Lamond muttered, staring ahead with glassy eyes, as if in shock.

"*Everyone* in this town is my people," Anderson growled at Deck, her eyes blazing. "That's a huge variety of personalities to keep happy—and safe. And that's what I'm working on doing. I'll handle things on my end, and if you really care as much as you claim, you'll work with me, not against me."

Deck didn't have time to respond. Anderson stormed out.

"Jeeves, could you please draw the curtains?" Lamond asked weakly. "I'm not exactly feeling sunny right now."

Floodlights created a beacon of white at the top of the cliff where Weeping Manor sat, with dozens of cars parked in a huge gravel lot on the side of the mansion. To those who lived in the city, it looked as if Lamond was throwing one of his huge parties. Present were the gayest of celebrities and the most beautiful young men, who would never be believed by friends and acquaintances if they claimed to have slept with, if not just met, any particular megastar at a gay party.

However, there was no party tonight. Tonight, they all came to remember Benjamin DuPont, one of the most charismatic, warm, and inviting men any of them would ever meet in their lifetimes. They could only reflect on the positive because Ben's entire life had been immersed in having fun and good times, sharing his joy with those he met. Not unlike small-scale wakes, this one was filled with light chatter and laughter as men paid their respects. However, the wall-to-wall testosterone filling the ballroom created decibels of communications that only further impressed upon the mind the sense of a party.

The sill of the great hallway picture window was now lined with men whispering about the arson incident that afternoon, many questioning what the police were doing about it, and some speculating on who could possibly be behind it. The BeNelly name was dropped several times.

The crowd was casual in attire, the way Ben DuPont would have wanted it, because he rejected formality in every possible instance. Deck was now wearing a simple white cotton V-neck T-shirt, which highlighted a glowing summer's worth of tan. Basic low-riding jeans hung from the top of his ample derriere—and slightly under his belly. He stood in a corner against a wall, eye on the doors, waiting for the arrival of one particular person.

"You're getting lots of looks again," Don said as he came up beside Deck. "Especially from those two."

Deck took note of Officers Soloman and Bembury, who were once again dressed down and appeared to be off duty. They stood in a corner by a big floral arrangement. When Deck caught their eyes, both cops simply tilted their heads in recognition of his existence. He returned the silent salutation.

"Why are they here again?" Deck asked.

Don shrugged. "They're good guys at heart. I think they're probably the only cops in this city who really give a shit about us. And there are a lot of famous faces here tonight. They probably want to make sure they don't get harassed by fans."

Before he could respond with his own suspicions as to their reasons for being at the wake a second time, Deck was completely drawn to a man who entered the ballroom. Only, it wasn't the person for whom he'd been waiting. In fact, any eyes that had been on Deck were equally drawn to the magnetic presence of the man wearing a tight black turtleneck and black slacks under a trendy beige blazer. High cheekbones and a long, sharp nose created the ideal platform for piercing black eyes and finely shaped eyebrows. Thick, soft lengths of hair were magically combed back with a lavish sweep.

"Who's that?" Deck asked as Healy, Lamond's onsite footman (pedicures, massages, foot reflexology, and more) passed by.

The short, stocky blond foot master said, "Proc, our new neighbor," just as Deck put two and two together upon seeing a big towering black figure behind the new arrival. It was Wilky, who had been nice enough to chauffeur him around the other night. Wilky was in a light gray suit that was practically tearing at the seams because he was so bulky. He was an incredibly flattering sidepiece to the smooth and pale complexioned Proc.

"Isn't he fuckin' hot?" Healy asked, nearly growling as his beady little hazel eyes pulsed.

"You know it, honey," a nearby lanky visitor sipping a martini responded.

Wilky waved at Deck over the crowd, a big grin on his face as he directed Proc in Deck's direction. Deck's mouth went dry. The excessively polished and pretty Proc wasn't even his type, but he now understood the concept of getting weak in the presence of beauty— mind-altering beauty. People parted for the majestic man and his large black shadow, giving the illusion of some sort of celebrity being tailed by his bodyguard.

The thin-lipped smile that was flashed at Deck as a cool hand gripped his came so smoothly and easily that it was almost unnatural— subtle, relaxed, and confident in its message.

"Great to finally meet you," Proc said to Deck. "Wilks told me you were one sexy man, and now getting a look at you, I can see he was so right."

You've gotten a look at me before, Deck thought, immediately feeling distrust of him, anticipating ingeniousness.

"I *think* I saw you standing on one of the balconies the other night when we were doing some moving, but it was so dark, I had no idea what I was looking at." Proc rolled his eyes. "From where I stood, it looked like a hot bear, but from that distance, we fags tend to fill in the hazy areas with what our horny little imaginations want to see."

Deck was caught completely off guard by the confession—and the actual logic to it. Bottom line was, he had been staring at them and sizing up the aesthetics of their forms as well. "Yeah, that was me. I guess I was doing the same thing. Sorry."

"Aah, no biggie. We caught each other in the act. Seeing you up close now, I'm not complaining." Proc's intense gaze was devilishly sexy and seductive.

"Thanks." Deck's face turned red.

"Told you how adorable he is," Wilky said.

"We must have you over one of these nights," Proc said. "You know, after things settle down with the tragedy. The whole Lamond clan can come see what we've done so far with Pale Shelter. On an off night, before things pick up in The Caves again."

"They're phenomenal." Wilky grinned from ear to ear as he dropped a heavy arm on Deck's shoulder. "We'd love to see you down there."

"Indeed, we would." Proc winked at Deck.

Deck was so about to be seduced by this couple. He could see himself going home with them right then—until his eyes drifted over Proc's square shoulder to a new entry into the ballroom. So lean and sleek, gently exotic, in tight tweed pants and a red V-necked designer tee.

"Gentlemen, if you'll excuse me," Deck said quickly. "Proc, it was nice meeting you, and I'll definitely attend your get-together. I'd love to see the place."

"Wonderful. It's a plan." Proc rubbed his shoulder.

"Later, Deck," Wilky said.

Deck worked his way through the growing crowd. He recognized faces from Dirty Harry's, including the adorable owners of the club, Harry and Jimmy. At last, he was standing beside Maru.

"Hey," he tried to say nonchalantly, hoping his voice would carry to Maru, who was busy nodding to familiar faces. He didn't want to be too forward (or appear eager) by making any physical contact with Maru.

"Hey!" Maru's face brightened.

"You look…refreshed," Deck said, appreciating the bright sheen of Maru's spiky black hair.

"Refreshed. You're quite the charmer," Maru said.

"No really. You look very nice." Deck fumbled over his words.

"You, on the other hand, look ridiculously sexy," Maru said directly.

"Thanks." Deck turned red for the second time in a few short minutes. "You wanna go to that teashop?"

"Um, I'd kinda like to pay my respects first. Get in some star sightings while I'm at it and, you know, check out Ben's eternal crib. Comparison shopping."

"Let's go over to Lamond," Deck said, still unsure of how to react to Maru's morbid and highly unfunny sense of humor about death. "Then we'll get going."

Deck and Maru stood behind a line of men waiting to see Lamond, who was up near Ben's pedestal with Jeeves. When Don walked by, Deck grabbed his arm and leaned in to whisper, "Hey. Would you do me a favor? I want to sneak out of here. I think those two cops might be keeping an eye on me. Could you distract them for a while?"

"You got it," Don said. He winked at Deck and raised his eyebrows teasingly in Maru's direction. "Have fun."

❖

As Deck tried to maneuver his car out of the large parking area on the side of Weeping Manor a while later, he realized it wouldn't be easy getting it up the long road to the front gates because there were cars everywhere. So he targeted the desolate road that connected Weeping Manor to Pale Shelter Estates.

"Where you going?" Maru asked from the passenger seat.

"Shortcut," Deck answered.

"Wow. You learn your way around fast," Maru said. "I like that in a man."

Deck shot a glance in Maru's direction, just in time to see Maru's eyes widen.

"Watch out!" Maru pointed.

Deck looked forward to see his headlights picking up a very large white presence. He quickly yanked his steering wheel to avoid it. It was Wilky's white Hummer, which was parked on the shoulder of the narrow road.

"We could've both died and gone to heaven," Maru quipped. "Wouldn't be the worst way to go."

Deck wasn't sure if Maru meant going with company or by crashing into a giant white Hummer.

"That's Wilky's," Deck said.

"As they said in your day, no duh," Maru responded.

Deck was insulted, and wanted to argue about not being that old, but unfortunately, "no duh" *was* the term they used in his day.

"I was just saying," Deck said sheepishly. "I guess they couldn't find a spot in the parking area. Hey, wait."

"What?" Maru asked as Deck drove slowly along the dark path between the two estates.

"Any chance we could make a detour on our way to the teashop?" Deck asked.

"I thought this *was* a detour," Maru pointed out.

"No. I mean, more like…a mission," Deck said.

"Like, detective work?"

"Yeah."

"Hell yeah! We can be like the Hard Boys," Maru said brightly.

"Um, that's the Hard*y* Boys," Deck corrected him.

"Um, that was dirty talk," Maru said.

Deck blushed profusely as he turned into the Pale Shelter driveway.

❖

"You're stopping here?" Maru asked as Deck parked the car on the cobblestone.

"We're gonna check out Proc's place," Deck said. "Can you grab the flashlight from my glove compartment?"

"Um, I don't think Proc and Wilky killed my boyfriend," Maru scoffed.

Deck hadn't even thought of the relevance of his snooping around to Maru. This was personal for Maru. But there was a whole lot more going on in Kremfort Cove than just his boyfriend's death.

"Chill." Maru handed him the flashlight. "I was just saying. I know you have a lot of other stuff you need to investigate. I've been dying to see their place. Let's go in!"

Maru jumped out of the car. After removing his tools from his key ring, Deck swiftly followed, leaving the car running.

"Hold on there," Deck said, closing the door quietly. "You're not going in with me."

"Well, then what?"

"You're going to stay out here by the car, peering in *that* direction." Deck pointed down the road they had just pulled off. "And if you see the *slightest* hint of light coming this way through the trees, you get in my car and take this driveway *off* the premises to the road and wait for me."

"Shouldn't I signal to you or something to warn you?"

"Yeah. I guess that will be fine. I'll leave the front door open."

"What's the signal?" Maru asked as Deck turned on his flashlight and headed up the walkway leading to the front door of the Pale Shelter mansion.

Deck walked backward and responded, "Talk dirty to me. And that's dirty with two r's."

Deck's teeth gleamed in the moonlight. Now it was Maru's turn to blush at the pop culture reference Deck knew he would recognize instantly. It was the spelling of the controversial Christina Aguilera hit "Dirrty."

"Don't think you can be getting your private dick all up in my business so easily!" Maru tried to counter his embarrassment with a smart response, but Deck was jogging up the walkway already and pretended not to hear him.

Deck crept onto the front porch, which was illuminated by a dim bulb in a fixture set into the underside of the awning. He found the handy detective tool on his key ring that he needed to pick the lock. He needn't have bothered. The front door was unlocked.

"What are these guys thinking?" Deck muttered. He didn't want to side with Anderson, but he was seriously concerned about how these well-off men skimped on practical safety precautions— especially considering the questionable city to which they had moved.

Deck entered an extremely hollow home. He wasn't faced with creepy cobwebs, dust, and sheet-covered furniture, which his overactive imagination had expected. Instead, his flashlight beam picked up a lovely scroll rug sitting in the middle of the foyer's highly polished wood floor. Over to his right were French doors that happened to be open, revealing a large room in a beautiful rich wood finish. Inside the room, there were thick, ornate drawn drapes between empty bookshelves. Several chairs and a gorgeous bulky desk were the only items in the room, and all looked equally antique.

A desk was always a good place to start. Before moving over to it, Deck pushed aside one of the heavy, musty smelling curtains and peered out at the dark driveway. The weak halo created by the front porch fixture allowed just enough light for him to barely make out the shape of his car and Maru leaning against it. No sign of lights coming through the trees at all.

"Front door open, desk locked," Deck said in the chilly echoing air of the room as he tugged on a drawer. It didn't take him long to open the middle drawer with his handy tool. The large interior looked like the shelves at a stationary store—paperclips, pens, pencils, pads, scissors. *Was it necessary to lock that drawer?* He relocked it and focused his attention on the three drawers on each side of the desk.

Chances were that if he went systematically from the top left drawer down and then across to the top right drawer and down, anything worth finding would be in the very *last* drawer he opened. So he targeted the bottom right drawer first and worked his way up.

"Argh!" Deck finally groaned. *Every* locked drawer had been empty except for the top left drawer—which happened to be loaded with what looked like personal documents. Now he was getting somewhere. He sifted through the top sheets of the stack of papers within. They were simple receipts for furniture, electrical work, and other new home money-draining necessities. He pointed his flashlight back into the drawer. With a bunch of the papers off the stack, he could now detect a blue folder at the bottom. He instinctively went for that one.

He opened the folder on the top of the desk and pulled the top document out of the inside pocket. Holding his flashlight up to it, he realized it was some sort of legal letter that had been notarized. He read the contents quickly and then looked at the signatures at the bottom. It was a simple and straightforward agreement. Proc and Wilky did not own Pale Shelter. They were leasing it from Lamond and DuPont. At least Proc was. Wilky had not signed the letter. Proc hadn't even signed a last name. It was a simple felt-tip pen scribbled John sans Hancock.

Deck moved to put the letter back in the folder and stopped abruptly.

Staring up at him from the folder was a large, handwritten note: *Greetings, Deck. What do you think of the place?*

Deck's face burned with blood, his hands grew cold. He jerkily swung his flashlight from one corner of the empty room to the other. It was like there were eyes searing into the hairy flesh at the back of his neck. The shadows created by the beam seemed to come to life and stretch across the floor toward him. He hastily but carefully replaced the letter in the folder and tried to organize the stack of papers in the desk just as they had been. He closed up shop, relocked the drawer, and shook with shock as he heard something raucous scratching against one of the windows on the other side of the room.

"Maru!" Deck gasped, not bothering to investigate what was trying to get into the house on the other side of the drapes.

There was no time to worry about not being able to search the full extent of the mansion. Deck bolted for the front door.

"Eek!" he screamed as he slammed full force into a body that was coming at him as he pierced the threshold.

The much smaller body skidded across the painted wood planks of the porch with a guttural bark. The porch light revealed Maru.

"Shit! Sorry!" Deck reached out a hand. "Get up quick! We have to get out of here."

Maru was yanked onto his feet, the front door was yanked closed, and they raced to Deck's still idling car.

"What happened?" Maru asked.

"Did you see anything on the side of the house?" Deck asked as he sped out of the driveway.

"Yeah! There was this big black thing bumping up against the window!" Maru exclaimed. "I didn't know what the hell it was. That's why I came to get you. Did you find something?"

"Nothing," Deck said flatly, still trying to catch his breath. "That noise just scared the hell out of me. And I'd sure like to know what it was."

"Aren't you supposed to be a big brave detective?"

"I'm also smart and know when to run from danger. Especially when I don't have a gun. Not even a big brave detective could take on a gang of the dudes in black sheets that people have been talking about," Deck said as he drove them toward the town.

"Good point," Maru said. "Do you think that's who it was?"

"I don't know," Deck responded. "I'm not the one who was outside. Did it look like a bunch of guys in black sheets to you?"

"It looked like some sort of moving, floating black cloud," Maru said. "Is this city haunted?"

"I never rule it out," Deck admitted.

❖

"This whole town is probably going to be loaded with ghosts soon if this stuff keeps up," Maru said from the passenger's seat as he directed Deck into the city and toward Chai Tea, the Asian teashop he had mentioned that morning on the phone. "I really can't believe Ben is gone too."

"Yeah. And look at how many people are affected by the loss of one person," Deck said, glancing at Maru from the corner of his eyes.

"Man, you *suck* at subtlety." Maru giggled, a sound Deck found refreshing.

"What?" Deck played coy.

"I don't know. Out of nowhere, your innocent words seemed to spark this realization in the back of my head about all the people who will miss me when I'm gone. Let's see. There's my mother. Nope. She withered away from cancer before she was fifty. And my boyfriend. Nope. He fucked around on me behind my back then set himself on fire, causing me to nearly be arrested for his murder. Yeah. I'm good to go. Everyone I'd affect is already on the other side."

"Harry and Jimmy clearly care about you," Deck pointed out.

"Yeah. The two men who pay me to whore myself out to every man in Cremation Cove," Maru scoffed.

"I don't think they would throw you out on the street if you decided to stop dancing tomorrow," Deck said.

"Excuse me if I don't have faith enough in mankind to test that theory, because from my experiences, people and life suck."

"Yeah. Life sucks. You don't have to tell me."

"Oh yeah? What happened to you that was so bad?"

"I got kicked off the police force in Chicago," Deck said. "I was gonna be a star, moving my way steadily up the ladder. And then it all fell to shit on me. But you pick up your life and move on."

"And what exactly happened to your heart?"

"My heart's fine," Deck said shortly, glancing over at Maru, whose expression was unreadable.

"This is it. We just have to drive around and find a parking spot," Maru said.

❖

The trendy red, black, and beige interior of Chai Tea had a flamboyant Asian edge, but it was somehow subdued and tranquil at the same time.

"Mr. Chai designed this all himself," Maru said as he and Deck sat at an isolated corner booth, sipping delicious herbal teas and sampling from a tray of mini Asian desserts Maru insisted Deck try.

"This place is like a Chinese Starbucks," Deck said, noticing the large crowds of gorgeous gay men filling booths and couches around the large space.

"It's everything Asian," Maru corrected him. "Not specifically Chinese. Mr. Chai lives an all-inclusive life."

"Whoops. Sorry." Deck rolled his eyes.

"You're funny with your 'whatever' attitude about everything."

"That's not true." Deck defended his honor. "I care deeply about a lot of things."

He was just reaching for another dorayaki, a sort of cream filled pancake sandwich he had found he liked the best on the plate. Coincidentally, Maru had been reaching for the same sample. Maru's smooth, small hands brushed over Deck's. Deck felt the hairs on his knuckles raise, and even felt shivers at the hairs on the back of his neck.

"Sorry. You take," Deck said.

Maru drew his hand away. "No, you can have it. It's the last one, and I can tell you like those the best."

Before they could get into a tiff about who should enjoy the final dorayaki, a distinguished and reserved looking older gentlemen, graying at the temples, approached them.

"Maru, my friend, I'm so glad to see you," the man said warmly, rolling up the sleeves of his striped button shirt.

"Hi, Mr. Chai." Maru greeted the man by standing and hugging him. "This is Deck Waxer,"

"Hunky!" Mr. Chai winked at Maru as he shook Deck's hand.

"No, I'm just a—" Deck began.

"A detective," Maru cut him off. "He's a detective who's looking into Lance's death. As well as the other cases in town."

Deck felt his hand go limp in Mr. Chai's palm at those words. He could see Mr. Chai staring at him as if sensing the vibe through Deck's fingers: the disappointment, the soft hurt at not even being referred to as a friend, the wonder as to Maru's reasons for being so blatantly cold in giving Deck a title. Deck pulled away uncomfortably from Mr. Chai.

"Well, then, I will let you two get back to business," Mr. Chai stated, placing a hand on Deck's shoulder and giving it a squeeze, sending him an unspoken message of hope.

"Bye, Chai!" Maru playfully rhymed the two words, smiling charmingly at Mr. Chai as he strolled off.

"He seems to really like you." Deck tried to act nonchalant in falling back into conversation with Maru.

"Not enough to hire me when I came looking for a job," Maru said.

"He didn't?" Deck was shocked. The man really seemed to adore Maru.

Maru shrugged. "He said I deserved better than to be a tea servant. So I aimed high and became a male stripper."

"Well, what are your actual dreams?" Deck asked.

"Is this a professional question or personal?"

"It's a question I would be interested in hearing the answer to," Deck said evenly.

"Wow. You're good," Maru said as he poured himself another cup of tea from a small pot beside his dessert plate. "I wanted to be an actor. Of course. That's why I can't do anything else. Because we 'actors' can't imagine ourselves doing anything else."

"Well, PontMond Enterprises—"

"Lance wouldn't let me get involved with them," Maru said. "He was a therapist in town. He'd heard enough stories from clients about the parties at Weeping Manor to believe that they would be more interested in exploiting me at home than promoting me in the industry."

"Did he always make decisions for you?" Deck asked.

"He didn't make decisions *for* me," Maru corrected him. "We were partners. We decided together what was best for us. Just because he was thirteen years older than me—"

Thirteen years older, Deck thought fleetingly while Maru was still talking. *Didn't look it in the picture. So Maru likes older men.*

"—doesn't mean we played that whole father figure game."

"I wasn't assuming anything," Deck said.

"Yeah, right. Young guy, never knew his father, lost his mother before he was twenty, needs a male role model in his life." Maru went through the list. "I know how you guys think. I was practically married to a shrink, remember?"

"I didn't know you didn't know your father," was all Deck could think to say.

"Yeah. American sailor she met back in Korea. He told her he wanted her to come to America to be his wife. She gets here, practically barefoot, and most definitely pregnant, and he never shows at the airport to greet her. Never spoke on the phone, just letters—none of which he ever answered after that. Luckily, he happened to be part Italian and part Korean, not all white."

Deck blanched at that comment.

"Oh, no offense. It's just not good for the Asian ego when a woman gets knocked up by an American sailor. Just way too cliché. Because she was done wrong by one of her own, it just empowered her to prove herself, especially since her family disowned her, told her never to come back to Korea. She was very Americanized before she even got here. She was totally from a new generation of Koreans. Spoke almost flawless English, was attracted to Western ways. So she stayed. Became a citizen, got a job, an apartment, and raised me on her own. She was amazing."

"And how was she with the gay thing?" Deck wondered, truly engrossed.

"Biggest hag, EVER!" Maru giggled. "She had a close gay friend from college back home. He became quite successful over there, and he would send her money when times were rough. She dreamed of him being my surrogate father. But I never met him. He died young. You know…"

Deck simply nodded in understanding.

"She adored my Lance. I was like *just* legal when we met, but she overlooked that. She truly believed he was going to be good for me. So did I." Maru looked sad. "And he was. But then we moved here, because it was up-and-coming and there were so many fucked up men floating around that he believed he could make a difference. And he wanted to write a book about the transformation of a gay ghetto. And that's when he changed."

"In what way?" Deck asked.

"He became obsessed with his job, with the book, with the lives of the people here. He would go out every night, to do 'research.' He really believed he was heading toward a Pulitzer. And then he went up there."

Maru gestured with his head in the general direction of what Deck assumed was Weeping Manor.

"After he told you to stay away from them?" Deck was stunned.

"I'm telling you, he was a man on a mission. He needed to be at every problem area of the gay ghetto to see the damage being done to people firsthand. And I trusted him. I had no reason not to."

"So he thought that Lamond and DuPont were problems, causing damage to the city?"

"No. Their pioneering the cleanup was part of his focus, and they knew that. He was upfront with them about being unbiased in reporting the pros and cons of their actions to the community."

"A con being what? That a monogamous man like himself could get sucked into the allure of the free love subculture?" Deck found himself feeling angry for Maru.

"It was never intentional!" Maru suddenly snapped. "He didn't go up there looking to get involved in their orgies. But we're fucking men, you know? You put us all together, and create this sense of caring between us, and we're going to get into a dangerous comfort zone that might make us do things we never would have otherwise. It's exactly one of the things he was trying to show through his observations."

"So you forgave him for that?"

"I understood it. It's all around us in this place. I'm not gonna deny that I struggle to fight the temptations every day. And he was human. He made a mistake. I loved him. I didn't want to lose him over a mistake."

"You never hated him for it? Not even for a minute?"

"I didn't *kill* him!" Maru growled. Men at nearby tables turned quickly and stared. They knew who he was. They knew all about him. And so the whispers began.

"That question was of personal interest, not professional," Deck responded calmly.

Tears sprung to Maru's eyes. He looked like he was going to slide under the table with embarrassment as he choked out, "I hated myself. I'd become what my mother never had. The submissive Korean housewife to the manipulative, dominating white man."

Maru tried to hide behind a red cloth napkin as if he was merely wiping crumbs from his mouth.

"We're getting out of here. I'm just going to pay the check, and then I'll take you—"

"Home?" Maru whispered hoarsely.

"I'll take you anywhere you want to go," Deck whispered back, feeling his throat constricting with shyness. Or perhaps that was fear. "Just let me go get rid of some of this tea pee."

He smiled, and Maru let out a small laughing cry of relief.

"I'll be right back," Deck said. It was like he wasn't in control of his own instincts as he reached up and gently stroked the shorts spikes of hair at the side of Maru's head. There was an electric blast of emotion at contact, and goose bumps exploded from that contact: through Maru's scalp, along Deck's fingertips, and over his hairy forearm.

Without another word, Deck walked to the back of the teashop, check in hand.

"Damn bathroom signs," Deck grumbled as he found himself winding through a bland hallway that was clearly a part of the restaurant Mr. Chai didn't want customers to know existed. Deck was sure he'd been properly following the arrows pointing toward the restrooms

"I'm lost," he muttered to himself. Then he heard voices coming from a doorway down at the end of the dreary corridor.

Probably the kitchen. I'll just ask them how the hell to get back to the bathrooms.

He was surprised to hear urgency in a strained voice as he moved closer to a small oval glass window in the center of a door. What he saw through the pane was like something out of one of those twisted Asian exploitation movies.

Bent over a desk was a completely naked, tightly athletic, hairless body. The cheek pressed up against the top surface of the desk belonged to the handsome young Asian man who had brought Deck and Maru their tea earlier (batting flirty eyes at Maru the whole time, Deck had noticed). He was gagged, his eyes wide with terror. Surrounding him, firmly implanted into the wood of the desk, was a series of erect, razor sharp Ginsu knives, the blades all only inches from the young man's vulnerable, flawless skin.

Holding him down by the neck was one of the giant BeNelly brothers, the tight black shirt that was their trademark hugging every rippling muscle. Other BeNellys watched with excited gleams in their eyes.

"Please!" cried Mr. Chai, who was cowering in a corner by a bookshelf. "I will get you the money tomorrow! I just have to wait for a check to clear."

"You know the deal," came the voice of another BeNelly, tall like a basketball player, with tight curls and a thick goatee. "You pay back the agreed amount every month on the last Tuesday of the month."

"Please. I can't lose my restaurant," Chai tried to explain.

"Don't worry. You won't lose your *restaurant*," the goateed man said, thick arms crossed in front of a square chest.

"I—" Mr. Chai was nearly in tears as he looked at his young employee's dangerous predicament. "Please don't take—"

"He's ours. Just like agreed," the BeNelly brother said. "Time to hire yourself another waiter in case you can't pay again next month."

"You can't take him." Mr. Chai sounded like he still didn't believe that whatever deal he had made with these devils was actually true.

"Don't worry. He'll be living in a gorgeous estate at the corner of the Cove, with a great private beach, and all the cock his faggot ass can handle," the BeNelly brother promised. "But we gotta see if he's worthy of such luxuries. And if he can handle what he'll be getting every day."

The BeNelly leader of the moment was handed an ominous looking samurai sword. Deck feared a horrific impaling as he watched the terrified young man's tiny pale tush quiver. Instead, the blade was positioned horizontally just behind the back of his neck and held in place by the tall, goateed man. The purpose was obvious. The slightest movement from the naked waiter and he'd be dicing himself.

"Knock him up, Knockwurst," the goateed BeNelly ordered the giant man whose hand was crushing the naked waiter's spine.

"He's done nothing to you!" Chai cried, and then went sailing across the room, crumpling against a wall after being backhanded by one of the BeNellys.

The origin of Knockwurst's nickname was soon revealed. There it was, a purple black piece of meat, sticking straight out from the lowered zipper on the tight black pants that were neatly wedged right between the big man's huge ass crack.

Knockwurst wrapped both hands around the base of his monster to help keep the blood in it, and spat a large white glob onto it. That was the extent of the lubrication.

The squeal through the gag was so loud it almost sounded as if the kid had busted a lung. Deck wished more than anything that he had a gun right now, so he could stop this. Knockwurst ripped into that compact derriere viciously, right to the zipper of the pants, and Knockwurst, who had the face of a big dumb football player, grinned with pleasure. "Tiiiiiiight."

"Fuck him hard," another BeNelly egged Knockwurst on.

"Plant your seed in him!" the goateed leader said, standing alongside the situation with the giant samurai sticking straight out from his crotch.

The savage BeNelly tore into what had probably been a perfect slit of a pucker. Deck could actually see the once taut rectal muscles weakening and being drawn out with every machine gun speed withdrawal. Knockwurst had grabbed those petite hips to do the pounding properly. Sweat dripped from his chin and nose, and Deck could only hope that they perhaps landed on his thickness, adding even the slightest bit of lubrication.

The naked waiter's face had gone blank. He stared ahead with no expression in his eyes as he was used as a fuck hole. Perhaps he was trying to stay as prone as possible so as not to move an inch for fear of being sliced by the frame of blades. But Knockwurst was ramming him so hard, huge thighs banging against his ass with painful sounding thuds, that his body was automatically thrashed about a bit. Deck could see a sliver of blood mar the flawless skin covering the young man's ribs under the armpit, where he'd gotten nicked a tiny bit.

"I'm plantin' that seed!" Knockwurst announced, and the others cheered him on. He yanked his hips against the naked waiter's ass, grunting and groaning savagely as he came up inside the warmth surrounding him.

The naked waiter's eyes finally shifted, sending Deck a message that he was still alive. They actually landed right on Deck, and the young man's eyes widened, trying to warn Deck to get away.

But it was too late. A dark shape that had snuck up on Deck came in for the kill.

CHAPTER SIX

The blackness descended on Deck as his eyes fluttered open. The deep tangy musk that smothered his mouth brought memories flooding back of the sharp, sweet wetness that had enveloped his mouth right before he'd passed out. He'd been drugged.

"Toss that salad, you white bitch," a deep bass voice grunted from above.

Deck's cloudy vision gave him snippets of his story. He was centered under a rim chair. Tufts of crotch hair tickled his face. And his nose was being engulfed by a big black asshole. His scalp screamed as his hair was yanked, a handle that made it easy for the man sitting on his face to move his limp head about as if to simulate eating.

"Lick it, fucker!" the bass voice came again. Deck was lifted by the hair deeper into that tangy man smell.

He did as he was told, lapping at the fuzzy flesh, tasting the fresh funk of a man's usually sealed orifice.

"That's right! You the new boy! You got a lotta asses waitin' to get a turn," said the man attached to the giant ass.

"Let me get some," another throaty voice nagged, and for a moment there was light, giving Deck a second to start making out the details of his predicament.

He was basically a human toilet bowl, on a platform in the middle of a room painted all in black, with a row of large, open animal cages lining the far wall. There were men everywhere doing—

And then he was smothered by another black ass.

Amazing how different every man's ass tastes, Deck thought as he lapped up a purer taste. This slightly smaller ass with less crack hair may have come from a more recent shower.

After seeing a flash between asses of a young blond white man suckling passively on the swollen purple nipple of a BeNelly brother who had him in a headlock, Deck tried to clear the fog as he went to work on a third ass that had fallen in place. The latest pucker danced spastically on Deck's lips as he nipped at its sensitive circumference.

Coming up for air, through his haze he could make out a gym bunny of a man on all fours, with a giant black forearm deeply embedded between his meaty butt cheeks.

Dark, dark chocolate flesh enveloped Deck, two of the biggest ass muscles so far, playfully squeezing and crushing his face as he feasted.

More precious oxygen. He could taste the pungent flavors building up in his thick beard. He spotted a bearish redhead on his knees in another corner, hungrily gagging and choking on one of many massive black cocks waiting to fuck his round, pink-complexioned face.

"Tickle that ass with that beard!" The next face looked through the rim seat at Deck before crash-landing on his face. He recognized his latest meal. It was Knockwurst. He did as he was told, roughly rubbing his whiskers into a kinky mass of crack hairs before coating the dark flesh he was irritating with his healing salivary ointment. Knockwurst was groaning as loud as he had when he'd planted his seed in the naked waiter.

Speaking of, there, on the floor off to the side was the naked waiter, ass way up in the air, being leapfrogged by another BeNelly brother, spreading his own cheeks apart to allow for deeper access. He seemed to be adjusting quickly to his new role in society.

As the tightest black ass so far fell into the circle above Deck's head and right onto his waiting tongue, he realized that this abundance of BeNelly brothers was working the room, going from one sex station to the other: Sitting on Deck's face, getting a cock sucked by the redhead, pounding the fuck out of the naked waiter, ramming a fist up the gym bunny's ass, breastfeeding the hungry little blond.

Releasing his latest meal with a pop, Deck circled his upside down eyes to the last station within his field of vision, where each BeNelly brother was spanking bright red welts onto the smooth ass of a tattooed and pierced punk with a Mohawk, who whimpered and pleaded for his black daddies to give him more.

And finally, Deck learned where each BeNelly brother was going to release the last ounce of his testosterone in this high-energy orgy. Thick white cream saturated his beard as the ass that had just dismounted hunched over and burst forth with a stream of spunk.

"NOT in the mouth!" a stern voice ordered almost simultaneously with Deck stretching his mouth wide in an effort to snatch the wads out of the air. "It will be weeks before he has proven himself worthy of our gifts."

He was taunted with quick attacks with which he could not keep up as one BeNelly brother after another mounted the platform and lowered a large cock into the rim seat opening to shoot precious squirts of Deck's favorite beverage all over him, but never in his snapping mouth. Although, an initial translucent, sweet liquid drop would occasionally fly uncontrolled onto his guppy-pursed lips, which he would tongue at greedily just in hopes of sampling that magnificent flavor that is as varied from man to man as is the taste of the anus.

Deck's cock throbbed between his naked thighs as he was saturated. He could feel thick, heavy gobs slipping off his cheeks, seeping from his forehead into his scalp, coagulating in his beard, clogging his nostrils with the incredible bleachy aroma, even drizzling through his sideburns and into the wells of his ear canals. His eyes burned from the intentionally cruel aims, so he was forced to shut them, sensing that they were crusting shut as the glue took hold. He reached a hand toward his crotch to release his own pressure as the never-ending stream of BeNelly brothers doused him in their secretions.

His hands were violently ripped away from his sex, torturing him by forcing abstinence in this combustive situation.

And as the last of perhaps twenty BeNelly brothers shot a starchy stench into his nostrils, everything went black again.

❖

Shouts of ecstasy morphed into barks of confusion as the entire dungeon was plunged into complete darkness. In his inebriated state, Deck grappled his way out from under the rim chair and fell from the top of his perch with a knee-bruising thud onto hard floor. Moist, rank flesh brushed against him as chaos ensued, men trying to find their way out. Deck swiped his hands across his face, attempting to remove the dripping juices as he rose to his feet, using the table he'd been on for leverage. His tongue instinctively crept from between his lips and circled the circumference of his whiskers trying to sop up some of the pungent substance.

Suddenly, hands were on him, brushing over his furry chest and swollen nipples gently. They slipped up to his beard, feeling him, smearing the mess in his whiskers, crawling over his ears and through his thick head of mussed and sticky hair.

"Who—" he tried to speak.

"Let's go," a soft voice whispered, finding one of his hands and pulling him deeper into the current black hole of his existence.

The hand gripping Deck's held tight as if for dear life, his unseen guide leading him through frantic bodies that nearly knocked them over. Finally, the ruckus was left behind and he was being carefully coaxed up a flight of stairs as his guide moved alongside him and put one arm around him for support, warning him in a whisper to watch his step. When he was on the verge of tumbling backward, a tight, lean muscle bulged against his bare, sweaty back to propel him up, even slipping underneath one great big hairy buttock and squeezing tightly to coax him.

"We're almost there," the voice assured him, and then he felt himself reaching level ground.

"Who are you?" Deck whispered back as he was propelled through the darkness swiftly.

After several more steps, a light beamed brightly in his eyes, blinding him. He shied away from the sudden burst of brilliance.

"You're a mess," the voice behind the light said. The beam bounced spastically for a moment, and then he was being handed a shirt. A very familiar shirt: a red V-necked designer tee he had been trying to magically see through not two hours ago. "Clean yourself up."

"How did you?"

"We have to keep going," Maru said, wiping globs of BeNelly emissions from Deck's face with his shirt. The light beam from Deck's own flashlight, which Maru was clutching, followed his all-over treasure trail to the crotch. "Nice. Now let's get you somewhat covered."

Without waiting for suggestions, Maru insisted Deck hold the flashlight and aim it down. Deck did as told. Maru helped him step into the T-shirt, lifting a calf and placing the foot attached to it into one of the shirtsleeves, then repeating the process with the other leg. Maru hurriedly yanked the soiled shirt up, pulling it over his thighs, causing an echoing rip.

"Could your shirt be any smaller?" Deck asked, watching mesmerized as Maru dressed him, Maru's now bare torso gleaming in the flashlight beam, which caused beautiful shadows in every tightly defined valley of the smooth physique.

"It's these huge muscular thighs of yours," Maru said as he ripped the cuffs of the sleeves open to capacity, making the tight fit slightly less extreme.

"You're cutting off my circulation," Deck said as his thighs were choked. The material finally reached its max about three-quarters of the way up his thigh.

"If only we had the time to help you with your problem," Maru said as he pulled the material up and over the object of his comment.

For the first time, Deck realized that he was still rock hard erect. Maru slipped the material over Deck's groin area, covering his privates, and then wrapped his hands around the "waist" of the shirt, following the line until his arms were around Deck, so he could pull up the back flap.

"Damn, your ass is huge," Maru said, yanking on the material that had gotten stuck under the meaty flesh.

Deck tried to ignore the sensation of Maru's chest rubbing against the bottom of his up-pointed shaft through the T-shirt material. It was useless. His cock throbbed as he replied, "It's muscle."

"I can feel that," Maru said, and Deck wasn't sure if he was referring to his ass or his cock, which was throbbing against Maru's heart.

"OW!" Deck cried as the material was tugged over his butt—and right up into his crack. "You're giving me a wedgie!"

"Sorry." Maru rose from his squatting position and took the flashlight from Deck, who now looked like he was wearing a tattered, tight red Tarzan loincloth. "We gotta go."

Maru took Deck's hand again and they ran down a creepy gray hall until a big metal door greeted them.

"Almost there," Maru said, reaching for the handle of the door.

It was pulled from his grasp as they were bathed in bright moonlight.

"You motherfuckin' faggots are mine," said a BeNelly monster who greeted them outside the entrance, gun in hand and pointed right at them.

❖

Deck was still incredibly woozy from whatever the BeNelly brothers had used to drug him, but he tried to push Maru behind him to act as a shield against any gunfire. The last thing he expected was for Maru to bully past him and right up to the BeNelly brother.

"Fucking do it, man!" Maru screamed, expressing a fury Deck would never have imagined. "Blow my fucking brains out! Try and threaten the willin' with a killin'!"

The confused BeNelly's eyes were wide with shock, but he did manage to keep his large presence from backing away from the onslaught.

Maru grabbed the BeNelly's gun hand and, to Deck's horror, slipped the barrel of the gun between his own taut lips.

"What the fuck?" the BeNelly brother stammered.

"Fawkin Duh eht!" Maru garbled around the barrel of the gun, his expression blazing. "Yooh pufhy!"

Garbled or not, it was clear to Deck that Maru had just called the BeNelly brother a pussy. The expression of murder on the BeNelly's dark face made it clear he had understood the message too.

The menacingly large man grabbed the back of Maru's head and forced his piece deeper into Maru's mouth.

"I'll fucking KILL you!" the BeNelly yelled, spittle flying from his full lips and speckling Maru's cheeks.

"Duh eht!" Maru gagged on the gun in his mouth as he grabbed a thick black wrist and seemed to force the gun even farther down his throat.

Deck was immobile, propped up against a wall as the two men grappled in the doorway in a psychotic standoff. He feared the slightest rash move would create a knee-jerk reaction from the BeNelly brother, which would surely leave at least one person dead.

But much to Deck's surprise, the BeNelly brother visibly relaxed the tension on Maru, his eyes softening with discomfort. "I'm not gonna."

Deck had to act while the BeNelly brother was faltering. He found his nerve—and strength—and thrust himself off the wall and at the big man.

But before he could reach the gun-toting BeNelly, an even bigger body burst in, the door swinging completely open and slamming against the outside wall. Moonbeams flooded in, shedding even more light on the situation. The gigantic body grabbed Deck around the neck and smashed him back up against the wall, knocking what little wind was left out of him.

"I'll take care of these two ass eaters! Get the fucking lights back on!" the new arrival growled at the BeNelly attached to Maru, thrusting a flashlight in their direction.

As if waiting for an escape from the scenario, the BeNelly brother yanked his gun from Maru's mouth and took off without another word, disappearing up the hall from which Maru and Deck had just come.

"Fucking BeNelly nigger can tell us apart even less than a cracker," the man with a chokehold on Deck griped as he loosened his grip. "You okay? I'm so sorry. Just had to make it convincing."

Deck clenched his raw throat and coughed as his assailant tried to hold him upright.

"You saved me….again." Deck gasped for air, clutching Wilky's bulging arm.

With his other arm, Wilky reached down and righted Maru. "Time for thanks later. Let's get the fuck outta here. Those BeNellys are gonna catch on pretty fast."

❖

The man is a real life Hercules, was all Deck could think as he was propelled through the dark woods. He was entirely cradled in Wilky's arms as Wilky dashed through the vegetation dodging trees Deck could barely make out until the large trunks were right upon them.

Maru was keeping pace, once again clutching Deck's flashlight.

"What's that sound?" Deck muttered as the biting cold made his flesh burn.

"What sound?" Maru asked, running beside them and looking around frantically.

"Up there." Deck tried to point to the trees above. Silhouettes created by the moonlight made the leaves high above look like they were moving, circling, swirling, fluttering maddeningly.

"It's like the thing I saw," Maru said, then stopped talking abruptly.

Deck had shot him a warning look, fearing he might mention that they'd been at Pale Shelter Estates at the time of the previous spotting of the mysterious black mass.

"He's delirious," Wilky said to Maru, not even looking up to see what Deck was referencing. "They must have given him some strong shit."

They broke from the trees into a clearing, where Wilky's car was waiting. Deck was quickly loaded into the backseat of the vehicle.

"Do you mind if I…" Maru began, pointing to the backseat.

"'Course not, my man." Wilky nodded, a slight smirk creeping across his beautiful lips. Got a blanket in the compartment under the seat back there you can cover him with," Wilky spoke into the rearview mirror as he drove them out of the woods and onto the main road leading back to Pale Shelter Estates. "Although, he looks pretty good like that, huh?"

"Yeah, he does," Maru agreed.

"I'm cold," Deck said, nearly pouting.

"What a big baby," Maru said. He found a wool blanket where Wilky had described and tucked Deck in.

Deck rested his head on Maru's naked shoulder and closed his eyes.

❖

When Deck opened his eyes, he was convinced he had somehow slipped back through time to an earlier century. He just wasn't sure which one. There were cathedral ceilings floating way above him in patterns crafted with fine detail. His gaze traveled down to walls bursting with floral prints. Majestic statues and classic art accented the space. And he was on a rich maroon couch across which one might expect to see Cleopatra sprawling.

"Here, use this to wash off his face." Wilky offered a soft cloth and a bowl of warm water to Maru.

"Thanks." Maru took the cloth and dipped it in the water as Wilky placed the bowl on a marble end table.

Maru, sitting on the edge of the couch beside Deck, who was under a thick wool blanket, gently tried to wipe most of the now crusty remnants from Deck's face. "You're really going to need to shower this stuff off."

"Where are we?" Deck asked.

"What do you think of the place?" a sexy voice spoke.

Deck realized a lean yet imposing man was standing behind Maru, smiling almost ironically. The expression quickly melted into a gentle look of concern. "How are you feeling?"

Proc, who was now in a silky red robe, looked incredibly dashing, like some sort of classic movie star, his perfectly slicked back dark hair bringing out the contours of his sharp, stunning features.

"I'm okay." Deck sat up, pushing the blanket to the side. He was still in his makeshift red loincloth.

"Wilks, can you get Deck something to wear?" Proc asked.

"Sure thing," Wilky said, exiting the room, which Deck assumed was the living room—a room he hadn't had a chance to explore on his first visit to Pale Shelter.

"Why didn't you just take me to Weeping Manor?" Deck wondered, slightly suspicious.

"It's really late. We didn't even tell Hayes what happened. Not what he needed to hear after the funeral—and this afternoon's little arson show on his lawn," Proc said.

"How did you know where I was?"

"Mr. Chai was nearly hysterical," Maru chimed in. "He said the BeNellys got you. I called Wilky. I didn't know who else to turn to."

"And I'm glad you did." Proc patted Maru's shoulder. "You don't want to mess with those guys by yourself."

"Well, now I know why Mr. Chai doesn't want you to work for him," Deck said. "His staff is used as backup funding if he can't pay the rent."

"What do you mean?" Proc asked, his thin eyebrows furrowing with a hint of anger.

"Meaning, he borrowed the money to open his business from the BeNellys, and if he doesn't have the monthly installment available, they take one of his staff instead, who is then forced into white slavery. And, um, Asian slavery," Deck corrected himself, looking bashfully at Maru.

"They need to be stopped," Proc muttered, his penetrating eyes almost looking yellow.

"Well, I have a feeling the men Chai hires know the risk of working for him, because tonight's catch seemed to be enjoying himself," Deck recalled.

"Even so, they are like a virus in this city, and the police won't do a damn thing about it." Proc scowled. "And if they aren't going to do something about it, we will. This city is about to combust and we can't just sit here and let it happen. And *you*," Proc turned to Maru. "You need to watch yourself with these BeNellys. Wilky told me what you did in there. You're going to need to look over your shoulder at every moment. In fact, I would feel better if you stayed here. They're not going to come near you in here."

"Let 'em kill me." Maru shrugged. "Then the police will have to put them away."

"Life is a precious commodity," Proc stated evenly. He placed one finger delicately under Maru's chin and lifted his face. "Your beautiful life is precious."

There was something sensual and seductive about the gesture and the words, even if it was not intended that way.

"You can stay with me," Deck blurted out.

Maru's and Proc's heads turned slowly, and Wilky, who happened to be re-entering the room with a folded sweat suit, froze dead center in a grand archway, his full lips circling into an O.

"I mean…with us. At Hayes's home," Deck tried to clarify.

"Asian slavery, huh?" Maru teased him.

"Thank you for being such a wiseass," Deck muttered as Wilky handed him the freshly pressed garments.

Proc grabbed a tight hold of Deck's full head of hair and looked him straight in the eyes. "And thank you for saving my life tonight."

"Yeah. That too." Deck looked down at his new clothes to avoid any eye contact with anyone.

"I guess, theoretically, I owed you one," Maru said.

Proc looked over at Wilky and rolled his eyes. "I don't know which one of these two's heads I want to bite off more."

"Wilky, could you take me home?" Maru asked, standing.

"Really, Maru." Proc stopped him. "Please consider my offer. The place isn't completely done yet, and some rooms are still gutted and look like a crypt, but I have space to accommodate you."

"I really rather just go back to Harry's," Maru said. "Besides, they have an alarm system."

"I'm gonna get dressed and get back to Weeping Manor as well," Deck said.

"You two are impossible." Proc threw up his hands. "Do what you want, but I want you both to check in with me by dusk tomorrow so I know you're both still all right, you understand me?"

"Here," Wilky said, grabbing a bag from the backseat of his Hummer and handing it to Deck as they pulled into the parking area alongside Weeping Manor.

"What's this?" Deck asked.

"It's your stuff." Wilky winked.

"What? Wait. You went back to the BeNelly's place?"

"It's easy. I blend right in with them."

Deck thanked Wilky, then stepped out of the Hummer, wearing just a pair of baggy, oversized gray sweats Wilky had lent him. The bag of his clothes in hand, he climbed the steps to the kitchen entrance of Weeping Manor, furiously pondering how the man could possibly have gotten back into the BeNelly place *and* found his clothes without being caught.

Once the alarm system was deactivated, he turned and quickly waved to Wilky's Hummer, not sure if Wilky or Maru waved back. The Hummer drove off slowly.

Deck pushed the door open, but stopped midway in upon hearing that flapping sound again. Leaning out the doorway, he glanced up in the darkness. Way above was the bulk of the balcony that belonged to his room. It must be those birds again. Or maybe bats? Exhaustion made him dizzy as he stared into the near blackness above. He clutched the handle of the door for balance and pushed himself upright. He hurried inside. His window of opportunity before the alarm would sound was closing.

Inside, more darkness greeted him. But his instincts came alive in the slight green glow of digital numbers from a clock on Don's industrial oven.

He wasn't alone.

"Deck."

Deck's entire lower region clenched with fear, from his asshole to the tip of his dick. But his mind was already registering the owner of the voice.

"Hayes?" Deck called into the shadows, finally making out a man sitting at the kitchen table behind the large cooking island in the center of the room.

"Yes, it's me. Just sitting here having some warm milk. I couldn't sleep. Come, sit with me."

Deck heard a chair being pushed out from the table.

"I'll give us a little light to see by," Hayes Lamond said before a warm orange glow filled the sparkling kitchen, bouncing off steel and ceramic.

Hayes had lit a vanilla scented candle on the table. And although the orange licked at his sharp features from below, it didn't come off creepy like one might think. Hayes actually looked vibrant, his skin smooth and taut, his white hair brushed back and glistening with a just-washed sheen. He was wearing a silk robe, completely open at the chest, exposing a barely haired chest that could have belonged to the body of a twenty-year-old volleyball player, aside from the speckles of aging freckles.

Deck felt the fullness of his own fuzzy belly brush against the edge of the table as he sat down, dropping his bag of clothes on another empty chair.

"You okay?" Deck asked, taking one of Hayes's cool hands from around the warm mug he had been caressing.

Hayes glanced over at him and smiled warmly. "Yes. I actually am. I feel so incredibly at ease. Like Ben is with me. Wants me to go on. To keep the dream we had for Kremfort Cove alive. All those beautiful men who attended tonight. We're here to make them love life. That's why I've decided we can't put off opening The Caves for another weekend. Saturday night, we're back in business. I will have Jeeves spread the word. You are going to love this party."

"I've looked forward to witnessing one," Deck responded, thinking it odd that Hayes hadn't even asked him what he was doing sneaking through the kitchen door in the middle of the night in just sweats. "But are you sure you're up for it?"

"Oh, I'll definitely be up for it. And you will be too," Hayes said provocatively, leaning in close and taking Deck's beard in his hands. "You are so beautiful, Deck. I can't thank you enough for being here to help see me through this."

Before Deck could react, thin, firm lips were pressed against his own. Deck's mouth instinctively opened, allowing suction to connect him to Hayes. Their nostrils breathed in each other's exhalations. Hayes was off his chair and pushing down on Deck until his large body was on the cold floor. Deck shivered as Hayes's face nuzzled into the crook of his neck.

"Mmmm." Hayes hummed. "You smell good enough to eat. What are you wearing?"

"BeNelly brother," Deck quipped.

Hayes didn't seem to hear him. He was kissing down Deck's kinky mess of chest hair, so Deck flexed his big, round pecs to highlight their size and shape. Then his knobby, rubbery right nipple was being gently but firmly suckled, which brought Deck's butt right off the floor as his groin gyrated with uncontrolled excitement at much needed physical contact that had been denied him by the BeNelly brothers.

Deck knew exactly what was going on here. He was being used to fill a void in Hayes's life. It was a safe using, because they knew each other, and Hayes knew there would be no hurt afterward, that they wouldn't desert each other, but that they expected nothing more from each other beyond this moment of ecstasy. It just didn't get any safer or better than this.

"You're such a man," Hayes whispered, moving over and chewing on Deck's other knob, which was still healing from his first encounter with the BeNellys. Deck's hands were flat against the floor gripping them to hold in the cries that wanted to escape his mouth.

With the agility of a teenager, Hayes was on his knees, straddling Deck's big body and crawling his crotch forward toward Deck's mouth. Soft, cool balls ran up Deck's cleavage, and a perfectly straight and erect, sleek, rod-like penis moved to his face. He brought his head up and opened his mouth to receive it.

"Yeeeessssss!" Hayes moaned above him.

Hayes, his robe now completely open in front, placed his hands down on the floor, on either side of Deck's head, lifted his ass off Deck's tits, and began to gently fuck Deck's mouth.

Deck took in every amazing carved indent of definition in Hayes's fatless physique, the evenly trimmed white chest patch, the perfectly designed fluff of white pubic hairs above his cock. Deck's hands found Hayes's incredibly lean and muscular buttocks and relished every flex as they worked in and out of his mouth. There was a brushing of soft hairs on that smooth flesh, and Deck pictured a symmetrical pattern of white back there.

Being face-fucked was rarely such a smooth experience as right now. Hayes's hard cock slid in and out of him like a fruity flavored ice pop on a hot summer day. The roof of Deck's mouth and his tongue formed a tight tunnel for the lean phallus, the hard ridge of the head tickling the upper regions of Deck's oral cavity. Deck created a salivary suction to squeeze on the shaft, its pure, clean taste enticing Deck's palate.

"I'm ready, Deck!" Hayes growled, then his narrow eyes were bursting wide as heavy cream filled Deck's mouth.

Deck had to keep his teeth in check as his jaw automatically tried to clench due to a stream of excitement that burst from his own untouched cock. The twisted eroticism of the night had clearly built up in him, giving him a waking nocturnal emission.

"That's it. Every ounce of it." Hayes closed his eyes as he drained his fluids down Deck's hungry gullet in graceful gyrations. "I just love how you love the sweetness of man."

When they both recuperated from the expelling, Hayes hopped off Deck and helped lift him to his feet. "Oh boy, you made a mess of your pants."

Deck looked down at the large wet stain at his crotch. He could feel it gluing to his thick tufts of pubes.

"Come, let's get you showered," Hayes said, taking Deck's hand.

When Deck finally arrived in his bedroom, he dug into his bag of clothes. Shirt, shoes, pants, wallet, phone, keys were all still there. He'd need to get Don to drive him back to Chai Tea in the morning to pick up his car.

Deck grabbed his phone, intending to text Maru to make sure he'd gotten home okay. He got his answer from a text he had received, simply saying, "I'm here safe. Hope you're there safe."

After acknowledging that he was, Deck, too wired from the crazy night to pass out yet despite exhaustion, fired up the computer alongside his giant television (which happened to be the monitor for the computer) and Googled two words: spontaneous combustion.

CHAPTER SEVEN

Despite the abuse he'd taken the night before, Deck was feeling incredibly invigorated the next morning after being subjected to the ultimate spa treatment—sauna, hot tub, massage, and more.

And now he was lounging in a silky robe, head back on a plush pillow and eyes closed. He'd just had a pedicure, and now his feet were up on padded stirrups. Foot master Garth Healy was masturbating them with a warm, moist lubricant.

"Wow. That feels incredible." Deck groaned as the thick pads on the bottom of his feet were tenderly but firmly rubbed by strong fingers.

He opened his eyes to look at the short and stocky man, who was dressed in casual white shorts and a white tank top, revealing a fuzzy and finely formed chest and arms, ruddy from years of tanning. Garth's face was equally worn, with sexy dark whiskers, bushy sideburns, and a shaggy head of dirty blond hair with noticeable streaks of sun-bleached damage. Crow's feet pulled deep glowing hazel eyes into knots, and heavy lifelines swelled under thick lashes, a clear sign of much partying over the years.

"You've got the sexiest damn feet." Garth serviced with a smile, revealing incredibly straight and white teeth that automatically washed away the wear and tear and allowed his true age to show through—probably about thirty-eight or thirty-nine. Deck's age. "I love the toe pubes."

Garth gently tugged on the strands of hair on Deck's toe knuckles.

"Ooooh!" Deck wheezed as Garth hit a spot on his sole—a spot that seemed to tickle Deck's loins.

"Reflexology." Garth chuckled mischievously. "Every inch of your body can be traced back to a nerve in your feet. I could make you have an all-out full body orgasm if you wanted it."

"Are you propositioning me?" Deck asked.

"I just can't get enough of your feet," Garth nearly growled.

Deck watched as a swell in Garth's baggy white shorts was brushed back and forth across the bottom of his feet.

"I wanna fuck your feet so bad," Garth said, swallowing hard.

One of the flaps of Deck's robe slipped off his thigh as his own erection grew. His raised and parted legs were now uncovered, revealing the mass of black hair that coated the backs of his thighs, vegetating up into his crotch, over his balls, and up the base of his shaft.

"What a view," Garth whispered, using one hand to slip the elastic waistband down on his shorts until it came to rest just below his balls. A cock of about seven inches was released, nice and thick, and oddly, almost the same tan color as the rest of Garth's body. The upward curve was so extreme it looked painful, like someone had grabbed it in both hands at one time and bent it. If measured in a straight line from base to head, the distance might only be about five inches.

"That's quite a curve you got there."

"The better to hook you with." Garth winked.

"What kind of whore do you take me for?" Deck played mock insulted.

"Just wait until you see the arch of my load. You open that pretty little mouth, you may just get lucky," Garth said as he adjusted the stirrups, closing the gap between Deck's feet.

Deck's soles were pressed together, and Garth applied more of the slick, warm lotion. Then, finding the slit created by the meeting feet, Garth slowly wiggled his index finger into the crack.

"Tiiiiight fuck hole!" Garth gasped as his finger popped out the other side.

Deck watched with interest as the finger worked its way between his feet. He intentionally clenched them, pressing big toes and heels together to seal the gap between his feet even more. Garth slipped two fingers into the smaller opening. Deck found it bizarrely erotic, as if it was actually his asshole that was getting the finger fuck, and he was on the inside witnessing it.

"I want in," Garth said, moving closer and lubing up his curved cock.

"Be gentle," Deck cooed. "It's my first time."

"Love a virgin," Garth said quite seriously.

Deck appreciated Garth's ripped muscles and the light sheen of sweat that glistened on his golden body hair as Garth pushed his thick, swollen head against the flats of Deck's feet. Deck had to fight to not giggle at the tickling effect. But that tickle didn't last long. Garth's cock head forced its way between his tightness until the piss slit was winking at him as it poked its way through. He could feel the hard ridge of the head on the insides of his feet, could feel the length of the shaft passing through. Garth expertly maneuvered his narrow hips so the curve would seem to be traveling a straight path as it hooked its way in. At last, Deck felt a patch of pubes tickle the tender bottoms of his freshly scraped feet. Garth let out a sigh of pleasure.

"Fuck me," Deck pleaded, feeling kind of awkward there on his back with his legs up—and a dick between his feet instead of up his ass. No matter how hard Garth pounded him, he sure wasn't ever going to hit the A-spot.

Garth powerfully wrapped his hands around Deck's feet as if he was grabbing the reins on a horse, squatted slightly at the knees, and began to do a dipping grind down and then back up into the crevasse between Deck's feet. The man definitely knew how to maneuver that curved cock, getting a major hip workout as he created a rhythmic thrusting that looked like some sort of dance. Deck was mesmerized by the masculinity of the body movement.

Garth didn't even make eye contact. His complete attention was focused on the objects of his affection—the feet. He was squeezing them together harder and harder, practically crushing Deck's toes. Luckily, all the lubricant he'd applied was ensuring regular slippage.

Deck could feel the heft of the arched phallus digging its way into him and got to watch it come out the other side blindingly fast. It was fascinating.

"Tighten that hole for me!" Garth ordered. He released Deck's feet, bringing his hands up and running them through his thick, dirty blond locks, showing off bulging biceps and sweaty tufts of pit hair.

Deck focused his mind on forcefully cramming his feet together while keeping his knees apart so as not to crush his own balls, which were now draped over the bush of his asshole.

"That's iiiiiiit!" Garth groaned, throwing his head back, his shaft benefiting from the attempted meeting of the bones in Deck's feet.

"Blow your load up my foot chute!" Deck ad-libbed, not sure if that was the right terminology for this particular fetish.

"Open your mouth!" Garth demanded.

Unsure of what to expect, Deck simply did as told, even flattening his tongue as if having his throat checked by a doctor's wooden stick.

Garth's body shifted in mid-thrust, his shoulders hunching slightly, his groin readjusting, and his hands once again grabbing Deck's feet.

It was astounding: Deck felt the first sweet splashes awaken his taste buds and sprinkle the upper lip whiskers of his beard. He turned his attention to that hooked cock as bursts of cream shot from the piss slit, arching through the air before landing almost solely on his tongue.

"Yeah! Yeah! Yeah!" Garth cheered each score as his entire body tightened with the expulsions.

Deck wanted so badly to swallow, but any slight movement of his tongue would cause his mouth to close. It wasn't until the distances began to shorten, sprinkling over his chest then crotch and then missing him completely and disappearing between his legs, that he closed his mouth and let the noticeably watery semen melt against the roof of his mouth before swallowing.

Looking back to his feet, he watched Garth's thrusts slow, the final spurts of cum oozing messily out and scraping off on the bottoms of his feet as the cock was withdrawn. Much to Deck's amazement, Garth grabbed his feet again and began to massage the mess right in like it was a lotion.

"So how's the foot business?" Deck asked.

"Kinda slow this week, for obvious reasons," Garth answered. "In fact, really slow. I'm so hungry for some action that I keep thinking I see someone out in the waiting room, but when I go out there to call him in, there's no one."

"Really?" Deck pondered the comment as Garth brought him over to a chair with a jet massager in front of it.

"It's kinda spooky." Garth sounded like he had something he wanted to get off his chest. "The presence is so strong. And familiar."

"Familiar how?" Deck asked.

Garth's carefree features suddenly tightened. He smiled—and not with complete ease. "Oh, you know. Like Jeeves is lurking around or something. He likes to jump out of corners and make the staff jump a mile. So I guess my mind is just playing tricks on me, expecting one of his games."

As Garth leaned down to place Deck's feet in the jet massager, Deck looked over his back into the empty waiting room just outside the door. As warm speeding bubbles tickled his feet, a chill ran up his spine. And it wasn't because he thought he might glimpse Jeeves in there. He knew a quick cover-up story when he heard one. So who— or what—had Garth really seen? And why didn't he feel comfortable talking about it?

Deck looked at his cell phone four times before deciding it wasn't cool to call Maru again. He had dialed him first thing in the morning after waking to genuinely thank him for his foolish rescue effort, but all he'd gotten was voice mail. He would have loved to have just hung up, but modern technology made it impossible to do anything anonymously anymore. His number would be flagged in Maru's phone under "missed calls."

Therefore, it was crucial that he not even dial since he couldn't guarantee Maru picking up. He was going to visit the Glouster twins, and according to Don, who referred to them as the Glouster cabróns, their gym was right around the corner from Dirty Harry's. He thought he would give Maru the option of going with him to do some sleuthing—to live a little.

Heart beating annoyingly overtime, Deck pocketed the phone.

He would head for the Glouster gym. Alone.

❖

Deck was thrilled when he came downstairs to find his car keys dangling in Jeeves's hands. He was even more shocked to see Jeeves dressed in jeans and a sweater. Jeeves had just entered through the kitchen door.

"Your car awaits." Jeeves smiled, handing over the keys. As soon as his hands were free, he began stripping.

"You went and got my car?" Deck asked. "Thanks."

"Don was heading into town for some special ingredients for a dinner he's making, so I went with him to get it. Chai Tea was nearby," Jeeves answered as he quickly undressed.

Deck planted a kiss on Jeeves's bald head. "You're a sweetheart. I owe you one."

"Can't wait." Jeeves nibbled the tip of his tongue playfully before bundling up his clothes and popping them into a nearby cabinet.

"Well, just announce yourself before you make an appearance in my room. I scare easily when it comes to hiding games," Deck said.

"I always knock on your doorframe," Jeeves said, looking concerned that he may have somehow annoyed Deck.

"Oh, I know. You do." Deck played it off. "Just saying, don't get any ideas of trying to scare me for fun."

"Believe me, I won't!" Jeeves assured Deck. "I hate being scared myself! This place is so big it's easy to suddenly run into someone when you think you're all alone. Just promise you won't do it to me either."

"Deal." Deck winked.

"Well, have fun today." Jeeves stood on his toes for a quick lip peck and then turned and walked off.

Deck watched that perfect pale ass jiggle back and forth as Jeeves left the room. When it was finally out of view, he stepped out into the daylight.

❖

Just as Deck's car was bouncing over a small wooden bridge that signified the transition from the wooded back road leading to the estates and the jungles of the city, his phone rang in the cup holder next to him.

"Hi." Deck fought to hide his absolute joy at the call.

"So did you lose your wallet last night? If you pick me up for brunch, I'll treat," Maru suggested boldly on the other end.

"Actually, I'll treat. I don't think the BeNellys need the petty cash. Wilky found my wallet too. I'm on my way into town right now. I'll pick you up in about fifteen to twenty. But I'd rather not do Chai Tea," Deck joked.

"Okay, but I hope that doesn't mean I won't get a chance to see you naked again."

Before Deck could respond, he realized Maru had played coy and hung up.

As he pulled behind Dirty Harry's, Deck caught sight of adorable club owner Jimmy in only tight jeans and a wifebeater as he tossed a bag of garbage into a Dumpster. He waved as he recognized Deck.

Deck rolled down his window. "What are you doing out here with no shoes or jacket on? You'll get sick."

Jimmy strolled over to the car and leaned down to the window. "I'd say you sound like my father, but he never gave a shit. Maru should be out in a minute. I think he was trying to get extra pretty for you."

Jimmy winked and Deck blushed.

"Hey. I just was wondering." Deck changed the subject. "Have you and Harry, you know, talked to Maru about his issues and maybe getting some professional help?"

"Absolutely. We even offered to pay since the kid has no health insurance. And you know, Hayes is working to get some social services up and running in the city for the community, but until that is in place, no one really has anywhere to turn for affordable assistance. But we did try to get him to go talk with Father Merrin."

"Father Merrin?"

"Yeah. Great man. He's starting a Catholic chapter in Kremfort Cove—an all-inclusive church. He's openly gay and wants to make a difference for the community. We had talked to him about Maru, and he has been urging us to get the kid there, but Maru is kinda mad at God these days."

Before Deck could nod his understanding, there was the industrial sound of a metal door. Jimmy turned and saw Maru coming out.

"Well, you get inside, and get some shoes on," Deck scolded Jimmy in an effort to cover up any hint that they had been talking about Maru.

"Okay." Jimmy waved as he stepped away from the car. "You two have fun."

Jimmy patted Maru on the shoulder as they passed each other.

"Hands off my daddy," Maru said to Jimmy with a playful nudge.

Deck, sipping on a flavored hot coffee, watched as Maru picked daintily at his plate of pancakes and sausage smothered in sweet syrup. The diner they were in was rather quiet at the moment since it wasn't quite lunchtime yet and this was a business day. They were tucked into a booth near the back of the place.

"You sure eat slow," Deck said, having already polished off his plate of eggs and hash browns.

"I like to take my time and enjoy it whenever I eat something," Maru said, then licked some syrup off the edge of a sausage link speared on his fork. Despite its suggestive nature, Maru's boyish expression made it seem innocent.

"I'll note that in my sleuth book. Could come in handy later," Deck shot back.

"So now that you've had some caffeine to wake you up," Maru said, "Wanna hear something unbelievable?"

"That's pretty much all I have been hearing since I got here," Deck pointed out.

"I know. But despite being unbelievable, it's something I have a feeling you'll *totally* believe."

"Probably. Hit me."

"I'd love to hit that," Maru said. "Oh…you mean, tell you the unbelievable thing."

Deck had no control over his face muscles as he grinned sheepishly.

"I saw Lance." Maru's words made Deck's smile fade immediately.

"What? Where?" Deck asked without the least bit of cynicism.

"At the end of the hall by my room when I was coming in after Wilky dropped me off last night."

"A ghost?" Deck asked.

"I'm thinking an angel. I mean, he wasn't much of an angel when he was alive, but I've really been reading up on guardian angels, and I just felt so comforted when I saw him. I wasn't scared at all."

"So God's okay today?" Deck spoke without thinking.

"What's that supposed to mean?" Maru raised an eyebrow.

"Oh...I was just..."

"Talking to Jimmy this morning." Maru called him out.

"I'm sorry. You mad?"

"Not if he's the one who started the conversation," Maru prodded lightly.

"Totally. It was all Jimmy."

"Okay then." Maru's playful expression changed as his eyes drifted over Deck's shoulder.

He looks like he's seen a ghost. Deck turned quickly, but all he saw was a half wall with a trellis covered in plastic vines in the corner of the diner. He looked back at Maru. "What is it?"

"I swear I just saw him," Maru stated flatly. "He was standing right there, and then disappeared behind the wall."

"Stay here," Deck said, sliding out of the booth quickly.

Heart racing, Deck moved swiftly to the trellis. There was no one in the hallway that was created beyond it. But there were two doors to the restrooms. Out of habit, Deck pushed open the door to the men's room first. It was a small room. Only two urinals and two stalls with both doors open. No windows. And no ghosts.

Deck stepped out into the hall, knocked on the door to the ladies' room, got no response, and pushed it open slowly. *Damn. It's like a five-star hotel in here.*

The frilly and perfume-filled room had six stalls; the last had their doors closed. *Shit. I gotta check them.*

Deck propped the door open with a nearby waste bin just to prevent any shock if a woman should walk in—although, he had yet to see a woman other than Yvette Anderson in Kremfort Cove. *Doors should probably just be labeled "Men" and "Drag Queens."*

Deck was so ready to be scared pissless by a ghost as he shakily approached the closed doors of the far stalls. He didn't see any feet underneath, but that didn't mean much if he was dealing with a ghost.

Rather than pulling a movie move, where the detective slowly reaches with his hand to the door to push it open, Deck found his nerve and quickly punched it with his palm. It swung inward with a bang. *Empty.*

Deck breathed a sigh of relief and turned to step out of the stall.

A hideous face with bug eyes, flaring nostrils, and a stretched mouth revealing rows of straight white teeth stared him in the face.

"Aaaahh!" Deck cried, nearly falling back into the toilet bowl.

A stream of laughter escaped the monster as its face morphed into the face of Maru as he released the hold his fingers had on his ghoulish expression.

"Are you kidding me?" Deck stammered with controlled annoyance as Maru doubled over with laughter.

"Oh man, you should have seen your face!" Maru giggled as he tried to contain himself.

"So were you fucking with me?" Deck asked haughtily.

"No...no...I really saw him," Maru said as he caught his breath. "But I'm telling you, he's not a ghost. You shouldn't be scared of him."

Deck hurriedly checked the last stall, with Maru right behind him. Finding nothing, they stepped out. And they both screamed, instinctively clinging to each other.

"Did I miss anything?"

There stood the waiter who had been serving them.

"You know, we prefer you have any fun in the men's room," the waiter said. "We wouldn't want to have to deal with the commissioner and her bullies if a woman did happen to come in and catch you."

"We weren't—" Deck began.

"Sorry. I just couldn't wait any longer. That sausage made me horny and this bathroom was closer," Maru said as he took Deck's hand and led him out of the room.

"Uh-huh." The waiter smirked, following them out, with Deck looking over his shoulder and trying to mime that absolutely nothing had happened.

"I'll bring you your check." The waiter winked as they sat back down at their table and he passed by.

Deck gave Maru a stern look.

"What were we going to tell him?" Maru shrugged. "That we were looking for ghosts and angels?"

"You got a point," Deck said. "But seriously. I want you to listen to me. I don't know what's going on here in Kremfort Cove, and I'd really like to find out if anyone else involved in all this has experienced the same thing you have."

"Which means you should ask Hayes Lamond."

"Yeah, but how do you do that tactfully, considering he just lost the love of his life? You volunteered the info. Which is why I'm going to tell you, please don't try to connect with this apparition in any way if he appears again. Seriously. I know you'd like to believe—"

"Wow. You really do believe in monsters," Maru said before sipping from his glass of orange juice.

"Yeah. I do," Deck admitted. "Until proven wrong. So you call me, any time, day or night, if you see him again, and you turn and pretty much run away for now. Go knock on Harry and Jimmy's door if you have to, just so you won't be alone."

"If guardian angels are real, I never am alone," Maru replied, and Deck felt his stomach sinking, because he wasn't sure the seemingly fearless Maru *would* run away if someone—or something—beckoned him from the other side.

CHAPTER EIGHT

As summer was becoming autumn, the daylight hours were dwindling faster and faster. By the time Deck parked on the street of the Glouster Gym, darkness had fallen. He'd spent a majority of the day with Maru, who showed him the town—meaning, the many stores and shops it had. They'd only parted because Maru had to get ready for work. *Why does that bother me so much?*

Deck pretended not to know the answer to that one.

The gym shared one side of a street with a deli, a couple of currently dark bars/lounges, and a large health products store right next to the gym. Storefronts on the opposite side of the street were still boarded or caged up.

Due to the scarcity of businesses, Deck was able to park only a couple of spots away from the gym. He admired the amazing gay bodies going by in shorts and tank tops as men left the gym, some disappearing immediately into the health products store.

"Now that's a brilliant business partnership," Deck muttered.

He blushed as he realized a twinkish twenty-something passing him on the street with a pug on a leash was staring at him oddly, probably thinking, *crazy old homo,* or something of that sort. The twink was quickly distracted by an approaching person. Deck could hear the two trying to exchange pleasantries, but the pug began to bark furiously. Deck looked back and saw the dog twirling its leash around its master's legs in an effort to get away from the other person, a man who looked like he may have had a really late night. He also heard the dog owner saying, "Bitch! What are you barking at! It's just Terry!"

Deck slipped through the gym doors, leaving the barks outside. He was greeted by bright track lighting and industrial shades of silver, white, blue, and black. His eyes shot to the tall, physically perfect physique of the bleach blond, blue-eyed beauty standing behind a welcome counter, smooth, sun-soaked skin contrasting wonderfully with a glaring white stretchy gym leotard, the straps of which barely covered raging hard nipples.

Unfortunately, Deck's work of art appreciation was interrupted.

"Waxer," a mustached, boxy-big black man said from the doorway of a nearby juice bar. It was Officer Soloman, along with his sidekick, Bembury. They were in casual shorts and sweatshirts with the sleeves ripped off.

"What you doing here?" Bembury asked, arms crossed in front of his broad chest. Deck noticed the thick swirls of hair on his swelling triceps, a growth spurt not uncommon amongst men of their age. Deck had often considered shaving his, but learned to just live with it.

"Hi, officers," Deck said, approaching them. "So, you *are* following me."

"We were just here working out," Soloman said. "But yeah. We're keeping an eye on you."

"Let me guess," Deck said. "Commissioner Anderson put you up to it."

Soloman and Bembury exchanged glances.

"Let's talk," Soloman said, gesturing Deck into the empty juice bar area and signaling the blond behind the welcome counter to stay put.

They sat at a small circular table in a booth with leather seating.

"So," Soloman began, "Anderson did ask us to keep tabs on you. What's your deal? We can't figure out if she loves you or hates you."

Deck shrugged. "Little bit of both."

"So you chase ghosts or stuff?" Bembury asked directly.

"Or stuff," Deck said.

"Yeah? How many ghosts you caught?" Bembury asked, but it sounded more like he was mocking the idea.

"None yet," Deck admitted.

"So," Soloman said, "This could be your big break."

"Why do you say that?" Deck asked. "You think there's something supernatural going on in Kremfort Cove?"

"We didn't say that." Soloman shook his head. "We're just wondering why you've come to town. These cases are a little weird. Maybe you think you can sensationalize it and sell your story to the *Enquirer*."

"Is that what Anderson thinks?" Deck asked, fearing that might be just what she thought. He hadn't expected her to be thrilled when he showed up in her city, but the last thing he wanted was for her to not trust his intentions.

"We didn't say that," Bembury said.

They all stared at one another for a minute.

"We're not really getting anywhere here," Deck said. "Was there something specific you guys wanted to talk to me about?"

"Can we trust you?" Soloman asked.

"Can I trust you?" Deck asked.

"We want to keep the entire population of this city safe," Bembury said. "We're not sure that everyone who should feels the same."

The statement seemed to hang in the air for a moment and then drop onto the round table with a thud.

"Are you saying Anderson—" Deck stopped in mid-sentence. "Let me guess. You didn't say that."

The cops both shrugged.

"She's my friend," Deck said, going on the notion that they *were* saying it. "I've known her for years. She was practically a gay activist."

Soloman and Bembury actually had troubled looks on their faces. Deck got the impression that they were really conflicted, either about thinking about their boss that way, about admitting it to him, or both.

"Any chance either of you are looking to fill a vacated position if it opened up in the police force?" Deck asked directly.

Soloman's thick black mustache twitched as he pursed his lips. He took a moment, and then said, "We might have dreams of how we would do things different. How we'd make sure all subcultures felt safe and secure. We've watched this city change. People—my people—being pushed to the fringes because they can't afford to keep up with the gay Joneses. Families forced to move away because the conditions were so bad here they had to shut down the schools. No more kids in Kremfort Cove. And maybe that's for the better. This is becoming a different place. An adult place. It's no place for little ones. And that's fine. I appreciate what men like Lamond Hayes and Ben DuPont are trying to accomplish. It happens. But not always at the cost of lives. This is serious shit. And it doesn't feel to me like we're doing what we should be doing to facilitate the transition. People change. Loyalties change. Motivations change."

"Pressure takes its toll. Helplessness takes its toll. Inexplicable deaths approached only with the logic of criminal science never get solved," Deck challenged in an attempt to defend Anderson's reputation.

"We've seen things," Bembury said. "Questionable things."

"Like what?" Deck asked.

"We think she's got a thing going with a local thug," Soloman said.

Deck scoffed at the idea. "She wasn't into young guys even when we were young. She liked them big and burly."

"I didn't say he was young," Soloman said. "I said he was a thug. They come in all sizes and ages."

"So what makes you think this is going on?" Deck asked.

"Everyone at the station talks about it," Bembury said. "He gets brought in constantly for different misdemeanors. And he walks out scot-free every time."

"You know you can't hold every man for every little thing he does," Deck said. "Cells get crowded. It costs the city. It can ruin a not-so-bad guy's chance at cleaning up his act."

"He's been seen going to her place," Soloman said.

"Yeah?" Deck's tone was accusing. "By who?"

Without answering the question, Soloman said, "She doesn't live in an area where guys like him go unless they're up to something. She's got a quaint little bungalow on the outskirts of the city. There are a handful of houses in the woods, for those who want to experience the best of both worlds. And have the money to do it."

"Maybe she's trying to help him out," Deck suggested. "She was big on good causes even when we were in college. Maybe she put him to work, doing some odd jobs around her place."

"At night? All night?" Bembury asked.

"Wow." Deck shook his head. "You guys are unbelievable. That's her personal life. She's your boss."

They almost looked ashamed of themselves, but Soloman said, "We're just covering every angle. We're looking out for your people."

"My people," Deck said. "Says the two Village People hanging out together at the big gay gym in town."

Soloman slammed his big black hand down on the table and stood up. He leaned in close and Deck could feel the heat of his breath. "Fuck you and the Trojan you rode in on. This is a dangerous city to be in all by yourself. So you'd best not get caught with your pants down."

Soloman strode out of the juice bar area as Bembury stood up. "You blew it, man. We were trying to work with you."

Bembury chased after his partner. Deck hastily jumped from his seat and exited the juice bar just as Bembury was catching up with Soloman, who was waiting inside the front door of the building.

"Guys!" Deck called. "Just give me some time. I'll get to the bottom of this."

Soloman didn't even look back as he ushered Bembury out the door and flipped Deck the bird.

Deck turned back into the main area of the gym. He was caught off guard by the model-like blue-eyed blond behind the welcome desk, who was staring at him with total bitch face.

"Looks like you're not getting to the bottom of anyone," the blond said snarkily.

"Um," Deck spoke, trying to ignore the rude comment, "I'd like to get a membership."

"I can see why," the blond muttered.

"Did you just—" Deck started, looking at the blond in shock.

"You're too late. We're closed," the blond interrupted him, pointing to a sign on the wall behind him that listed the business hours.

"Come on." Deck played nice. "I really need this membership. Can't you see why?"

The beauty gave a bitchy smirk at hearing his own words played back. "Yeah. In the hands of my brother Sherk and I, you can become a whole new man."

Deck noted how pure the man's English was. Almost too pure. It was the sign of a European who had learned proper English instead of the gritty slang and dialects of the current wave of "native" Americans.

"Do I have to fill out some forms or anything?"

"Well, it depends on which membership you want—"

"Premium," Deck cut him off.

"I knew it." The pretty boy rolled his eyes. "It's always the same with you tired queens."

"You treat all your clients this way, they may just walk out," Deck said, watching the blond's perfectly taut and solid physique as he moved from behind the counter to the front door to lock up.

"You'll stay, you'll pay, and you'll ask for more," the blond said.

Cocky son of a bitch! Deck followed the wonderful white body in the leotards as he gestured to a set of steps.

"Sherk was not feeling so well earlier, so we may have to postpone your introductory offer for another time."

"Could I ask your name?"

"Zims," the beauty said, actually turning around and shaking Deck's hand. "Nice to meet you, Deck Waxer."

"Of course. You've heard—"

"And I'm assuming you are here to probe our feelings about Weeping Manor and its state-of-the-art gymnasium that threatens to steal away all our clients?"

"Well…"

"Let's discuss how fine we are with the competition after we fulfill your introductory offer," Zims said as they breezed through a lavish hallway adorned with artistic, erotic, silver-framed posters of men.

As much as Deck wanted answers after that teaser line, the posters on the wall were clearly there for a reason, and now he was thinking it would be fine to get what was coming to him before getting those answers.

Just as Zims went to knock on a door at the end of the hall, it was pulled open.

"You scared the hell out of me," Zims gasped at the virtual mirror image of him that appeared.

The only difference between the twins was that the tight buzzed sides and back of Zims's head were just as bleached as the spikes on top of his head, but Sherk had his spikes dyed a totally synthetic shade of black, giving him a reversed skunk look. And then there were the crowns of thorns tattooed all around Sherk's ankles, very noticeable due to the mere fact that Sherk was completely naked, a long, thin, uncut cock swinging between veined, muscular legs, surrounded by only a thin line of golden pubes, shaved so close they were straight rather than curly.

"A newbie?" Sherk asked, glancing at Deck.

"It's Waxer," Zims said and Sherk nodded. "Are you up for it, or still feeling under the weather?"

"Feel amazing," Sherk said, letting them into a fully mirrored room that appeared to be for aerobics classes, with a thick red mat covering the polished wood floor. "I napped for a few hours, then got up and hit the elliptical before showering. I'm ready to satisfy our new member."

"Credit card or cash?" Zims asked.

"What?" Deck was taken aback.

"For the membership." Zims rolled his eyes again. "Nothing comes for free, you know."

"Oh, right. Cash." Deck pulled his wallet out of his pocket.

"Five hundred," Sherk said from the mats, where he was now stretching his mouthwatering physique—a full-body tan that somehow had a pale edge to it as compared to Zims's darkness. Apparently, a tanning booth they had passed in the hall wasn't having the same effect on these identical twins.

"Five hundred gives you unlimited access to the show for two months. You just have to call a few hours in advance to schedule a time. We only perform from closing until midnight," Zims explained.

He removed his white leotard to reveal another flawless physique and an uncut cock that was indistinguishable from his brother's other than the fact that it was actually already plumping up nicely. He folded his garment on top of a table with a stereo system and some bottles of water, then tucked the cash between the folds.

"You also get to use the gym any time during our business hours, currently six a.m. through eight p.m., soon to be twenty-four hours a day." Sherk stretched into his words.

"And when is that change taking place?" Deck asked.

"As soon as we bring in enough profit to cover the overhead and pay more staff," Zims explained, now joining his brother in the stretch routine. "You can just relax on that easy chair. There's lube and clean-up cloths in the dispensers on the wall."

The comfortable chair was only feet away from the "stage" where the twins were stretching. Deck sat back and relaxed, watching the splendor of the veins, tendons, ligaments, muscle, and epidermis working together to create living art.

Simultaneously, the twins spread their legs and bent over completely, folding in half and staring at Deck from between their legs. He enjoyed the perfect lines that split them up the middle, and the caramel-colored scrotums that swung in the breeze. Zims was rock solid already, his thick foreskin dangling past the top of his head. Sherk was getting there, but clearly not as sexually charged as his brother.

"Don't even think of touching us," Zims said from underneath his package. "We aren't looking to be handled."

Your words say "no." It was so damn obvious that the bitchy twin was practically begging for it, despite his repeated snide comments about Deck's physical being. Deck unzipped his shorts (he wasn't wearing any undies) and pulled out his already hard cock. "Yeah, yeah. Just get on with it."

"Ugh," Zims said with disgust as the brothers rose back up. "Look at that hairy mess. Makes the dick look even smaller."

Deck so wanted to fuck this cunty bitch.

The naked brothers proceeded to absolutely wow Deck with the unexpected, doing a routine like something from Cirque du Soleil, holding acrobatic poses using each other as the equipment, leaving nothing to the imagination. The focused intensity on their gorgeous faces with each new movement and balancing act captured the intimate eroticism of the performance for what it really was—the total trust in each other's bodies and concern about the other's safety. It was the most sexual experience two brothers could share without actually doing anything incestuous.

And just as fast as it had begun, the show seemed to be over. The brothers dismounted. Sherk stood first and helped Zims up from the mat like a courteous gymnastics partner.

"You two are amazing," Deck said sincerely, blown away by their talent.

"I know," Zims said arrogantly just as Sherk flashed a surprisingly genuine and adorable smile and said, "Thanks!"

"What's the matter, old man? Having problems getting off? Look, Sherk. He didn't even take care of himself." Zims raised the corner of one smooth and shiny lip in a snarl.

Deck had forgotten he even had his cock out. His hands were actually placed lazily on the armrests of the comfortable chair, which at some point had begun vibrating and sending a warm heat into his back.

"Time for the heavy artillery," Sherk announced. He opened a closet door off to the side of the room and pulled out a glass display case on wheels. Tacked to a board inside were tags marked with dollar amounts ranging from one hundred to five thousand. And the price plan made total sense. Under each dangling tag, a double-headed dildo was cradled in a plush purple pillow. The lowest prices had "starter kits" barely the size of a piece of licorice. As the dollar amounts increased, so did the size of the double-headers, up to the five thousand dollar monstrosity that was about the diameter of a standard log of wood in a fireplace.

"How much can you afford, Sugar Granddaddy?" Zims said through tightened eyelids, as if skeptical of getting even a one hundred dollar dildo shoved up his ass.

"How about you surprise me?" Deck said.

"Huh?" Zims's cold exterior defrosted in confusion.

"*You* decide how much I can afford tonight," Deck responded, still sitting with his hands on the armrests, sort of like a king on a throne, his cock jutting from his shorts. It pulsed spastically of its own accord, creating a bubble of pre-excitement at the piss slit.

"What should we…" Zims gaped at his brother.

"Uhm…" Sherk looked just as bewildered. ""We'll take the—"

"This one." Zims's smug attitude seemed to falter as he reached for the one thousand dollar double-header. It wasn't small, but it was only about the size of a slightly above average penis on each end.

Deck felt the shift of power in his favor. *They don't have the guts to suck up the five grand bitch for the money if they aren't forced.*

Sherk took it from Zims and held it toward Deck, as if asking for acceptance.

"That will be fine." Deck shrugged. "Now I want you to stack your asses one on top of the other, on all fours. I don't care which of you is on the bottom."

"We only do it back to back—" Zims argued.

"I'll give you the five grand, even for the chicken shit size you picked," Deck said, standing and reaching for his wallet.

The brothers looked at each other doubtfully. Sherk was the first to give a hesitant nod. "Fine. You go down first."

Zims didn't argue. He dropped to his knees on the mat, facing away from Deck. His tight butt muscles tensed, then relaxed and swelled as he dropped forward onto his elbows, arching his back. His foreskin once again draped over his swollen erection.

Typical bottom. Bitchy, defensive façade that will soon be whimpering for more, Deck thought as he shoved a wad of bills into Zims's discarded white leotard. He wasn't one to go throwing his money around for sex. This cash wasn't his. Hayes had hooked him up good, telling him to have a great time with the twins and get some answers while he was at it.

Sherk kicked a leg over Zims's body as if mounting a horse, then leaned forward and dropped his hands to the mat beside Zims's elbows.

Now Deck could see the slightest difference in the identical twins. Sherk was definitely a hint more filled out, like he might be more of an athlete, whereas Zims had a more compact physique that hinted at the build of a dancer. And as the two muscular asses parted before him, he could see that while they were both naturally hairless for the most part, Sherk had a thin hair outline framing his caramel-colored fuck slot.

"You two are precious," Deck said.

"Worth every penny," Sherk said. "So make sure to get your money's worth."

"Oh, I will," Deck said, getting on his knees, his cock still poking out from the gap in his shorts where he'd lowered his zipper earlier.

"That's right, crawl for it, pig," Zims said as he watched from between his legs.

Just as quickly, Zims cried out. Deck had given his hard ass an openhanded whack.

"You asshole!" Zims barked as the redness rose to the surface on his glute.

"No, *your* asshole," Deck said, slipping an index finger in his mouth quickly and then drilling it smoothly into Zims's winker.

"Aaaa....ooooh." Zims gave a vocal performance that went from shocked and almost uncomfortable to surprisingly pleased in a flash.

Deck relished the power.

"You're supposed to be using the dildo," Zims said, but his attitude seemed to have come down a notch.

"I'm just getting my money's worth," Deck said, implanting his other index finger in Sherk's hole.

Sherk grunted less with appreciation than with the sound of a man who's taking one for the team. "Damn, you're much tighter than your brother," said Deck.

"Fuck you," Zims spat.

"Fuck YOU," Deck said, snuggling his middle finger up against his index finger inside Zims and wiggling them tensely.

"Oh!" Zims cried.

"Good whoooooore," Deck crooned.

"I'm no one's fucking whore, you tub of lard!" Zims growled.

"No? Then maybe I should be doing this for free," Deck said. "Shall I take my five grand back, or are you my whore for the night?"

"You wi—"

Deck hooked his fingers inside Zims's tunnel and pressed down hard on his prostate.

Zims wheezed in shock, his asshole clenched tight, and Deck could hear him slurping saliva back in from the corners of his mouth.

"Yes! I'm your whore!" Zims's voice rose to a higher pitch.

"Good. Now keep your piehole shut while I sample your brother's tight cornhole. I like 'em with a little hair."

With that, Deck sank his tongue into the sweetness between Sherk's cheeks. Sherk once again let out an almost uninterested groan—as if he didn't want to reveal that it actually felt good to have a fuzzy beard and swirling tongue working over his anus. Deck grabbed on to the steel-like glutes and pried them apart. The pucker was up-front and center, not one of those recessed assholes. It pursed its lips for him so he kissed it, making it sink inward.

"This asshole needs to be fucked," Deck said, rising off his knees to get his crotch lined up.

"Man, go easy," Sherk said from his hovering position over his brother. The blood should have rushed to his head as a result, but he actually retained a smooth, creamy complexion.

"Oh please. You're hardly going to feel a thing that small," Zims said.

"Shut up, bitch." Deck moved with great ease despite his size, swiftly dropping back to his knees on the mat and forcing his prick up Zims's unsuspecting pink ass instead.

"Oooowww!" Zims cried out, his voice wavering.

"Maybe you're tighter than I thought after all," Deck said, grabbing Zims's non-existent waist and pulling himself deep inside the incredible warmth.

"Take it easy!" Zims pleaded as Deck put all his ass weight behind the thrusting, his thick, hairy thighs pounding violently against Zims's muscular cheeks.

"Shush now, whore. It's so small you can barely feel it," Deck said.

"You hairy moose," Zims said with little of his bravado as the pounding began to loosen him up and massage his innards. "Fuck me."

The turn to submission was just what Deck was going for. He pulled out and rose back up and slipped inside Sherk. "That's right. We're gonna use your brother's ass juices as lubricant."

Tension and fatigue built in Deck's calves and toes as he perched on them to leapfrog into the muscular twin, but he ignored the discomfort. The tender flesh of Sherk's anus clung tightly to his prick as he watched it slip in and out: a beautiful sight and sensation.

"Easy, man," Sherk instructed him, and Deck was delighted to feel Sherk's sphincter muscles contracting in an attempt to control the invasion, making it all the more tight a ride for him.

"Just getting my money's worth," Deck breathed out as he exited with a popping sound and dove back inside Zims, latching his hands around the crown of thorns tattoos on Sherk's nearby ankles for leverage.

"Please, fuck me hard," Zims begged him, now completely in the moment. His mind was useless to protest against what his rectum needed.

Deck spun a record in his head so he could create a rhythmic gyrating with his hips. The song of choice was a remix he used to hear at clubs for the cover of "Lady Marmalade" by Christina Aguilera and a bunch of other divas.

"Oh, wow!" Zims wheezed. "What are you doing to me with that little thing? It feels soooo gooood!"

"That's right. You want this hairy moose to cum up your ass?" Deck asked.

"Please. Fill me."

"I'm ready to blow!" Deck growled.

"Fill me!" Zims pleaded.

Deck withdrew and shoved his cock up Sherk's ass, where he let his gusher go. He felt the muscles inside Sherk sucking up the juices greedily.

"That's right. Drink it all," Deck said, gently rubbing the swelling muscles on Sherk's back.

"You son of a bitch!" Zims whined from down below. "I told you I wanted it!"

"What difference does it make?" Deck asked as he exhaled heavily, escaping Sherk's grasp and dropping heavily onto the mat. "You got your money. Now I want some answers."

Sherk, now in a pair of tight shorts, blended Deck a smoothie in the juice bar where he'd had his little confrontation with the cops. Deck sat at a counter stool and took the offered pink drink, the cold nipping at his fingers as condensation sucked on the tips. He needed the energy boost, because he was beginning to feel a bit drowsy. He preferred not to blame the exhaustion on the physical exertion of his recent interlude.

"We have no interest in bringing down Hayes's gym, nor did we have anything to do with the Other Way Triple K burning on his lawn. And if you're looking for someone to blame all these human torchings on, you've definitely come to the wrong place," Sherk said before coating his pretty lips in a rich red froth of smoothie, which caused him to scrunch his face as if it was bitter and push the glass aside, even though Deck found it quite sweet and yummy.

Sherk's eyes and stance appeared slightly haggard, which actually made Deck feel a bit better about his own sluggishness: the same sluggishness that seemed to be dulling his senses. Which is why he couldn't wrap his thoughts around everything Sherk had just said. "What...Other Way?"

"You're going to live in Cremation Cove, you're going to have to stay on top of all the catchphrases. The guys in town are constantly coming up with them," Sherk explained.

"Well, I already heard 'Cremation Cove,'" Deck said proudly, remembering Maru throwing around the phrase the other night.

"The Other Way Triple K is what everyone in town is calling the black guys in black sheets who seem to be terrorizing anyone white," Sherk said. "You know, like the KKK in reverse."

"Yeah, I get it. But how can people be sure it's black guys under those sheets?"

"Well, they are targeting rich white men," Sherk pointed out.

"So you just assume all black people are resentful of rich white men and must be responsible for the incidents?"

"Don't look at me." Sherk raised his muscular arms in a defensive gesture. "I never said that. But that's the kind of thing that's being whispered around town. Just because everyone's gay around here doesn't mean they don't have some sort of prejudice against other minorities. Everyone needs a scapegoat. Someone they can feel better than."

Damn, this gym bunny is actually intelligent.

"So why doesn't it bother you that Hayes has his free gym open to the public at Weeping Manor? Doesn't that threaten to ruin your business?"

"Are you kidding? This is a huge gay community. There could be a gym on every corner and they would all be packed twenty-four hours a day. And everyone is looking for something different. Hayes has hit the 'exclusive' market. You basically need to be on a guest list to get access to everything Weeping Manor has to offer, if you know what I mean. Not every man in this community is drop-dead gorgeous. But they all need an outlet, for both exercising and the other reason gay guys go to the gym. And that's where we come in."

"That makes sense," Deck said.

"And with rich men like Hayes cleaning this town up, the population is just going to grow, and that can only benefit our business. Before long, two gyms aren't going to be enough. You'll see."

"I really hope to," Deck said.

"Me too. I only wish we could bring the level of pride to this community that he and Ben were bringing, and I just hope Ben's death doesn't slow down Hayes's efforts too much."

This was clearly a dead end. There was no doubting Sherk's sincerity—and respect for Lamond and DuPont.

"So since you haven't done anything, would you mind if I looked at the names of some of the people who have frequented your place for the after-hours specials?"

"Because you want to see if any of them went up in smoke," Sherk stated flatly.

"Um, if you don't mind, I work alone," Deck fired back.

"Only one human torch came here frequently. Lance Freeman." Sherk pointed to Deck's almost empty glass and pushed his own barely touched drink toward Deck. "You want another one?"

Deck felt an anxious knot in his stomach at the mention of Maru's deceased lover—almost like he just found out he had been *personally* wronged.

"Hey. You still with me? That was great, that stunt you pulled on my brother." Sherk finally showed a sign of personality. "He really needs to be taken down a notch every now and then. And believe me, despite everything he said to you, he would be putty in your hands if you wanted to make him your bitch. He's got serious unresolved daddy issues."

"Haven't we all," Deck said, standing and pulling a card out of his wallet to present to Sherk. "Would you mind calling me if you remember any other 'human torches' that were here?"

"Not a problem," Sherk responded, grabbing Deck's empty glass from the counter as he read the card. "Cute calling card. You know, I'm no Nancy Drew, but if I were you, my next stop might be Milkman Stan's high-rise over on Fourth."

"Milkman Stan?"

"You'll understand soon enough. Anyway, he's another mogul buying up the places around here, converting derelict buildings into gorgeous apartment and condo complexes. He's everything you want in a lead on your case. He's fallen victim to the Other Way Triple K. And his partner was the first to burst into a cloud of smoke."

❖

The air had a frigid edge as Deck stepped out of the gym and back onto the now quiet street. It must be social hour for all the boys in town. Deck imagined getting back to Weeping Manor and either slipping into a hot tub or perhaps doing something more communal with Jeeves and Don.

He dragged ass over to his car, still feeling extremely exhausted.

There might not be many people around, but just like in any city, the streets were now lined with cars, probably due to the growing number of apartment complexes.

Just as Deck was about to start the ignition in his car, he was greeted with the sight of a limo pulling up to the front of the Glouster Gym.

He leaned forward in his seat and squinted to better make out a series of BeNelly brothers exiting the limo and scoping out the general area before crowding into the gym. Deck ducked quickly so he wouldn't be seen, even though he was a few cars away and it was dark out. He was just thankful that he hadn't yet turned on his headlights or his car.

Deck couldn't be sure how many BeNellys remained in the double-parked limo, so he couldn't risk creeping his car up to the gym to look inside. Which meant he'd have to do it on foot.

I'm so dead, he thought as he reached for the handle of his door, wishing he were still permitted to pack heat. Before he could get the door open—or unlock it, luckily—a frightening black figure slammed against the window, rocking the car violently.

Deck's head spun from the impact. Or was it the momentum of the car being hit with such force? His vision blurred as a force bashed into the other side of the car. He willed his head to turn in that direction, where another black-sheeted figure was dancing wildly outside the passenger door, arms flailing.

Deck's equilibrium was off—way too much to be a result of the car rocking. He tried to reach for his keys in the ignition as more bodies swarmed the car from every direction, darkening the interior. The eyes circled by cutouts in the black sheets were practically sizzling into his ear through the pane on his left. More eyes glared at him as figures mounted the hood of his car and clawed at the windshield.

He desperately struggled to turn the key in the ignition. Finally, he heard it click in place.

And that was it. The car didn't start. Didn't even cough an attempt.

Deck tried again, pumping the gas with a weak foot, feeling his eyes closing, as if he was being sedated slowly on an operating table. He feared flooding the engine, but he still kept tapping.

He heard an explosion behind him. His head rolled lazily on its axis to see what the commotion was.

Fists pounded like thunder on the roof of his car. An arm reached inside his now smashed backseat window—heading for the lock. Deck brought a limp arm to the controls on his driver's door panel and pressed a finger against the switch to try to keep the door locked. But it didn't matter. Hands grabbed his head from behind, clawing at his face, nearly poking out his eyes. He tried to scream, but he was fading fast. He couldn't even bring his arms up to fight off his attacker.

Then the hands were gone, leaving blood on his cheeks where fingernails had tried digging into his face. He now heard shrieking, but it wasn't him. He lifted his eyelids, desperate to see what was happening. It was like the black figures were being yanked or plucked away from the car.

As his pupils shrunk toward oblivion, he saw red saturating black. White, so beautiful and bright, was taking over, destroying the darkness, bringing back the light.

CHAPTER NINE

"Chief! We got a live one over here," a thick voice called. "It's Waxer."

Deck's eyes opened at the sound. His face was on fire, the remainder of his skin chilled. He looked over to see Officer Bembury, now fully uniformed, leaning into his car.

"You okay?" Bembury asked, intimately close, fluffs of his mahogany goatee whiskers nearly tickling Deck's face.

"What happened?" Deck asked, trying to force saliva into his mouth, squinting as bright daylight beamed through his car.

"That's what we'd like to know," a gruff female tone greeted him.

"Anderson," Deck said, hating himself for feeling relief at her presence.

"Waxer, what in Buddha's name happened here?" Anderson said.

Deck pushed his way out of his car.

"Maybe he needs a paramedic." Bembury actually sounded concerned. "I got Teddy on speed dial."

"He's fine," Anderson said, chasing after Deck as he stumbled for a mob scene in front of Glouster Gym. "Bembury, stay there and examine Waxer's car."

Deck was pushing past spectators that were pressed up against police barriers. It was all too familiar. Only now, Deck was going to have to cut through all the yellow tape, literally.

"Just let him go!" Anderson actually called to officers who moved to block Deck from entering the crime scene. She huffed up behind him, attired in her usual business suit.

Deck took in the scene. The sidewalk. The pile of near white ashes. The foot. Just a foot. And at the charred top of the foot, he could make out a tattoo. A crown of thorns. A crown he'd had his hands on only hours ago.

"Sherk," Deck gasped. "What happened? What happened to him?"

Deck had grabbed the bony broad shoulder of the man bending over the foot and forceping it into a clear plastic bag as photos were snapped all around, both professionally and on spectators' cell phones. Others were merely gasping at the sight.

Over the lenses of his large glasses, Zimmerman, the forensics expert, looked up at Deck, his blue eyes wide. He scratched his wavy dark hair and said, "No sign of arson. No smell of any flammable liquids. No matches. No lighter. No cigarette. Like the others. I'd say it's another case of comb—"

"Zimmerman, that's enough," Anderson said sternly, and he retreated like a scolded dog. "Waxer, come with me inside. I need to talk to you."

"Yeah," Deck said distractedly, glancing at the remains of the gorgeous twin blowing in the breeze as the examiner tried to hurriedly sweep them into a pan for evidence.

Cool air-conditioning made Deck shiver as he followed her through the gym's interior to a private office.

"Well. Here we are again," Anderson said flatly.

"What? What am I supposed to say, Anderson?" Deck said defensively.

"Deck, there's a young man torched to death on the sidewalk. Your car is not half a block away, window smashed, sides dented, and you passed out inside with scratches all over your face. What am I supposed to think?"

"Coincidence?" Deck said halfheartedly.

"And two of my men saw you come in here after closing last night." Anderson raised an eyebrow in annoyance.

Snitches!

"Oh yeah. That."

"Yeah. That."

"I don't know, Anderson," Deck said. "I left not an hour later. But I passed out."

"Come on, Deck. Was this before or after something apparently attacked you in your car?"

"It was those things," Deck said, remembering clearly now.

"What 'things'?"

"Not things. I mean, people," Deck corrected his odd word choice. "The ones in the sheets. The black sheets. Who lit the fire at DuPont's funeral."

Anderson's face dropped. "So where did they go?"

"I told you, I don't know. I passed out."

"Deck, they did a job on your car, smashed your window in, did a job on your face—"

"And I think they tampered under the hood or something so I couldn't get away."

"I'll have one of my men get Otto here to check that out," Anderson said, calling in an officer quickly and relaying the request. Once they were alone again, she said, "So then what happened? Why did they just stop at that?"

"You mean, why didn't they torch me too?" Deck asked.

"There's no evidence that 'they' torched him," Anderson said. "This only happened an hour ago, in front of a couple of witnesses, including his brother."

"An hour ago?" Deck was baffled by the time lapse. "What time is it?"

"It's nearly eight in the morning."

"I don't get it."

"Me either," Anderson said.

"Zims. The brother. What happened to him?"

Anderson pointed to the doorway of the office. There was the lean and gorgeous twin, in a T-shirt and more conservative shorts than the night before, being led by police—in handcuffs.

"What are you doing to him?" Deck moved toward the door. Anderson grabbed his arm to stop him.

Zims looked up at the sound of Deck's voice. His face was streaked in fresh tears, and his eyes were bloodshot. They swelled in magnifying pools of liquid at the sight of Deck.

"Deck! Please tell them I didn't do this!" he cried hysterically, trying to skid to a halt with his feet, but being dragged out by the cops.

"Someone fucking killed my brother!" he shrieked as he disappeared from view.

Deck moved forward, but was blocked by another cop. "Anderson! What are you doing to him for fuck's sake! His twin brother was just killed!"

"It's a formality, Deck," Anderson said, trying to take his arm gently. He yanked it away angrily, and she paused, seeming to be hurt by the gesture. "We are pretty confident he didn't have anything to do with it. But witnesses said he was standing in the doorway speaking loudly, possibly shouting, at his brother when the fire started."

"And naturally, some witnesses claimed they saw him dousing gasoline and lighting a match, right?" Deck asked angrily.

Anderson sighed. "Yeah, something like that."

Deck shook his head with disgust.

"You can come and pick this one up too when we're through with him. Seems like you've landed the role of suspect protector since you got here," Anderson said.

"Yeah. Well, I'd also appreciate if you'd fill me in on whatever information you've gathered after this whole investigation scene is sealed for the day," Deck grumbled, now pushing past the cop who had restrained him.

"I will…" Anderson started, then hurried to the door to call after him, "when you come down in about an hour so we can get your statement as well! Deck! Did you hear me?"

He heard her. But he was too upset by the way she was handling the situation to even look at her, let alone respond. The concerns Soloman and Bembury had expressed during their conversation were suddenly weighing heavily on his mind.

With his car in Otto's shop, Deck once again found himself crashing indoors for the day, with the exception of having Don chauffeur him to the precinct following a call from Anderson herself demanding he show up. She had actually seemed quite worried about his physical well-being when he'd arrived, demanding he let her accompany him next door to the medical center for a checkup, but he had passed on the offer. He had been more concerned about his emotional well-being, because Anderson showing her caring side made him feel guilty for suspecting her of taking sides in the city's social wars.

He had, however, made sure that Zims was released without a problem, and he and Don had personally dropped Zims off to stay with a close friend. It had saddened him when the previously arrogant Zims had clutched on to him throughout the entire ride, and then hugged him tightly—almost desperately—for several minutes before saying thank you and good-bye. He had even given Deck his cell phone number with no explanation as to why. Without thinking, Deck had planted a soft, gentle kiss on his forehead, promising to call and check up on him.

Once back in the secluded safety of his room at Weeping Manor, Deck called Maru with a good excuse. Zims had expressed anxiety at not being able to keep the gym running, wishing for some helping hands. Deck thought this could be an opportunity for Maru to make money without dancing. Unfortunately, Deck had to leave a message, and hated himself for wondering what the hell Maru could be so busy doing that he couldn't answer the phone. He even imagined Maru seeing his name and number on the phone and opting *not* to answer.

Heavy lids and a heavy heart dragged Deck to dreamland, his exhausted mind wondering why he was feeling so sluggish lately—and fearing it might be a sign he was nearing age forty.

By that evening, Deck was feeling invigorated and alive, just in time to go see Milkman Stan. Hayes had personally called Stan for him. Stan said he'd be thrilled to talk to Deck, but that he was personally showing apartments all day because he was still looking to hire a good real estate agent to do the legwork for him. He invited Deck to stop by his penthouse loft at ten that night.

Otto had promised Deck he would have his car up and running by day's end with the broken window replaced, and he proved to be a man of his word. Deck was shocked when Jeeves called him downstairs announcing the arrival of Otto and Teddy, who had driven to Weeping Manor together to drop Deck's car off to him. Naturally, the promise of a future tryst was a topic of conversation, metaphorically built around an offer of Otto doing bodywork on Deck's car, but tonight, Deck had a date with a dairyman.

CHAPTER TEN

Deck had seen his fair share of growing areas of Kremfort Cove already, but when he had his car valet parked by a handsome chap with a tight ass, he knew he had entered the ultimate upscale area of the city. This gorgeous, brightly lit block, abuzz with voices, sounds, colors, and sights of nightlife, was Milkman Stan's incredible contribution to the effort Hayes had pioneered.

The equally handsome young chap at the front desk in the lush lobby immediately greeted Deck by name (Mr. Waxer) and led him down a long art nouveau hallway, through a door he had to unlock, and to an elevator. He bid Deck a fond farewell and pressed a button for the penthouse.

Gorgeous classical music streamed through the freshly scented elevator as Deck was whisked upward. He glanced at himself in the mirrored walls. He sure felt underdressed to be in such a formal building. He was wearing tight jeans that once fit but now gave him an embarrassingly noticeable wedgie. He wanted badly to untuck his polo shirt so his semi-noticeable little belly wouldn't look so...big. But he feared he was already too casual to be in the presence of a man who demanded such formality from his living space.

The elevator released Deck directly into a perfectly gaudy living space that made him even more uncomfortable about his attire. It was sheer elegance, from classic statues and paintings to complex crystal chandeliers and lamps.

"Hello?" Deck called to the large empty room. It was so quiet it almost seemed as if his voice bounced off the hammers inside the sparkling black grand piano in a far corner of the room, which was surrounded by a round wall of windows that looked out on the stars. He couldn't help but mutter, "Wow."

"Deck Waxer, is that you?" a voice echoed down a hall to Deck's right.

"Yes! It's me!" Deck called awkwardly, leaning his body toward the hall, hoping his voice would travel.

"Well, come on in! I've been waiting for you!"

Deck was put at ease by the jolly tone, so much so that there was actually "jolliness" in his stride as he went in the direction of the voice. He aimed for the only open door in the long hall.

His eyes bugged out at the sight that greeted him.

In the beyond-luxurious bedroom with monumentally elegant décor was a giant California king-sized bed, covered in a black latex sheet that spread out across the floor as well. And on top of that black latex sheet on all fours was a giant bull of a man whose naked skin was as pasty white as milk. Was that why they called him Milkman Stan?

As the gigantic man looked at Deck, Deck recalled the huge crush he used to have on a young John Goodman when he was on the *Roseanne* show. Deck couldn't count the number of times he had envisioned the pleasantly corpulent actor in just this position. Milkman Stan's grin was centered between the same full jowls, and his soft eyes squinted into the same wrinkly crow's feet, his cheeks dimpling adorably. A full head of wavy golden brown hair on his head looked fluffy and freshly blown out.

But another reason for the nickname could be the near cow-like size of the giant man. Milkman Stan's body was swelling with the wonderful flab of manly heartiness. Every inch of his body was cushioned by thick hunks of flesh resulting from years of culinary enjoyment. Character-building stretch marks rifted through beefy arms, swollen love handles, and a planet-sized ass that rose majestically into the air, straining at the seams as it took on its roundest shape.

"Am I interrupting something?" Deck asked, moving forward.

"I apologize," Milkman Stan said, reaching out one hand to shake Deck's while holding his excessive weight up with just his other elbow. "It's just that you're almost an hour late, and I'm due for my milking. I would love it if you'd join us and lend some helping hands."

"O…kay," Deck said quizzically. "Who's 'we'?"

"This is my new farmhand, Ralph," Milkman said. "Ralph, stand up. Deck can't see you over my fat ass."

Finally, Deck did see Ralph. A cute, orange-blond haired young man with gentle green eyes and a smooth, white complexion, wearing only overalls, stood up behind Stan on the bed and reached an arm above Stan's extra wide back to shake Deck's hand. Ralph's exaggeratedly pink lips didn't separate as he smiled at Deck. Deck took a moment to appreciate the pale, hairless, athletic chest and arms, and the hint of fiery hair peeking out from the armpits.

"If we can just relieve my milk buildup, I will be able to discuss other issues more clearly," Milkman Stan said.

"What can I do?" Deck asked.

"Just pull up one of those stools." Stan gestured with his thick head of hair to a couple of milking stools sitting at the bedside. "Scoop some of that cream cheese onto your fingers, reach your arms below my underbelly, and squeeze my teats. It helps to relax my nerve endings and open me up for the milk delivery."

"O…kay," Deck said again, grabbing a stool and squatting onto it, which brought him way down near the floor.

Now, with his eyes below the shadows of Milkman Stan's enormous dangling belly, he got a better look at what was dangling from Stan's chest area: two enticingly swollen man breasts, drawn to conical points as a result of the tug of gravity on Stan's meaty chest. The massive nipples looked like they were ready to burst.

Deck grabbed the small tub of freshly opened cream cheese from a nightstand and scooped the creamy smooth substance onto his fingers. He noticed Ralph placing a milking stool at the foot of the bed, behind Milkman Stan, a larger tub of cream cheese in his own hands.

"Isn't it such a wonderfully smooth and milky sensation?" Milkman Stan asked as he watched Deck prepping.

"It is. I would have never thought of it," Deck admitted.

"Okay, now reach under…that's right." Milkman Stan beamed with anticipation as Deck worked his big arms between Stan's tricep and belly. "Ooooooooh."

Stan's entire glowing complexion reddened as his eyes rolled back. Deck had grabbed a slippery hold of each of those bullhorn-sized tits. He started at the dense tops and gently squeezed his way down the surface of each in a milking fashion. He felt the even silkier areolas between his fingers at the bottom and the swollen hardness of the nipples when he reached the tips of the tits. A huge dip appeared in Stan's back as his belly dropped even closer to the mattress in his relaxed state.

"Perfect," Ralph finally spoke from somewhere behind those hog-like haunches. He had a noticeably heavy hick twang. "You made his milk spout expand nearly to its full opening. Do it again."

"My pleasure," Deck said as he once again squeezed the chunks of flesh.

"Wonderful," Milkman Stan sighed. Deck watched as beads of perspiration broke out on his temple.

"Your teats are fantastic," Deck said.

"Oh, Deck, you are a pro at *this*!" Stan cried as Deck built up speed, yanking more firmly and vigorously with each consecutive downward yank.

"Nice big hands. Oh…oh….oh…oh…oh…oh…OH!" Stan wheezed, his large body going limp with pleasure.

Deck could hear the vertebrae snap in Stan's back as his belly dropped to its limits, and Ralph cried out, "His spout is larger than we've ever gotten it!"

Deck was entranced by his own rhythmic tugging of Stan's teats as the cream cheese dried up, offering less lubrication. It took three shouts from Milkman Stan before Deck responded with a dazed, "Huh?"

"It's time," Stan puffed. "Please. Those fantastically large hands. Could you do the honors? You've got my spout so relaxed that Ralph's small hands will not do."

Deck looked over to Ralph, who held up his small, adorable hands with a shrug.

"Sure. What do I do?" Deck asked.

"Ralph will guide you. Deliver what I need, and I'll make sure to let you taste the sweetest milk."

"Sounds good," Deck said, rising off the stool and moving behind the giant rump.

He was practically knocked breathless by the incredible immensity of the cheeks, a shiny bright white, and the valley-like, shadowy butt crack. And none of it had even a hint of hair on it. And it wasn't that this 500-plus pound man shaved, he was just naturally hair-free back here.

"It's a masterpiece," Deck found himself muttering at the larger-than-life model of posterior perfection that should be the mold for all other posteriors, no matter what the size. You just wanted to get lost in it, get sucked into its depths.

"Wait 'til you get a look at this," Ralph said from beside him.

Ralph splayed the fingers of each hand apart to create a larger handhold, then grabbed the inner part of each cheek and moved the mounds of flesh in each direction.

"Ho-ly…" Deck spoke volumes as he got a look at the hole before him.

It was actually more like an irrigation canal. Of all the asshole slits Deck had seen in his life—and there had been many—none of them ever measured upward of an inch. Until now. From bottom to top, Milkman Stan's anus had to be about three inches long. It was a perfectly formed crevasse, taut pale peach skin folding inward to create the two side walls, with a gaping pink epicenter.

"It's the biggest I've seen it in the three weeks I been on the job," Ralph spoke in his southern accent. "I had no idea it could get that big. No wonder he wants your big-assed hand up there."

"How's that?" Deck said, caught off guard.

"Just gotta use the whole container," Ralph said, handing Deck the large tub of cream cheese. "Get the arm up in there and just kinda wiggle it around to cause friction on the walls, and then I can grab hold of that thing and milk it."

"What thing is that?" Deck asked, looking to where Ralph was pointing, which seemed to be the massive thunder thighs under Stan's ass.

"Milkman Stan, can you part the legs more so I can show Deck here the master valve?" Ralph twanged.

"Yeah," Stan said from up front.

As the large legs danced apart on the mattress, causing it to sink more on the edges, springs squeaking, Deck caught sight of some hefty bear-sized testicles coated in a modest fuzz of hair.

"Can't see it yet. Push it back for us," Ralph said.

"What the—" Deck stammered as "it" came swinging through.

"Ain't it great?" Ralph asked. "Big as the damn bulls back home."

One thing was for sure. Milkman Stan might have packed on the pounds over the years, but it was probably a necessity to make him appear proportionate. Deck crouched and moved in for a closer look.

"That thing is nearly the size of my arm!" Deck exclaimed, dangling his forearm next to it to compare.

"I know." Ralph beamed. "And it's as hard as a rock too. Painfully hard."

"I can imagine," Deck said, taking in Ralph's compact body. "It fits in you?"

"Oh yeah. But it huuuurts something awful at first. I go slow, until it starts feeling good, then I bounce up and down like a pogo stick."

"I assume it's safest for you to be on top," Deck noted.

"If I'm lucky, Stan will sit at the edge of the bed so I can get on all fours and back up on it. That's my favorite!" Ralph said happily.

Why do I feel like I'm talking to Tom Sawyer?

"I'm all ready to go!" Stan said anxiously.

"Oh. Sorry." Deck refocused.

He coated one arm in wads of cream cheese while Ralph painted the space between Stan's cheeks as if he were buttering a baking pan. Finally, they were ready.

"Brace yourself," Deck said, making a fist, tucking his thumb, and pointing his knuckles to create a head.

Ralph held the cheeks apart so Deck could press his lubricated fist against the slot. The opening pulsed excitedly, sinking invitingly. Deck used a steady and firm forward action. Milkman Stan engulfed him effortlessly. He could feel the incredible warmth within, and the muscles contracting around his hand. He sensed a slight curve as he popped through the sphincters and opened up into the cavernous area beyond. He let the path be the guide as he pushed forward, his arm being taken on a journey. The heat rose steadily toward his elbow as he made his way deeper and deeper.

"UUUUUUUNNNnnnnhhhhhh!" Stan could be heard wheezing somewhere ahead.

Deck could see Stan's arms draped lazily over the sides of the bed, which meant he was holding up all his front weight with his face. Deck could detect the relaxation and shifting of body weight as Stan's back once more arched, creating an extremely receptive tunnel inside.

"Now jiggle it around!" Ralph said.

Deck gave his arm quick, short, twisting motions to massage the sides of the walls that held him. Stan let out a much longer, wet-sounding growl.

"Damn, that's fast!" Ralph exclaimed. "You're getting him right where it counts. You want the milk, you're gonna have to work your mouth under the udder."

"I can do that," Deck said, thrilled at the prospect of the offered beverage.

Deck jumped into action, twisting his arm inside so he could flip over on his back on the mattress and limbo his way under Stan's crotch. He slid his face between Stan's thighs.

"I'll guide the opening into your mouth," Ralph said, and soon Deck felt the scalding heaviness of the cockhead pressing against his lips. "You ain't gonna really be able to get it in your mouth, so we just wanna keep the opening lined up so it'll all go straight in."

Deck was in no position to respond or even nod his head. He simply focused on tickling Stan inside with his arm. Ralph had grabbed the monstrous shaft with *both* hands and was now stroking up and down on the giant tube vigorously. Deck couldn't very well hear any verbal signals from Ralph or Stan, so he had to go on intuition as to when it was going to happen. The spasms that clenched his whole buried arm were the giveaway.

That and the gusher that exploded in his mouth.

Deck immediately thought several things. First, there was even further meaning to Milkman Stan's name, because this tasted nothing like cum. It most definitely tasted just like whole milk. Second, he had died and gone to heaven. Third, he was about to seriously die and go to heaven, because this wasn't stopping, and he couldn't swallow it fast enough. He began to choke on it, the excess spilling over the sides of his lips, dripping down his cheeks, saturating his beard, slipping between the hair follicles and drooling down his chin. He tried to gurgle a cry for help.

Suddenly, he was yanked by the shoulders out from under the heft, streams of Milkman Stan's beverage sloshing over his nose and forehead as he was dragged below the spout. Once he was free, he scooped the milky substance across his face with his fingers and tried to cram it into his mouth. He made his body erect in hopes that everything would make its way down his throat with more ease.

"Dee-LISH, right?" Ralph grinned as Deck was licking his fingers clean. "Makes you just want to stir in some Nesquik!"

"It's unbelievable," Deck said, taking a damp cloth Ralph fetched him from a nearby basin of warm, wet towels. As he began to wipe cream cheese off his arm, he asked, "Why—how—does it taste like that?"

"Don't nobody know." Ralph shrugged. "I believe it's a gift from the Lord. Everything about Milkman Stan. He's just beautiful with so much to give."

Ralph placed a hand on one of Stan's lard-engorged ass cheeks and gave the meat between Stan's thighs a long palm stroke, almost like he was petting a dog. Stan's entire body quivered from the sensitivity of having just unleashed.

"Will he be functional enough to talk to me now?" Deck asked, knowing how tired he would be after such an explosion.

"Sure thing. I gotta replenish his inner ecosystem." Ralph was busy wheeling in a big silver tank with a thick hose attached. "We use only pure organic strawberry kefir smoothie. It's sort of like yogurt, but even better for the digestive tract. Milkman Stan also believes it gets absorbed into his system to help make sure he always tastes so delicious."

"Anyone else remember that Crazy Cow cereal back in the seventies?" Deck joked to no one in particular as he tried to absorb the insanity of this situation.

Meanwhile, Ralph lubricated the big shiny silver nozzle of the hose with cream cheese, then slid it deep into Milkman Stan, who moaned gutturally.

"He likes the coldness of the metal," Ralph explained as if Deck had asked. "Okay. I'm gonna start the drip."

"Fill me," Stan muttered.

Ralph twisted a large knob on the top of the silver tank, and the flaccid hose stuck in Milkman's Stan's ass expanded like a quickly growing erection.

"You can go take a load off." Ralph flicked his head toward the front of Milkman Stan.

Deck grabbed his milking stool and moved up beside Stan, whose friendly, chubby face was resting on one cheek on the mattress. Stan looked at Deck with the warmest, most endearing eyes. His crow's feet were filled with perspiration, and his face was glowing with a coat of the moisture.

"Thanks for making my milking so special tonight," Stan said, his full face beginning to turn red, veins popping out on his wide forehead as his insides received a flood of the kefir smoothie.

"Any time," Deck said.

"You're sweet."

"No, really. Any time," Deck said very seriously.

"I knew you would like it. I've been told of your love for man milk."

"Yeah, but this is like nothing I've ever experienced before."

"Well, I'm in this position every night at ten. You're always welcome with those big arms of yours. OH!" Stan finished as his guts convulsed in reaction to the liquid filling him.

"You do this *every* night?" Deck asked.

"Yes. I have to. If I don't release my milk, I get downright bullish. There's so much it actually hurts if I don't expel it daily. And I really need several hands to do the job, as you can see, and it's been tough finding a second farmhand."

"You okay up there?" Ralph called from behind the behind.

"Yes, thank you, Ralph. Keep it coming. I feel incredibly open tonight, thanks to Deck here. I think we will be going for a record fill. You will be absolutely saturated."

"Wahoo!' Ralph cheered in response, and Deck wondered what was meant by all that.

Stan visibly shivered. "It's so well chilled tonight!"

"I knew you'd like it!" Ralph said. "It'll warm right up in there."

"So I don't know if you are okay with talking about this," Deck began, watching the strained look on Milkman Stan's face as he gulped down the smoothie from the opposite end.

"I am at total peace with Gerald's death," Stan said with an expression that backed it up. "I've worked closely with my psychic, and he has truly been my guiding light. I've already urged Hayes to consider talking to him, because I don't think he is dealing with Ben's death as well as he likes to front."

"Yeah, well. I don't either. It's only been a few days. How long has it been since your partner—"

"Gerald. He was one of my live-in farmhands more than a traditional partner. The other farmhand quit and never came back after seeing what became of Gerald, which is why it's been so hard finding a second replacement."

"I can see how you're man enough for two guys."

"You're sweet. I have the distinction of being the first man in Cremation Cove to have watched someone he cared about go up in a puff of smoke," Milkman Stan noted before letting out a loud groan, half pleasure, half pain as his intestine swelled with smoothie.

Deck could clearly hear the loud sloshing of the substance in Stan's gut that time.

"You're doing amazing," Ralph interjected from his post in the back.

"How long ago did Gerald...pass away?" Deck asked, his inflection extra high on the question since he was also asking himself if pass away was the right choice of words.

"Twenty-nine days ago tomorrow morning at ten a.m."

"What exactly happened? I mean, if you don't mind, could you explain?"

"He'd been feeling under the weather for a few days. Tired, pale, weak. We had been through a long bidding war for the building on the corner of this block, and it had taken a toll on him, I thought. See, he kept all financial and legal records for me. He was such a brilliant young man."

"Bidding war against who?"

"The BeNelly brothers, who else?" Stan asked, swallowing his focused breath, which made the puffy cheek he was resting his face on expand.

"It's not the first bidding war you've had with them?"

"Third, to be exact. They won't win, even if I have to sell my properties in California. You do know that they buy these buildings and then bully the men who rent them, right?"

"Yeah, I kinda figured that out."

"Yeah, well, some of those men who can't pay, disappear. And the police aren't putting much effort into finding a bunch of faggots trying to make a living," Stan huffed. "Especially with Commissioner Anderson so torn between protecting the gay citizens of the community and remaining loyal to her own struggling race."

"You think she would help instigate tensions?"

"Let's just say that I know how deeply set I am on bettering the lives of my own here, and I wouldn't blame her if she feels the same. It just so happens that the heterosexual element that lived in this community was predominantly black before the gays started moving in. And you know how the gays are. A few of us start cleaning things up, and soon nobody can afford to live in a damn community because it's so affluent. But that's what Hayes and I were trying to prevent here. We were trying to make this an affordable place for the down-and-out gay boys to come and survive."

"And tough shit to the black lower class that already lived here because they were straight?" Deck asked.

"The plan was never to push them out and take over the whole town. Things just snowballed really fast and the gays started coming in droves—just like the straights do after we clean up a place. The residents who already lived here began moving out from personal dislike of us as much as for financial reasons. And they also started acting out at us with violence, which is where Anderson found herself with a big problem. We all could have tried to live here together peacefully, but the bottom line is, neither group really wants that."

"Which is why the BeNelly brothers may have stepped in, to do what you're doing, but for their own. But at the same time, they want to put as many of us at their mercy as possible," Deck thought aloud.

"I'm not so sure they don't like things just the way they are," Stan said. "Personally, I think they much more enjoy living in a community where they can make gay white men their bitches than in a predominantly straight black community. It's a power trip to be financially thriving black residents of the city, with white men at their mercy. They get off on it."

"If that's so, then who are the guys in the black sheets?"

Stan shrugged his meaty shoulders. "Who's to say they aren't the BeNelly brothers in disguise? Are you aware of what happened to one of my ventures?"

"No. I was going to ask you," Deck began. "I, um, heard you had a run-in with the Other Way KKK."

"Well, one of my buildings did."

Stan clenched his jaw for a second, concentrating on keeping his G.I. tract in reverse. Deck knew exactly what that felt like thanks to his session with Phillip at Weeping Manor.

When his face relaxed again, Stan continued. "Big derelict place on what they call Diesel Drive. Don't know if you are familiar with it. It's the block where Otto's Auto is."

"Totally know it," Deck said and thought he saw Stan give a little smirk as if to say, "Of course you know Otto."

"Well. The building right across the street was constantly being raided by the cops because it housed pretty much all the homeless people in the city who were just looking for nightly shelter. Since it's sort of on the outskirts of town, I knew it wouldn't be a particularly appealing place to create apartments. So I decided to get a bunch of investors to help renovate it and turn it into an official homeless shelter. Had big plans for it, but they went off course when the place was completely vandalized from basement to top floor. So much money and work had gone into getting the skeletal frame of the place back in order. They broke in and caused tens of thousands of dollars of damage to walls, floors, windows."

"How do you know who it was?" Deck asked.

"They left some very clear messages spray-painted all over the walls to assure it. Several of my investors got scared and pulled out. And I couldn't get Anderson or her force to provide me any patrol because they apparently don't have the funds to stretch police protection that far through the city. So now I have to look into hiring a private security firm to guard it before I bother trying to make any more improvements. But there are already homeless people moving back in."

"I know," Deck said and then turned red since he hadn't mentioned having smashed out a window of the building himself and breaking into the place while running from the creeps in black sheets the night he'd met Otto.

"Yeah. News spreads fast around here," Stan said without a second thought. "And to think, all I was trying to do was create a safe haven for the very unfortunate people who are probably the ones dressing up in black sheets and rebelling against me."

"You think they are the ones who killed your farmhand?"

"No one killed my farmhand. He just burst into flames. He had been sleeping in for three days straight. When I woke up that last morning, I insisted he get into his swimsuit and join me on our roof for a morning dip in the pool. I told him I would bring us up some mimosas. When I carried the tray up there, right at the top step leading to the patio, there was a large pile of ashes and the two big gold hoop earrings he always wore. The ashes were still smoking. That gorgeous man gone in a flash."

"You don't think someone may have, I don't know, targeted him from a distance with some sort of—"

"Long-distance flamethrower?" Stan scoffed.

I was going to say pyrokinesis. But we'll go with what you said. Deck offered an apologetic frown for the presumed ridiculous suggestion.

"Deck, this is the highest building in the area. No one can see you up here. No, I believe what my psychic told me. It has to have come from the sky."

"This psychic..." Deck began.

"Right there in that middle desk drawer." Stan pointed with his clear blue eyeballs, which seemed to be swimming in smoothie right about now. "You should really see him. He'll not only answer your questions and shed some major light on this, but he'll change your life."

"If he has all the answers, why hasn't he helped the police?" Deck asked as he grabbed a card from a nice supply of them he found in said spot. While doing so, Deck also noticed a DVD in the drawer with the title *The Combustion/Close Encounter Connection*. The ominous and realistic artwork on the case depicted a man writhing in pain in a bed surrounded by flames, while a traditional bug-eyed alien glared coldly through a window, a UFO hovering in the background near a half moon. It was the kind of illustration that could easily worm its way into the minds of young children and scar them for life.

"Oh, believe me. Quest went to them. Commissioner Anderson was as interested in *his* help as she is in *yours*," Milkman Stan said.

"How did you—"

"My psychic told me." Stan winked, then clenched his giant ass cheeks, the mounds of flesh shuddering as he strained to hold back a gusher of kefir. "I don't think I can take much more! Get in position!"

Deck saw Ralph turn off the canister valve and pull the nozzle from Stan's ass while simultaneously stepping out of his overalls, crying, "Hold it in a bit longer!"

When Deck got a load of Ralph's tiny pale derriere, he couldn't imagine how it could accommodate Milkman Stan's giant pipe of man flesh. The total length of Ralph's ass crack was about the same size as Stan's entire shaft width.

"Hurry!" Stan choked.

"What's about to—" Deck began as Ralph, now naked, squatted behind Stan on a milking stool, his face perfectly lined up with Milkman Stan's ass.

"White wash!" was all Stan could gasp out.

"I'm gonna get going!" Deck backed away hurriedly. "Thanks for your help. I'll be back for a milking as soon as I can."

Without waiting for an answer, Deck spun on his heels just in time. There was a booming gastro-intestinal explosion, and then it sounded like a water main bursting. A flood of liquid could be heard splattering forcefully against Ralph's face and body.

As Deck hurried down the hall and toward the elevator that had brought him up here, he even heard the happy giggling and gurgling sound of Ralph, who clearly had his mouth open wide when the gusher struck.

Maybe it was power of suggestion or just that his stomach was in knots lately, but the next morning, Deck decided to visit Phillip for a colonic of his own, minus the smoothie. He was glad that his entire session with Phillip's comforting soul was uninterrupted by Don, Jeeves, or anyone else. Phillip verbally coaxed and congratulated him on his progress as he relaxed his bowels for a highly effective flush.

It helped release the tension he'd felt after exiting Milkman Stan's the night before. He'd gotten such a sense of déjà vu as he'd stood alone on the street, waiting for the valet to bring him his car. He had jumped at every shadow and even checked his backseat after being handed his keys. The feeling of unease hadn't lessened when he'd gotten home to Weeping Manor and heard that damn flapping and scratching outside his balcony door. Although he'd known he should have investigated it, he'd been too exhausted—and a little bit spooked—so had opted to just turn up the volume on his television and ignore it. Surprisingly, he'd slept deeply and dreamt of another overflowing session with Milkman Stan. It had been the first thing on his mind when he woke in the morning, which was what prompted him to head over for a fill-up from Phillip.

Flushed, showered, and back in his room, Deck dug jeans and a long-sleeve polo shirt out of his drawer based on a weather report on his television announcing unseasonably cool September temperatures. "Fall has arrived!" the weatherman announced authoritatively.

Just as the thick cotton of the polo shirt hugged Deck's body warmly, making him *feel* the sense of autumn, his cell phone rang on his bureau. He picked it up.

"Maru." Deck decided on the brazen approach as soon as he saw the name appear on his window. "I'm just about to go grab some breakfast in town. Wanna meet me?"

Disappointment turned to surprise as Maru explained why he was calling and why breakfast wasn't a great idea at the moment.

"Crap. I'll be right down."

The only consolation was that Maru responded with, "I'll look out for you."

Maru looked casual-comfortable in form-fitting jeans, sneakers, a Christina Aguilera concert T-shirt over a thermal long-sleeved shirt, and a knit raver hat. He was sipping from a Styrofoam coffee cup as he leaned against the wall of an apartment complex a little farther down from the one Deck had been in the evening before during the "milking" session.

With the tanned tones of his skin, the pine green tee with yellow silk screening, and the orange thermal sticking out from underneath, the rich prism in which Maru was wrapped brought to mind the looming autumn months—and the thought of cuddling up under a blanket by a fire to escape the chill.

Maru pushed off the wall with a foot that had been tucked up against it in flamingo fashion. He strolled over as Deck slowed his car to a halt in the street, taking in the scene of lights a few buildings up as he lowered his window.

"You're not gonna get any closer than this, so you might as well back up and park around the corner," Maru said.

Deck did just that. When he walked back onto Milkman Stan's street, Maru was waiting.

"It's hazelnut," Maru said, extending his arm and offering up his coffee, thick white streams of mist billowing out the small sip slit.

"Smells delicious, but no thanks. Haven't been staying away from the caffeine enough," Deck responded.

"Oh yeah. The stomach problems," Maru said.

"Which is in turmoil over this." Deck pointed to the crowd ahead.

"Another one bites the ashes," Maru said. "Lucky stiff."

"So what are the police saying? And is Commissioner Anderson here?" Deck asked as they pounded up the street.

"She's not here, but your name did come up," Maru said. "Officers Soloman and Bembury were asking Milkman Stan if you had been around to talk to him."

"Crap," Deck muttered.

"What exactly is going on? Do the cops think you have something to do with this?"

"Where's Stan now?" Deck ignored his question.

"They took him inside for questioning I think. I couldn't quite hear because they started to push all us nosy queers back to cordon off the sidewalk."

"So it happened in broad daylight again?" Deck was flustered.

"Yeah. Right in front of the doorman," Maru said. "Ralph was a cool kid, for a hick. He auditioned at Harry's place the day I started there, but they thought he didn't have enough of an erotic edge. Or any kind of rhythm. We don't exactly square dance on those speakers. So he ended up landing this gig with Stan."

"There he is." Deck heard before he saw the mustached cop who had been riding his ass lately break through the throngs of onlookers and approach with his sidekick in tow.

"Crockett and Tubbs," Deck remarked smarmily.

"Who?" Maru asked quizzically, and Deck practically clutched his chest in agony.

"Just kills ya when our pop culture references are lost on your boy toy, huh?" Bembury slapped smarminess onto his own expression.

Before Deck could respond and try to deny the implications of his relationship with him, Maru threw his arms around Deck's large frame.

"Daddy's still teaching me," Maru said without flinching, and then reached down and cupped Deck's crotch in his hand.

Deck nearly jumped out of his pants at the touch, but Maru squeezed a lean, muscular arm tightly around him to hold him still. Deck forced a strained, embarrassed grin in an attempt to play along.

"Damn, don't know which one of you sons of bitches is luckier," Soloman muttered, stroking his mustache.

"Uhm," Bembury broke the reverie, "We need to ask you a couple of questions, Waxer."

"Why am I not surprised?" Deck said, awkwardly shrugging Maru off him. He fought not to look at Maru—or smile—when Maru gave him sad, pouty lips and puppy dog eyes.

"Well, were you with him last night?" Soloman raised his eyebrow and used it to point in the direction of Milkman Stan's complex.

"I came to *question* him," Deck said forcefully, nerves on edge with Maru standing right there. "Men, can we go inside and talk about this? I'd like to see Stan as well."

"Yeah. Let's go. But the Thai toy has to stay out here." Bembury laughed at his own wisecrack.

"I'll be here waiting for you, Daddy," Maru said as he leaned in close so his warm breath was tickling the whiskers of Deck's beard, which still couldn't prepare Deck for what Maru pulled next.

Maru stuck out his tongue in a flaccid point and ran it in one swift circle around the inner perimeter of Deck's lips, leaving them opened in a shocked O when he was done. As Maru pulled away and squeezed Deck's hand good-bye, Deck awkwardly cleared his throat and cast his eyes down while passing Soloman and Bembury, who were both staring with drooling desire at the display of public affection.

"Man, you got him groveling at your feet!" Bembury taunted as they led Deck past the crowds and into the building.

"Shut up. It's not like that!" Deck said.

"Decky's in lo-uve!" Soloman singsonged.

"I don't do love," Deck said sharply as they rode the elevator up.

"You don't do love; love does you," Soloman said, and Deck noticed him staring intently at Bembury.

"Not if you stop the nonsense before people get hurt," Bembury shot back.

This was getting way too personal, so Deck interjected with, "What are they doing with Stan?"

Just then, the elevator doors opened to familiar territory. And there was Stan, even more of a visual presence standing than he had been when in milking position. He had to be nearly nine feet tall, something Deck had been unable to comprehend when he had been in the milking position. Stan had to have been born with some sort of genetic anomaly. Yet, despite his enormity, in a powder blue denim shirt and giant jeans (probably custom made) even his width and height could not detract from the gentle depth of his being.

"Stan?" Deck said, recognizing an all too familiar stance—Stan's arms drawn behind his back. He was bookended by two cops. Deck turned to Soloman and Bembury. "You can't fuckin' keep arresting men who have just lost men who are extremely dear to them!"

"Deck, just calm down." Bembury grabbed his chest.

Handcuffs wouldn't fit on Stan's wrists, so as he passed, Deck could see they were actually *tied* together with thick rope. Deck pushed past Bembury and shoved one of the arresting officers—hard. "UN-FUCKING TIE HIM!"

Deck's every muscle was shaking with adrenaline.

"Deck, don't," Stan spoke softly.

"You *don't* want to do this!" Soloman warned him, jumping forward with Bembury as the downed officer righted himself and the fourth officer was already reaching for his gun.

"He's cool!" Bembury said as he and Soloman grabbed Deck's arms with extreme force and yanked him back.

"How can you two stand here and watch this?" Deck glared at the partners.

"It's not our call, man." Soloman shrugged, and even with the darkness of his skin, Deck could see him blush with embarrassment.

"I should rip your throat out!" the attacked officer growled, punching Deck hard in the stomach, making him double over.

"ENOUGH!" Bembury was the one now pushing the cop. "We said we'll take care of this! Just take Stan out of here."

"Guys, please," Deck begged, not even struggling out of their grasps as he tried to regain his breath.

"I'll be fine, Deck," Stan said as he was moved into the elevator, which must also have been custom made to accommodate Stan's size when he had the building renovated. "My psychic told me this would happen. That there would be more fire and heartburn for me before the sun came out again."

With those last words, the doors closed.

"I know we should be the ones following up on this fire-predicting psychic, but it sounds like it's more up your alley. And I imagine you already know how to find him." Soloman looked at Deck, letting him go.

Deck didn't respond, just clutched his gut with gritted teeth.

"*But*," Soloman said aggressively, wrestling a hand into Deck's pocket, "You get back to us with what you know the minute you know it, you hear me?"

Deck watched as Soloman forced Deck's cell phone to kiss and swap phone numbers with his own. That done, he handed the phone back to Deck and punched the elevator button.

"Yeah, I got it," Deck said. The elevator doors opened, and he entered them, punching the lobby button quietly.

"You're welcome!" Bembury said sarcastically, leaning along with the closing of the doors to keep an eye on Deck until they sealed shut.

❖

When Deck stepped back outside, the crowd had dispersed and the investigative crew was shrinking. It was easy for him to pinpoint the thin, eye-glassed forensics expert Zimmerman. He got cuter with every new spotting.

Deck walked over to him, noticing that while thin, his straight-waist white pants and tailored blue and white checked button shirt had a streamlined look, meaning he probably had an obnoxiously lean and muscular physique. His shoulders were actually square, suggesting one of those high built backs and probably an elevated chest. *He carries all his meat in his upper physique.*

"Aw, crap," Zimmerman said as he spotted Deck and quickly closed his note binder.

"I just want to talk," Deck said casually.

"I *know.* That's the problem."

"Zimmerman, right?" Deck asked, flashing his most charismatic smile. He could actually see it working as those high shoulders drooped a bit.

"Deck, you know how she is."

"And she knows how I am, so she *expects* you to eventually give in to me."

"No! I told you before, I can't talk to you!" Zimmerman spoke with exaggeration as a cop breezed by, barely even giving either of them a glance.

"That was *goooood!*" Deck praised falsely, winking at Zimmerman as he moved in closer.

"Just…" Zimmerman held up one hand in defense, a pen still jammed between his index and middle finger. Then he dropped his voice to a whisper. "Wait two minutes before going to your car."

With that, he rushed away.

"What, was he intimidated by your beauty?"

Deck turned to see Maru had crept up on him.

"No, it was, um, business stuff," Deck said, feeling somehow guilty.

"Don't worry. I'm not the jealous type," Maru said, taking Deck's hand like it was the most natural thing to do as they strolled down the street.

"Do yourself a favor and don't get yourself to a place where you'd even need to be jealous. It's not worth what will amount to just a blip of bliss in your life," Deck said haughtily.

"I've experienced the blip, remember? And I'd risk it to experience the blip again if the opportunity would allow me to. The blip keeps the heart beating."

"Sure you're not confusing it with sex?"

Maru stopped just as they were reaching the corner around which Deck had parked his car. "Deck, I think you're the one who's got it confused. See, sex gives you an instant and short-term hard-on when a guy grabs your crotch unexpectedly with two cops watching. The blip gives you a hard-on that will last all the way down the length of a city street simply because a guy is holding your *hand*."

There was just no way for Deck to hide the truth that beat so prominently against the crotch of his jeans.

Maru, still holding Deck's hand, raised it to his mouth and placed a soft kiss on the large, hairy knuckles. "I've gotta get to work."

He walked off without looking back.

And Deck just stood there. His throat was too constricted to say anything, to even call Maru's name. Finally, when Maru was gone from view, Deck felt his heartbeat slowing, his emotional erection fading. He also could swear he still felt the imprint of Maru's palm pressing into his own palm where their lifelines had crisscrossed.

Turning to his car, feeling sort of lightheaded in the morning sun, Deck saw something tucked under the windshield.

He pulled out a folded piece of loose-leaf paper and opened it up.

Zimmerman had scrawled his address and phone number on the paper along with a message to come to his place that night at eight. The message continued with two quick sentences: "We need to talk about spontaneous combustion. Burn this note as soon as you've read it."

CHAPTER ELEVEN

"Spontaneous combustion. I *knew* I was on to something."

Deck spoke the words proudly as he drove to the other side of town. He'd gotten Don's help in mapping the occult shop of Milkman Stan's psychic, which was in what Don called Kremfort Cove's freak zone: a district full of the more artsy and mystical types of cabrónes.

And boy, was Don right. While the streets were small, quaint, and maze-like, the personalities were as big as they get. It was as if Deck had stepped into the middle of the glam/punk/new-wave transitions of San Francisco or New York. Naturally, it was Deck who got all the stares when he took his hulking physique out of his car. At a nearby café, a drag queen sitting at a table with gothic friends screamed, "Aaaah! A bear!"

Heads turned, people laughed and stared, and one multicolor-haired young guy sitting alone reading Kerouac actually lowered his new-wave sunglasses and checked Deck out carefully, a small smile of hunger crossing his lips.

With Deck sort of frozen against his car, the drag queen grinned through cakes of theatrical makeup and said, "Big Daddy, I'm just flirtin' with you. Everyone's welcome to the Glitter Dome as long as they don't mean no harm."

She actually waved Deck over, so he hurried across the car-less street to the lunching crowd.

"Hey, honey!" The drag queen put out a sequin-gloved hand. "They call me Missississi. As in, 'this missis is a big sissi.' Glad to meet you."

"Hey, I'm—"

"Deck Waxer." She winked and must have noticed his concern at being identified. "I'm a friend of Jeeves! Don't get your panties in a knot!"

"Ah," Deck said. "So could you point me to a shop called Quests?"

"Easy enough, Big Daddy. Down this street." She pointed down the sidewalk her dining table was on. "Make the first right, and you'll be in a little cozy cul-de-sac thingy. And right in the center of it, you'll find Quests in all its spookiness."

"Great. Thanks."

It was indeed a cozy cul-de-sac, with a stone pavement lined with small trees (not a hot commodity in the more metropolitan part of the city) and no people in sight. Businesses included an old-fashioned barbershop (less of a commodity than trees in a gay metropolitan area), a small adult bookshop (a major commodity if there were sex booths in the basement), a tiny diner (even gays have to eat), and an antique store (a staple in any gay community). Dead in the center of the sac was Quests.

The store was indeed spooky. The front windows were filled with all the clichés right out of the magic shop on *Buffy*: lit candles of both the black and white arts varieties, hideous gargoyle statues, polished crystals of various iridescent colors being clutched by decrepit steel claws on chains, Ouija boards, tarot decks with the two most notorious cards—the devil and the death card—prominently displayed, and numerous books on the occult. And of course, a couple of dusty, long-dead bugs were sprinkled around the clearly low-maintenance display.

Deck pushed on the front door and entered into the magical realm: burning incense, mystical music, and a general hypnotic atmosphere. He expected a little bell to chime, but no such sound shattered the mystique.

The place was empty. He approached a counter at the back of the store, looking for a dingable bell. Amongst all the paranormia littering the counter was a pile of business cards featuring an image of an eye and the words "Quests for Answers" written on it. It listed services Deck was well aware of, including Tarot readings, palm readings, scrying, past life regressions sessions, and a whole load of other bullet points about which Deck knew nothing.

"I'll be right with you, Deck!" a deep but youthful voice called from behind a beaded string curtain in the far corner of the store.

"Of course he knew I was coming," Deck muttered, amazed at the way gay men talked in this city.

Behind the counter were some plush chairs against the back wall, clearly there for waiting customers. Deck was about to move around to sit in one when he spotted a date book opened on the countertop. This was his opportunity to see who some of this psychic's clients were. He spun the book so that it was facing him.

That was as far as he got before he heard voices coming. He looked up and quickly turned the book back the way it had been.

"Be with you in a sec, Deck." The long and lanky young man who stepped into the room walked over to the counter, followed by a small and quiet older man with a comb-over.

"So we'll put you down for same time next week," the psychic said, reaching for the date book and a pen.

Deck watched with bated breath as the psychic reached for the book—not seeming to notice that it might be slightly out of place. He began to scribble a name and time in the book. When he was done, he said good-bye to his client, who patted Deck on the shoulder as he walked by.

"He's amazing. He'll change your life," the man said in the tone of one who's had decades of ups and downs and feels like he has finally seen the light.

With that, the man left the store and left Deck alone with the psychic.

"Hey," Deck began.

"I'm Quest." He reached out a hand and Deck shook it, his eyes traveling up veined forearms covered in skin art.

New Age themes were evident on both of Quest's arms, and Deck noticed something wrapping its way up the back of Quest's neck. It was hard to see from here, because Quest had bushy, thick, scraggly, dirty blond hair that masked most of it. He had a prominent Adam's apple, and above it, a deep cleft in his chin that couldn't be hidden by a light soul patch. Above his thin lips was a mangy mustache, and his long, wide sideburns were just as unkempt. He had a long, thin nose, thick eyebrows, and dark eyes that contrasted beautifully with his sandy hair. He was clad in jeans and sandals, with a simple black T-shirt that seemed to get sucked into every crevice of his lean musculature.

"Nope. I don't do drugs. Never have. And I don't really work out much," Quest said. "Genetics I guess."

"I—"

"Didn't say anything," Quest interrupted. "Not out loud."

"You probably just get that all the time," Deck tried to explain it away.

"Maybe." Quest shrugged. "But to answer your other question, yeah, I do have the V-cuts right here."

Deck watched as Quest lifted his T-shirt, revealing not only a fuzzy navel above low-cut jeans, but also revealing the beautiful ends of the V-definition that divided his leg joints from his abdomen at the crotch.

"God, how you'd love to stick your tongue in my hairy little belly button," Quest said.

"Okay, just STOP!" Deck insisted, completely unnerved.

"Sorry. Just had to prove to you that I'm not a fraud. I'm refocusing, so I won't hear anything you think," Quest assured him.

"Yeah, you *say* that, now that I'm terrified to think."

"Here, wear this," Quest said, grabbing a crystal on a chain from a rack on his left. He dropped the necklace around Deck's neck, where it landed right between his pecs, which swelled against his shirt.

"What is it?" Deck asked, taking a hold of it and looking down at it.

"It tends to cloud the aura. I guess you could say it keeps in the mystery, makes it difficult for me to read you."

"I guess I'll have to take your word for it," Deck said. "And I suppose you know why I'm here?"

"I could be a suspect because you're discovering that some or all of the victims of the fire seem to have consulted me for one reason or another."

"Yeah," Deck said. "So how do you explain it?"

"Well, if you'd gotten a chance to get through my appointment book before I came in." Quest winked at him. "And if you happen to have the times of death for all the victims, which Commissioner Anderson probably hasn't even supplied you with despite the fact that she expects *you* to help *her* by turning over information, you'll know that I have an alibi for where I was during every incineration. I begin with my clients early in the morning. So many lost souls in this world. Oh. And no. I don't have pyrokinesis. I just read minds."

"I thought you said you weren't going to do that," Deck said.

"I heard you thinking it from the minute I started reading your mind."

"So being all psychic and stuff, why haven't you helped the police? Do you know how these men have fallen victim to 'incineration' and who's to blame?"

"The cops would never believe me," Quest said with frustration, and along with his drug addict image and build, his body was now jittering like one.

"Why not?" Deck asked. "Who do you think did this?"

Quest circled around his counter, walked right up to Deck, grabbed him by the shoulders, and shook him while saying, "It's fuckin' aliens, man!"

Quest's face was only inches from Deck's, his dark, deep eyes bugging out.

Deck couldn't help himself. He burst out laughing, pulling away from Quest to keel over with the force of it.

"Dude! I'm telling you!" Quest said as he followed Deck, who was now pacing around the aisles of the occult shop. "I feel a non-human force in Kremfort Cove. It's *like* a human life form, but it's somehow…different."

"So you're telling me…" Deck wiped tears of laughter from his eyes, "that little green men are running around with laser zap guns incinerating gay men?"

"Be serious!" Quest looked frustrated. "I thought I could be honest with you, man. You've experienced some weird shit in your past."

That sobered Deck up fast. He got himself under control. "You're right. I'm sorry. But you gotta see it from my point of view."

"No, I know. I know it sounds crazy. But I *feel* it." Quest punched his chest with a hollow thud. "Right through my chakras. There's a growing force in this area that is not like us."

"So who do you think it is? The BeNelly brothers?"

"Nah. Those are just some horny-assed black dudes who like having the white man over a barrel," Quest said offhandedly.

"The guys in the black sheets. You get any vibes on them? Is it the BeNelly brothers?"

"No. They're a really hazy, disjointed entity. They're human all right, but there's no personal ties there, or sense of community, so I can't get a reading on motive. It's almost like a conglomerate of different ideals and desires. Clashes of interest, but with one common enemy that pushes them to band together. I need to get closer to it, to feel out one individual, get him out from behind this cloak."

"Well, if I catch one of the fuckers, you'll be the first person I drag him to see," Deck said. "*Before* I turn him over to the cops."

"Yeah. I'd advise that. Things ain't right with that bunch."

"You don't have to tell me," Deck said. "But I can't take on an entire police force."

"Or an old friend."

"Stop that," Deck said, shaking the amulet around his neck as if it weren't blocking his aura properly.

"Well, here's some foresight. You might *have* to take them on," Quest said, and Deck could only nod, discouraged. Quest changed the subject. "Now, I'd also suggest that, for your own spiritual sake, you take some time to explore personal paths."

"Like what?" Deck was skeptical.

"There's an aching in your heart so deep it's practically making my brain explode."

"I don't know what you're talking about," Deck said too quickly. "Look, I have my reasons."

"It's not often enough that the powers that be thrust two souls together with such precision. And when they do, there's no doubt it's real as can be, and that those two souls are meant to save each other. But he already told you something along those lines, and if he can't convince you, then I can't," Quest said, looking almost sad for Deck.

Which annoyed Deck. "If you're done, can I ask you if you have any—"

"Yeah. They're right here. I put them aside when I felt you were coming," Quest said, bringing a small stack of books on spontaneous combustion and pyrokinesis out from under the counter.

It sent chills up Deck's spine.

"Read away, but I'm telling you, that's not the problem." Quest punctuated his statement by pulling another item out from under the counter and throwing it on the stack of books.

It was a very familiar DVD, the one entitled *The Combustion/ Close Encounter Connection.*

"It's the one you saw in Stan's nightstand when you were—"

"How much do I owe you?" Deck interrupted the mind reading, reaching for his wallet.

"You know, your boyfriend was in here soon after his former boyfriend died."

"He's not my boyfriend," Deck said.

"Okay. That stripper from Dirty Harry's," Quest gave a dig, "was in here buying a book about interacting with guardian angels. I tried to talk to him about it, but he wasn't really willing to go into it with me, and I'm a little concerned about what it is he really might be communicating with. So if you could perhaps bring the subject up with him…"

"Yeah, sure. If I see him anytime soon." Deck shrugged nonchalantly, as if he had no intention of contacting Maru in the near future. Unfortunately, he could tell by the expression on Quest's face that he was being called out on his lie. "Outta my head."

"Sorry. I'm just concerned about the guys in this community. Just like you. All I ask is that you listen to the things I tell you," Quest said, putting the books and DVD in a bag.

"You can bet on it." Deck finally relaxed a bit and smiled, which in turn made Quest do the same, so Deck continued, "I think I can read *your* mind right now."

"Yeah, well, you don't realize it, but when you let down your guard, you are so fuckin' hot, dude. You gotta tap into that aspect of your persona, because it's like a magnet."

"I do okay."

"I believe it." Quest winked.

Deck's ears perked up, and his instincts had him ready to reach for that gun that had not been on his hip for years. He quickly put his finger to his lips to silence Quest as he looked toward a door at the far right corner of the occult shop.

"That's just my partner," Quest assured him.

"Partner?"

"Yeah. Ezra. We live upstairs. He usually does various types of readings as well, but he cancelled his appointments for the day because he was feeling like shit."

The door opened slowly, creaking as if it were purposely designed that way to add to the creepiness of the shop.

"You okay, baby?" Quest called out.

A young man with incredibly dark features peeped out of the door. He had olive skin, thick black eyebrows, piercing green eyes, and a head intentionally shaved down to stubble. He was in just shorts, showing off a tall, lean, smooth body type similar to Quest's.

"You still look a bit pale," Quest said.

Pale? Deck thought, looking again at the marvelous dark complexion. Ezra appeared to be of some sort of Middle Eastern descent, with his facial features smooth, slightly sunken, and glowing.

"I'm okay," Ezra said. "Is this Deck?"

"Yeah," Quest said. "Deck, this is my partner, Ezra."

"Hey, Ezra." Deck waved with the hand holding his bag of books.

"Quest, why not lock up the shop for a few and invite Deck up for a little something?" Ezra suggested.

"I was going to, but I didn't know if you were up to it," Quest replied.

"I'm *always* up for it." Ezra raised two eyebrows at Quest in what was obviously common banter between them.

"You got time?" Quest asked innocently enough, but Deck was getting a psychic vibe of his own.

"Sure."

"You can just leave the books on the counter and grab them when you leave," Quest said, locking up the shop and hanging an "Out to Lunch" sign.

Deck did as told and was led up to their apartment.

❖

Upstairs, Quest and Ezra's apartment wasn't decorated much differently from the shop. The main room was covered in fabrics, so much so that Deck wasn't even sure there were any windows, although from the outline, he sensed that one section of thick material was covering some sort of sliding balcony doors like the ones in his room at Weeping Manor. Providing the only light in the room were candles that oozed wax all over shelves around the perimeter of the space. The aroma of sweet incense was almost dizzying in its pungency. Shelves were lined with bottles of potions just like the shelves downstairs in the store.

"Damn, you're juicy," Ezra said in what was just about the sexiest, most alluring tone Deck had ever heard whispered in his ear.

Ezra and Quest had immediately sandwiched him in, their tall, thin bodies smothering his stocky one. Each of them was nestled in his neck on either side from the front and the back, licking and sucking his whiskered flesh, tickling his beard with their nuzzling, removing his shirt until his thick, hairy physique was being consumed by warm air.

"Woooh, guys, that feels amazing," Deck gasped, his muscles letting go of their tension as Ezra and Quest nibbled on his shoulder, back, and chest flesh.

"It relaxes the sphincters," Quest whispered before licking Deck's ear. "You're going to need it."

"Who says I'm going bottoms up in this scenario?" Deck asked.

"You do." Quest smiled, dangling in front of Deck's face the protection amulet, which he had apparently removed while seducing Deck into submission.

Deck's nostrils were clogged by the tangy scent of youthful sweat.

"Look at the size of this mondo ass," Ezra said, grabbing chunks of buns once he'd dug his hands down the back of Deck's pants. His fingers burrowed into the fuzz between Deck's cheeks, hunting for the warm slit that hid underneath. "Take 'em off and let us see that barrel butt."

Deck had to grab Quest's sharp shoulder blades to keep his balance as Ezra wrestled Deck's jeans down to his ankles. Deck was penguin-walked over to a fabric-covered ottoman by a sectional couch in groovy psychedelic colors and pushed firmly to his knees at the foot of the ottoman, which was just the right size to accommodate his torso and belly, leaving his head hanging off the opposite end once they'd draped him over it.

"Magnificent!" Quest exclaimed at the site of Deck's big furry round ass as it swelled and parted.

"Thank the fertility gods for this gift we are about to receive!" Ezra prayed like a horny frat boy.

"Guys, just take it easy. It's been a while." Deck tried to play down his concerns. These two may be serious about their magic arts, but clearly, their libidos were all guys gone wild.

"Now stop getting all anxious like that or you'll tense up," Quest said as he circled around the ottoman, now totally naked.

Deck looked up. "Aw crap."

Quest was smirking down at him from around a gi-normous, hard as steel cock, beneath which dangled two low hangers, all covered in a thin layer of tangled dirty-blond hair that wasn't all that different from the mop on Quest's head. Deck craned his neck to give them a lick.

"That's right, suck them balls." Quest's eyes closed and his head dropped back, making his Adam's apple more prominent and every ridge in his almost emaciated musculature throb. He crouched down onto the edge of the couch cushion slowly and tea bagged Deck's open mouth, tucking his sack neatly into the orifice.

Deck did his best to circulate saliva and tongue around the tangy treat, feeling the slightly sticky skin and hair adhering to his mouth's interior.

"You wanna suck my dick while my baby fucks that mondo ass?" Quest asked, looking down at Deck.

Deck bobbed his head up and down in response, so Quest removed his balls, which were now coated in layers of glistening spit, and shoved his cock into Deck's mouth, practically choking him. Deck had to wonder if these earthy spiritual types took baths on a regular basis, because Quest was quite musky and spicy. Tears sprang to his eyes as Quest fucked his mouth with youthful exuberance, determined to bury his way to the balls every time, his arms extended behind him and planted on the couch back so he could thrust forward with his hips.

Just as Deck was wondering what had become of Ezra, he felt the cold smear of lubricant in the cavern of his ass crack. Gagging on Quest's pistoning cock, Deck held up one finger, trying to send a message to Quest to relay to Ezra that he would like to be warmed up with at least a finger if there was going to be no tongue involved prior to entry.

Without slowing his rhythmic gyrations, Quest said, "Just focus on relaxing, because if you think I'm big—"

"UUUUUUNNNNNNNHHHHHHHHHH!" Deck squealed in agony around the heft of Quest's shaft.

It might not be anywhere as big as Milkman Stan's monstrosity, but Ezra was probably runner-up in terms of biggest cocks Deck had ever come in contact with, let alone had rammed to the hilt into his guts without warning. All the lubricant in the world couldn't have made it feel any less like sandpaper being rubbed up against his innards. Deck instinctively tensed up and tried to jump off the ottoman.

Quest held Deck's head in place and stroked it simultaneously, crooning, "I know, I know. It's a shock the first time. Believe me, I've been in your position many times. And he's a little more anxious because, well, neither of us has back like you do. Phenomenal."

Deck had grabbed Quest's smooth thighs and was squeezing them tightly in an effort to will the pain away as Ezra began to saw away at him with no regard for his comfort.

Quest just kept plugging away at Deck's mouth, fingers entwined in the thick hair on the back of his neck to keep him in place, and promised, "It will start feeling amazing soon. You'll see. He's fantastic at what he does."

Deck felt like a piece of meat on a shish kebab. He had one giant rod piercing each end of him, and he was pretty much stuck in place. He squeezed his eyes shut and tried to endure the agony of the ripping he was receiving from behind (thank heaven he had evacuated with Philip this morning) and trying to breathe through his nose with Quest's cock filling his mouth. He was determined not to look conquered by these two young guys. After all, he was the man here.

"Take it, bitch," Ezra grunted from behind. "He's taking it all the way."

"Let me see some of that," Quest said, leaning forward with his cock still in Deck's mouth. He pressed both palms down on the hairy tufts on either side of Deck's spine. "Come on. Arch that back and open up more. There we go!"

Deck had let the tension whoosh out of his tummy so it would go flaccid and squish against the ottoman more, which in turn arched his spine. He indeed felt his own rectum expand to accommodate the cargo better.

"Look at that hairy fuck hole suck it up!" Ezra exclaimed. "Right there, Questy baby!"

"That's right! You stay put, Waxer," Quest said. He pushed off Deck's back to swing his long body all the way back down onto the couch, never slipping from Deck's mouth.

Quest reclined into the couch cushions, sneered at Ezra seductively (he was so dirtbag sexy), and said, "Play frogger with his ass."

Deck felt the redirection of the meat packing his ass as Ezra got up on his tiptoes, grabbed hold of Deck's hairy shoulders, and begin to jackhammer down into him.

The pounding on Deck's inner pressure points was beyond anything he had ever experienced—and he had experienced a lot. How was this young man, nearly half his age, so good at what he was doing? Did he realize what he was doing, or was it just a coincidence that what he needed to do to make himself feel good happened to trigger all the right nerves in the person on whom he was inflicting his satisfaction surge?

Deck was being taken to a place beyond his capacity to comprehend. His guts convulsed, unable to digest the stimulation as quick as it was coming. His eyes glazed over and began to cross as he stared up at Quest with confusion.

Quest just nodded with a knowing look, and opted to remove his cock from Deck's mouth—as if he knew it needed to be empty so Deck could let out the high-pitched squeal that slipped uncontrollably from his vocal cords the moment his oral cavity was vacated.

Everything just went to mush in Deck's being. A pulsing numbness spread all the way to his extremities as his abdomen convulsed. He whimpered like a puppy, struggling to find enough adrenaline to turn his neck so he could look over his shoulder at Ezra.

Sweat glistened on Ezra's smooth olive features, his green eyes burning with intensity. But it was not so much the intensity of a man hell-bent on getting off—it looked like he was trying to get a job done. The challenge—the goal—was truly for him to extract some sort of reaction from Deck.

"You got it," Quest said, and it was unclear if he was speaking to Deck or Ezra.

Deck began to hyperventilate, a deep, whistling wheeze scorching his esophagus, his eyelids fluttering uncontrollably. His hands found Quest's ankles and squeezed desperately.

"Ez, he's about to pass out," Quest told Ezra. "Let up some."

It was almost as if Ezra hadn't heard him. He bounced even more viciously and began to hungrily suck on the back of Deck's neck, pulling in the flesh with the power of a vacuum.

"EZRA!" Quest released a shout while pushing with force against Ezra's forehead to detach him from Deck's immobile body.

The outburst seemed to break Ezra's spell. He slowed his pouncing to a crawl and then finally stopped, without removing himself from Deck's insides. He dropped across Deck's back, and Deck's asthmatic sounding inhalations and exhalations made Ezra's body rise and fall. Ezra kissed the sweaty hairs on the back of Deck's neck before running his tongue over them. Deck shivered uncontrollably as he tried to recover his motor skills.

"How about you cool off and then we let you take control?" Ezra whispered seductively in Deck's ear.

Deck could only nod in response. Ezra and Quest patiently watched as Deck's heart and breathing rates returned to a more normal pace. At last, Ezra rose from Deck's back, their sticky skin peeling apart.

"Come on, big guy," Quest said, and they lifted Deck up by his arms. His erect cock had soaked the ottoman fabric with precum, which stretched to a fine line before finally snapping in the gleam of the candlelight.

"Hold him up," Ezra said, putting the burden of Deck's barely vertical stance on Quest's shoulders. Ezra then dropped to his back on the ottoman, his butt at the edge of the piece, and pointed his enormous cock, surrounded by a surprisingly thick bush of matted black pubes, straight in the air.

"You wanna straddle it?" Quest asked, and Deck simply nodded, feeling like he was doped up. Quest steered Deck so he was above and facing Ezra, his legs on either side of both the ottoman and Ezra. "Just lower yourself down, and we'll guide it in for you."

There wasn't any lowering to do before it was on its way in, considering it was already poking at Deck's derriere. Deck grabbed Quest's tattooed arms to steady himself as he sank slowly down to Ezra's balls.

"That's it. Just ride it until you're ready to gush all over me," Ezra said.

Deck closed his eyes and did just that, feeling the strain in his leg muscles as they began to fatigue from the up and down spring motion. But he was too involved in the sensation tickling him inside to care. Doing a vertical back arch, which made his hairy chest and nipples poke forward, he reached his arms back to pull his cheeks apart so he could better engulf the magic wand that was again stimulating all his senses. He didn't open his eyes, but he did jump slightly and feel his rectum twitch when someone, either Ezra or Quest, began to roll his giant nipples between thumb and index fingers.

Deck began to build momentum, lifting nearly all the way off the cock then plunging swiftly back down on it. The last thing he expected was the colon-stretching second cock that suddenly joined Ezra's cock. There was no opportunity to bounce away from the extreme sport, because all his heft had been slamming down on Ezra's cock. Deck's eyes burst open in shock as his already aching ass was nearly torn in two. "Yeeeeeooooouuuuccchhhh!"

"Relax, you got it," Quest whispered into his ear. He had snuck up from behind and gotten into a position between Ezra's legs that allowed him to hold his slightly smaller cock parallel to Ezra's.

"It hurts!" Deck cried while simultaneously lifting off both cocks and then coming back down on both of them, determined to prove what a man he was.

"WOW!" he gasped, doing it again and again, mentally focusing on relaxing his guts.

"Keep going!" Quest wheezed from behind him, hot breath tickling the hairs on his neck.

"You're bringing us there!" Ezra shouted.

Arms snaked around either side of Deck as the partners took hands as if they were performing a séance and Deck was the crystal ball between them. Veins burst from forearms as they both cried out in ecstasy.

Deck felt the heated moistness saturate his insides as the cocks dueling inside him exploded, creating a slick and messy lubrication. He bounced up and down ferociously, draining them while grabbing his own cock and yanking furiously.

"That's it!" Ezra exclaimed as Deck's lust splattered across his lean stomach and chest, even drizzling down his chin and neck.

"Damn, you needed that!" Quest said.

When it was done, Quest pushed against Deck's back, sending them forward until Deck was sandwiched between them in a horizontal position, sweat and cum working as the condiments, the two big cocks still crammed in his ass. Quest and Ezra extended their heads over one of Deck's shoulders to kiss, and just waited until their cocks had shrunk enough to fall out of their own accord.

Without hesitation, Quest pushed off Deck's back and disappeared. Or so Deck thought. He suddenly felt a mouth clamp onto his loose, swollen, and exposed anus and suck powerfully. His sphincters were just too weakened to fight back, and he sensed them releasing streams of cum.

Within seconds, Quest had mounted Deck again, grabbed his chin to turn his head back, and clamped his lips on Deck's lips like he had on Deck's asshole. The recycled swirls of Ezra and Quest's intermingling semen flooded Deck's mouth. He swallowed, feeling his Adam's apple bulge determinedly.

"You read my mind." Deck said when they released the lip lock.

"You know it." Quest smiled.

❖

Deck was still in Quest and Ezra's apartment getting dressed when his phone rang. He fished it out of his pocket before he'd even gotten his pants all the way up.

"Hello," he said into the phone.

"Deck. It's Teddy. EMT Teddy."

"Yeah. What's up?"

"Do you have a minute to talk?"

Please don't let this be the night he and Otto want to hook up. My ass is way too sore.

"Um…sure."

Officers Soloman and Bembury told me to call you," Teddy said.

"Oh. Um, can you hold on a sec?" Deck asked. He looked over to Ezra and Quest, who were in a small kitchen area mixing some concoction that they promised would help him absorb psychic vibes. "Hey, guys. I gotta take this. It's kind of private. Is there anywhere I could go?"

"Sure," Ezra said. "Go back down into the store. You can even sit in the reading room. Back corner. Through a beaded curtain."

"Oh yeah. I know where it is. Thanks," Deck said. "And Quest?"

"Shutting off the powers," Quest said, mimicking a turn of the switch next to his temple.

Deck exited the apartment, stomped quickly down the steps, and went back into the shop. He crossed to the beaded curtain and stepped into what looked like a classic fortune-teller's room, complete with all kinds of future predicting tools scattered on a table in the center of the space. He sat at a heavy wooden chair with plush cushions and finally spoke into the phone again. "Sorry about that. What's up? Is everything okay?"

"So," Teddy began. "You really believe in supernatural and unexplainable stuff?"

"Word gets around fast. I'm very open to the possibilities. Yes."

"Deck, I don't know what the hell I witnessed today."

"You saw a combustion?" Deck asked without thinking.

"Um. Yeah. If that's what you call it," Teddy said.

"What happened?" Deck asked.

"Look. You can't tell the commissioner I told you this. I told Soloman and Bembury to just talk to you themselves, because they were there."

"They're mad at me. I guess I'm getting the silent treatment," Deck said. "So what happened? I'm not telling her anything at the moment."

"Okay. We had an incident at the police station today. They got this guy in there because of some sort of domestic violence situation. He hasn't eaten for three days since he's been in there. And he lost his shit. Became violent. Me, Soloman, Bembury, and a couple of other cops and medics. We could barely hold him down to tie him to a gurney. His strength was unbelievable. Especially for someone who's been starving himself. He was maniacal. Like a caged rat."

Deck hardly knew EMT Teddy, but he could tell the man was completely shaken up. "You have no idea what was wrong with him?"

"He just, I don't know...first we tried to give him an I.V. to hydrate him. But he fought us off. So when we finally were able to hold him down—*six* of us—we tried to sedate him. Dr. Chandler from the medical center. He was there. I watched him try to get the needle in. But the skin on this guy's arm. It was like every time the needle almost went in, the skin pushed it out, and the vein sealed back up. And there was nothing. No blood. Not a drop. He had to have stuck him half a dozen times in each arm."

"What does that mean?" Deck asked. "From a medical perspective?"

"The nearest thing would be what's called hypovolemia, which is a huge lack of blood. But that usually comes from hemorrhaging, externally or internally. This guy hadn't bled at all. He was on the giving end of the domestic abuse."

"Gay couple?" Deck asked.

"Yeah," Teddy answered. "We would have explored the possibility of blood loss, but we never got that far. He was ranting on and on about something flying outside the barred windows of his prison cell the night before. And he kept saying 'We're the same' and 'We can be together.' Deck, it was creepy."

"So how did he light on fire?" Deck asked.

"His body was freezing. His skin was so cold. So I got a blanket to put over him for the trip from the police station over to the medical center. We had him strapped down on a gurney and we rolled it out into the back lot. And I saw it happen. He just ignited, Deck. Like he'd been doused in gas and someone had thrown a match on him. And he shrieked in agony. It was like nothing I'd ever seen or heard before."

"If this is some sort of paranormal phenomenon, I will figure it out," Deck said. "But if you get any kind of leads involving a medical explanation, would you let me know? This will be strictly in confidence. I just need to know the whole story so I know I'm not barking up the wrong tree. I don't want to come out looking like a fool if there's a reasonable explanation for this."

"Of course," Teddy said. "I will. But after what I saw, I don't think there's anything reasonable about it."

❖

Deck left the occult shop a while later after drinking Ezra and Quest's potion and dabbling in some chatter about afterglow auras with what he dubbed the Psychic Boyfriends Network. He'd hoped the light conversation would get his mind off the horror story Teddy had shared with him. Outside, the night was rapidly approaching. The sun's shadows stretched across the pavement.

"Damn. How long were we going at it?" he spoke to himself in the quiet cul-de-sac of storefronts as he cut right up the middle to make his way back to his car, his bag of spontaneous combustion books in hand.

His still-pinched insides reminded him of just how long they'd been going at him. He would have stayed for dinner, as the boys had offered, but when Ezra had inquired about the upcoming night at The Caves, hoping Deck had some details about the return of Weeping Manor's main attraction, Quest had gotten argumentative— aggressively so, considering his gentle demeanor. He was firm on the idea that they not attend the revival, without giving explanation as to why.

That had been Deck's cue to leave. Lovers' spats were just not his thing.

Chills ran up Deck's spine. Perhaps it was the creepy shadows created by the quaint lantern-style streetlamps. Maybe it was the evening cool down. It could most definitely be the echoes of Teddy's voice still bouncing off the dome of his mind.

No.

It was the sound.

Deck stopped. Looked up. He heard the faint high-pitched squeals and flapping. Growing louder. Coming closer. Descending. He saw darkness on top of darkness as the black orb of movement blocked out a near full moon.

He began to run.

And realized he should have run back to the shop instead of out into what was clearly a deadly desolate street in the Glitter Dome. Where was all the life that had been populating this street only hours before? It was like a ghost town. He began to huff and puff as he sped past closed shops on the main street he had originally turned off, his heart pounding in time with his feet on the pavement.

The beating wings and chirps of angst were upon him. He choked on his own fear, spittle building at his lips. He dared not look back. Horrific thoughts of alien abduction had been planted in his head, and now they were developing into thoughts of tractor beams and anal probes even larger than the ones to which he'd just succumbed.

He nearly twisted an ankle slipping from the curb to cross the street to his car, which was looming in the distance. He wasn't paying much attention to the dark van parked on the side of the road as he was passing it.

Until arms reached out and violently yanked him inside.

CHAPTER TWELVE

The side door of the van was yanked closed—right before it was rocked violently from the outside.

"Get drivin'!" a deep voice exclaimed, and in the darkness, Deck was aware of one large man getting up from a crouched position in the back of the van while the other man held him down. He was too drained from running to even fight. He found relief in the fact that the voice sounded human and not alien.

Then the van was moving. Fast. It was still convulsing as well, and those horrible squealing sounds were like a cyclone around the entire vehicle. Deck tried to glance out the back windows of the enclosed vehicle, but they were deeply tinted. He needed to know what was making that sound. He struggled off the floor of the van and crawled to the front seats.

"Don't worry, Deck. It's us," a familiar voice said from behind him. It belonged to Officer Soloman.

"I have to see what it is," Deck said, feeling surprisingly dizzy.

His crossing eyes saw a glimmer of red swinging from a rearview mirror on the windshield. It was a rosary currently in a tangled mess.

"What the fuck?" Officer Bembury gasped from the driver's seat of the van as some sort of large creature attached itself to one of the unmoving wipers on the other side of the windshield.

Deck focused his vision as he grasped hold of the dashboard between the seats to raise himself onto his knees.

Soloman brushed up beside him and landed in the passenger seat. "It's a fucking—"

"—bat," Deck surmised as they stared at the large, hairy, rat-sized body.

A pig-like nose flared and fangs gleamed from an angry, open, and hungry-looking mouth. Wings splayed across the windshield from the force of the wind hitting the glass, and the creature's span took up almost half the width. It struggled to keep its foothold on the wiper, but its body was slowly moving up the angle of the outside glass, allowing its eyes to pick up the gleam of the ruby red rosary's reflection. There was a single squeal that was nearly as piercing as all the squeals combined, and then the bat was gone from view. Its body could be heard thumping against the metal roof of the van as it tumbled over the top before falling off the back.

"Something seriously ain't right in this God damn town," said Soloman "It's like *The Birds,* only with bats. You all right, Deck?"

"I think you guys saved my life," Deck stammered.

"We're cops. It's our job," said Bembury.

"I thought you hated me," Deck said. "You made Teddy call me instead of telling me yourself."

"But we made sure you got told," Soloman said. "We didn't want to be seen running right to you after what we witnessed today. Anderson would have known what we were up to. If she doesn't tell you that she saw it with her own eyes, then you really better start questioning her integrity."

"She was there?" Deck asked.

"Yeah, she was there," Bembury said as he continued driving. "It was some fucked up shit. I never saw anything like it in my life. It's not just the bats that have gone wild. We need to talk. See if any of this makes sense to you. Because it sure as hell doesn't to us."

"Let's pull into the spot," Soloman said to Bembury.

Bembury drove them into one of the still-seedy parts of Kremfort Cove and down a long narrow alley. At a dead end, he stopped the van and turned off the engine. After making sure all the doors were locked, they climbed into the back of the van. Soloman pulled across a maroon curtain that hung from a rod behind the two front seats.

They sat in a circle on the floor of the van.

"So—" Deck started.

"So," Bembury cut him off. "On top of all this other craziness, we've been having a slew of complaints about dog bites."

"Dog bites?" Deck asked, confused.

"Yeah," Soloman said. "Friendly neighborhood pets that know and love everybody are just going all Cujo and shit and taking healthy bites out of people on the street, in apartment buildings, even some attacks on the damn owners of these mutts."

Aliens disguised as dog owners? "I don't see how this is related—"

"Neither do we," Bembury interrupted Deck. "But the human torches, the dog attacks, the fuckin' bats just now—"

"The guys in black sheets—" Soloman added.

"And the BeNelly brothers," Deck threw in.

"Well, yeah," Soloman said. "Add it all together, and no one is frickin' stepping outside their doors."

"Businesses are suffering," Bembury added, "and the whole town is feeling it."

"So you're saying that the tax dollars needed to keep Anderson's precinct up to par…"

"Yeah, Deck. That's part of it. Maybe we're coming down too hard on her. Maybe she's struggling to keep good men on the case and get this shit solved so people will feel safe again in this community," Soloman said.

"So what? She wants me to join the force?" Deck said haughtily.

"We think maybe she wants you to step up your game," Bembury said. "But we think she's afraid to ask you. It's like she has a personal block on actually recognizing your talents."

"Well, that's true," Deck said. "So she sent you to ask for her?"

"Nah. We're here on our own," Soloman admitted. "We want to stick closer to you. Work kinda together."

So that's why they're softening on the Anderson issue. They want to get back on my good side because they want something from me.

"We think something big is going to happen this weekend at the reopening of The Caves," Bembury added.

"And why is that?" Deck asked.

"Couple of reasons," Soloman said. "For starters, the precinct has been getting anonymous messages—untraceable e-mails, phone messages, typed notes—about how Gomorrah is going to cause its own descent to hell this weekend."

"And inside sources say the BeNellys plan to crash this weekend," Bembury said. "And the stars are aligned—"

"Can it!" Soloman interrupted, punching Bembury's beefy bicep.

"You two have been to Quest!" Deck exclaimed.

"The guy's good," Bembury said sheepishly. "He predicted both of our cock sizes to the millimeter."

"*That's* why you went to him?" Deck laughed.

"No, man!" Soloman looked flustered as he shot Bembury a dirty look. "We went to question him about his obvious connection to several of the fire victims. He offered the cock size info up voluntarily."

"And you couldn't prove his predictions wrong." Deck smirked.

"He made us whip the damn things out to measure them before he would answer our questions willingly," Soloman explained.

"He and that terrorist boyfriend of his give some fuckin' great head," Bembury let slip, which won him another punch in the arm from Soloman.

"You know I hate that racist shit, bitch," Soloman said. "Just 'cause the color of his skin, don't mean he's a terrorist."

"You were the first one who said it," Bembury said.

"Oh…yeah. But those terrorists are all about the Buddha, Allah, or whatever and don't do that cocksucking stuff so he can't be one."

That gave them both a chuckle.

"Guys!" Deck interrupted, not cool with conversations about who was more racist.

"What?" They broke out of their side conversation.

"What's the game plan here? What do you want to do?"

"Well, we want to tail your ass to The Caves," Soloman said.

"How can you tail me there when I'm *staying* there?"

"So we want to tail your ass *around* The Caves," Bembury said. Soloman shot him a dirty look. "What? He's got a fine ass."

"Wait a minute. Do you guys really want to see what goes on in The Caves, or are you just looking to get me into a compromising position?" Deck asked, feeling the electric pulses of unspoken sexual energy floating through the enclosed space of the van.

"You need to invite us. We don't particularly make it onto Hayes's guest list," Bembury said.

"Fine." Deck nodded. "Consider it done."

"Now, about that whole compromising positions thing." Bembury raised one thick mahogany eyebrow.

"Aw, damn. Guys, I'm not much in condition for anything too hardcore tonight." Deck gulped, which automatically made his butt hole clench (and ache). It was practically on fire from the "psychic impressions."

"Don't worry your little head," Soloman said with a wickedly sexy-savage expression on his delicious black face.

Deck was scared: almost as scared as when the bats banged at the walls of the truck. Bembury reached into a nearby toolbox behind the driver's seat and brought out a long nightstick, a bottle of lube, and a pocketknife. At the sight, Deck crawled back on his knees. "This isn't gonna get violent, is it? I don't like mixing blood and sex."

Without speaking, and with an evil gleam in his eye, Bembury held up the blade, which glinted in the barely available moonlight. Soloman, meanwhile, assumed all fours, his derriere creating a bubble in his tight uniform. Bembury stabbed the knife right into the center of the seat of Soloman's pants.

Deck's heart leapt to his throat—until he saw the amazing control with which Bembury had targeted the seam, and how the knife had barely punctured the material. The knife was withdrawn and Bembury swiftly stuck an index finger into the asshole-level slit and yanked the tear bigger. He took the finger and stuck it under Deck's nose. The faint whiff of black man ass brought to mind Deck's involuntary feast on just about every BeNelly butt in Kremfort Cove.

Bembury inserted two index fingers into the widened hole and tore the pants in two directions. Large meaty black globes exploded out of the pants, covered in swirls of kinky black hair. But before Deck could enjoy the view, the men swapped positions and Soloman was stabbing at Bembury's swelling ass. Deck swallowed hard again, but the butt was left intact as the jeans were torn apart.

Without a word, Soloman grabbed the nightstick, held it horizontally, and lubed each end. They got on all fours, back-to-back. Soloman handed the stick to Deck. "Hold it steady for us, man. That's all you gotta do. Feel free to whack off if you want."

It was all so perfectly choreographed that it was clear they had probably been doing this same song and dance for years with numerous men.

"No." Their heads swiveled Deck's way with dog-like curiosity and shock at his one syllable refusal. "I wanna see you fuck him."

Deck pointed from Soloman to Bembury.

The uproar of expletive-filled protests practically made the van quake as they both rose to their knees, seeming traumatized and disturbed at the mere thought of it.

Deck threw the nightstick to the floor of the van, where it bounced metallically. "Then fuck yourselves. It's what you're doing anyway. You don't need me to hold it in place."

"It ain't the same doing it to yourself," Soloman griped, looking bummed about the way things were going.

"Yes, it is," Deck said. "Just grab the nightstick and ram it up your own ass."

"It wouldn't feel the same, man," Bembury argued.

"Why?"

Soloman and Bembury looked at each other, neither able to think of an answer. Finally, Soloman cracked. "We like it better when we share."

"Share what?" Deck asked. "Share a piece of painted wood? There's a whole lot more you could be sharing if that nightstick wasn't in the way."

Bembury scoffed. "Yeah, like you're the authority on—"

And then he stopped.

"On what?" Deck asked.

"Just shut up!" Soloman ordered, starting to walk on his knees toward Deck, a fist coming up.

"What are you scared of?" Deck backed away, grabbing Soloman's fist to hold it from swinging at his face.

"Soloman, wait." Bembury kneed his way into the fray. "He's right."

"Right about what?" Soloman looked hotly at Bembury, who was only inches away.

"You gotta tell me you know," Bembury said.

"Right about what?"

"Don't make me say it." Bembury cast his eyes down, swallowing hard.

"Say it, man." Soloman's commanding voice showed a hint of faltering, and Deck felt the raised fist in his hand go slightly limp.

"I want you," Bembury began.

"What do you want from me?" Soloman's voice softened, and now his arms went lax, so Deck let go of his fist.

Soloman and Bembury faced each other.

"I want you. I want you in me. All the time. It's all I think about." Bembury choked on his nerves.

Soloman pounced on him, his full lips smashing against Bembury's. Their muscles strained through their tight shirts as they hugged the life out of each other.

Deck just dropped back and watched. And felt. He felt blood racing through their veins, the pulse pounding in their temples, the fluttering in their chambers that seemed to be draining all life energy, then filling back up in a rush of adrenaline that was more than the heart could circulate safely.

Soloman lowered Bembury onto his back on the floor of the van.

The long-squelched desires bubbled to the surface so Deck could vicariously suck the energy from them as they converted the overwhelming feelings into the most primitive form of communication in this instant when words were too frightening to speak.

Soloman's forehead beaded with sweat as he lifted Bembury's booted feet until the soles faced the ceiling, causing Bembury's round rump, coated in mahogany pubes, to bulge from the makeshift chaps his police uniform had become. They were practically still dressed, which forced Soloman to dig his hefty, deep black cock out of the zippered crotch of his pants. He let saliva drool from his full lower lip onto the shaft and polished it, coating the entire length as he kneeled on his knees before Bembury's white ass. In response, Bembury reached his hands to his cheeks and yanked them apart to reveal his deeply striated asshole, which was clearly worn from years of nightstick encounters.

Soloman put pressure on both of Bembury's thighs to bring the hole directly into the air, then let another string of saliva stretch its way down to the target. Large drops of the sweat on his forehead dripped off and drizzled into the cavern as well.

Finally, Soloman lined up his mushroom-like cock head, much bigger than the thickness of his cock, and simply plunged it right in. Bembury cried out with shocked surprise—not an unpleasant cry. Soloman didn't hesitate. He sank all the way up to the balls and dropped his shoulders down on the back of Bembury's thighs, crushing them to Bembury's chest. He smothered Bembury's mouth with his own lips and sucked greedily on the tongue he encountered as his hips began to buck rhythmically.

Deck wasn't watching a cock puncture an asshole. He was watching one soul sink itself deep into another. It was stunning. It was the most passionate sex he'd ever witnessed. The partners did not take their lips from each other's mouths; they did not close their eyes, which were only an inch away from each other. Bembury's hands squeezed the meaty black ass cheeks that were pumping into him, trying to draw them even closer.

It only took a few minutes for Soloman's love to gush out. At that moment, the breathing between their mouths sounded more like gasping for air. Deck actually heard their teeth clank together.

And then, it was done. Soloman's ass, coated in the moisture of exertion, stopped its undulating thrusts and jiggled to a stop as he just stayed with his monstrous mushroom head crammed in Bembury's hole. Deck watched the messy overflow spill out around his thin shaft and travel in streams through Bembury's ass pubes. His immediate thought was to leap over and lap it up, but he knew it wouldn't be right to intrude on this couple's first time, so he just stayed quietly on the sidelines even though he wanted so badly to bust a nut himself.

The private moment was shattered by a digital jingle coming from Bembury's pocket. Soloman quickly pulled up and out of him. Bembury lowered his legs and dug the cell phone from his pocket.

"It's the commish," he said, looking guiltily at Deck and Soloman before answering and listening. They could hear the raucous voice of Yvette Anderson drilling into his ear.

"Yeah. Okay. We will," Bembury finished.

"What is it?" Soloman asked.

"Waxer, we're supposed to find you and take you in," Bembury said flatly, digging into his trunk of tricks and pulling out two fresh pair of uniform pants.

❖

"So am I under arrest too?" Deck asked as he sat in front of Anderson's desk.

The commissioner had just entered the room, pulled all the blinds dangling from the office windows, and closed the door to shut out the sounds of a busy night of petty crimes at the police station.

Yvette stepped behind her large desk, but didn't sit. She crossed her arms across her big chest, which was framed by the blazer she was wearing. It now looked like her arms were holding up the bulging bosom. "Deck, what am I supposed to do? Every time someone gets torched, it seems you were with them only a matter of minutes before."

"Yvette, I'm investigating the paranormal. That's why I was at Quest's shop. That's why I *offered* up that information."

"So it's just another coincidence," Anderson said.

"Okay. So I guess I could be a prime suspect. Other than the fact that I didn't arrive in town until you already had a handful of flaming faggots on your hands," Deck said. "What about Milkman Stan? Are you still holding him for something you know he didn't do?"

"Just like the others, he's been freed with strict orders not to leave town," Anderson responded. "And exactly how do I know they aren't involved? Just because these all seem like isolated incidents with unrelated men doesn't mean there's not some weird underground cult thing going on here. Men sacrificing their own partners and family members in a burning ritual. Hell, it could even be some sort of conversion cult that has each man take a life of another gay man to help cleanse his own soul."

"Come on!" Deck shook his head. "You really are reaching for explanations here."

"Yet, your mind is whirling with how great an explanation that is," Anderson said.

"Yeah. But you forget, Yvette, I was with some of these guys right before the tragedies, and I can tell you, *none* of these guys had any qualms about being gay. *Believe* me. And Maru—"

"I know. He was destroyed by his partner's death." Yvette's domineering persona softened. "If nothing else comes out of you being in town during all this—"

"So why did you really call me down here?" Deck stood, almost as if his soul tried to jump out of his skin, which was forced along in order to keep it in place.

Deck could see through her thick makeup to the strain and stress that had stolen her youth—the skin, smooth and flawless in the days when they'd felt like stars at every club they entered, was now etched with age that was attempting to hide under some thick foundation. She looked tired, worn, and unhappy. Soloman and Bembury had to be wrong. There was no way she was getting laid nightly.

"I saw it happen," Yvette muttered, not looking at Deck.

"You saw what?" Deck began, acting ignorant as her strong eyes looked up at him weakly. "Oh God…"

"God couldn't possibly have anything to do with this." Yvette shook her head, almost as if to deny she'd seen what she'd really seen.

"Who was it?" Deck asked, hoping to get more information about the prisoner than Teddy had been able to supply.

"Another local," Yvette said. "There'd been a disturbance in his apartment the other day. Neighbors called us. My men got there, found this guy curled up in a corner crying, with blood running out of his mouth, his partner locked in a bathroom, covered in bites but sleeping like a baby. And it's a fucking mess and none of it makes sense!"

"Well, what happened?" Deck asked.

"What happened is, the neighbors said these two were madly in love, together for years, never had a fight before. The victim was taken next door to the medical center and heavily sedated because he was babbling about demons taking over the biter, who was being held here until we could get either of them to talk about what had happened. Instead, a nurse finds the victim's room empty last night with a window open on a second floor and nobody down below. And today, the biter, who has been starving himself since the attack, just… bursts into flames. And no one knows what it means, not even the doctor who was working with him."

"Starving himself," Deck said. "You think it was intentional? Maybe a suicide pact?"

"Neither of these guys fits the profile. They were successful owners of a chain of catering halls." Yvette answered Deck's question for him. "And now I got these two witches or whatever they are..."

"Quest and Ezra were two really nice guys who seemed to live life to the fullest together," Deck assured her.

"I'm giving you permission to go talk to Zimmerman, my forensics guy next door. He's going to examine the bodies and remains. Since you were with these two last, I want you to chime in if anything seems out of the ordinary based on what you experienced before you left them. Because all I got right now is some eyewitnesses who said they heard a quarrel and then Quest forcing Ezra out their balcony doors by smashing a bottle over his head."

Deck still couldn't believe the report. He couldn't picture Quest suddenly turning on Ezra. They'd seemed a real team. Although there had been the little tiff over a visit to The Caves. But that had been a simple lovers' quarrel. There was no way that had led to a murder/suicide. The mere thought gave Deck the chills.

"Who were these witnesses?" Deck asked. "When I left the place, the area was dead quiet."

"They'd rather remain anonymous for now," Yvette answered. "Now why don't you get over there? Take the elevator to the basement. Zimmerman's expecting you."

❖

Deck was soon walking up to the medical center's front desk, where numerous male nurses were scurrying around as if there had been some major outbreak in town. Taking in all the patients sitting in chairs lining the walls of the gray room, Deck figured he must have walked right into the emergency room. In fact, it felt like the medical building was simply one big emergency room.

"Sorry. Could you just point me to the elevator to get to the basement? Commissioner Anderson sent me to meet with, uh, Zimmerman..." Deck leaned over the counter to talk to a burly, red-haired, mustached nurse typing insurance information into a computer.

"Hey, Waxer," the redhead greeted him. "He's expecting you. Head down the hall, all the way to the end, make a left through some swinging doors. Just when it starts to look really creepy, you'll be at the service elevator. Pick up the phone next to it and you'll be connected right to Zimmerman. Announce yourself, and he'll buzz you into the elevator."

"Great. Thanks…Steve." Deck smiled after noticing the name tag on the nurse's chest, but his charm and personalization was wasted, for the nurse had already looked back down to his data entry.

"Waxer!"

A lithe body lunged at Deck and a clawing hand grasped at him as he turned away from the counter. Deck stepped back, taken by surprise. He knew immediately by the bloodshot, wild eyes and the glossy, sweaty facial features that the man was strung out on something.

"You've got ta help uuuuus!" The man, who looked like a forty-year-old who'd lived himself to a sixty-year-old condition, groaned as if in agony.

It was then that Deck caught sight of the bandage haphazardly wrapped around a stump where the man's other hand should have been.

Two nurses moved in and pounced on the man, yanking him off Deck quickly and apologizing as the big presence of Nurse Steve arrived to give the man a sedative. Everyone waiting in the emergency room had shifted their focus away from their numerous pains to the action taking place center stage.

"Pleeeeaaaaase!" the man howled. "I'm not like you anymore! We're all going to chaaaaange! Someone has to stop iiiiit! Loooook what it's done to me!"

The man began to wave his bandaged stump around until the sedative made him go lax in the nurses' arms, simply shaking and whimpering as he clung to them with his one hand.

"This should have knocked him out completely," Nurse Steve murmured as he stared at the syringe he was holding.

"What happened to him?" Deck asked no one in particular.

"Crack accident most likely." Nurse Steve shrugged. "Burned his own hand off. It was bound to happen eventually."

"Noooooooooooooo…" The one-handed man sobbed as if giving up all hope that anyone would ever believe him. "Different now… becoming one of the flyers…"

The man's voice trailed off as the nurses carried him out to remove his drama from the room full of anxious people already concerned with their own ailments.

"I couldn't get the needle all the way in…." Nurse Steve was murmuring to himself as he stared at the syringe in his hand.

Deck backed away from Nurse Steve as he tried to mentally shake off the incident—and to will the goose bumps on his arms to shrink back into his skin after more references to "flyers" and needles that wouldn't go in.

Calming his nerves was proving to be harder to do than Deck expected once he followed the path that led right to the creepy hall Nurse Steve had described.

"Yeah, it's Waxer," he said into the old-school phone on the wall beside the elevator, then he hung up as the doors parted for him.

"This thing needs some oil," Deck murmured as his stomach lurched and the elevator creaked on its way down to the basement.

"Hello?" Deck called loudly through the dimly lit, echoing hall after stepping off the elevator.

"Down here!" a voice echoed back, and Deck saw a shadow on the checked floor outside a doorway several yards away.

"Why does this place have to feel like a morgue?" Deck asked as he entered the coroner's office to find Zimmerman dressed in a lab coat, standing up while typing into a computer before turning around to hover over a body on the table behind him.

"It is," Zimmerman said with a certain ignorant charm. "Right now, I'm kind of a one-man show in this city when it comes to dealing with dead bodies. I do it all. Except in the day when I have my interns helping out."

"Well, that would explain why you have this place down as your address," Deck remarked, remembering the note Zimmerman had left on his windshield. "I guess you're always here, huh?"

"Yeah. The good news is, you're only a little late getting here, and now we don't have to be secretive about it since the commish requested that I talk to you. Which makes me wonder if she knew I was going to anyway."

"Oh, geez," Deck murmured, taking in the lump of what remained of Ezra on the table under a bright overhead lamp. He was reminded of that old joke, *Why did the girl from* Jaws *have dandruff? Because she left her head and shoulders on the beach.*

He looked away quickly, and told himself it was to avoid the glare of light bouncing off a shiny crucifix that was lying on the chest of another corpse nearby.

"Geez," Deck said again, swallowing hard as he pictured Ezra alive. *I had this guy inside of me only a few hours ago. He was so young. So hot.*

"This is great," Zimmerman said, almost as if talking to himself.

"Huh?"

"Oh, sorry. I mean, this is the first time I've had something more substantial than a hand or foot to examine. Looks like he must have been struggling to get back in the room. He must have ignited out on the balcony and was trying to work his way back in, getting just his head and shoulders in before Quest was able to close the balcony door and leave most of the flames outside."

"So you don't believe Quest lit him on fire," Deck asked as a statement.

"I believe he was trying to put him out," Zimmerman said.

"What?"

"There was a large, gothic decanter smashed on the floor and liquid all over. It was water. Just water."

But Deck knew it was more than just water. He'd seen a shelf of the decanters in Quest's store. It was blessed water for warding off demons, hounds from hell, and God only knew what else. As Deck considered the information, his gaze was drawn to a body that was completely covered by a sheet. Deck thought he saw the sheet move, almost as if an air current had blown it. But the sheet seemed still as he held his eyes on it for a moment. "So you believe it was—"

"Spontaneous combustion," Zimmerman finished. "I just don't know if Anderson is going to believe it even though she saw it with her own eyes today."

"She told me she saw it happen, but she didn't mention combustion as a possibility. Did you suggest it to her?" Deck asked.

"I'm definitely not the right person to talk to her about it. I'm a scientist. If I talk about anything considered more of a paranormal phenomenon by most, I'll lose all credibility."

Deck easily read the meaning in the expressive blue eyes behind the large glasses. "Oh, *no*. I'm not going to tell her. Hell no."

"Come on, Deck," Zimmerman pleaded, his puppy dog eyes sinking to new levels of adorably pathetic. "She warned us all about you. She's used to you coming up with all these crazy theories that sound like something out of a bad horror movie."

"It's not the horror movies that are bad; it's the people who close their minds to them."

"See, that's just it!" Zimmerman pointed out. "You believe in this stuff. You have passion for it on your side."

"You seem pretty sure yourself."

"Yeah, but I have to explain it from a scientific angle. I can do that once the seed has been planted in her head, but I can't present what is basically an urban legend as fact from the start."

"Wait a minute." Deck gave Zimmerman a hard look. "Why do I get the feeling you don't want to tell her because you actually aren't sure?"

"Well…" Zimmerman paused. "I'm pretty sure I'm sure. It's just that, well, I don't know much about spontaneous combustion, and what I've found online both supports and contradicts some of my findings."

"Such as?" Deck asked.

"Okay. The victim is often left as a pile of white calcined ashes. Check. That would require a temperature over seventeen hundred degrees Celsius. We're talking hotter than a crematorium. There doesn't seem any possibility that anyone could have access to such excessive temperatures to off someone and then disappear without a trace. So I'm convinced this isn't murder or suicide by fire."

Deck was both relieved and even more confused. "But how can we be sure that this is a combustion thing? You wouldn't believe some of the theories I've come up with."

"Like what?" Zimmerman asked.

"Pyrokinesis for one. But I'm beginning to question that idea myself."

"Because there's no one person who has been present at every fire," Zimmerman said.

Deck swallowed hard at those words, because *he* had been present just before quite a few of them.

But clearly, Zimmerman wasn't thinking along those lines, because he shrugged and said, "It was one of my first theories, too."

"Well, our friend Quest has another one. He thinks it's aliens," Deck said bluntly. "Said people are acting differently in Kremfort Cove. Not to mention dogs are acting out against their—"

"Aliens." Zimmerman's brow furrowed skeptically.

"You wouldn't consider aliens, but you believe spontaneous combustion?" Deck said. "Not for nothing, but this Quest guy was seriously psychic. He was responding to things I never even said out loud."

"Okay. So let's say there's some sort of body snatcher invasion going on," Zimmerman played along. "Now we have alien clones that are bursting into flames. You know, combusting. Two New Age theories in one."

"So whacked a theory it could just be true." Deck shrugged. "Maybe the aliens are having a reaction to our air or something, which would explain the unnaturally high burning temperatures."

"So then how do I know you're really you? And how do you know I'm really me?" Zimmerman asked.

The room grew dead silent as they stared at each other until the hair was standing up on the back of Deck's neck.

"Let's get back to this." Deck broke the tension nervously.

"Yeah." Zimmerman nodded, moving shakily over to a body under a sheet. As he turned his back to Deck, he suddenly snapped around quickly.

Deck raised his hands up defensively as he sensed Zimmerman's distrust. "Just checking out the ass."

They began to laugh, the nervousness draining out of them.

"Well, clearly we're both having emotional reactions to overactive imaginations." Zimmerman giggled, pointing to the swelling in Deck's jeans.

"Yeah. You look pretty emotional yourself." Deck winked at the sight of a growth in Zimmerman's pleated pants resulting from the flirtation.

"All right, I'm on the clock."

"I know this is a stretch, but—" Deck began, and Zimmerman gave him a raised eyebrow.

"Okay, *another* stretch," Deck continued. "They said that dude in the prison cell"—Zimmerman pointed with some sort of prodding tool in his hand to a cloaked table in a far corner, which Deck took to mean the remains of the very dude of whom he was speaking—"seemed strung out. And I just saw a guy up in the ER blabbering in hysteria about how we're all going to change...and *fly*. So either this dude was talking about peapod shit or there's some sort of mass delusion going on here, maybe drug induced. Is it possible that some sort of new drug, the latest trip, is hitting the market—"

Zimmerman picked up Deck's line of thinking excitedly, his words firing rapidly from his lips. "Maybe being distributed by someone like the BeNelly brothers or the Other Way Triple K, that's supposed to essentially brainwash people into following one leader, some sort of cult, but is instead having some sort of chemical interaction with the body and essentially making people ignite."

The BeNelly brothers. Drugs. They drugged me. Oh, shit. I also drank that witch's brew Quest and Ezra gave me. All I need is to fucking burst into flames.

"Great minds think alike," Deck said to distract himself from his own fatalistic thoughts.

"Or crazy conspiracy theorists think alike," Zimmerman said.

"Okay, crazy. But is it possible?"

"I guess it could be if I hadn't tested and retested the mounting remains that are being sent my way for any sign of any kind of foreign substance. Nothing foreign. Either clean or very familiar substances like booze, pot, or other recreational favorites of the gay ghetto," Zimmerman explained. "While many supposed cases of combustion have found large quantities of liquor were consumed beforehand, which I feel is an attempt to suggest the flammability of the alcohol is to blame, that only applies a few times here. And there's one other problem. Something I tested today because of an issue Dr. Chandler was having with the guy we had in the prison cell, He wasn't able to inject him with a sedative. Said the vein was literally rejecting the needle."

"That hot daddy red bear nurse upstairs just now said something about not being able to get the needle in a guy," Deck said, making sure not to let on that he knew many of the details of what Teddy had witnessed that afternoon.

"Really." Zimmerman's eyes widened behind his glasses as he moved to his computer and began typing. "I'm e-mailing Steve to see if he can even get a blood sample from the guy. I tested the blood of Dr. Chandler's guy from next door. Luckily, I had enough upper remains that didn't fry. I was thinking maybe there's some sort of virus going around. Something so powerful that it can reject foreign bodies trying to enter the bloodstream, maybe assuming everything foreign is a threat to its existence."

"*And*?" Deck asked excitedly.

"*And...*" Zimmerman raised his eyebrows dramatically. "What little blood was left running through this man's system wasn't his own."

"Huh?" Deck asked. "I don't understand."

"He's a resident of the area. I got his medical records from his doctor's office. He was A positive. The only blood in what remained of his system was B positive. The blood type of his partner." Zimmerman's eyebrows arched upward again. "And unfortunately, the partner has gone missing, so I can't do any other exploration of that information until the police find him."

Deck's mind was whirling with several frighteningly fictional possibilities.

"Now let me show you Quest." Zimmerman pulled back the sheet Deck thought he had seen blowing in the breezeless room earlier.

It was worse for Deck seeing a man he'd just been with looking almost perfectly preserved and not like a piece of charcoal. "Fuck me," he grumbled, swallowing his sadness.

"Notice the darkness of the bruises on the neck," Zimmerman said with a pen in his hand. "He was choked with amazing strength. They must have been fighting beforehand."

"They weren't fighting." Deck shook his head. "They weren't the type. They were good together."

"Didn't you just meet them?" Zimmerman asked. "How would you know what they were like together when people weren't around?"

"It's something you just know," Deck said sternly as he looked at Quest's bruises. "What if...what if Ezra was trying to get back *in* to the apartment? What if he was grabbing frantically for something, anything, while he was on fire, and the thing he happened to grab was Quest's neck?"

"Enough to choke him to death?"

"Who knows what you're capable of if you're set on fire? What if it *was* the air, or something about being outside that caused him to burn? What are the situations of all the other victims? Were they outside? I know the Glouster twin was. And Milkman Stan's farm boy."

"And the guy from the prison cell was wheeled outside to be brought over here. But not Ben DuPont," Zimmerman reminded Deck. "He was in his bed. And none of the witnesses saw Ezra go up in flames outside. It appears that happened inside. They only saw Quest throwing a couple of bottles at him on the balcony. But I'm glad you noted the frequency of outside combustion. Because that's another complication in the theory. Recorded cases of combustion have almost predominantly taken place indoors. That's the exception rather than the rule here."

Zimmerman moved over to his computer again to type in some information. "I've reached out to some supposed experts on spontaneous combustion with my findings, and I'm keeping them updated with each new situation, so I want to fill them in on today's occurrences and see if there's any correlation with cases they've studied. It could take a while to hear back from them. And if there is the possibility of some sort of new drug doing that"—he pointed to Ezra's remains—"we're going to bring in higher levels of expertise."

"Zimmerman, you got to promise me you're going to let me know if you find something—and that you won't tell Anderson I know." Deck handed over one of his cards, and Zimmerman read the copy printed on it:

> Deck the Dick
> The whole package
> 1. Go deep undercover
> 2. Finger the suspects
> 3. Crack it wide open

"How can I resist with a calling card like that?" Zimmerman said. "Although, don't you need one for your paranormal investigating?"

"It's the first thing I'm going to do if I actually *solve* a paranormal case," Deck said.

"Well, you have to promise me that you won't tell Anderson anything *I* tell you unless you're ready to solve this whole thing beyond a shadow of a doubt."

"Of course." Deck nodded, thrilled that they had an understanding. "Now I gotta get back to Weeping Manor and get some sleep."

They jumped in surprise at a sudden swift movement in front of them. One of Quest's arms had slipped from the examination table and now dangled off the side.

Deck rolled his eyes as he wiped a hand over his beard. "I don't know how you stay down here alone."

Zimmerman nonchalantly put the arm back up on the table, but his hand was noticeably shaking. "It happens all the time. You get used to it. But that one kind of got to me for a second."

"Me too," Deck said. "So I'm definitely gonna go now."

Damned crucifix, Deck thought as he was walking out and got lasered in the eye again by the exaggerated shine of the cross on the dead body. He was most definitely not the most religious of men, but he gave the crucifix a second thought. *What are you trying to tell me, God?*

"Hey, Waxer," Zimmerman called as Deck headed for the door. "Maybe I'll see you in The Caves this weekend?"

"You got it." Deck made one last promise, feeling butterflies inside at the thought of the uptight looking Zimmerman letting it all loose in God only knew what kind of situations The Caves had to offer.

CHAPTER THIRTEEN

Leaving the medical building, Deck considered going back into the police station to talk to Anderson, but he had too many mixed emotions about her right now. Plus, he really needed to get some sleep.

As he walked past the precinct and into the lot of the police station, he scanned the vehicles to see if he could spot the van belonging to hot cops Solomon and Bembury underneath the streetlights that illuminated the space. He didn't see it. He could sure use Wilky's Hummer pulling up right now.

He'd have to call a cab. He pulled his cell phone out of his pocket. As the screen lit up, he caught a hint of movement beyond his close-focused vision. He looked over the phone to a series of trees that lined the back of the police station parking lot, running alongside a wall of the right wing of the building.

"Zimmerman?" Deck said quietly as he squinted to make out the shape that seemed to be floating (flying?) between two trees in the darkness. He got a case of goose bumps at the odd illusion, and then swallowed hard before calling, "Zimmerman? That you?"

Deck could clearly make out an arm lifting, a hand gesturing, beckoning him to the distant location. He paused warily. How could Zimmerman possibly have gotten to such a location from the basement of the medical center without passing him somewhere along the way on the sidewalk? Was there some sort of secret entrance connecting the medical center to the precinct?

The dark shape still beckoned, and Deck's eyes were playing a mean trick on him, because it seemed to be floating out from between the trees, dancing along the edge of dark just outside the reach of the lot's backmost streetlights.

Deck began to back away, remembering the dark bodies that had chased him through the city more than once. But would they dare try to pull a stunt right outside the police precinct? Deck looked left and right, taking in the shape of each car in the lot as he backed up…and felt his ankle catch on a curb. He tumbled backward. He landed on a soft cushion of grass and leaves between the parking lot and sidewalk, but his body and senses still felt jarred. As he refocused, he saw two faces looming over him and coming down at him.

Deck let out a high-pitched yelp of fear.

The two faces began to laugh.

Solomon and Bembury picked him up off the ground by each arm as they tried to contain their laughter.

"It's not funny!" Deck growled, embarrassed as he brushed any dirt off his bruised butt. "You scared the hell out of me."

"Our buddies Regan and Damian would call that a Scream Queen." Bembury giggled. "We gotta give them a call and tell them that we're finally an official couple. Maybe they'd be willing to do a foursome now."

Bembury winked at Soloman, who seemed to imagine the fantasy in his mind before asking Deck, "Why so spooked?"

Deck returned his focus to the back of the parking lot. There was no one there. Just darkness. "You guys mind driving me back to my car?"

Something about returning to the vicinity of the Quest/Ezra tragedy sent a surprising melancholy through Deck's soul. Even having spent just the past few days in Kremfort Cove, he felt as if the atmosphere of the thriving gay Mecca was quickly degrading before it even had a chance to fully develop. It seemed to be negating the work of devoted men like Milkman Stan, Lamond, and even the mysterious Proc.

Wilky might be next…Deck realized that the partners of two of these three men were already victims of this combustion situation.

But none of them, as far as he knew, made drugs a recreational activity. Which would negate the possibility of it being a drug ring, unless somehow the drug was being unknowingly introduced into the systems of men here in the Cove.

Like how? Through the water supply? Then he remembered allegations of Quest throwing those blessed bottles of water at Ezra. *Or is water the cure?*

Then there was the pyrokinesis angle, which seemed like way too big a stretch. Because if there was a pyrokinetic master in town, as Zimmerman had pointed out, he'd have to be at every scene of combustion to make it happen. *Or would he? Can it be done remotely if the fire starter wishes hard enough? Or is there maybe a whole cult of homophobic fire starters torching gays?*

A cult. *A group of men under some sort of spell? Or hallucinogenic drug? One with combustive side effects?* Deck hated that he was thinking it, but the most obvious cover for a cult would be The Caves that everyone talked up so much. Hayes Lamond was such a powerful man, both financially and sexually. He was alluring, charismatic. Everyone seemed to love him. He himself had fallen for Lamond's charms. What if Lamond's plan for "homosexualizing" the city was to brainwash the community for a takeover? *Am I getting way too Syfy Network original now?*

There was only one way to find out if he was really buying into his own hype as a paranormal investigator. It was time to poke around in the very place he was staying; invade the personal space of the man who had welcomed him in.

There was a beep behind Deck as he reached the turnoff into Lamond's estate. Solomon and Bembury had insisted on trailing him safely home. They flashed him a good-bye with the lights of their police van before pulling away as he continued on through the gates and up the weeping willow-flocked road.

❖

When Deck entered the mansion, it wasn't quite dawn yet, but there was already a dim light on in the kitchen. He was almost expecting to see Don whipping up a delicious breakfast. Instead, it was Phillip, preparing a cup of tea. He was wearing a comfortable pair of sweats and a T-shirt, which meant he'd probably been doing yoga already.

"Well, hello, Deck," Phillip greeted him with his usual formal air as he pushed his glasses up on his nose. "Just getting in? Would you like a cup of tea?"

"No. I haven't slept in what feels like days and the caffeine will just keep me up," Deck said.

"Oh. I don't drink caffeinated tea. It's poison. This is a wonderful herbal tea that helps cleanse toxins from the body. Here, smell." Phillip held a steaming mug to Deck's nose.

"Mmmm. Smells like some sort of pumpkin spice."

"It's good for digestive problems, too," Phillip said. "And speaking of, I really have to get down to my office. Tomorrow night's the big reopening of The Caves, and I usually have a line of men waiting to be cleansed before the big event."

And we're back to The Caves again. "Well, make sure you squeeze me in."

"What are you doing now?" Phillip asked. "Are you too tired to go for a session?"

Deck thought about it. "Actually, I could go for it. It really has been working wonders on my digestion."

"I can see that," Phillip whispered, leaving his tea on the counter, untouched.

Was he trying to get me to drink tainted tea?

As they headed for the far wing of the mansion, Phillip said, "Your belly is definitely looking flatter."

"Really? You think so?" Deck whispered in the echoing halls, flattered by the flattery about his flatness, yet still inadvertently sucking in his tummy as Phillip looked him up and down.

"Absolutely. You look wonderful," Phillip said, leading the way into the isolation of his office.

"I'm going to use the shower room to rinse off. I feel grimy," Deck said, holding his shirt away from his chest with just the tips of his fingers to signify the strength of the stank.

"Sure thing. Fresh towels and robes in that closet right there." Phillip gestured as he began to set up the colonic machinery.

In the shower oasis, Deck sensed something was very different. Aside from a twinge of loneliness at not having Don's perfect fur-covered body next to his, the room was noticeably dark. Then Deck realized why. The giant window wall at the back of the shower room was somehow closed up. It was now two giant, solid doors. He assumed they must slide out from the slots in the walls. It really changed the incredible sensation of showering in the open that he'd experienced before.

Once showered, refreshed, and robed, Deck returned to the room, where Phillip was perched on his stool waiting.

"Okay. You can disrobe and mount the table whenever you're ready," Phillip said.

Deck blushed a little as he dropped the towel to reveal a full erection.

"Well, someone's already looking forward to a happy ending." Phillip bent and spoke directly to Deck's erection as if it were a child. He even gave it a little pat on the head.

"Sorry. I don't know what it is about this atmosphere," Deck said as he climbed onto the table and got in position.

"It's pretty standard for men to have an erection during this process," Phillip said. "Colonics are a highly erotic practice."

"Wait…you…" Shocked that this sterile personality would make such a claim, Deck shot a glance over his shoulder as Phillip lined up behind him with a colonic hose in hand.

"Oh, Waxer. I'm a professional, but do you really think that the sight of an ass like yours in my face doesn't drive me wild?" Phillip smiled politely. "I'm only human. My, my. You have seen some impressive action recently, haven't you?"

"Um…yeah."

"Yes, if I know my Kremfort Cove cocks, I'd say this is the work of Ezra," Phillip said as he pulled Deck's cheeks apart and inspected the anal tissue.

"Yeah," Deck responded quietly as he felt Phillips gloved fingers swirling around his perianal area, applying cold jelly lube. He didn't have the heart to tell him the sad news.

"I'm going to have to use a larger nozzle this time. You haven't quite recuperated yet, so the usual will pop right out of there!" Phillip chuckled.

"Okay, but go gently. It's really sore."

"Oh, I'm sure. You're not the first lucky man to take him on."

Deck wondered if Phillip himself had taken on Ezra at some point.

"OOOOOHHHH!" Deck cried out as a hefty and thick nozzle was slipped inside him.

"Come on, tighten it up," Phillip instructed him.

The nozzle was sliding back out, so Deck put all his energy into grabbing the intrusion with his exhausted sphincter. Phillip eventually seemed satisfied that it wasn't going anywhere, and let go.

Deck closed his eyes and breathed air into his pelvic area as Phillip had been coaching him to do, expanding his belly, opening up the spaces within his system, allowing the warm water to flow and wash away angst and tension. He didn't even focus on the heaviness in his lower regions as he was filled, just closed his eyes and relaxed.

"Deck, I think you nodded off. Are you ready to release?" Phillip's voice seemed to whisper seductively in Deck's ear as a hand rested gently on his ass cheek. "This is the longest you've ever held in. Almost forty minutes."

"Yes, I'm ready," Deck answered through a fog of comfort, even though he didn't exactly feel full yet.

As Phillip reversed the flow, Deck's intestines gently pulsed and released the water from inside him instead of convulsing to get it out as in the past sessions. He was left feeling evacuated and refreshed.

"One more rinse should do the trick." Phillip decided for him, and he began to get a warm, wet internal sensation again.

The room's isolation was hyper-peaceful. Deck began to drift off again, his face nuzzled between the comfy head cushion on the colonic contraption. He began to have a wonderful sexual nap dream in which his ass was just completely lubricated and open for intercourse, with no resistance, an unseen phallus moving swiftly and smoothly in and out of him like a jackhammer, stimulating and awakening all his rectal senses.

A weight on Deck's back woke him, and it took him a moment to reclaim his sense of location and situation as he saw only floor tiles beneath him. He tried to lift his head, but felt hands that were incredibly comforting—yet firm enough to keep him from moving— pushing at the back of his skull.

"Couldn't…resist…this…ass…" a voice gasped into his ear, covering his lobe in warmth.

"Phillip?" Deck croaked, realizing the seemingly abstinent man was inside him, riding him rapidly.

"I'll bring us to the point together," Phillip whispered, and his heated breath in Deck's ear canal made Deck's dangling testicles crawl.

Deck didn't move, allowing Phillip's cock to ravage his asshole. There was no telling how big or small he might be, because Deck's rectum was so perfectly dilated for receiving. Had he emptied out again, or had Phillip entered him while he was full? And how was Phillip so high up on the contraption? There were no footholds with Deck's knees firmly planted in the reversed stirrups of the oddly designed table. Deck could feel Phillip's triceps pressed against his back, but it was definitely not the entire weight of him. In fact, Phillip felt light as a feather—and hairier then Deck would have imagined.

The physics of it all washed from Deck's mind as he was treated to the good old reach around. Phillip's dry hand circled his cock and stroked vigorously, causing an immediate burning friction against Deck's shaft. Combined with the constant internal rubbing of his prostate, the sensations drew his testicles into tight balls immediately.

"Holy…fuck!" Deck howled as the cum speared its way out of him, the bursts capturing the spirit of the first-time orgasm of a teenage wet dream, a sensation one forgets after years of overuse.

Phillip, as proper and quiet as ever, huffed quickly into Deck's ear as he released his own liquid into Deck's ass gullet.

As Deck heaved out his last ounce, Phillip's presence disappeared from his back. Within seconds, Phillip, still wearing his sweat suit with just his cock and balls hanging over the lowered waistband, had crawled into the space under Deck's belly, where Deck could see the stainless steel basin beneath him.

Like a dog, Phillip lapped ravenously at the pearly white puddles Deck had released onto the surface of the basin. Deck gawked. Phillip was a total cum slut! Amazing how easily a man's sexual energy could completely change your attraction to him.

Without a word, Phillip, on all fours beneath Deck, turned his head upward and licked any remaining cum drops from Deck's sensitive cock head. Deck's groin convulsed from the feel.

"Come, I'll help you down," Phillip said politely as he righted himself and took one of Deck's hands to aid him in the dismount.

That was it. No more flattering comments about Deck's ass, not even a thank-you.

Just as he was leaving the room, Deck's paranoia set in. He turned back to look at Phillip, who was simply busying himself in cleaning up the hosing he'd used for Deck's colonic. Nothing too guilty looking about that.

I passed out during the colonic. Could that be how drugs are being pumped into men's systems?

On his way back to his room, Deck noted one of numerous gigantic grandfather clocks littering Weeping Manor and realized it was the time of morning when Don, Jeeves, and Samson usually worked out in the gym, before any of the men from town began to show up. He took a detour to go say hello—and to see if any of them had gone for a recent colonic and how it might be affecting them. When he entered the fully equipped gym, the large flat screen televisions lining the walls were already running the *Today Show* (the inhabitants of Weeping Manor had a thing for one particular host who was often self-deprecating about his large nose and balding head), but Don, Jeeves, and Samson were nowhere to be found. Deck noticed some towels and water bottles, so he knew the men had already been in the room.

Perhaps they're having some fun in the locker room?

Deck sprinted to the locker room doors—the most exercise he'd gotten in the gym of the mansion so far. But he slowed his movement as he reached out for one of the swinging doors; he was in the mood for some frisky voyeurism. He decided not to announce himself, hoping to play the silent spectator game so as not to interrupt whatever kind of rhythm they had going.

As Deck pushed the door slightly open, he was surprised at the lack of sexual sounds. He weasled his way into the naturally echoey room and quietly crept down the first row of lockers. Where were they?

Then he heard the tickling tones of a whisper coming from a far corner of the locker room, closer to the showers. He brought himself to a silent screeching halt as the conversation whistled into his ear.

"It didn't feel like a dream to me," Jeeves was nearly hissing. "I'm telling you, I feel like Master DuPont visited me. He floated into my window and talked so sweetly to me. He said soon everything would be okay and we'd be together."

"You miss him so deeply," Don was responding now. "Believe me. I've lost people and had them appear to me...*in* dreams. Maybe it is somehow their spirit coming to give you a message, but it really is just in your dream."

"I've had it happen too," Samson finally spoke up.

"See?" Don said before Samson could continue. "It's just a dream."

"No," Samson responded, his voice dropping to more of a hush.

Deck leaned in closer to the edge of the row of lockers behind which he was hiding, not wanting to miss what the hair whore was going to say.

"I saw Ben too," Samson said bluntly. "In the hall outside his bedroom."

"What are you saying?" Don asked.

"Floating. Like Jeeves said," Samson continued. "I thought I was imagining it, or dreaming. But I wasn't in bed. I was heading back to my bedroom after a late night shaving session with a hottie I'd brought home from Dirty Harry's. I'd just let him out the front door and as I was walking up the stairs in the front hall, I saw something at the top of the stairs, so I followed. And I finally caught up to him when I got near the master suite. I thought it was a ghost. And then he turned and looked at me. I was scared. I ran. Back to my room."

"A ghost?" Don said, his mind clearly filling with paranoia.

"No," Samson said. "It was him. When I got to my room, he was already there waiting for me. He told me not to be afraid. But I was terrified."

"Jeeves," Don interrupted. "Don't cry. Samson, please. You're upsetting him."

"How do we tell Master Lamond?" Jeeves's voice was a hoarse whisper.

"Listen to me!" Don's voice was a huffed whisper. "Don't say *anything*. Either of you. I can…I'll ask around. I can talk to Quest. Tomorrow. I'll do it. Just keep quiet about this. And I'll talk to Waxer. He believes in this stuff. Maybe he'll know some answers."

Deck blushed with guilt. Here he was spying, eavesdropping on their conversation, and Don expresses trust and a willingness to confide in him. It was time to make a quick retreat before they caught on to him.

As Deck worked his way quietly back to his own quarters, he was close to having no doubt that things were as bad as he'd imagined. And he was terrified of running into Ben DuPont on his way back to his room.

When Deck returned to his room and shook off some of his fears (turning on the television helped bring a sense of normalcy), he threw his balled up clothes in the hamper. He noticed the sky outside his balcony was just turning reddish-purple as dawn poked up above the watery horizon. He drew the curtains closed to bring darkness to his room, disrobed, and flopped face-first onto the luxurious comforter on his bed. Within seconds, he was completely out.

He had a deep, dreamless sleep, until it seemed like a voice had entered his mind.

"Hey, cabrón."

Deck groaned.

"Cabrón, you got a visitor," Don's voice whispered in his ear.

Deck grunted an automatic acknowledgement as he drifted between the sleeping and waking realms.

Don waved the bottom of the cooking apron he was wearing in Deck's face to supply him with rejuvenating air. Deck lazily swatted him away. He shrugged then moved to the door to usher the visitor, still in the hall, into Deck's chamber.

"Well, he's all yours," Don said to Maru, putting an arm on his shoulder. "Be gentle with him. He's a big boy, but he's got a fragile ego."

"Thanks, Don."

"And just tell him I was up here and need to review the dinner menu with him if he's eating in. You're welcome to stay too."

"Okay."

"Of course, you two may want to eat out instead of eating in." Don walked off.

"Deck? Deck, it's me. Maru."

Deck looked over his shoulder with his eyes half open, then groggily whispered, "Maru?"

Maru nodded.

"Am I dreaming?" Deck asked, blinking lazily.

"I don't know about you." Maru smiled genuinely. "But I think I am. Because you're showing me a whole lot of something totally worth living for."

Maru's death humor made reality click in for Deck. And that's when he remembered....

"I have no clothes on!" Deck stated the obvious. On his belly, he could feel his legs were spread and all his junk was sticking out below his ass. He clawed at the big comforter in an effort to hide himself under it.

Maru stood up and grinned boyishly. "Not a problem."

Deck was hastily fixing the comforter over his body as he turned red. He was now wide-awake.

Maru plopped down right beside Deck. "There's nothing I didn't already see over at the BeNelly place, remember?"

Maru grabbed the comforter and playfully tried to peek underneath.

Deck slapped his hand away and clutched the covers to his chest. "That was different. That was a rescue mission and I had to swallow my modesty out of necessity."

"The bare necessities," Maru said.

"What are you doing here?" Deck asked as he relaxed and leaned into his pillow. He practically winced as he realized his tone was anything but relaxed when the words hit the air. "I didn't mean it to come out like that."

"No prob." Maru shrugged. "The indifferent, annoyed, and brutish act gets me hot."

"Seriously. I'm glad to see you." Deck smiled as Maru slid back on the mattress and leaned against the headboard beside him. "I actually might have a possibility for some employment that will make an honest man out of you."

"Really?" Maru asked. "You jealous of my bad boy behavior?"

"Worried for your welfare," Deck said stubbornly. "They need help at the Glouster Gym."

Maru laughed sarcastically. "What? Where my dead boyfriend used to go to get his rocks off? Where I can go be part of *their* show?"

Deck's mouth went dry. "Oh shit, Maru, I didn't..."

"Wait. You want me to go undercover for you, don't you?" Maru said excitedly.

"Nah. I just fucked up and didn't think it through," Deck admitted. "With one of the Glouster twins gone, the other one is really going to need some help keeping that place running. And I don't think there's gonna be any backroom shows going on there for a while. I felt bad for him and my immediate thought was that you could kind of be supports for each other."

"Deck Waxer, are you trying to set me up with a Glouster twin?"

"No!" Deck said too quickly.

"Aha! You are jealous. And a little insecure."

"I'm *not* the jealous type, and I'm *not* insecure." Deck completely fell into Maru's trap.

"So," Maru continued, "I was wondering if you were going to The Caves tonight."

"No!" Deck answered way too quickly.

"It's not a big deal." Maru shrugged as if indifferent to Deck having any extra-curricular activity. "I don't expect you to miss the grand reopening. Would you mind if I came too?"

"Why?" Deck's face turned red with uncontrollable emotion.

"Calm your big hairy man pits." Maru gently touched Deck's arm. "Not to hook up. I just, you know, really want to see what goes on down there before I'm gone. Word around town is that my lying, cheating Lance was quite popular with The Cave crowd."

"I don't want to even think of you being exposed to what goes on down there."

"I won't be. I'll have you to protect me," Maru said. "We can role play. I'll be your Asian bitch. That will drive them wild."

"Okay."

Maru smirked. "Well, I guess I better get in line with all the other guys already here waiting for the big Phillip flush fest. So what time do you want me to come back?"

"You're leaving?" Deck couldn't fully hide his disappointment.

"Well, yeah. Don invited me for dinner, said it's just you and him eating together tonight, but I have to do an early shift at Harry's. Mostly a crowd of weekend rejects who can't get clearance to The Caves."

"Maru." Deck grew serious. "Forget that job. Don't perform today. Or ever again."

"Look, I'll consider the gym thing. But I have to perform at Dirty Harry's for now if I want a place to stay."

"Come here," Deck said. "Just go back to Dirty Harry's, pack up your stuff, and come stay here."

"Come on. Do you really think Hayes is going to let me take a room in his mansion without some sort of payback?" Maru asked.

"Yes, I do. You can stay in here, with me," Deck suggested with a dry mouth.

"You're still half asleep," Maru said uncomfortably. "I'll be back later."

"Call me as soon as you're through," Deck said, afraid to push the issue. "Do you need me to come pick you up?"

"There are so many guys heading this way, I'll catch a ride with someone. You better go talk to Don. He wanted to know about your dinner needs for tonight. I'll see you later."

"Later." Deck watched him go. His heart was racing. Aching. Why hadn't he just pounced on Maru just now?

"Ugh," Deck huffed. "I respect him too much."

Chapter Fourteen

Deck felt cold enveloping his naked body and making his skin prickle. He looked to either side of him. He seemed to be floating through a dark tunnel.

"Yeesh. Can this dream be any more Freudian?" his dream self said, as his sleeping mind lucidly contemplated the symbolism.

He seemed to be levitating as he was carried along, the tunnel in front of him getting smaller and smaller, with only a black spot at the end.

"Guess it's better than seeing white at the end of the tunnel," dream Deck muttered. *Unless...aw, shit, I'm seeing the black light at the end of the tunnel to hell?*

Dream Deck felt warm hands on his legs, and suddenly, his body was no longer moving forward. It was actually bouncing up and down. He felt a pillow of cotton beneath him, but there was a heavy weight pushing down on top of him repeatedly. Mostly on his pelvic area. He lazily lifted his head from the cushion beneath his skull and looked down the length of his naked body.

"Don?" Dream Deck murmured as he took in the burly, nearly black back hovering over him, muscles rippling through thick forests of hair.

The head of the form floating above Dream Deck turned.

"Just lay back and enjoy, cabrón." Dream Don winked.

Dream Deck could see—and feel—that Dream Don was sitting on his cock. It was a beautiful vision. As Dream Don squatted on him, bouncing up and down on his crotch, Deck stared in amazement at how the contrast of Don's black coat made his own cock look blindingly white as it disappeared into the excessively furry muscle buttocks repeatedly.

Dream Don had folded Dream Deck's body, pinning legs to chest with his powerhouse arms to keep them in place so Dream Deck's full crotch was open and exposed for Dream Don's ass ride.

"Damn, you're a hairy motherfucker!" Dream Deck could barely spy a centimeter of human flesh through the all-over coat of Dream Don, whose tight fuck hole was pleasuring his cock. Dream Don's massive body writhed ever so gracefully, the back and butt muscles swelling and rippling in dark, hair-filled cuts as he did some sort of anal dance, rectal muscles squeezing and sucking on Dream Deck's shaft to the point where he felt like he was about to explode, at which point the muscles would relax and the tickle would dissipate.

Dream Deck's fingers curled tightly around the plushness beneath him each time he was about to release. Left almost breathless (possibly also a side effect of his knees being practically drilled into his lungs), he gasped, "You're a fucking animal!"

"We're all animals," a calm and confident voice spoke from somewhere behind Dream Deck's head.

Deck rolled his neck to get a look behind him. Where the cave walls had been, there was now a transparent sheet of glass, and a host of gorgeous naked men were clawing at the glass voraciously. Deck recognized some of the faces from his time on the town in Kremfort Cove; others might just be composites of men he'd seen or imagined in his fantasies in the past.

"Cum inside me," Deck heard Don request, which brought his attention back to the beautiful man riding him.

There before them were two more guests in this dream orgy. Hayes Lamond had his beautiful bald slave facedown in the soft fluff, and was fucking the youthful bottom hard, Jeeves whimpering with delight. Jeeves turned his head up just enough to glance at Don and utter, "Stick your fingers up his ass."

As if for Deck's benefit, Don turned his head to the side to expose his profile as he stuck his index and middle finger in his mouth and sucked on them momentarily. When he removed them from his mouth, they were glistening wet with saliva. Don's head dropped and it wasn't long before Deck figured out where his attention had gone.

Two fingers jabbed aggressively into Deck's fully exposed, wide-open ass crack and began to stab savagely and determinedly at his prostate. With his legs firmly pinned down by Don, he didn't have any choice but to allow the invasion. At the same time, Don's rectal muscles were at it again, treating his cock to peristaltic action like he'd never experienced before.

"This is unbelievable!" Deck growled through clenched teeth.

Déjà vu flooded Deck's mind as cum flooded from his penis. Not the first time since entering Kremfort Cove, Deck felt like he was fourteen again, experiencing his first real nocturnal orgasm.

And suddenly, he was awake, still cumming, and witnessing a real-life sex scenario not unlike the one he'd just been dreaming. And he was wishing he'd been conscious for the whole thing as he caught the tail end of a show of which he was apparently the star.

As he gushed up Don's hairy ass, he could see that Don was hunched over and sucking down a load being delivered by Hayes Lamond, who stood naked at the foot of the bed, hands pulling Don's head down onto his cock. Other visual clues told Deck that somewhere between his and Hayes's crotches was Jeeves, for Don's head seemed to be surrounded by two swelling, completely hairless ass cheeks, and there was a gulping, gagging sound coming from somewhere, which probably meant Jeeves's bald head was currently impaled on Don's cock, swallowing his load.

Deck could barely get his wits about him as the gorgeous trio of bodies before him unfolded and reformed. Now Don was on all fours at the foot of the bed, swallowing Deck's cock to suck out the remaining remnants of cum, Jeeves's hairless face was smashed into Don's forest of ass, and Lamond was swiftly slipping his cock back up Jeeves's ass to wipe away any mess that Don had failed to swallow.

"Release it into his mouth," Lamond's voice carried over both Jeeves's and Don's daisy-chained shoulders.

Don pulled away from Deck's cock with a sensitive lip pop and then stared right at Deck, the dilating pulse of his eyes incredibly familiar—just like the expression he made when the two were side by side, releasing on the colonic tables. Only now, Jeeves's lips were suctioned tightly onto his asshole. Don gave Deck the raunchiest of smiles as he relaxed his sphincter muscles, sending the flood of Deck's cum from his ass into Jeeves's mouth.

"That a boy." Lamond stroked Jeeves's back gently. "I told you you'd be getting your favorite dessert tonight."

When he was finished indulging, Jeeves lifted up on his knees and threw his head over his shoulders to give Lamond a taste of his dessert. Lamond received the offering, and after swallowing some, he moved over to Don, who had also raised himself up on his knees, and passed a sampling to Don.

When their lips parted, Lamond walked casually over to Deck, who was still on his back on the bed, taking everything in.

"What would existence be without human male flesh?" Lamond asked as he bent over to place a kiss on Deck's lips. "I thank you all for that wonderful experience. Now let's all get ready for tonight!"

Grinning from ear to ear, Lamond trotted off enthusiastically, Jeeves following right behind him.

"You fully awake yet?" Don asked, dropping on the bed next to Deck.

"I think so," Deck said. "What just hit me? What time is it? What *day* is it?"

"Cabrón, you slept through dinner. I came to get you after Maru left, and you were out again. You didn't miss much. I ate a light salad by myself because everyone else is pretty much too anxious and excited about tonight to eat," Don said. "There's leftovers in the fridge if you want me to throw some together for you."

"No. I better get ready," Deck muttered, standing in an attempt to come back down to reality.

"Hey, you're not mad about what just happened, are you?" Don asked.

"Huh? What? No, no. It was fantastic. I kinda just wish I had been awake to enjoy the whole experience."

"Look, it didn't start out that way," Don explained. "I came up to check on you, and you were just laying there completely naked with this raging hard-on, and I've been so fucking horny for you to fuck me since you got here…"

"So you decided to just mount me while I was sleeping?" Deck laughed.

Don laughed too. "Hey, what can I say? You're so hot. So I'm just there bouncing up and down on you, enjoying the fuck out of your cock, when Jeeves and Lamond appear out of nowhere—I've barely seen them for days—and they hop right in on the action. But damn if that didn't make it hotter."

"You got that right," Deck said as he rummaged through his bureau for something to wear to The Caves.

Don walked up behind him. Deck could smell the intense aroma of sweat-soaked, matted body hair. "Shit. You feel guilty because of Maru."

Deck turned quickly. "What? Are you fucking kidding me? No way. I'll go at it again with you right now. But this time we satisfy my fantasy and you ram your cock up *my* ass."

Deck's words spilled out of him so fast he nearly tripped over them.

"That's an offer I'd love to take you up on," Don said, moving in close. "But I think I missed my chance."

Deck looked away.

Don grabbed Deck by the beard and gently yanked his face up until their eyes met. "It's okay to be in love."

With that, Don planted a gentle kiss on Deck's lips and, without another word, walked out of the room, leaving Deck alone with his fluttering heart. He had an unexpected new respect for the man. It was amazing how it could take just one aspect of a casual exchange with another person to make you realize that person was someone you wanted to have around you, in your life, for a long time.

Deck pulled out jeans and a button-down shirt, and then moved to grab sneakers from his closet. That's when he noticed the blinds of his balcony doors were open, letting in the nighttime moonlight. They had been closed earlier to block out the daylight when he was sleeping. Did one of the men open them to give the neighbors at Pale Shelter a show?

Still completely naked, Deck slid the glass door open and stepped out onto the balcony. He was so heated from not only the sex, but the intimate exchange with Don, that the chilly breeze felt good.

He reached for a switch inside the room beside the glass door and flicked on the exterior light, which gave off a warm, yellow glow. He padded across the cool cement to the balcony rail. Through the trees, he could once again make out the entrance of Pale Shelter, which was well lit, revealing a person standing on the front porch. From the shining white color of the shape, it was clear the figure was naked. Deck squinted into the night as if that would help him make out illicit details.

A long arm on the far off figure reached to the sky in a hand wave. Deck waved back. It was Proc, being the polite neighbor as usual. Apparently, he wasn't modest either. Deck wasn't even sure if he'd be seeing him later. Would Proc and Wilky be participants in the goings-on down in The Caves this evening?

As Deck turned to go back inside, his eyes were drawn to light bouncing off the panes of the balcony doors. He moved in closer to examine a series of streaks running down the length of the glass. It almost looked as if the glass had been touched by hands. Many hands.

Deck turned back to look across to Pale Shelter Estates. Proc was gone. The porch was empty.

There was a rustling in the weeping willow closest to Deck's balcony. He moved closer to the edge and felt a pinch on his foot. He looked down to see he had stepped on a twig. He bent and picked it up then placed it on the little table on his balcony so he wouldn't step on it again. In the tree, which was about five yards away, he saw little dots of light glaring at him. He once again squinted to get his aging eyes working—then jumped back with fright as a flurry of black burst from the branches and up into the air before swooping downward and out of his sight to somewhere below the balcony.

"What the fuck?" he stammered.

Something fluttered past the yellow light, swirling around it and then grabbing on to it. Deck glanced around the warm, glowing bulb attempting to identify the small thing attached to the side of the light.

It was a bat. And it was no bigger than Deck's fist. It crawled to the top of the light fixture clumsily with its wing claws.

"What are you doing, little fellow?" Deck asked gently as he approached the light. "Don't you want to join all your friends?"

He reached out a hand slowly, his index finger jutting out like a tree branch, and was amazed to see the bat crawling toward it.

"There you go, little fellow," Deck whispered as the bat, an impressively cute little critter, made its way boldly onto his finger, looking at him as if very taken with him. "Well, you're a gentle soul."

Deck eased himself into the chair beside the balcony table and rested his forearm on the table. The bat crawled casually off his finger and onto the table.

"You're surprisingly attracted to a big bear like me," Deck cooed, easing his hand out of the way and nonchalantly onto the twig he had placed on the table a few moments earlier. He wrapped his fingers around the twig, his heart beating overtime, and whispered, "If I'm wrong about this, forgive me, God."

His words seemed to have a significant effect on the bat. The little creature's eyes glared at him and its ears spiked up as its little mouth opened in a screech, revealing rows of fang-like teeth. Without hesitation, Deck raised the twig up and brought it hammering down to pierce the body of the little bat.

The bat's screech seemed to jump an octave as it was impaled, its wings spreading out to a surprisingly lengthy span—

—and then it burst into a flame, forcing Deck to yank his hand away. As quickly as it ignited, the flame went out.

There on the table was a pile of dust that swiftly blew away, leaving just a claw-like bat foot behind.

"Lord help us," Deck gasped, jumping up and stumbling back into his room. He slammed the balcony door behind him and double locked it before yanking the blinds closed.

Grabbing the pants he'd been wearing earlier, which were thrown over a chair, Deck dug through his pockets for his cell phone. Before he could dial, the phone notified him he had a text message.

"Stream Btwn Wpng Mnr n town. Mdnt. Zmmrmn."

Deck's instinct was to immediately call Zimmerman and warn him of the danger, but he had a feeling Zimmerman had probably figured out exactly what he had.

Deck jumped to Maru's listing and called him.

"Are you still naked?" Maru asked.

"Huh? Um, yeah," Deck responded, looking down at his nudity.

"Really?" Maru laughed.

"Look, that's not important," Deck said seriously.

"If you're worried about me, then you'll be happy to know I didn't dance this afternoon. I told Harry and Jimmy I'm going to stay with you and they were thrilled—"

"I don't want you to come here," Deck cut him off with the first words that came to mind in his heightened state of panic.

The silence on the other end spoke volumes.

"I didn't mean that," Deck quickly continued, not sure of how he was supposed to explain to Maru why he didn't want him to come to Weeping Manor. "Um, Harry and Jimmy. Did you see them at all this afternoon?"

"I told you, I talked to them and told them I was leaving," Maru replied, sounding confused.

"No. I mean, did you see them today? When it was light out. Did you see them in the sunlight?"

"You know, it's not like you asked me to move into *your* house," Maru tried to joke. "You're getting all crazy on me."

"I'm serious, Maru. Did you see them in daylight?"

"Well, I…yeah. Actually. When I was leaving to come see you, they were on a ladder changing a couple of burned out bulbs on the Dirty Harry's sign."

"Okay. Good. Then they're safe to be around. I want you to stay with them. Just until morning."

"Does this have something to do with the murders?" Maru asked. "Do you know who killed my Lance?"

"I know what killed everyone. But I can't talk about it now. But believe me, his death was a blessing. Do you own any religious items?"

"Religious items? Like, you mean Jesus statues or something?" Maru asked.

"Like a crucifix."

"Well, yeah. I do. My mom was determined to Westernize me, so I went to religion classes, made my communion—"

"Put the crucifix on and stay at Dirty Harry's tonight, around as many people as you can at all times. And don't go outside in the dark alone. Do you understand me?"

"Why do I feel like I'm in an episode of *Vampire Diaries* or something?" Maru said. Deck was caught off guard by the accuracy of his joke and paused too long. "*Am* I in an episode of *Vampire Diaries*?*"

Maru sounded scared. Deck's mind raced with the implications. One, it meant there was a part of Maru that was afraid to die. Two, it meant he was observant and keen enough to put two and two together, even if the solution to the mathematical problem meant Deck was talking about something everyone believed to be myth.

"Holy shit," Maru said. "I want to come and be with you."

"NO!" Deck said like a parent scolding a child who has just run into the street without looking, the abrasive tone being the result of fear, not anger.

"Do *you* have any religious items, like a crucifix?" Maru responded. "If that even works. Bram Stoker made that stuff up...I think."

"All right. I'll come pick you up," Deck said, the surreal reality actually sinking in as he imagined himself crawling through the throngs of men in The Caves wondering who was alive and who was undead. He recalled the bloodbath scene that opened the movie *Blade,* with a techno song blasting and blood pouring from a sprinkler system as vampires began to devour all the dancers at a club. Would that be the situation in The Caves tonight?

"Okay. Give me like an hour to get all pretty for you," Maru said. "You can come to the rear entrance. I'll be waiting for you."

"Inside."

"Right. Inside. But what do I do if you ask me to invite you in?" Maru said. It didn't sound like he was just teasing.

❖

Deck felt intensely paranoid as he showered the scent of sex off his body, not even closing his eyes when he shampooed his hair or daring to stick his entire head under the water. He hastily dried off, barely feeling dry as the water drops were replaced by sweat of fear. Yet, despite his terror, realizing he was about to meet up with Maru, he made sure to select jeans and a shirt that would accent his broad shoulders and big butt while drawing attention away from his belly.

Deck looked at his cell phone on the bureau while scrubbing his towel over his thick head of hair. He'd barely killed any time. The need to have Maru close to him so he knew he was safe was pounding through his blood. There was no way he was going to be able to just stay here and wait for the time to pass.

Should he take a few minutes to explore the desolate halls and rooms of Weeping Manor? For what? Exactly what was he looking for at this point? Coffins to verify what he feared most? That his host was probably already sucking more than cock? But if that were the case, how come Lamond hadn't taken a bite out of him?

Deck ran to a dressing mirror in his closet and did a quick body search for any kind of fang marks, even bending over and spreading his butt cheeks for signs of any kind of literal ass eating. He was relieved to see everything was intact—although, his asshole, bruised and battered from his frequent encounters since arriving in Kremfort Cove, had seen better days. *And I hope it gets to see more.*

Deck got dressed and stepped out of his room. The mansion was eerily quiet as he entered the hall.

"Holy fuck, this is scary shit," he muttered under his breath as he attempted to casually stroll his way toward other wings of the mansion—in particular, the wing that was the site of Ben DuPont's vampiric combustion. He noticed something that made his mouth go dry: the absence of certain statues and paintings that had adorned the long corridor wall. Specifically, any art that had any kind of religious theme, including a series of reproductions capturing highlights from Michelangelo's Sistine Chapel masterpiece.

This reality was a game-changer. Life would never be the same for anyone.

Deck gulped audibly while passing a dark door on his right. A pale white shadow seemed to float out from the doorway. Deck screamed.

"Sorry, sir." It was Jeeves, naked as usual, and with what appeared to be a slightly amused smirk on his face.

"Je—Jeeves!" Deck quickly turned the "Jesus" that was on the tip of his tongue to Jeeves's name. Assuming Jeeves was already a vamp, he wouldn't take too kindly to the Son of God's name, and Deck wasn't yet ready to stab this little hottie through the heart with a spike without proof positive.

Oh, shit. Can vamps read minds? Deck put a strained smile on his face. "You scared me. I thought everyone would be in The Caves already."

"They're getting there," Jeeves said. "I'm just tidying up the place. Are you lost?"

"Huh?" Deck asked.

"You're heading toward the back of the house to Master Lamond's suite," Jeeves noted, and Deck was convinced there was an accusatory lilt to his tone.

"I...am?" Deck stammered, and his own fear at having been caught played to his advantage as he followed that with a lie. "I have a horrible sense of direction. You'd think I'd know my way around after being here this long."

"Well, let me show you the right way," Jeeves said. "Maybe you're just too distracted thinking about Maru."

Deck blushed.

"He's delicious..." Jeeves paused. "To look at. You two deserve to be together. Forever."

Jeeves stood on his toes to place a kiss on Deck's bearded cheek.

Deck distinctly heard the inhaling of breath as Jeeves dropped back on his heels, allowing his nose to pass over Deck's jugular.

Goose bumps crawling over his skin, Deck managed to act nonchalant as he and Jeeves parted in the main hall. He even went so far as to not immediately bolt for the front door, but alluded to going to the kitchen to see if Don was around and what kind of sexual uniform he might be wearing to The Caves.

It was once Deck was alone in the kitchen with no other person in sight that he bolted for the back door. Outside, the autumn was definitely taking hold of the thermometer. He shivered as he walked along a well-lit stone path that led through the grass on the side of the house to the parking area. He found his heartbeat slowing upon discovering that the large cement arena was hopping with action. Numerous cars were filling the space, with four or five men climbing out of each one in various states of dress (more like undress), laughing and chatting, flirting with those emerging from other cars, and even swaying to dance beats pumping from the stereos of some of the cars.

If Deck weren't so terrified, he'd be completely turned on by the variety of role-playing on display. Aside from your usual twinks, muscle queens, and bears, there were firemen, wrestlers, army soldiers, football players, male nurses, and even some cops. But two cops in particular stood out as they leaned up against a familiar van. Deck hurried over to them as he received various pinches, spanks, grabs, and attempts at tearing off his shirt by the throngs of men.

"You guys actually showed," Deck said to Solomon and Bembury.

"Hey, we're horny men too, and guys *really* go for *real* cops," Bembury said as a gang of guys walked by, whistling and winking at the burly uniformed men and calling them by name.

Once the group had passed, Solomon leaned in closer and said, "Well, you kinda forgot to invite us officially, but Anderson asked us this morning to come out here tonight to make sure things stay cool. We haven't been able to get in touch with her to make sure that's what she still wants, so we figured we'd go on with the original plan. We'll join the fun in The Caves a little later. We just want to make sure none of those sheeted crazies are hanging around in the shadows once the lot clears out."

Deck realized he needed to be more careful. Quickly looking around the ground, he located two sticks. After glancing to make sure no one was watching, he crossed them and then held them up to Solomon and Bembury.

"What the fuck?" Bembury looked confused.

Deck quickly placed the makeshift crucifix to Bembury's forehead, right below his mahogany curls.

"Dude, have you gone nuts?" Bembury pushed Deck's hand away.

Deck didn't hesitate. He pushed the sticks to Soloman's forehead. The only result was a seriously pissed off expression as one dark eye peered from either side of the main shaft of the cross.

Deck was overcome with a moral dilemma. These two men— every man in this town who wasn't already infected—could be walking into an orgy of the dead right now. But no one would ever believe him if he jumped up on the truck and started to scream "Vampires! Vampires!" How in hell was he supposed to take this on himself, though?

The lot was quickly emptying as men disappeared through hatch trap cellar doors at the side of the house. A car just pulling into the lot cast a beam of headlight over the area. The glare bounced off something sparkling in the window of the cop couple's van. It was the red rosary.

Deck threw the sticks in his hand back to the ground.

"Quick. Get into the van," Deck said, trying to thrust the burly bodies in by pushing on their backs. But Soloman and Bembury didn't budge.

"Hey," Bembury said. "Thanks, but we don't play the nightstick game anymore."

"It's not that," Deck said, looking around nervously as the lot was becoming more and more desolate. "This is important."

Finally, Soloman and Bembury climbed into the open sliding door on the side of the van, Deck right behind them. Once inside, he pulled the door closed and crouched on the floor as the two men took the front seats.

"What's going on?" Soloman asked.

"Which one of you is religious?"

"Huh?" Soloman asked. "What the fuck is this about, Deck? You're acting like you're looking for Dracula or some shit."

"Neither of us is like a fanatic or anything," Bembury piped up, "but, you know, I was raised Catholic and it kind of stuck with me. So, you know, I keep the charms around to ward off evil spirits."

He giggled uncomfortably, as if embarrassed to show any sign of faith.

"Remember the bats?" Deck asked. "The way that one shrieked when it saw that rosary?"

Their heads swiveled slowly to where Deck was pointing, to the beaded ruby chain hanging from their rearview mirror. Just as slowly, their heads swiveled back to stare silently at Deck.

"I know it sounds crazy." Deck put up his hands in a stop motion before they could say anything. "But please, just one of you wear it around your neck—under your shirt though, so no one sees it—while you do your patrolling. And if you have anything else like it in your possession, keep it in reach. In one of your pockets."

"Oh, fuck me," Solomon groaned, wiping sweat from his thick black mustache as he looked out the van windshield and then hunched over. "Get down!"

Soloman pulled Bembury onto the floor between the front seats. Deck crawled up beside them and they all lifted their heads just high enough to see over the dashboard.

Outside, a long black object seemed to materialize from the trees. In actuality, it was a large limousine pulling out from the nearly hidden shortcut that led to Pale Shelter. Its headlights were off.

"Is that?" Bembury whispered.

"It's the BeNellys," Deck said.

They watched as the limo came to a stop only a few yards away. The doors opened, but the tinted windows still didn't allow any view of the occupants. Finally, familiar bulging bodies exited from every door, until ten BeNellys were out, wearing their usual black attire.

"They're the Other Way Triple K," Bembury surmised in a whisper, assuming that was the only reason the men would be sneaking up on The Cave party.

The words were barely out of his mouth when some sort of large cloaked forms appeared seemingly out of nowhere. The BeNelly brothers didn't have time to react. It was as if they were enveloped by the flap-like cloaks and swept away, down the cellar stairwell.

Deck didn't hesitate. He threw his arms around Soloman and Bembury and slapped his hands over their mouths to keep them from crying out in shock.

The parking lot was almost empty again. One man, dressed in leather and chains, stood in the center of the parking lot, looking around, moonlight making his striking pale features glow yellow and his white hair shine like a halo.

It was Lamond. They all swiftly ducked below the dashboard level as he directed his gaze to the van. Deck could feel the sweat bursting from Soloman and Bembury's upper lips into his palms. He used his hands to turn their heads in his direction, then looked up at the red rosary that hung from the rearview mirror on the windshield.

There were two loud bangs outside that made them freeze with their eyes locked on the religious item.

It was nearly a minute of silent staring before Deck whispered, "I think it was the cellar doors closing."

He slowly removed his hands from their mouths.

"We're supposed to serve and protect. We need to look," Soloman said to Bembury.

Bembury just pointed at Soloman. Soloman shook his head in terror and pointed back. Bembury shook his own head in terror.

"On the count of three, we *both* get up and grab for that rosary for dear life," Soloman whispered, pointing to the red protection dangling only a few feet above them.

Bembury nodded and Deck crawled back into the heart of the van to get out of their way. At the same time, Soloman began a finger countdown while mouthing, *one…two…three!*

Bembury popped up and clutched the rosary…alone. Soloman had stayed in his crouched position below dashboard level. He was now grinning guiltily up at Bembury.

"You bitch!" Bembury murmured as he realized he'd been tricked.

Soloman shook his finger in front of his lips to shush Bembury.

"Is he there?" Deck asked urgently.

Bembury quickly crouched back down as he peered out the windshield. The parking lot was empty, the hatch trap doors closed. "He's gone."

"Okay, Deck," Soloman whispered. "You're the monster man. Now what the fuck do we do?"

"I don't know, but I have to get Maru," Deck said. "And Anderson needs to know."

"She's never gonna believe this shit," Soloman said. "And I don't think we should be splitting up."

"Please," Deck said. "There's not a lot of people I care about in life. Go find her."

"She's probably getting screwed senseless by her ghetto boy toy," Bembury said haughtily.

"Come on, guys. You don't have to tell her what's going on. Just keep her safe."

Soloman looked torn. Finally, he said, "Fine. But you better keep in touch with us. You call us as soon as you get to Maru so we know you're both safe."

"You got it," Deck said, ready to sneak out the side door of the van.

"Wait," Soloman said, pulling his keychain out of his pocket and detaching something from it. He handed it to Deck. It was a medallion. "It's blessed. It's from the driving club. My grandmother gave it to me years ago when I first got a car. It's an image of Jesus so he can watch over you when you're driving."

"Thanks," Deck replied, actually feeling relieved having the piece of metal in his hand.

"Do you want us to drive you to your car?" Bembury asked.

"I got my...driving medallion," Deck said uncertainly. "I'll be fine. I'll call you."

Deck slowly opened the sliding door and stepped back out into the night.

❖

Why the fuck did I split up with them? This is the kind of stupid shit they do in horror movies!

Truth was, despite the bloodsuckers that were probably crawling all over the city, all Deck could think about was being alone with Maru. But first, he had to meet up with Zimmerman. He wondered if Zimmerman had figured out what was really going on as well.

He circled around the front of Weeping Manor and made his way to the private carport for guests, which was on the other side in front of the garage. He shivered while his eyes darted to every dark shadow created by all the moon-drenched weeping willows. As he stepped onto the pavement, a motion-activated spotlight at the peak of the carport's roof came on, practically blinding him and totally blowing his cover.

"You're leaving us?" a confident voice emitted from beyond the glare of the light.

"Who's there?" Deck asked, placing a hand in front of his face to cut out some of the glare. He could see it shaking in the halo of light. His other hand slipped into his pocket and wrapped around the driving medallion.

"Oh, sorry," the voice came again as two men emerged from under the light. "Didn't mean to scare you."

It was Proc, sounding incredibly casual and non-threatening. He looked spectacular, in a form-fitting black latex suit that hugged his lean physique and especially accented his impressive bulge, bright silver zippers ready for unzipping in all the right places. One stray lock of his classically debonair dark hair dropped across his forehead, creating an odd complementary contrast with the futuristic cybersex feel of the shiny suit. Clutched in Proc's hand was a metal dog leash, and attached to the other end of it was a large hulking man who was crawling along the pavement, completely naked. It was Wilky.

"Hey, men," Deck said, managing to keep his voice even-toned. "I'm going to pick up my date."

Proc approached, smiling warmly as Wilky crawled obediently beside him. "Maru, I hope."

Deck shrugged sheepishly in response.

"Well, I hope the two of you will be coming back to enjoy this experience together," Proc said.

"Absolutely. I wouldn't miss this for the world."

"Good. Wilky was hoping you'd be here, weren't you, my big chocolate bitch?" Proc tugged roughly on the leash. "He so wants a taste of your ass. As do I."

Wilky ran his tongue up the length of one of Proc's latexed legs.

Without removing his intensely erotic gaze from Deck's face, Proc reached down and back with one hand and slipped his index finger up the deep slot between Wilky's massive black muscular buttocks. Wilky wince-moaned, and Deck realized Proc had swiftly inserted his finger into his anus. Wilky groaned as it was removed.

Proc took the index finger and brought it to Deck's mouth, slipping it between Deck's lips.

"You don't want to miss the taste of that either." Proc winked as he slowly slid his finger over Deck's tongue. "I don't suppose you and Maru would like to stop by Pale Shelter for a cocktail first? We're not drinkers, but we could relax and chat for a while. We're in serious need of a normal couple to hang out with. You know, movie nights, game nights."

Deck stared blankly for a second. What was going on here? Why was this man so filthily forward one moment and now back to being the charming, charismatic guy next door? Was this a trap? For a foursome? Or a man buffet?

"Well, there's just so much happening tonight, we're kind of anxious to get down there," Deck said nonchalantly. "And we're already late."

Proc's cold hand wrapped tightly around Deck's wrist, squeezing it. "Are you sure you don't want to come with us first? This is no place for you and Maru."

Deck instinctively pulled his hand away—hard. Proc let it go, but just as quickly, Wilky reached out one of his hands (which was currently functioning as a paw). But before he could grasp Deck, Proc had blocked the move and wrapped his bright white hand around the dark hand.

"We'll do it another night," Proc instructed Wilky sternly, pushing his hand back to the ground before looking back at Deck. "Now go get your man. We'll see you inside, hopefully with less clothes on."

"Yep," was all Deck could manage as they walked (and crawled) off.

Deck jumped into his car, fired it up, and backed out of the carport.

Blood coursed into his raging hard-on at witnessing the master/servant scenario just now, and in complete contradiction, his heart was nearly stopped from the terror of the confrontation.

❖

Deck was surprised at just how desolate the road was, considering all the cars that had been pouring into Weeping Manor. Still flush from the victory of escaping from the estate without two hole punctures (or more) in his neck, he had the window rolled down to let in the cool night air. That's why he was able to detect the sound of a motor and music coming around the corner.

Unfortunately, the gang of gays in the car—a convertible with the top down, no less—hadn't bothered to turn on their headlights. The car was nearly upon Deck before the bend in the road allowed his headlights to pick it up. He cut his steering wheel hard while slamming on the brakes and slid into a ditch on the shoulder.

"Party's this way, chubby hubby!" a voice from the car yelled over the blaring dance beat as a bunch of guys laughed and hooted, the sound trailing away as the car just kept going.

"It's muscle!" Deck yelled back futilely as his car came to a crunching halt in the ravine. "Dammit!"

Turning on the interior light of his car and leaving on the headlights, Deck threw his door open and climbed out into wet, marshy earth. He circled his car, which was perfectly wedged between inclines on either side of the ravine, the wheels seeming to be sunk into the mud like it was cement. He was only about twenty feet from his destination, the stream that ran through a pipe under the road.

"Fuck me!" Deck exclaimed.

His words had barely echoed through surrounding trees before he heard another motor approaching. At first, it seemed to brake up ahead, but then began moving again, in his direction. He jumped, tripped, and slid up the embankment back to the road, and was bathed in headlights.

He didn't even need to wave the approaching vehicle down. It slowed as it pulled up alongside him. Narrowing his eyelids to see the driver, his mind and heart wondered if he'd just presented himself as dinner for feeding time. There was no telling who was a vampire anymore.

The driver's side windows of the four-door rolled down. There were five young men sitting inside.

"I didn't see any bear crossing signs," a playful voice instantly calmed Deck's nerve, but only slightly.

"Maru," Deck said. "What are you doing here? I told you to stay put!"

"Ooh," the young driver of the car said. "That's one strict daddy you got. Why don't you hop in? We can call Otto to rescue your car with his tow truck."

"No," Deck said quickly. "He's, um, already on his way, and I told him I'd wait here for him."

"Okay," the driver said. "Well, we'll see you there."

"Wait!" Deck said, grabbing the side view mirror before the car could pull away. "Um. Party's overcrowded. They're not letting anyone else in."

The driver of the car looked at his buddies. "Um. Okay. Sure. We'll go back home."

"I'll wait with you," Maru said hurriedly, jumping out of the car. "Thanks for the ride, guys."

Maru waved good-bye to the young men inside, who waved back before pulling away.

"What are they doing?" Deck said. "They're not turning around!"

"Deck," Maru said, sticking his hands into the single front pocket of his hooded sweatshirt. "You've never been to The Caves before. Apparently, anyone who gets an invite gets in. They have ways of making room for you."

"Why did you come here? I told you not to come," Deck said angrily.

"They were heading this way. I finished early. I was worried about you, and I didn't want you to be here alone." Maru looked around. "Wow. It sure is dark out here."

"Maru!" Deck said, grabbing his arm. "Do you understand what I told you? There are *vampires*."

"I know. I know what you said. And you pretty much have me convinced. But I wasn't sure. And, well, it kind of did bother me to think that maybe you wanted to go down there by yourself tonight and just made that up to keep me away. When Lance—"

"Let's get in my car, quick," Deck said before Maru could finish. He pulled him down the incline on the side of the road. As they neared his car, he was surprised when Maru steered himself to the back door.

"What are you doing?" Deck asked as Maru opened the door as much as the inclined barricade would allow and began to climb in.

"You have bucket seats." Maru shrugged. "I want to be close to you while we're waiting for help to arrive."

Deck climbed into the backseat with him, his heart gasping for air. "There isn't any help coming. I made that up. I'm supposed to be meeting Zimmerman, the forensics guy."

Maru's expression sombered in the shadows of the car.

"To talk about the case," Deck said. "But I'm glad I'm not alone."

They stared at each other and smiled. Deck leaned between his seats to punch off his headlights, hoping the darkness would be their cover from any creatures of the night.

"Youch!" He jumped as he felt a firm pinch on his right buttock. He dropped heavily into the backseat.

Maru was grinning. "Sorry. It just looked good enough to eat."

"You bit my butt? I tell you there are vampires running around Kremfort Cove, and you bite my butt?"

Maru giggled, reaching into the collar of his sweatshirt and pulling something out. "Look. It's a crucifix." He yanked his collar down to expose his smooth chest. "See? Not branded. I'm safe."

"Me too." Deck dug the blessed driving medallion out of his pocket.

It slipped from his fingers and dropped to the floor as Maru pounced on him. Maru's lithe body splayed across his torso, firm mouth landing heavily on his lips.

"Deck Waxer, I want to be with you so badly," Maru whispered as he came up for air. "I don't feel alone. For the first time in a long time."

"Oh Jeez, Maru," Deck gasped between returning the face suck. "I don't know what it is. What you do to me. They way you make me feel."

Maru straddled Deck's thighs, grabbing Deck by the beard as they continued to eat face. "I just want you to hold me. To love me."

"We have to...Zimmerman will be waiting at the bridge..." Deck tried to insist, but his hands had plans of their own, already feeling up Maru's round, tight butt.

"We'll only be a few minutes," Maru said, thrusting his tongue deep into Deck's mouth as his hips rotated on Deck's lap, the motion creating a fantastic butt flex in Deck's hands.

"I last more than a few minutes," Deck said during pauses in their tongue dance.

"Good," Maru muttered, pulling away from Deck and smiling. He turned around and flicked his shoes off and onto the floor of the car, then began to work at the buttons at the crotch of his jeans.

"I can't believe this is happening." Deck slipped his hands under Maru's sweatshirt and pulled it up and over his head. "I never thought you'd really want me."

Without getting off Deck's lap, Maru pushed his jeans down and lifted one knee at a time off the car seat to push the jean legs down and off.

"Damn!" Deck gasped, holding on to the naked body straddling him. "You're beautiful."

In the moonlight, he could see the exotic depth of Maru's eyes gleaming in his direction. Maru looked happier and more alive than Deck had ever seen him.

"Aren't you cold?" Deck asked, pulling Maru against him as he leaned up front and turned the ignition to utilities so he could crank the heat. But his finger never made it to the heat button.

"You'll keep me warm," Maru whispered, wrapping his bare arms around Deck's head and pulling him close.

Deck rubbed the thickness of his beard against the hairless flesh of Maru's tight chest. He began kissing it. His tongue worked its way over to one of Maru's pert little nipples. Maru moaned and dropped his head back. Deck could feel the heat from Maru's cock and balls resting against his belly. He reached between their bodies to feel the genitals. Maru was amazingly rigid, his balls taut with minimal peach fuzz. Deck stroked Maru's lengthy shaft, found the head, and discovered a pool of precum streaming from it. He used the emission as a lubricant on his index finger and reached behind Maru to find the incredibly warm spot between Maru's meaty little buns.

"Everything about you feels so hard. So tight and young," Deck whispered around Maru's nipple, his finger circling the tense slit of Maru's anus.

"It's all yours," Maru whispered back, kissing the top of Deck's head.

Deck was crazy with desire at the way that Maru was surrendering himself, giving himself completely, getting off on being completely naked in the cold air on top of a beefy, hairy man body.

"I want to be in here so badly," Deck looked up at him and whispered as his sticky index finger circled the smooth flesh surrounding Maru's anus.

"I need you in there," Maru spoke with his mouth and eyes as he leaned in to kiss Deck's lips again, holding the kiss as he arched his back to open his buttocks more.

Deck tickled Maru's perianal area with the tip of his finger, making him groan and shiver in his arms. He pushed his index finger gently against the taut asshole, feeling it pulse in response, attempting to suck on his finger.

"You're driving me crazy," Maru gasped, his exhalation steaming the car windows.

"Good," Deck said.

They needed no words to change positions. It was almost as if they each knew how they had to proceed. As Deck was shifting his weight to sit sideways on the backseat with his back against the passenger door, Maru swiveled off his lap to straddle him in sixty-nine formation.

A moon in the moonlight, Deck thought as Maru's compact buns were practically shoved in his face. He placed his hands on each cheek and spread the tight crack. He blew a breeze of warm air up the crevasse.

Maru sighed and his upper body went lax as it dropped between Deck's legs, Maru clawing at his jeans.

Deck stretched his neck forward, his tongue out, and licked slowly up the length of Maru's asshole. He was amazingly clean and fresh tasting, lacking the type of musk that could be expected from a hairy man. Deck lapped at the inside of each cheek, his cock pulsing at the way his actions were making Maru quiver and squeeze his calves. Deck reached his hands around and pushed down on the smooth skin over Maru's spine, provoking him to arch his back deeper, which caused the crack to open, bringing the anus to the forefront. Deck hardened his tongue and poked at the center of the slit, firmly spiraling out from the center. The tight anal muscles weakened, pulsing and dancing on his taste buds.

"Please take me," Maru said through short breaths as Deck worked on him. "Everything I have is yours."

Deck's tongue probed and prodded, moistened and saturated. His lips, wet with saliva, sucked in the tight flesh of Maru's buttocks as he nibbled on each one, which seemed to make Maru squirm with delight.

"I need you inside me." Maru offered himself up again, dropping his body onto the backseat of the car with his groin raised.

Deck didn't hesitate. He lifted himself on one knee, the foot of his other leg planted on the floor of the car, his body hunched over to keep his head from hitting the car's ceiling. He quickly unzipped his jeans and dug out his plump, drooling cock. He released a wad of saliva into his mouth and spat it into his hand, which he then used to polish the head and shaft of his hairy cock. He steered his erection down toward the puckering hole waiting for him. Just as his piss slit met the warm, pulsating flesh, Maru looked over his shoulder and into Deck's eyes with complete trust.

"You'll go easy," Maru said, a confident statement of fact.

Deck winked. He hunched his body over Maru's horizontal form to direct his cock into the welcoming hole. Its grip fed on his short shaft as he was engulfed very slowly into a vacuum of warmth, until he felt that wonderful puncturing of the tight ring within. They sighed in unison as Deck draped his heft over Maru's tight frame, covering him.

"You're so fat," Maru wheezed, then quickly followed it with, "Your dick, I mean."

"I know." Deck smiled, familiar with how surprised bottoms were when he stuck his mere five-inch dick in them and they realized that length isn't everything.

"Just stay inside me for a minute." Maru craned his neck to accept a kiss from Deck.

"You're amazing," Deck huffed with intense pleasure. "You feel amazing."

"You feel so right. So perfect," Maru murmured, closing his eyes and allowing his innards to release all tension to accommodate Deck.

Deck smothered Maru's lean, naked body, their mouths locked, tongues sparring moistly. So they were literally tongue-tied in fear when there was a knock on the rear passenger side window of the car. They breathed into each other's mouths, neither of them moving. The steam on the window made it impossible to recognize the face peering in at them.

"Deck, it's Zimmerman," a muffled voice came from the other side.

"Tell him you're kind of in the middle of someone," Maru joked, squeezing his rectal muscles around Deck's dick playfully.

"Stop!" Deck gasped and giggled at the same time. "You're going to make me shoot!"

"Deck! I'm sorry to catch you two…you know…but it's really important," Zimmerman said, his mouth nearly pressed against the outer side of the window.

"Crap," Deck muttered. Without moving, he made sure his entire body was carefully cloaking Maru's nakedness before reaching one hand to the passenger door and pushing the button for the automatic window, which buzzed as it lowered. Zimmerman's face looked pale in the moonlight as he crouched down to peek into the backseat.

"Oh, man. Sorry, guys. You're really deep into it, huh?" Zimmerman asked, sounding like he was blushing, but without his face going red. He also seemed to be talking through sealed lips rather than fully forming the words with them.

"Uhm, you could say that," Maru chirped from underneath Deck.

"Just get in the front seat quick and give us a moment to get dressed," Deck said, hitting the lock button on the door panel. "You don't want to be out there alone."

"Um, you don't want to invite me in," Zimmerman mumbled through tight lips again.

Deck and Maru shivered against each other in terror, their bodies totally synchronized as they tried to crawl backward away from the window while still in fucking stance.

"You're…"

Zimmerman raised one lip slightly as he smiled in what appeared to be sheepish embarrassment, revealing two incredibly long, pearly white incisors. "The fuckers kinda got me just as I was putting it all together."

"Oh shit!" Deck exclaimed, slipping a hand between his and Maru's bodies in an effort to dig into his pocket for his Jesus medallion. But it wasn't there. It was still on the floor where he'd dropped it.

In the meantime, Maru had risen up as much as possible and pulled his own crucifix off his neck, and now thrust it at the window in Zimmerman's direction.

Now Zimmerman just seemed annoyed. Reaching in and taking the crucifix in his hand to demonstrate, he shrugged and said, "It doesn't work for me. I learned that the hard way. Quest got me. I grabbed one of these from the nearest body in the coroner's office to fend him off. I'm most definitely not a Jew for Jesus."

Zimmerman pulled the collar of his shirt aside to reveal two puncture marks.

"I missed it Deck. He had them, too. They were camouflaged by the choke bruises."

"Please," Deck said, pulling Maru even closer to his body and wrapping his arms tighter around Maru's nakedness.

"Sorry!" Zimmerman said, turning away from them. "I'm not looking. I didn't see anything. You guys can get dressed. But hurry up."

"What? What are you talking about?" Deck asked. "I mean, please don't hurt us!"

"Oh!" Zimmerman turned back to them. "No. I'm not going to hurt you. I wanted to warn you—"

Before Zimmerman could finish his sentence, he burst into flames. Deck and Maru finally worked their way out of their compromised position, Deck grabbing Maru by the shoulders and tugging him away from the scalding heat. They watched the flames quickly dissipate as they crammed up against the other side of the car. There was a clink on the floor of the car as the crucifix Zimmerman had been holding fell from midair. It coincidently landed right beside the Jesus medallion Deck had dropped earlier.

And there, behind the spot that had once been taken up by Zimmerman, stood Don, hulking, hairy, and handsome in what appeared to be a black fur coat, but which was mostly just his own body hair and a tiny black G-string. In his hand he was holding a long, pointy piece of carved wood. A stake.

"That fucker was a vampire," Don said, staring through the light cloud of smoke at Deck and Maru.

"No shit," Deck said, feeling his body relax and his grip on Maru's shoulders loosen. "Get in here quick."

"I thought you'd never ask." Don's eyes blazed yellow as he parted his lips to reveal pointed fangs. He yanked the door open, grabbing a hold of Maru's ankles just as Maru was leaning down to grab his pants off the floor.

"NOOOOoooo!" Deck screamed, lunging to grab Maru.

Maru also screamed as Don tugged him out of the car and onto the wet inclined earth. At the same time, the window behind Deck shattered and cold, pale arms reached in and grabbed him. His large body was pulled easily out the window. Before he could fight back or get his footing on the angled ground after his legs dropped, he was sent reeling forward with great force, his head smashing into the side of his car.

Everything went black.

Chapter Fifteen

It was as if Deck was in the Haunted Mansion ride at Disney. He was seated in a chair that was spinning back and forth 180-degrees as it moved steadily and slowly in one direction, giving him glimpses of alcoves that lined each side of The Caves. Before he could focus on the show he was getting, he looked down at his body. He was completely naked and bound to the chair, thick rope wound around his legs, snuggled into the clefts of his crotch, crossing over his chest multiple times, perfectly framing his giant nipples, and even digging into his neck, nearly choking him. His wrists were tied to the back of the chair and there was a ball gag filling his mouth, the leather straps secured tightly around his head.

Deck's cloudy vision began to sharpen slightly, a not so easy situation in the darkness. He first noticed how eerily like his dream The Caves were, but he also sensed that the rock-like tunnel wasn't actually rock at all, but a simple designer façade to give it that look. There was nothing basement-ish about it. It wasn't cold or damp or musty. Actually, it was hot, humid, and musky, like the back room at one of the many clubs he used to frequent when he was younger.

This was definitely a dick den. The scents were clawing—sweat, armpits, crotches, cum. It was that big conglomerate pheromone that provokes gay men into mob mentality.

Deck took in the man-sized, living dioramas as they spun slowly past his vision to give him an almost thirst-quenching taste of a diversity of fetishistic sex and scenarios: bondage, S&M, gang bangs, orgies, water sports, spanking, locker room, doctor's office, alleyway, bathroom stall, auto shop (with an actual car on a lift!), mud pit, leather, latex, rubber. The men were flawless, making it clear that this was definitely a VIP invite situation. The sex-crazed specimens, no matter how tame or extreme their situation, seemed oblivious to the bound spectator whirling down the center hall of the tunnel which echoed with grunts, groans, gasps, growls, commands, whimpers, and pleas for more (or less, for those who got off on lying). Much to his dismay, Deck noted familiar faces in certain scenarios: Phillip in a colonic chamber, filling up a line of men in the doggy position; Healy the foot reflexologist bouncing up and down on the extremely large foot of a man who had jammed his toed appendage up Healy's ass; Samson the hairstylist actually whipping his head in circles as he wound up to flog a chained man's back with his long locks. Each of the familiar faces didn't even break their fetishistic character as they flashed their fangs as if taunting Deck.

These flashes of white triggered Deck's senses enough to help him remember where he'd been last. His entire body convulsed with fear.

Maru. Deck futilely struggled, sweat bursting from his every pore.

His heart nearly shattered when his ears were assaulted by a harsh whoosh of air as whatever mechanics were moving his chair came to a skidding halt in front of a dark wall at the end of the tunnel. Deck stared in confusion at the blackness in front of him. He felt a change in air pressure as coolness swept in from his right. He turned to see a doorway had opened to another hall, into which he was soon being ushered. The new area was white, sterile, and quite bright. Deck had to squint to cut the glare.

"I hope you're not too uncomfortable," an incredibly sincere and calm voice seemed to come from all around Deck. "You've been a good friend to me, and I'm hoping we can come to some agreement on how to proceed."

Deck realized it was Hayes Lamond. What the fuck was going on? Where was Lamond? What was he planning to do? Had he done anything to Maru? *Damn this ball gag!*

"I know you must have dozens of questions for me," Lamond continued as Deck's chair once again stopped, this time in front of a blank white wall. "You have to understand that I've always made the welfare of this city and its population my top priority. And I still do. Things just haven't gone as planned. So many outside groups with their own agendas have tried to destroy all that a few of us have been building up. Including these two special interest groups."

Like a garage door, the white wall in front of Deck raised, revealing a large room behind. The stark white interior contrasted fiercely with the dozen or so naked black bodies inside.

Chained to the floor on all fours was a row of hunky and hung black men Deck recognized as the BeNelly brothers. Most of the muscle-bulging BeNellys were struggling with the heavy metal links that secured their ankles and wrists to the floor. Their chiseled faces showed expressions that ranged from angry to scared to confused as they glared at the wall that had disappeared in front of them, revealing Deck's bound body on the chair.

Deck's only recourse was to watch the proceedings. His eyes widened in shock at what was materializing—literally—before his eyes, and his expression was infectious, because the BeNelly brothers began to struggle even more violently, fearing what they couldn't see that Deck could.

A wall of naked black men seemed to rise up from the floor behind the doggy style BeNelly brothers until they were towering behind them, engorged cocks of different sizes, lengths, and thicknesses jutting out in front of them. These men weren't nearly as polished as the BeNellys, and Deck's mind compartmentalized them as "ghetto" compared to the stunningly packaged and marketed BeNellys. Everything about the men who seemed to be floating behind the BeNellys rather than standing behind them screamed anger, violence…and lust. They were already penetrating the BeNellys with their eyes, and that look went beyond a sexual desire. They looked hungry. Deck knew what to expect before the men even opened their lips to reveal their fangs.

"These are the men who have been terrorizing our city," Lamond's voice returned. "The Other Way Triple K, as they've become known by all our beautiful citizens. The ones who attacked you in your car before others like me came and rescued you. Theirs is a black empowerment movement—an extremely poorly organized mess of one, but one nonetheless. Their goal was not to steal this city away from its white citizens though. It ran deeper than that. They wanted to stop the upscaling of the community and the infiltration of gays— even black gays. Their true purpose wasn't a racial divide; it was homophobia. They felt that our people threatened their territory, the very territory we've been working to improve for all. But they didn't see it that way—and neither did your long-time hag, Commissioner Anderson."

Deck shook his head in denial. She would never have…

"Oh, yes. Corruption in our very police department. The woman we thought was on our side, trying to protect us, was instead working to stop our growth to benefit her own. Because you see, Deck, no matter how 'inclusive' any of us believes himself to be, as a result of the inherent instinct for survival in this 'humane' jungle, we all share a deep self-importance when it comes to the trait that makes us slightly different from everyone else. It was Yvette Anderson who sent these goons after our people."

A spotlight shined on a vampire standing in the center of the Other Way Triple K: a towering, distinguished looking vampire with a bulky body covered in salt and pepper fuzz.

"She's got taste. He's the best looking one of the bunch. We had him take care of her so we didn't have to dabble in female flesh. He *really* ate her out good. And then we have the BeNelly brothers, who were driven by their own power—black gay financial power. Their foolery was a mere acting out of fetishism. They didn't mean to bring down our community, merely to be the masters of it. But this community only has room for one master. Men, feast."

Lamond's words were a command to the vampires behind the glass, who were clearly now under his control. Deck watched as they levitated in the air, then gracefully swooped down on the BeNellys. Cocks were thrust deep into unprepared holes, BeNelly eyes bulged, bodies draped over backs, fangs sank into the napes of necks. There was no room for struggling as the BeNellys were used to satisfy sexual and culinary appetites at the same time. The parasites seemed to drain the BeNellys of their lifelines. Chained bodies began to collapse to the floor. Teeth gnashed, blood spilled and was then lapped off skin that stretched taut over thick muscle. The vampires thrashed in ecstasy as the liquid flowing into their mouths coursed through them, refueling the lust at their crotches, causing liquid to flow below.

"That's right, men. Enjoy your last supper," Lamond cooed.

The heads of the attackers lifted in the air, drool and blood dripping down chins as crazed yellow eyes blazed with paranoia.

It happened so fast the vampires didn't have time to react. Several attempted to shrink back down into bats to escape the crudely constructed grid of wooden spikes that suddenly fell from the ceiling, but it was too late. They were all pierced numerous times as the ancient looking contraption, apparently, a makeshift design and recent addition to the room, pinned them to the floor with the dead BeNelly bodies beneath them. Deck had to squint to protect his eyes from the bright blaze of the mass combustion. Seeing the gruesome results happen before his eyes, he felt the pain for all those men he'd met in Kremfort Cove who'd had to witness their loved ones disintegrate before their eyes. His eyes welled up with sadness. And then he thought of Lamond and the death of his own partner, Ben DuPont. Had Lamond been faking all his pain and devastation? Or had they both been vampires, DuPont accidentally thrust into daylight by Jeeves? No, that couldn't be it, because Lamond had been exposed to daylight—at least for the first few days Deck was staying at the house.

"Imagine our beautiful men having to experience that in this city," Lamond said resentfully as he pointed to the fiery massacre. "Having gone through it myself, I want to save others from it. The men I care about, love. I needed us to all be on the same page once again. Part of the same family. The same clan. And once you've gone Drac, you never go back."

Lamond giggled in his best Transylvanian accent.

"Sorry. A little vamp camp." Lamond laughed again. "I just want you to know, Deck, it's not the way I would have planned it. It just happened. It was beyond my control. And we need you. We need you on our side."

The room in front of Deck grew black, the wall came back down, and his chair moved on again.

❖

Deck's chair was steered through another doorway and halted in the middle of a dimly lit, small and empty room. He would never have imagined the complexities of The Caves that had been so hyped for so long.

There was another whoosh off to the side. A wall retracted into itself to reveal an opening. Seeming to materialize from the darkness beyond the portal, Lamond stepped forward.

Deck felt so naked. Not because he was naked, but because he was completely bound, unable to move, with no religious artifacts to fight the forces that clogged the veins of this labyrinth.

Lamond's face was stony, his features more chiseled than ever. The pale white of his skin and body hair drastically contrasted with the black of his leather attire—black chaps with nothing underneath them, the traditional spiked straps around his beautifully developed biceps, a black leather master's cap pulled down low, casting a shadow over his eyes and hiding most of his thick white hair. Just like everyone else in this underground hell, his cock was swollen, bursting in a bright pink from his perfectly manscaped pubic bush. The tone of his penis contrasted drastically with the rest of his ghostly flesh, as if all the stolen blood running through his system had coagulated in that spot to keep it in a rigid state.

Deck was mesmerized by his towering presence. Lamond moved up behind him and placed a cold hand gently on his shoulder. On Deck's other shoulder was the tickling sensation of Lamond's white pubic hairs and scrotum as the pink cock jutted over Deck's collarbone. Feeling somehow inebriated, Deck turned his gaze to it, taking in every ridge and ripple of the shaft, the smooth shine of the head. Urges built in him. He wanted it. Why did he want it?

"That's right," Lamond spoke softly, massaging one shoulder with his hand. "Just let your soul relax and go with the flow. What you're feeling is part of the incredible power the alternative life holds. It's like some sort of mass hypnosis. The more of us that are concentrated into one area, the more it grows and leaks out to those around us. It's infectious. Eventually, all the men in Kremfort Cove will fall under its spell. It's really the answer to all my worries about making us a strong community. And that's why I'm counting on you to join us."

Deck groggily shook his head.

"Yes, Deck. Yes. I care about you, and I want you to come comfortably, so I'm easing you into this, but you will come. You're already on your way. You've become so dedicated to all of us so quickly. You've shared with us, exchanged fluids with us."

Deck shook his head harder.

"Oh, but you have. You haven't even realized it. That's how painless—and actually, quite pleasurable—it can be. You've participated in practices you wouldn't outside of this domain. You've not used anything. Think back, Deck. Every man you've been with, including me. There was no barrier. In fact, it didn't even enter your mind. The fears—of danger, sickness, death even—they never surfaced. That's the way it always is, for all of us. We sense those infections, and we avoid them. So you were safe from them all along. Instinctively. We are all clean. You have the power in you now, growing in you, waiting to be fertilized. It's why you've become nocturnal. Sleeping more during the day, barely able to stay awake. Alive at night, prowling for flesh. For love. I want this to be a passionate experience for you. Both of you. But one of you has to go first. At the hand of another. He made the decision. For love."

Deck glared up into Lamond's yellowed eyes as they peered down on him, emotionless. Lamond's strong, cleft jaw gestured forward. Deck turned to face the wall, which disappeared into itself just like the one from which Lamond had emerged.

Deck became dizzy with grief as the lights came up on the other side of the glass wall that was revealed. The bonds were so tight it was useless to fight them. He tried to will his soul out of his body and through the glass. His vision blurred with tears that streamed down his face, pooling in his beard.

"He offered himself for you, Deck. He doesn't want you to go through it like that. And he sees there are options after death. He wants to go first, and then bring you in himself."

Maru's face was barren of any expression. His lips didn't quiver as they clung to his gag. His eyes didn't flinch, didn't even blink. He stared straight at Deck as if telling him that this was simply how it was going to be. His wrists and ankles did not fight with the chains that held him to the floor. Deck could see the smoothness of his lean back, the curves of his derriere as it pointed into the air behind him.

"He's beautiful," Lamond said, stroking Deck's hair. "A master-piece of nature. The perfect marriage of Caucasian and Asian."

The swarm took shape behind Maru. Deck fought not to reveal his horror on his face. There was absolutely no getting out of this. And he didn't want his terror to transfer to Maru. He internalized it, feeling it nearly bring his every organ to a grinding halt.

"It's going to be tough to watch, but believe me, these preliminary doses make you so much more receptive to the final bite. It doesn't hurt at all this way. And I will do the honors, because I'm your dear friend, and would not sacrifice him to just anyone. I will take wonderful care of him."

As much as Lamond seemed to be promising to go easy on Deck and have his best interests (and feelings) at heart, just how much of a heart was it, considering it no longer needed to pump recycled blood through it continuously to keep the man's soul alive? There seemed to be no compassion behind the selection of man-monsters that were in the room with Maru—all handsome, physically fit, mature men around Deck's age who were about to use Maru as their play toy in a hellish gang bang. The abnormal circumstances aside, Deck was racked with jealousy.

The first man-monster swooped down on Maru, and from the swelling of Maru's otherwise unflinching eyes, it was clear he had been pierced. The man-monster masterfully pumped in and out of him as the other dozen or so around him stood and watched hungrily, waiting for their shots while being visually fluffed by the act taking place before them. Some of them were even relying on the mortal practice of stroking their cocks in preparation for what was to come.

The first man-monster completed his task and swiftly removed himself so the next one in line could mount Maru.

"Look! LOOK!" Lamond said excitedly, moving closer to the glass wall and pointing. "See, on Maru's forehead? Those are beads of sweat. Of *fear*. You do know what that means, right?"

Deck, feeling woozy, wishing that this were a dream, just stared numbly at Lamond, waiting for him to answer his own question.

"It means you've gotten into this young boy's soul. Made him want to live again. He's afraid. Afraid of pain. Of death. None of that mattered to him before you came around. He was embracing it. But now he believes he has reason to live. But this conflict of emotion will soon revert back. He'll once again no longer fear death. Because death *will* be life. Eternal life. With you."

The second man-monster had finished his business, already replaced by the third, a bearded, ponytailed sex pig of a man who looked directly at Deck, his sparkling blue eyes turning yellow as he forcefully humped Maru like an animal, grabbing Maru's hair and yanking his head back, then licking the beads of sweat off Maru's forehead.

Deck was in agony. The depth of the humiliation he felt for both himself and Maru was beyond anything he'd ever imagined. He watched one man-monster after another use Maru's precious body for pleasure. Some took their time, went slow, a couple were vicious and violent, a few simply responded as if through uncontrolled instinct, like a dog humping the leg of a chair. One of the last reveled in doing Maru in standard on-the-knees doggy style without the help of any vampiric levitation abilities, grabbing his lean hips to grind deeply into him, and quite frequently landing openhanded smacks on Maru's tender ass cheeks, leaving bright red marks on the pale white skin.

It was as this slaphappy man-monster was inflicting damage that Lamond made his exit with a short, "It's almost my turn."

Deck watched him shrink until he was a small bat like the one Deck had killed on the balcony. Leather and metal dropped to the floor behind Deck. The bat disappeared into a vent in the ceiling. Seconds later, Lamond, naked, materialized in full human size as he dropped from a vent in the ceiling on the other side of the glass window. The simultaneous movement and metamorphosis made it look as if Lamond was actually oozing out of the vent like sand in an hourglass.

All the other vampires in the room stepped back slowly until they were pinned to the walls of the room, some of their hairy butts causing cracks in the glass wall through which Deck was watching as they pressed up against it, making room for Lamond to approach Maru.

Deck felt the slow-motion itch of a tear pooling over his lower eyelashes and down his cheeks. This was it. It was over...or had just begun if he wanted to look at it from a vampire's perspective, which he would soon be doing. He felt his world going black. Way too black.

And then he realized the lights had gone out on his side of the glass.

❖

The only light now was from the room on the other side of the glass wall. Was this part of Lamond's sick game to create drama and theatrics?

But no. Lamond looked confused. Lamond was no longer focusing on Maru. Lamond was peering with angry yellow eyes into the glass, into the darkness, past Deck.

And then Deck heard it—the 5.1 surround sound effect of hectic shuffling all around him. There was someone—or something—or a lot of somethings—in here with him. The hands—warm hands—that began to lay themselves all over him were proof positive if the sounds weren't. Out of the darkness, he saw a giant shape jettison at the glass wall. He expected it to bounce off the glass, but apparently Lamond, as rich as he was, hadn't shelled out the extra cash for shatterproof, mortal-proof vampire protectant glass. The giant shape smashed through the transparent divider, which exploded into the other room. The glass crasher hit the ground and curled up to avoid the rain of shards.

Without hesitation, what looked like a small army of men leapt into the other room, swinging their arms as vampires tried to shrink into bats to escape the attack. Most of the night creatures didn't make it, instead bursting into flames while in half-vamp/half-bat form as the rescue party pierced them with a variety of pointed objects. Lamond, completely defiant and fearless despite the onslaught, lunged for Maru's neck.

As Deck sensed his tight binds being sawed off him, he strained desperately against them in an effort to break them so he could save Maru.

It was as if Deck was having a vision—a holy vision. It was almost cartoonish in its ridiculousness. A priest in full black robe and white collar garb soared through the open space that was once the glass wall and slammed a sparkling silver crucifix about six inches long into the gaping open mouth of Lamond just as he was about to attach himself to Maru's neck.

There was an earsplitting screech as Lamond was thrown back, his naked body slamming up against the wall behind him, his arms spread at his sides as if it were Lamond who had been crucified. He stared right at Deck as his eyes turned a brilliant red.

And then he burst into flame, disintegrating within seconds.

"What-the-fu—" Deck stammered as the ropes finally untangled themselves from his body and fell to his feet.

Hands on either side of him helped him stand. They were much needed hands, because his legs were asleep, tingling as the blood returned to them. Warm, human blood. He felt so alive. Just that thought gave him the strength he needed to shake off the arms and tumble across the room and through the opening in the wall. He crashed into the priest as his legs gave out, and he clawed at the man's robes as he came crumbling to the floor, right in front of Maru. He kissed Maru's face while tugging at his chains furiously. "Get these fucking chains off him!"

The glass crasher was Milkman Stan. He moved in with heavy-duty clippers and easily snipped the chains that held Maru. Maru yanked the gag from his mouth and crawled into Deck's arms, sweat sealing their naked flesh together as they sank into each other from tongue to toe.

"Even with vampires taking over, this is a beautiful sight," Milkman Stan said.

"That's because it's love. And that's what life is all about," a deep voice responded. It was Soloman, who pulled Bembury close.

Other men appeared behind them as someone turned the light back on in the room where Deck had been tied to the chair, revealing a small army in black, covered in numerous tools, weapons, and religious items that were stuffed in gym bags and knapsacks or simply strapped to their bodies. Among the faces, Deck recognized Maru's bosses Harry and Jimmy from the club, the hot black bartender Lox from Dirty Harry's, the living Glouster twin, and bear daddy and auto mechanic Otto and his bearded partner, EMT Teddy.

"Is everyone okay? Anyone need medical attention?" Teddy asked.

"Everyone seems in one piece." The priest stepped forward, leaning down to retrieve the crucifix that had been in Lamond's mouth and was now sitting on a pile of ash. "Anyone bitten?"

The priest wasn't exactly expecting honesty, so he held the crucifix up in front of him as he slowly waved it past all the men in the group, including Maru and Deck. They stared up at him like he was crazy.

The priest, an attractive man with shaggy blond-gray hair shrugged in apology. "Sorry. This whole concept is really new to me."

"This is Father Merrin. He's just starting to establish a gay-friendly church here in town. We figured we could use him," Bembury explained quickly.

"Thanks. All of you," Deck said to the locals gathered around him.

Milkman Stan reached out his hands for Deck and Maru and helped lift them off the floor. "Well, we gotta get the fuck out of here now." Stan grimaced. "Sorry for the language, Father."

"I just killed a vampire. The F-bomb is the least of my worries," Father Merrin said. "Now let's get the *fuck* out of here."

Solomon and Bembury quickly draped several religious artifacts around Deck and Maru's necks. "Sorry, we didn't think to bring any clothes for you. We weren't even sure we would, um, find you. But we did raid the church, the police station, Quest's old psychic shop, a couple of antique stores, a hardware store, and a sports shop for everything we thought would be useful."

Maru and Deck took the stakes that were handed to them, crafted hastily from nightsticks that had merely been split in half to create sharp edges. With Father Merrin in the lead, the group retraced their steps, going back through the wall portal in the room in which Deck had been held captive.

Deck's heart was beating overtime as they followed a bland, quiet hall to a stairway. The large group mounted it, heading for a door at the top. God only knew what waited beyond that door.

At the stop of the steps, Soloman and Bembury tapped Father Merrin on the shoulder.

"Let us go first," Soloman said, holding up his rosary.

Father Merrin moved aside so they could get up front. Soloman grabbed the handle of the door and slowly opened it a crack. The hinge squeaked and might as well have shouted their names. Soloman froze and grimaced.

"We gotta do it," Bembury whispered.

"Okay. Same time. Count of three," Soloman suggested, glancing at the low light beyond the gap of the interior door.

"Yeah *right!*" Bembury shot him an unforgiving look.

"I promise this time," Soloman said. "I love you."

Soloman reached out and gave Bembury's arm a reassuring squeeze.

"Okay. Love you, too," Bembury said.

Soloman reached for the doorknob of the interior door and counted. "One...two..."

Bembury quickly thrust Soloman against the door, which flew open with a bang and sent Soloman stumbling forward.

"You asshole!" Soloman barked.

"It's clear," Bembury said, turning to the others as they waited on the stairs.

"Lucky for me! I could have been a dark meat dinner!" Soloman grumbled as he picked himself up off the floor.

"You had the rosary!" Bembury argued.

"Guys!" Deck said, moving up behind them. "Flight now. Fight later."

They were in a large room of the mansion that Deck didn't recognize. It appeared to be a stock room, but it looked more like a grocery store, based on the contents lining the shelves. There were toiletries, cleaning products, and food items enough to keep the mansion running for months.

"I'd suggest everyone keep an eye on any heat or air-conditioning ducts," Harry said from the middle of the group. He clutched a crucifix in one hand and clung tightly to Jimmy's hand with the other. "Those things can clearly get around that way."

Maru was clutching Deck's arm. He leaned in and whispered into Deck's ear, "I'm terrified."

Deck threw him a look that said the feeling was mutual. But Maru's fear seemed to heighten as his eyes widened. He was staring down the grocery aisle they were passing.

Deck looked, but saw nothing. "What is it?"

Maru shook his head. "I thought I saw Lamond. Then he just disappeared."

Deck squeezed Maru's hand reassuringly. "You're just scared. He's dead."

They wound through the storage shelves, finally exiting into a laundry room. This led directly into the kitchen: a very dark kitchen with only the light of the moon streaming through the picture windows.

"This is too easy," Bembury muttered.

"No, it's not," a young and mischievous voice said from above.

All heads shot up to take in the naked body of Jeeves, moonlight bouncing off his bald head. He was literally hanging from the industrial kitchen lights like a bat, his hands and feet currently morphed into talons, his balls tight against his body, and his erection pointing down at the huddled group. No one knew how to react as he revealed his fangs. His yellow eyes gleamed emotionlessly. He was too high up for even Stan's towering presence to reach, so they didn't have any way of attacking him with their weapons. Or so they thought.

Suddenly, Soloman pushed through the crowd and aimed something at Jeeves with both hands. "Bitch! Your Master is dead."

Jeeves's ghastly smile faltered.

"That's right, mofo! I'm your master now!" Soloman said.

"That's some blaxploitation talk right there," Lox muttered as Jeeves hissed in fury and Soloman squeezed the item in his hands, sending a stream of water shooting up at the ceiling. Soloman completely drained the water from the spout of the large bulb, narrowly missing Jeeves.

"Get him!" Father Merrin ordered, and a bunch of like-spouted bulbs were aimed at the ceiling.

Jeeves melted into bat form and flew for his living dead life, pinging spastically against numerous pots and pans that dangled from a rack over the kitchen's main island.

Holy water rained down on the group, and finally there was a horrific squeal as water made contact with the furry flying creature, which came spinning down toward the floor. The group scrambled frantically out of the way, creating a circle for the bat to land in. It slapped onto the floor, one of its wings completely singed off.

The bat's head transformed into a miniature version of Jeeves's beautiful, youthful face. Before he could cry, "Help me! Help me!" like something out of the movie *The Fly*, Otto jumped into the circle and brought a stake forcefully down into the little chest as if he were Vincent Price wielding a rock. The bat burst into flame and Otto quickly withdrew his hand.

They stared in silence at the absurdity of vampire bats and stakes being real.

Finally, Maru said, "Did you guys just kill a vampire with holy water ass douches?"

"Hey. You work with what you got." Otto shrugged, rubbing sweat from his bald head with the back of his hand. "And Kremfort Cove is loaded with anal douches."

"If all that fictional shit about vampires is true, then Lamond may not have been the head vampire," Deck pointed out.

"Aren't all the other vampires supposed to turn normal again or turn to dust or something if the king is killed?" Milkman Stan asked.

"I really think we should talk about this later," the Glouster twin spoke up, his fear seeming to bring out the heft of his previously limited accent. "We need to get out of here, now."

The others looked through the wide arch that led out of the kitchen and into an enormous dining room. On the other side of the grandiose table (as long and decorative as one you might see in a Transylvania castle in the movies) was another major arched doorway into the main foyer of the mansion. The entranceway's giant front window was allowing in plenty of moonlight to reveal running forms gathering in there and racing toward the kitchen.

"Everyone out. NOW!" Father Merrin said, pushing the gang out the back door of the kitchen and into the night.

CHAPTER SIXTEEN

Deck practically felt the approaching threat breathing down his neck—more like biting down it—as the group crammed through the doorway to get out of the mansion.

Milkman Stan stood to the side of the threshold outside and thrust men out of the house with one giant hand as he removed a backpack from his shoulders and let it drop to the ground with a thud. He quickly bent and pulled a large jug out of the backpack. He unscrewed the top hurriedly.

"Let's go! They're coming!" Soloman yelled.

Stan took the jug and dumped it over his head, moving it around so the rush of water drenched every inch of his gigantic body. He muttered, "This better work."

The other men, already near the edge of the woods about forty feet away, turned and stood with weapons raised, from crucifixes and garlic rings to crossbows and (holy) water guns. No one seemed to have the courage to run back across the lawn to help Stan as about a half a dozen shadows rushed the doorway, framed by its large molding.

"Close the door!" Maru yelled, stepping forward as if to run and help Stan.

Deck tried to grab his hand to hold him back, but was not fast enough. As Maru bolted across the lawn, his lean, naked body glistening in the moonlight, Deck and then some of the others chased after him. At the same time, they all witnessed the horror as Milkman Stan was thrown to the ground with a huge thud after creatures in half-man/half-bat form flew against his body and knocked him over with violent force.

One creature shot up in the air and off Stan with a bloodcurdling shriek, landing with a thud on the grass. This was quickly followed by another, then another, squeals of agony swirling on the tunnel of wind caught between the line of trees and the large walls of the mansion.

"Get them!" Father Merrin cried as the bodies rained down.

Men rushed to the crumpled forms sprinkled over the lawn and stakes were raised high before coming down with great power into hideously deformed specimens that had gotten caught between the bony, hairiness of bats and the defined musculature of men.

Otto handed several stakes to Maru and Deck, who ran over to the closest monster. Deck brought his stake overhead and was ready to thrust it down into the monster's chest when his eyes caught sight of the face of the creature, in agony, large chunks of its body and wings burnt to a crisp.

"Deck, please don't," begged the face, human but with pointed bat ears, a pug nose, and flaring nostrils. Beady human eyes, yellow in the iris, stared blankly at Deck.

"Oh my…it's Lamond's foot specialist," Deck muttered, frozen in place. The thin lips of Garth Healy, the pedicurist, split open to reveal animal-like teeth.

And then the body burst into flame, causing Deck to leap back to avoid the excessive heat. Maru sprawled onto the lawn beside him, having thrust the stake into the creature's heart since Deck had been immobilized.

Deck stared around at the carnage, at the couple of creatures still trying to assault Milkman Stan as he rolled around the lawn as if he were on fire. Lips pulled back, sharp teeth ready to pierce his flab anywhere accessible. Deck recognized the faces—Phillip the colonic therapist, Samson the hair man, and none other than Don the chef.

There was a visible and audible spark and sizzle as the teeth came within millimeters of Stan's flesh before the monsters leapt back like the Wicked Witch of the West after trying to grab the ruby slippers.

Harry and Jimmy were on it, running up behind the creatures and ramming large stakes into their backs and out the other side. More bursts of flame followed.

"Come on. We have to go." Maru had already sprung back onto his feet and was tugging at Deck's arm.

"They're taking all of us," Deck murmured, dazed with the reality of each of the men he'd shared so much time with in the past few days now being not only vampires, but dead vampires.

"There will be more coming," the Glouster twin said as he ran over to Deck and grabbed his other arm. Together, he and Maru brought Deck to his feet.

"Let's get out of here." Milkman Stan began to lead the charge again.

"Are you bit?" Father Merrin asked directly, stopping him.

Stan stretched his arms out wide to expose as much of his body to the moonlight as possible. "Not at all. Worked like a charm."

"Why don't we all cover ourselves in the holy water?" Teddy suggested.

"Don't think we have enough on us to cover everyone," Otto said.

"We gotta go. Now!" Soloman interrupted.

"Fuck me!" Lox exclaimed next to him, a crossbow cradled in his lean and muscular arms. "So what are the first victim rules when there are *two* black dudes?"

"We cancel each other out and *both* survive," Soloman spoke defiantly.

The fluttering sound was growing, moving closer. Everyone looked up in the sky, weapons raised. No one expected the great cloud to come swirling like a black tornado from a pipe somewhere near the foundation of the mansion.

"RUN!" Bembury cried, grabbing Soloman's hand and dragging him in the direction of the woods.

They all began to run without hesitation as a dark, flapping mass rose up and eclipsed the moon above.

Ignoring the incessant stabs at his soles, Deck pounded the ground in his bare feet as he and Maru disappeared into the thicket of the woods—and nearly crashed into three dark shapes just ahead of them. Maru cried out in fear.

"Keep running!" came Bembury's voice.

Deck and Maru followed Soloman and Bembury and one other man in front of them. Ominous noises came from all around, shadows danced in the beams of the moon that cut through the thinning late summer trees. There was a bloodcurdling shriek—or more likely, a blood-*sucking* shriek—that seemed to come from off to the left and almost stopped them in their tracks. It could only mean one thing. At least one of their crew hadn't made it—made it to *where* being another concern for all.

Soloman turned to the others as they all slowed to a stop, breathing heavy, but trying to keep the huffing to a minimum. "Let's proceed with caution so we don't run full speed into a bunch of those things. And have your weapons at the ready."

Everyone held up various religious artifacts, stakes, and artillery.

"Okay. Let's go," Deck said, grabbing Maru's hand.

"But where are we going to go?" Maru asked.

"If we can loop back around to Weeping Manor, we can get back to our van," Soloman whispered. "I mean, since all those vamps are out here looking for us, there probably aren't any back there."

"Okay, but which way is back?" Lox spoke up.

"Damned if I know," Soloman admitted, just his white eyes and teeth revealed in the dark as the shade of his skin blended with the absence of light in the forest.

They began walking mutely. Deck hoped they were headed in the right direction. The woods had become very silent. No flapping of bat wings, no screaming of victims. It was rather unnerving. Only the cover of the trees added some sort of feeling of comfort.

"There!" Deck barely whispered the word, pointing. They quickly crouched behind the nearest thick conglomeration of vegetation.

"What is it?" Maru whispered as they all watched a large silhouette passing through the woods on higher ground, outlined by the moonlight. "Are there bears around here?"

"Yeah, but not the kind you're thinking," Soloman responded, his voice almost sounding at ease. He proceeded to do a very genuine sounding impersonation of some sort of night bird.

The "bear" looked in their direction, apparently spotting them as Soloman dared to step out from behind the bushes.

"Are you crazy?" Maru gasped.

Bembury also stepped out as the birdcall was repeated. "It's okay. It's Milkman Stan. We set up a little signal in case we got split up."

Maru and Deck joined them. Stan was picking up speed as he hurried down the noticeably steep ground in front of them.

"Oh shit!" they all heard Stan cry as his massive weight attempted to resist gravity.

"Take cover!" Soloman tried to warn them, but it was too late.

Stan's legs got jumbled together and it was like watching a building being demolished. Stan crumbled to the ground while still moving forward. He landed in a layer of leaves and began rolling so fast no one had time to jump out of the way. Bodies went sailing into the air as Stan took them down like a bunch of bowling pins. The crash stopped his momentum, and just as he was coming to a halt on his back, five bodies showered down on him.

"OOF!" he gasped as he was smothered in men, two naked, three not.

They all tried desperately to right themselves.

"Under normal circumstances, I'd have a hard-on already," Stan mumbled from between Deck's furry ass cheeks.

"Sorry!" Deck said as he rolled off Stan's face.

"Anytime," Stan replied quickly as he tried to help the others off his body.

Once they were all standing, they struggled to help him onto his feet.

"Have you seen the others?" Maru asked, concerned and scared.

"They got him…" Stan choked. "The Glouster twin. I don't even know what the fuck his first name was. I never could tell them apart."

Tears glistened on Stan's big cheeks in the moonlight.

"And the others?" Deck asked.

"Don't know. They may still be out here." Stan gulped. "But we gotta get the fuck out."

"And go where?" Soloman exclaimed, seemingly desperate and disillusioned.

"Come with me," a gentle voice spoke from the dark behind the nearby bushes, causing the entire group to let out a chorus of gasps and cries of fear.

Out stepped the deep black body of Wilky, still wearing only the dog collar he had been leashed to when Deck had run into him and Proc in the driveway of Weeping Manor earlier.

"Stay the fuck back!" Deck demanded, holding up his crucifix.

Wilky immediately hissed, showing his fangs, his eyes flaring yellow at the sight of the horrific vision. "Don't be a fool!" he spat. "I'm not one of them."

"This ain't no Buffy and Angel good vampire bullshit," Soloman said. "We don't trust any of you fuckers."

"I ain't no angel," Wilky admitted. "Never was, not even before this. But I'm still looking for peace, and so is Proc. So just stop hiding behind the religious propaganda and let's just get on the same side here."

"Stake the bitch!" Maru cried, totally out of character, looking at Bembury, who had a stake-loaded dart gun in hand.

Bembury raised the gun to aim at Wilky's bulbous pec, which was like meaty armor protecting the spot where his heart should be.

"Fine. Just fry me. Then you'll be on your own out here." Wilky shrugged. "But I hear them heading this way already."

Everyone froze, listening. The flapping sound hovered in the distance.

"Aw, fuck. What are we going to do?" Stan almost whimpered.

Deck looked at Wilky, who had spent days showing up at just the right time to save him from harrowing situations—often in isolated locations where he easily could have made a meal out of Deck. They held each other's gazes. Undead or not, Wilky's yellow eyes still revealed a common decency.

"Follow him," Deck said, squeezing Maru's hand to reassure him.

"This is fucking nuts!" Soloman grumbled, ready to resist.

They all leapt with fear as there was a flash of movement and a screech. Deck tried to follow the swift movement and make it out in the dark.

A vamp-bat had appeared from out of the darkness and swept Lox across the open area in which they stood. His weapons had been knocked out of his grasp and showered to the ground. Now Lox was pinned to a tree, struggling desperately against a giant bat with a human head. The bat man turned to glare with yellow eyes at the group, fangs exposed.

"It's Old-Timer!" Maru gasped upon seeing the face that once belonged to an incredibly feeble body most often seen on a corner barstool at Dirty Harry's. Now, the purple bags under the eyes were gone, the facial skin was smooth and taut, the body was limber.

"Noooooo!" Soloman shrieked, raising his own crossbow to shoot as Old-Timer's head plunged into Lox's neck.

Lox's scream of agony melded into a whimper of pleasure as the bat penetrated him.

Wilky moved to attack Old-Timer, but Deck actually stopped him, instinct telling him the big black vamp—who he still kind of considered a friend—might get caught in crossfire.

"It's too late! We have to kill them both!" Bembury stepped up beside Soloman with his dart gun aimed.

"Get the fuck away from him!" Soloman slammed his open palm into Bembury's chest with so much angry adrenaline that Bembury fell on his ass.

Everyone froze as Soloman himself lifted his crossbow and let a wooden dart fly.

Deck shielded his eyes from the burst of flames. As the smoke cleared and glowing orange embers of ash fizzled out, he could see Lox's still body pinned to the tree by the wooden arrow that pierced his heart.

"I'm sorry, my brother," Soloman choked, looking quickly away from the dying man.

"You had to—" Wilky tried to say, but Soloman pushed past him. He walked over to Bembury and helped him off the ground.

Deck tensed for a fight, but Bembury simply squeezed Soloman's hand and said, "We're good."

"Get us the fuck out of here, Blacula," Soloman growled at Wilky.

❖

"Please, just keep your weapons at a distance," Wilky said as he rushed ahead of them. "It's very unnerving."

"Not like you got any nerves anymore," Bembury muttered.

"Believe me, it's not a lifestyle I chose," Wilky responded. "Just focus and keep up with me. We're almost at Pale Shelter."

"Don't you mean Dracula's castle?" Soloman asked.

They weaved through the field of pines that heavily guarded Pale Shelter estates.

"I have a bad feeling about this," Bembury said as the large mansion moved closer.

"Do you know that line was used like six times throughout the course of the *Star Wars* series?" Wilky said.

They all looked at their undead guard.

"What?" Wilky asked defensively. "I've always been a fan. And the upside to this whole vampire thing is, if they make a new trilogy every twenty years or so, I'll always be around to catch them. Some of you guys might be dead before they even get to episode nine. Suckers!"

Everyone was silent for a second, then the nervous tension seemed to finally find a channel of release, and the whole group began to laugh.

"A fucking man eater with a sense of humor." Stan shook his giant head as he wiped tears from his eyes.

"That seems to be a side effect," Deck said, remembering just how witty Lamond had become after his transformation.

"Ssh!" Wilky hissed. His beautifully plump lips curled up, revealing his glistening white fangs. It was almost as if he was using them to sniff the air. "Quick! They're coming."

He hurried them across the estate's cobblestone driveway and around the side of the mansion. They finally reached a large door that looked like it was straight off a barn. He swung it open and pushed them inside as fast as possible.

"Hurry! Pull that rope and lower the gate!" Wilky said.

"Wait! What are you doing?" Soloman said.

Several half-bat/half-man bodies clamped onto Wilky from behind, wings flapping wildly in an attempt to drag him out of the way.

"Close it!" Wilky commanded, trying to rip one attacker off one shoulder.

Deck and Maru leaped up and grabbed the thick rope dangling in the doorway and yanked. A loud grinding sound began as a grated gate descended. Just beyond it, Wilky tried to swing the barn door closed.

But the night creatures got past him. The men crammed backward into the minimal cubicle of space they were in as two vamps slipped past the closing door and grabbed on to the descending gate to stop it, their faces human, their eyes beady like those of a bat. No one needed to be asked to help as the bat men tried to fly up with their claws wrapped around the bottom of the gate. All the men grabbed the gate and yanked downward. The strength of the vamps was astonishing as even the weight of Stan failed to fully make headway.

Suddenly, a bat burst into flame and the men jumped back. Maru stood closest, a spike clutched in one hand.

"I got him!" he cried excitedly, but was quickly yanked into the confined space by Deck as the other vamp realized what had happened and tried to lunge for him.

"Get the fucker!" Deck cried, trying to shield Maru's naked body with his own.

"Close the gate and hit the button!" They heard Wilky barking from outside, amidst a cloud of floating bat men he was battling.

"You still got balls, you bastard!" Soloman screamed maniacally at the bat man as he swung one leg up as if playing kickball in a playground.

His leg made contact with the crotch of the bat man, who let out a high-pitched squeal before dropping to the ground, yellow eyes crossing. His wings completely molding into arms, the bat man clutched at his crotch as he writhed in pain.

They quickly slammed the gate down and Stan punched the button Wilky had mentioned.

Deck's belly sank as they were lifted up and a glaring fluorescent light flickered on. They were on some sort of freight elevator.

❖

They grabbed elevator walls with their backs, Maru and Deck on the left, Soloman and Bembury on the right, and Stan taking up the entire back wall, hunkered over so his head wouldn't hit the ceiling.

"Are they going to kill Wilky?" Maru asked.

"He's already dead," Stan pointed out.

"You know what I mean."

"It was kinda cool of him to do that for us," Bembury said just as the elevator came to a stop.

They raised whatever weapons remained in their arsenal as they looked into an octagonal room that had just a large round rug in the center and a bright chandelier hovering over its center.

There was a bald man curled up against the far wall, sobbing.

"Is that?" Soloman said as he lifted the elevator gate and stepped slowly into the room. "Oh fuck. It's Otto."

"Wait!" Deck grabbed him and held the others back with his arms. "It could be a trap. He could be one of them."

"I'm not fucking one of them!" Otto bellowed from under his crossed arms, where his head was tucked. "I'll fucking kill them!"

They hurried over to Otto, none of them fully lowering their weapons.

"What happened?" Stan asked.

"They got him," Otto sobbed. "Teddy. My Teddy Bear."

Otto was hysterical. Deck didn't know what to say, but Maru knelt and comforted him with an arm over the shoulder, tears in his eyes. Deck tried to restrain him from getting too close by yanking on his shoulder.

"Did those things put you in here?" Bembury asked.

Otto shook his head and struggled to stand, wiping streaking tears from his cheeks. He swallowed hard. "No. It was the only place I could find to hide. We almost made it. We lost Father Merrin. Don't know where he is. But me, Jimmy, Harry, and my Teddy. We got to a car in the driveway. I was just finished hotwiring it, and those monsters dragged Teddy out. I ran out to help him. Jimmy and Harry. I don't know. I hope they got away. The things were all over the car, and it sped away. A couple of those things had Teddy. They were biting him. Flying away. He was struggling. Screaming. Telling me to run. They were up so high. And he fucking fell. They dropped him. On the path."

Otto began to groan in agony.

"This is a nightmare," Stan murmured, staring blankly ahead like he was daydreaming.

Deck ran over to one of three windows that were spaced a wall apart on the octagonal shaped room. Each window was flocked by thick drapery. Deck slowly moved the curtain aside. He looked out of the tower-like gable of the mansion, but all he could see below were pine trees. "Maybe we should turn out that light. I don't know how safe we are in here."

A large shape smashed against the window just as he finished speaking. They cried out in terror.

They crammed into the center of the room, backs together. With their fists clenching the weapons in front of them, they appeared to be doing a reverse circle jerk.

Deck stumbled backward away from the window and landed on his butt on the rug, which caused some serious rug burn. The curtain he had moved aside left a small space for them to see out. A pale and beautiful face was peering in at them, seeming to glow white compared to the dark locks of hair on his head.

"Aww, fuck!" Soloman groaned. "This is some *Salem's Lot* shit right here."

"It's Proc," Deck said, realizing the main inhabitant of Pale Shelter was somehow defying gravity outside the gable window.

"I'll fucking kill him!" Otto suddenly burst out in fury, his bulky body swelling, veins popping out on his bald forehead as he yanked a crossbow from Soloman's hands and rushed toward the windows.

Unfortunately, he tripped over Deck's body and came crashing to the ground.

"Deck!" Proc said loudly enough to be heard through the window. "You're an intelligent and level-headed man. Calm them down and let me talk."

"Fuck him!" Otto cried out, trying to scramble off Deck's body and over to the crossbow, which had skidded across the floor.

"I'm deeply sorry for your loss. All your losses. The losses of this community," Proc spoke passionately.

Deck grabbed on to Otto's arms and tried to calm him down.

"Let me go! He's the fucking master!" Otto argued, beginning to fight it out with Deck. The others rushed over to stop them.

"You give me way too much credit," Proc said, his pale face seeming to float outside the window. His hair blew in the breeze caused by the altitude, causing an even creepier effect.

"This all started when you got here!" Otto barked.

"He's right." Bembury stepped forward in full police officer stance, a crucifix out before him instead of a gun.

Proc hissed, revealing his fangs as he turned his head away. "I've lost a lover as well." He managed to remain calm, even in the face of danger. "His parts are now scattered throughout these woods, being drained by the creatures he was protecting you from."

Bembury's grip on the crucifix faltered.

"Don't you have to stake a vamp through the heart or drown it in holy water?" Stan said.

"Technically," Proc said. "But tearing him from limb to limb and draining him of precious life force can do the job just as well."

"Should we let him in?" Maru, being no stranger to torment, pain, and the loss of a loved one, asked with concern.

"Screwdat!" Soloman said. "You invite one of those things in here, and everyone becomes the main course."

"Actually." Proc regained his vampiric composure, his dark eyebrows bowing into a powerful V. "You're in *my* home. I can come in any time I'd like."

"Oh fudge," Bembury muttered. "If you can really come right in, why didn't you? Why are you hanging—or flying—outside a window scaring the hell out of us?"

"Sorry." Proc's stern features seemed to soften to a beautiful tenderness. "I've always been somewhat of a prankster, and thanks to all the vampire lore in movies and books, well, let's just say it kind of tickles me to play along with vampire imagery that has been burned into the collective conscience of society. Watch this."

Proc's face morphed into a dramatic wide-eyed, eyebrow raised expression as he did an impersonation of a Bela Lugosi impersonator, quoting one of the most famous vampire movie misquotes of all, "I vaant to suck your blood!"

"Shoot the fucker!" Bembury ordered as the others made their weapons, which had gone slightly limp, rigid again.

"Put the weapons down," Proc said through the windowpane, sounding impatient now. "If I'd wanted to make a happy meal out of you, it would have been done already. Particularly you, Waxer. You look good enough to eat."

Deck's eyes grew wide.

Proc rolled his eyes. "I mean that in a purely objectifying sexual way. Not the Hannibal Lecter way."

"Uhm, thanks?" Deck said, confused.

"For hell's sake. You two spend more time naked then clothed. Would you take some linens out of that closet over there and cover yourselves up? There are sheets, blankets, towels, maybe even some robes. Moving is such a hassle. Everything gets lost in the shuffle. I was planning to convert this space into a honeymoon suite for guests, with a master bath and all."

"Nice," Stan said, looking around. "Brings up the home value. Plus, they'll have their own private elevator entrance."

"Exactly." Proc nodded.

"Um, could we get back to this whole vampires taking over the earth thing?" Soloman interjected.

"I am centuries old. If we were going to take over the earth, we would have done so by now. We're just trying to unlive our life." Proc chuckled, but received only blank stares. "Too soon?"

"A bit," Deck replied sarcastically.

"Sorry. Just get dressed. I promise, no vamps, ghosts, or werewolves in there. Just me." Proc's face disappeared from the window, and they froze in shock.

"Where the fuck did he go?" Otto asked, jumping up onto his feet as if ready for a fight.

"I'm in the closet," a muffled voice came through the door at the other end of the room. "And I'd like to come out of it, if you would all be so kind as to not persecute me for what I am."

"Oh shit! He's in!" Soloman raised his weapon to the closet door, and some of the others followed suit.

"And he's a fricking comedian," Bembury added.

Deck noticed a frosted glass windowpane across the top of the closet had lit up. He spotted dark movement creating a silhouette behind the pane, and then the window pushed out slightly.

Two white bathrobes appeared, clutched in a hand that was nearly as white, but sprinkled with dark knuckle hair.

"Take these," Proc said as the robes were waved like a white flag.

"Quick, shoot him!" Otto said, lifting his retrieved crossbow.

"NO!" Deck jumped in the line of fire and knocked Otto's weapon aside.

Maru scurried over to the closet and grabbed the two robes. Proc's hand quickly disappeared back into the closet.

"Get him away from there!" Otto struggled with Deck to protect Maru.

"I'm fine," Maru assured them, walking safely away from the closet and slipping into one of the robes after handing the other to Deck.

"What do you want from us?" Stan asked.

"I'd like to get you out of this fucking mess so you can all go on with your lives and continue to rebuild this town," Proc spoke through the door.

"And build up your feeding ground! You took away people that were dear to us," Stan argued.

"On the contrary, I helped protect you from the riffraff," Proc countered. "Deck. Who showed up every time you found yourself face-to-face with the baddies in this town? Those scary guys in black who were after you?"

"It was Wilky," Deck said to the others. "He was always there."

"Yes. You see, I've been roaming this planet for centuries, never having a place to settle, to feel safe and secure. And I've watched our people—gay, not vampire—suffer beyond anything you can imagine. I suffered. Society pushed me to the fringes. And I made a bad decision as a result that forever altered who I was and who I'd intended to be. And that's the story for so many of us. And so, I decided that if I had to continue existing by taking away from others, then I would take away from those who take away from us."

"Cool. You're like a gay vampire renegade!" Maru said enthusiastically. "Any way you could take care of Reverend Phelps?"

"I'd love to, but he always has so many damn religious relics on him," Proc said.

"So wait a minute. You're saying you're a *good* vampire?" Otto seemed to be getting his wits about him and cooling off. "Like the Robin Hood of the vampire world?"

"I do my best," Proc replied.

"So Lamond *was* the king of the vampires," Otto said.

"No. Just misguided." Proc sounded genuinely sad. "It can be a very powerful state for those who are freshly indoctrinated. Especially someone like him, who lived his life as a master. Metaphorically, sexually, socially, creatively. He was always in control of everything he did. So he bought into his own hype and it ruled his vampirism. It's quite easy to give in to the desire. Believe it or not, you actually feel so much more *alive* when you're undead," Proc said. "All the pains go away. You feel like a sixteen-year-old boy. You lust for life. You lust for lust. I tried to rein Hayes in, but once he lost Ben, the loneliness took over and controlled his desire. His desire to be surrounded by men. Men who would consider him their mentor. The bond we create with those we turn can be very genuine, yet still very slave-like. And some, like Hayes, are clearly turned on by that relationship. So it's easy for him to spread that infrastructure, which is what he was trying tonight. And in reality, those like me stand a better chance of existing if there are fewer of us."

"Food supply," Bembury said dryly to the others.

"Believe me. I wish you bleeders would really create some sort of *True Blood* so we feeders didn't have to…" Proc's voice trailed off behind the closet door.

Deck spoke. "Proc. What happens once you—once a vampire, combusts? Are they really gone?"

"Doesn't get any more gone than that," Proc answered.

"Why have people seen them?" Deck said. "Some guys in Weeping Manor spotted Ben DuPont. Maru saw his lover."

"And I think I saw Lamond tonight. After we killed him," Maru added.

The others stared at Maru first in shock, and then with slight annoyance that he had not told them.

"I wasn't sure," Maru said defensively.

"Spirits," Proc explained from the closet.

"You mean ghosts?" Soloman asked. "Are you saying they turn into vampire ghosts?"

"No. Just spirits. Freed souls," Proc said. "They're just regular spirits, finally detached from their physical bodies. Those who became vampires before being taken off the planet tend to have a lot more reasons to stick around. There's a whole what-the-fuck thing going on in their heads. No soul wants to believe it turned into a vampire before being released. But I assure you, there's nothing dangerous or vampiric about them."

They glanced at one another and there was silence again. Finally, Deck spoke to the closet door, pulling his robe tightly around him. "Proc? Are you still there?"

"I don't know how to fix this," Proc finally answered. "There are so many of them in town now, and they are not one with me. They were made by another through the incestuous goings-on down in The Caves. And they will be coming after me. I have to leave this town."

"Wait," Deck said. "What are we going to do? How can we clean up this town?"

"If I leave, they will follow me. It's really my battle. There *is* what you all might consider a king vampire. But he's much bigger than that. And much more dangerous than you could ever imagine. He's the Deceiver. He comes for you in any form he can come up with. And not always your traditional Hollywood monster. You never know what shape he'll take. He's taken way too many of those who have meant something to *me* through the ages. So I think it's really me he wants. Stan?"

"Wh-what?" Stan replied, his nervous voice a great contradiction to his menacing size.

"You must continue the efforts here. Make this the safe haven for gay men that we all wanted. Anderson and her men are gone. And I'll take the other threats with me. Things will be safe here for now. When the deaths started here in the Cove, Hayes and Ben feared what would happen to the gay community if they should die as well, before seeing the transformation through. So they willed their property to me in the case of their deaths should Jeeves perish as well, so that it would be kept 'in the family' and we could continue their work. Pale Shelter was not truly mine, as Deck knows." There was a pause as Deck blushed at Proc calling him out on his snooping, despite the note in the desk drawer that had done just as much.

"This was Lamond's property. But now it is mine. And I will turn it over to you. Expect to hear from some lawyers in a couple of days. They will draw up the paperwork and meet with you to sign it. Make good use of both of these properties, even if you sell it to others looking to stick to the cause. Kremfort Cove will no longer be called Cremation Cove by its residents. It shall be referred to as Comfort Cove."

"You're going to *give* all this property to me?" Stan stammered.

"Deck," Proc said. "You're a modern day Van Helsing. Your mind is open to all this. They need you in the Cove. Watch over them."

Deck reached for the doorknob. "Proc. Wait!"

Bembury, Soloman, and Otto grabbed Deck to hold him back so he could not release Proc from the closet, not that the door was really stopping that possibility.

"You'll all be safe in here for the rest of the night. Tomorrow, they'll all be gone," Proc said.

"No. Wait! Who's after you? Who's the Deceiver?" Deck shouted, yanking himself away from the men and grabbing the closet doorknob to quickly open the door.

Bembury and Soloman thrust Deck—and his fluffy white robe—out of the way with their weapons aimed into the closet. The closet was literally another room, lined with shelves, cabinets, and hanging rods, with wall-to-wall plush carpet and a full-sized mirror on the back wall.

"Where'd he go?" Bembury said.

Deck pushed past them into the large room, carefully examining every inch of the space. For starters, it was a relief to see all their reflections in the mirror. Next, he found a vent under a shelf way in the back of the room. "Here. Either an air-conditioning or heating duct."

"Does that mean others can come in this way?" Soloman wondered aloud.

"Not if the invitation rule really applies," Deck said, not feeling very reassured. "Let's grab a bunch of these blankets and have us a little sleep over."

They gathered thick comforters and pillows neatly stacked on the shelves and in the cabinets and exited the closet. Deck wedged a box full of folded sheets between the lowest shelf and the floor vent.

"Not sure if that will exactly stop a vamp," Deck admitted.

"Here. Hang this over it," Stan called from the main room. He tossed a rosary in to Deck.

Deck decided to lift the box and slip the crucifix on the rosary *into* the vent. He then wedged the rosary beads themselves between the carpeted floor and the cardboard box so it would stay in place. "Let's hope all the vamps around here believe in Jesus."

They returned to the main room, closed the closet door, and went about using some of the religious relics around their necks to create a barrier. Another crucifix on a chain went through the window above the closet door and was wrapped around a hinge so it would dangle against the inside of the closet door. Next, they adorned the three windows on the remaining sides of the room with religious repellents strung over window locks. They then pulled all the thick curtains tight.

"It's cold in here," Maru said, pulling his robe tighter. "My fingers and toes are freezing!"

"You're tired. And hungry. And probably in shock," Deck said, pulling him into a bear hug. "We're going to set up camp in the middle of the room."

They kissed.

"Ahem!" Stan broke through their smooch. "You lovebirds better behave tonight. Especially when you're on guard duty. I'd suggest we take shifts in pairs."

No one agreed to take the first sleeping shift because no one seemed at peace enough to actually sleep. So they created a bed out of the dozen or so blankets, using the pillows to create a circular, nest-like outer wall. Maru and Deck curled up in a reclined position, with Maru opening Deck's robe so he could snuggle up against the warm fuzz of Deck's chest and belly. The others kicked off their shoes and stripped down to their underwear before entering the circle.

Soloman, white boxer briefs tightly hugging his firm thighs and butt and contrasting beautifully with his dark skin, propped himself up against some pillows with his legs spread so Bembury could slip between them and use his body as a backrest. He immediately began to finger comb Bembury's thick mahogany curls.

After pulling off his army fatigues but leaving his army green tank on, Otto found a switch on a wall and used it to dim the chandelier over their heads to a warm glow. When he turned back to the group, they were all gawking at him.

"Have you been raiding my dancing wardrobe?" Maru cracked, and everyone started to laugh.

"What?" Otto asked defensively. "It's a thong! It makes me feel sexy!"

"A *pink* thong under your butchy military attire makes you feel sexy?" Bembury said.

"It's not pink!" Otto said, but then he looked down at his crotch. "Oh…shit. Teddy must have thrown it in with our red towels. Dammit! No matter how many times I tell him—"

Otto almost chocked on his breath.

"Come here." Stan, in nothing more than custom-made baggy boxers covered in a print of popular chocolate bars, thumped over to Otto and wrapped a giant arm around him as he began to cry. "Men, make some room for us."

Stan led Otto to the circle and everyone moved to create a space large enough to accommodate Stan. Stan grabbed his bag of tricks and dropped it near the circle, then brought his large body down to the floor with impressively graceful ease, sitting cross-legged.

"Come on, auto man. Just lay across my lap. Lord knows I'm more cushiony than any pillows," Stan offered Otto.

Otto didn't have much choice, considering Stan pretty much took up the remaining space on the blankets. He draped the back of his legs over one of Stan's enormous thighs as he brought his butt down between Stan's legs and then used Stan's other thigh as a back support.

Stan gently caressed Otto's head with one hand while rubbing Otto's thigh soothingly with the other. "How's that. You okay?"

"It feels good to be close to someone right now. But what… what's that against my…" Otto was squirming to make himself comfortable against Stan's crotch. "Wait a minute. Is that your—"

Stan's face turned red. "Well, don't call everyone's attention to it! It's very sensitive, and now it's beginning to…"

"What the FUCK?" Otto exclaimed as the chocolate bar print on Stan's boxers began to reach out, extending right over Otto's tight belly, pinning him to the floor.

"Holy shit!" Bembury gawked. "Is that really—"

"I have a mild case of gargantuanism." Stan sounded apologetic as his face grew redder. "It's a rare genetic disorder."

"Damn! I'm black, and I wish I had that kinda genetic disorder down there!" Soloman quipped.

Deck and Maru were giggling now, Deck trying to look as impressed and shocked as the others by the "reveal" of Stan's cock size. Maru really didn't need to know that he'd not only already seen the wonder of Stan's genetic disorder, but had actually had his hands wrapped around it and milked it!

"Stop talking about it," Stan said. "It's not exactly as modest as me. It kind of likes the attention."

"Get this thing off me!" Otto's tears of grief had turned to tears of laughter as his eyes grew wide at the thick hose stretching over his torso.

"Come on, Stan. Whip it out. Let's get a glimpse of the full Monty," Bembury said.

"Yeah!" Maru chimed in, and Deck raised a scolding eyebrow at him. "I just want to *see* it. I still love yours more."

"Bastard," Deck said.

"Whip it out! Whip it out!" Soloman chanted, and the others began to pick up the chant.

Now Stan was laughing too, tears streaming down his chubby cheeks, his big man tits jiggling wildly. Otto saw his opportunity and quickly grabbed the stretched waistband of the boxers and yanked them out further in an effort to finally reach the head of the monstrosity.

The others screamed in girlish delight at the magnificence of it. It looked like some sort of exaggerated giant dildo you'd see at a sex shop. Otto released the waistband of the boxers, but they only managed to slip *under* the cock instead of covering it again, so the heavy engorged appendage slapped against his belly.

"It's on me! It's on me!" Otto squealed.

Stan, still laughing hysterically, grabbed a hold of it and began to thump it loudly against Otto's taut belly.

"It's gonna blow!" Deck bellowed.

"There ain't enough mouths in this room to blow that piece!" Soloman said.

They laughed until they slept.

EPILOGUE

Disembodied faces floated outside the windows, finally head-butting the glass and swooping in from every side of the rounded room, dive-bombing the sleeping circle of men and attaching to their necks.

Deck woke with a start—actually forced himself to wake—just as he felt fangs puncture his neck. He reached for it, sure there was going to be a head hanging from his jugular, and only breathed a sigh of relief when his mind began to revert to a waking existence, accepting that it had only been the alternative reality of a dream. He was heated under his thick robe. Beads of perspiration spilled through his tufts of body hair as if melting away the fear. Maru was still wrapped in his arms, draped across his chest. And he was stirring.

"Are you okay?" Maru muttered with sleep in his tone. "I felt you shake."

"Bad dream," Deck said, kissing Maru's head.

"Where is everyone?" Maru pushed off Deck's body, alarmed.

Deck quickly got on his feet while taking in his surroundings. "It's daylight."

Deck pointed to the drawn curtains around the room and the rectangular halos created from light beaming against their backsides.

"So we're safe," Maru said, sounding only half convinced as he took Deck's hand.

"I hope so. And I hope everyone else is okay." Deck quickly pulled open the closet door, hoping for the best but expecting the worst. He got the best. The closet was empty and everything seemed intact. He then moved to one of the windows and peeked around the curtain, squinting in reaction to the glaring light outside.

Down below on the back lawn of the expansive property stood the other men from their group of survivors, along with a bunch of other Kremfort Cove faces, some familiar, some not. They were all looking directly up at the window and began waving at Deck with big smiles on their faces, gesturing at him to come down.

"Looks like we have a welcoming committee. Come on," Deck said, taking Maru's hand again and leading him to the elevator.

They smiled at each other as the dropping elevator left little pits in Deck's stomach. They reached for each other and hugged. Just as their lips touched, the elevator came to a stop. Deck raised the elevator gate and then grabbed the knob on the large exterior barn door and pushed it open.

When they stepped out onto the driveway into the crisp morning air, their bare feet greeted by hard stone, they turned to the crowd of men waiting for them. The men began to applaud loudly, and Deck noticed a large cloud in the sky above moving quickly past the sun, which explained the chilly shadow cast across the driveway.

"Looks like it's over," Deck said, squeezing Maru's hand.

They began walking across the stone pavement, almost as if dancing down the yellow brick road.

"Something's…wrong." Maru stopped.

"What's the matter?" Deck turned with concern to him.

"I feel…strange," Maru stammered. "Hot. Too…hot."

Maru keeled over, first gripping his stomach, then clawing at his body, wrestling the robe off and to the ground.

"What's happening?" Deck cried, reaching for Maru.

"Don't come any closer!" Maru growled in an uncharacteristically harsh tone as he threw his head up and stared directly at Deck.

Deck stepped backward in horror at what he saw. Blazing yellow eyes. A snarled upper lip. Fangs.

Deck felt the heat as the cloud behind him moved away from the sun, letting the beams blaze onto his back.

"Noooooooooooo!" Maru let out an inhuman screech.

Deck watched as the sun's rays sizzled into Maru's naked flesh, eating away at it and turning it neon orange for only a matter of seconds before he burst into a ball of flame.

A cloud of dust exploded before Deck's eyes, and he screamed in agony as the particles rained to the ground.

About the Author

Daniel W. Kelly is the author of the erotic horror collections *Closet Monsters: Zombied Out* and *Tales of Gothotica and Horny Devils*. His stories have appeared in erotic anthologies including *Manhandled*, *Just the Sex*, *Dorm Porn*, *Bears*, and *Best Gay Erotica 2009*. His short story "Woof" was awarded the first place honor in the bookpuppy.co.uk erotic writing contest in January 2006.

When not obsessing over his dogs (which is pretty much always), Daniel is a pop culture junkie, stimulating his ADHD by listening to music with a thumping beat and a catchy chorus, playing video games that involve blasting the heads off zombies, and watching bad horror movies in search of scenes featuring hot men. He also writes excessively about these subjects on his website: danielwkelly.com.

Books Available from Bold Strokes Books

Crossroads by Radclyffe. Dr. Hollis Monroe specializes in short-term relationships but when she meets pregnant mother-to-be Annie Colfax, fate brings them together at a crossroads that will change their lives forever. (978-1-60282-756-1)

Beyond Innocence by Carsen Taite. When a life is on the line, love has to wait. Doesn't it? (978-1-60282-757-8)

Heart Block by Melissa Brayden. Socialite Emory Owen and struggling single mom Sarah Matamoros are perfectly suited for each other but face a difficult time when trying to merge their contrasting worlds and the people in them. If love truly exists, can it find a way? (978-1-60282-758-5)

Pride and Joy by M.L. Rice. Perfect Bryce Montgomery is her parents' pride and joy, but when they discover that their daughter is a lesbian her world changes forever. (978-1-60282-759-2)

Timothy by Greg Herren. *Timothy* is a romantic suspense thriller from award-winning mystery writer Greg Herren set in the fabulous Hamptons. (978-1-60282-760-8)

In Stone: A Grotesque Faerie Tale by Jeremy Jordan King. A young New Yorker is rescued from a hate crime by a mysterious someone who turns out to be more of a *something*. (978-1-60282-761-5)

The Jesus Injection by Eric Andrews-Katz. Murderous statues, demented drag queens, political bombings, ex-gay ministries, espionage, and romance are all in a day's work for a top-secret agent. But the gloves are off when Agent Buck 98 comes up against The Jesus Injection. (978-1-60282-762-2)

Combustion by Daniel W. Kelly. Bearish detective Deck Waxer comes to the city of Kremfort Cove to investigate why the hottest men in town are bursting into flames in broad daylight. (978-1-60282-763-9)

Ladyfish by Andrea Bramhill. Finn's escape to the Florida Keys leads her straight into the arms of scuba diving instructor Oz as she fights for her freedom, their blossoming love…and her life! (978-1-60282-747-9)

Spanish Heart by Rachel Spangler. While on a mission to find herself in Spain, Ren Molson runs the risk of losing her heart to her tour guide, Lina Montero. (978-1-60282-748-6)

Love Match by Ali Vali. When Parker "Kong" King, the number one tennis player in the world, meets commercial pilot Captain Sydney Parish, sparks fly but not from attraction. They have the summer to see if they have a love match. (978-1-60282-749-3)

One Touch by L.T. Marie. A romance writer and a travel agent come together at their high school reunion, only to find out that the memory of that one touch never fades. (978-1-60282-750-9)

Night Shadows: Queer Horror edited by Greg Herren and J.M. Redmann. *Night Shadows* features delightfully wicked stories by some of the biggest names in queer publishing. (978-1-60282-751-6)

Secret Societies by William Holden. An outcast hustler, his unlikely "mother," his faithless lovers, and his religious persecutors—all in 1726. (978-1-60282-752-3)

The Raid by Lee Lynch. Before Stonewall, having a drink with friends or your girl could mean jail. Would these women and men still have family, a job, a place to live after…The Raid? (978-1-60282-753-0)

The You Know Who Girls: Freshman Year by Annameekee Hesik. As they begin freshman year, Abbey Brooks and her best friend, Kate, pinky swear they'll keep away from the lesbians in Gila High, but Abbey already suspects she's one of those you-know-who girls herself and slowly learns who her true friends really are. (978-1-60282-754-7)

Wyatt: Doc Holliday's Account of an Intimate Friendship by Dale Chase. Erotica writer Dale Chase takes the remarkable friendship between Wyatt Earp, upright lawman, and Doc Holliday, southern gentlemen turned gambler and killer, to an entirely new level: hot! (978-1-60282-755-4)

Month of Sundays by Yolanda Wallace. Love doesn't always happen overnight; sometimes it takes a month of Sundays. (978-1-60282-739-4)

Jacob's War by C.P. Rowlands. ATF Special Agent Allison Jacob's task force is in the middle of an all-out war, from the streets to the boardrooms of America. Small business owner Katie Blackburn is the latest victim who accidentally breaks it wide open but may break AJ's heart at the same time. (978-1-60282-740-0)

The Pyramid Waltz by Barbara Ann Wright. Princess Katya Nar Umbriel wants a perfect romance, but her Fiendish nature and duties to the crown mean she can never tell the truth—until she meets Starbride, a woman who gets to the heart of every secret, even if it will be the death of her. (978-1-60282-741-7)

The Secret of Othello by Sam Cameron. Florida teen detectives Steven and Denny risk their lives to search for a sunken NASA satellite—but under the waves, no one can hear you scream . . . (978-1-60282-742-4)

Dreaming of Her by Maggie Morton. Isa has begun to dream of the most amazing woman—a woman named Lilith with a gorgeous face, an amazing body, and the ability to turn Isa on like no other. But Lilith is just a dream...isn't she? (978-1-60282-847-6)

Andy Squared by Jennifer Lavoie. Andrew never thought anyone could come between him and his twin sister, Andrea...until Ryder rode into town. (978-1-60282-743-1)

Finding Bluefield by Elan Barnehama. Set in the backdrop of Virginia and New York and spanning the years 1960-1982, Finding Bluefield chronicles the lives of Nicky Stewart, Barbara Philips, and their son, Paul, as they struggle to define themselves as a family. (978-1-60282-744-8)

The Jetsetters by David-Matthew Barnes. As rock band The Jetsetters skyrocket from obscurity to super stardom, Justin Holt, a lonely barista, and Diego Delgado, the band's guitarist, fight with everything they have to stay together, despite the chaos and fame. (978-1-60282-745-5)

Strange Bedfellows by Rob Byrnes. Partners in life and crime, Grant Lambert and Chase LaMarca, are hired to make a politician's compromising photo disappear, but what should be an easy job quickly spins out of control. (978-1-60282-746-2)

Speed Demons by Gun Brooke. When NASCAR star Evangeline Marshall returns to the race track after a close brush with death, will famous photographer Blythe Pierce document her triumph and reciprocate her love—or will they succumb to their respective demons and fail? (978-1-60282-678-6)

Summoning Shadows: A Rosso Lussuria Vampire Novel by Winter Pennington. The Rosso Lussuria vampires face enemies both old and new, and to prevail they must call on even more strange alliances, unite as a clan, and draw on every weapon within their reach—but with a clan of vampires, that's easier said than done. (978-1-60282-679-3)

Sometime Yesterday by Yvonne Heidt. When Natalie Chambers learns her Victorian house is haunted by a pair of lovers and a Dark Man, can she and her lover Van Easton solve the mystery that will set the ghosts free and banish the evil presence in the house? Or will they have to run to survive as well? (978-1-60282-680-9)

Into the Flames by Mel Bossa. In order to save one of his patients, psychiatrist Jamie Scarborough will have to confront his own monsters—including those he unknowingly helped create. (978-1-60282-681-6)

Coming Attractions: Author's Edition by Bobbi Marolt. For Helen Townsend, chasing turns to caring, and caring turns to loving, but will love take five steps back and turn to leaving? (978-1-60282-732-5)

OMGqueer, edited by Radclyffe and Katherine E. Lynch. Through stories imagined and told by youth across America, this anthology provides a snapshot of queerness at the dawn of the new millennium. (978-1-60282-682-3)

Oath of Honor by Radclyffe. A First Responders novel. First do no harm...First Physician of the United States Wes Masters discovers that being the president's doctor demands more than brains and personal sacrifice—especially when politics is the order of the day. (978-1-60282-671-7)

A Question of Ghosts by Cate Culpepper. Becca Healy hopes Dr. Joanne Call can help her learn if her mother really committed suicide—but she's not sure she can handle her mother's ghost, a decades-old mystery, and lusting after the difficult Dr. Call without some serious chocolate consumption. (978-1-60282-672-4)